CONVALESCENCE

Can you forgive yourself?

CONVALESCENCE

Can you forgive yourself?

MAISIE KITTON

Other books by Maisie Kitton:

Opium

Praise for *Opium*

"Vivid imagery, and it pulled me in right from the start. Well done
to the author."

"The author plunges you straight into the action from chapter
one. Just like the book's namesake opium, the storytelling is also
very addictive."

"By the end of chapter one I was gripped by the characters and
hooked by the storyline – it got to the point where everything
else had to wait! The detailed descriptions of events, but most
of all the extraordinary depth of insight into the suffering and
feelings of the main characters made it compulsive reading."

"This is a well-written story and an emotional roller coaster."

"A very good first book that I would highly recommend!"

"This book has you on the edge of your seat, it's difficult
to put down."

To everyone who has yet to find their place in the world. x

<u>Content Warning</u>

Be aware that this novel contains graphic depictions of violence and abuse, including death. Be aware that this novel contains descriptions of depression and suicide ideation, and vague descriptions of self-harm.

Stay safe, and please read at your own risk.

Contents

Key Pronunciations

People
Felan – 'Fey-len'
Blaez – 'Blaise'
Accalia – 'Ack-ay-leah'
Randi – 'Ran-dee'
Convel – 'Con-vul'

Places
Guadalupe – 'Gwad-ah-loop'
Weisworth – 'Whys-worth'

Chapter 1: Foreboding

Felan had woken up with a pounding headache again.

He thought it was probably because he'd only slept for about an hour last night. It was also probably because he'd been ill on the days leading up to Blaez's departure from Weisworth. No one had been sure what had brought his sudden bout of illness on, but one morning he had woken up with a throbbing headache behind his eyes, and no energy or desire to do anything.

After Blaez had left, Felan had laid listless in his bed, thinking, *I thought you might've changed your mind. I don't want you to leave. Please don't leave me on my own. I don't know what I might do without you here to stop me.*

No. He'd never derail her from something she wanted to do, pun most definitely *not* intended.

Felan grunted and pulled his duvet tighter around himself. Despite being nearly summer, it was rather cold outside of his bed, and he didn't want to leave it before he had to.

Was it so bad that he just wanted to be left alone? In some ways, he was glad Blaez had left; she kept trying to get him to talk about his feelings. She was worse than Mrs Walters in that regard, and that was saying something. He didn't want to hear the kids shouting and running around the massive house. He just wanted quiet and solitude.

He was in a bed that had previously belonged to Zac, a fact that one of the kids, Elliot, had been sure to remind him of daily at the dinner table, much to Mrs Walters' chagrin.

'Mrs Walters, is Zac going to be given his duvet set?'

'He has everything he needs, Elliot,' Mrs Walters said.

*'But he chose it himself.' Elliot pointed at Felan. 'It's not fair that **he** –'*

Felan glanced down at the plate of food he'd barely touched, his fork clenched tightly in his hand.

'*Enough, Elliot.*'

'*But it's not fair!*'

'*I said that's enough!*' *Mrs Walters barked.*

It didn't make Felan feel any better about taking up space when he knew he didn't deserve it. He just didn't understand why nobody else had come to that same conclusion yet. He was unsociable and he took up space. People hated that in teenagers, especially a teenager like Felan. If people found out what he had done, if people found out what he was capable of doing, they would chase him out of Weisworth with pitchforks and torches and scream at him to never return.

As for the kids, they were all still wary of Felan… other than Gemma. Felan was bigger, he was defensive, and he was moody, however Gemma was a little unforeseen ray of sunshine. She'd pounced on Felan the first chance she had gotten and demanded he read to her with big green eyes. He had been in too much shock to decline and so five minutes later he was stammering out a tale about warrior princesses to a very excitable four-year-old.

And the rest was history, so to speak.

At the time, Mrs Walters had said it was a good sign. A month later, however, the other kids still hadn't quite warmed up to him. Of course, that was entirely Felan's fault.

'*They'll come around, Felan. Trust me.*'

But his trust had been broken one too many times to believe her. In some ways, he prayed the kids never did end up liking him. He prayed that Gemma stopped trying so hard to include him, and yet part of him was tired of being on his own.

The rest of him knew it was the only way things could be now.

After what he'd done, being alone was the least he deserved. After what he'd done, he would never end up like Zac: welcomed with open arms into a new home.

It was only natural that the kids missed Zac, but it didn't make Felan's life any easier. Every time he heard Zac's name, a wall of guilt hit him (a wall built up of broken bricks and crumbling mortar), and a ball of jealousy formed before he could stop it (a ball that twisted and pulsed in his stomach).

The sudden loss of April and Amelia, the two sweet sisters who had been moved to a different home within a week of Felan arriving, was another sore point. It was his fault they left. He knew it.

'Sometimes, a home isn't a right fit for certain children, and that's okay,' Mrs Walters said when they'd been picked up by foster parents. Felan pretended he didn't hear the wobble in her voice. 'There is always somewhere else for them to go.'

Felan had waved goodbye with the others, lost in his thoughts.

There wasn't anywhere else for me to go back in Guadalupe. I was on my own in a big city full of dangerous people. I was just a kid and I was on my own.

The kids, and Mrs Walters, missed the girls terribly.

Felan, not having known them at all, isolated himself and steered clear. Blaez had been the only one he really talked to and now she was gone. The kids tried to talk to him. Mrs Walters did too. They all still tried.

He wished they wouldn't.

Someone rapped on his bedroom door three times. 'Felan,' Mrs Walters said, interrupting his wallowing. 'You can't stay in bed all day.' Her footsteps faded away down the hall.

Oh, he so wanted to. He could. She wouldn't get angry at him, and she most definitely wouldn't force him (he had figured that out very fast into his stay in Weisworth) but she'd give him that dreadful, pitying look that he loathed. It was the same look the nurse gave him when his father put him in hospital – the same look that had started everything. The same look that had knocked over that first domino and sent the rest of them tumbling down in quick succession. He could still feel the shockwaves of the dominoes now; he feared he always would.

It wasn't bad, staying in an orphanage, but he hated that everyone was there for more or less the same reason as him: he was unwanted, unloved and alone.

A screech rang through the house.

Felan growled under his breath, threw off his duvet and headed to the bathroom. He had a cold shower, actually managed to brush his teeth, changed into clean clothes, and when he found the nerve to head downstairs, he ate dry toast for breakfast. He washed up his plate and stared out of the kitchen window in silence.

Mrs Walters had taken him to the doctors a few weeks ago for a check-up, despite Felan's insistence that he was fine. His teeth, according to the elderly doctor with white hair, were not in the best shape, and he was severely underweight. That was fine. He could deal with comments like that. His father and Nick had prepared him well for those.

What he hadn't been ready for, however, was the way that Dr Sampson had held his scars under close scrutiny. Felan's skin had crawled for days after. No one apart from him had ever touched his scars, not even Blaez, and to have some stranger come along and inspect every single one like they were some sort of extra-terrestrial phenomenon...

Felan abhorred them. Sure, he abhorred the people who gave them to him, but he abhorred what his scars represented even more so: failure. Every time he looked at his scars, he thought of them: Nick, his dad, and all of the others that contributed to the array of lines forever etched into his skin. They were a constant reminder of his failures.

Still failing.

Chapter 2: Disperse

Mrs Walters had noticed the hollow to his cheeks faster than he did, but that may have just been his steadfast refusal to look in the mirror. Despite sharing physical similarities with his mother, he had more in common with his father, and after that unsettling revelation, he hadn't looked at himself in the mirror since.

He had spent hours tracing his lips that were identical to his mother's, and his nose and his slightly pointed ears, but he couldn't look himself in the eye without seeing his father staring back – those same cold, grey eyes that glared at Felan daily. Even his hands were the same as his father's – capable of inflicting pain on others – and so was his hair. Felan knew what it looked like when it was dry and greasy and matted with dandruff. He knew what it looked like plastered to his face with sweat and stinking of cheap beer and cigarettes. Felan had made an effort to wash his hair daily when he remembered that particular image. His mother's hair had been blonde, and on his seventh birthday the strands had been stained red with blood.

So he avoided making eye contact with himself and traced the shape of his mouth with his eyes firmly shut. He traced the parts of himself that were his mother's and pretended.

He pretended that everything was going to be okay.

***

'Are you playing with us today?'

Felan blinked himself out of his reverie and turned around. At the backdoor stood Elliot, a rather timid eight-year-old. To be asked to play was a bit of a surprise. It was also a surprise that it was Elliot, out of all of them who'd asked. The eight-year-old had been the main advocate for reminding Felan about Zac every chance he got. His twin sister, Mary, sat quietly and watched the events unfold every time.

He didn't blame her. After all, he was a threat. A threat that had dared to step foot into the kids' sanctuary, a threat who had disrupted their day-to-day life, a threat who had taken the attention of Mrs Walters away from *them*.

Despite that, Felan considered Elliot's offer, weighing up his options. He didn't really want to play, but all he had planned for the foreseeable future was to dive right back under his covers and hide from the world. 'What are we playing?'

'We're on the climbing frame, then I think the others want to play IT,' Elliot said. He kept glancing over his shoulder at the other kids playing, like he was missing out on things in the time he spoke to Felan. Or, rather, like he couldn't look Felan in the eye.

'You go on ahead,' Felan said. He tried to sound engaged. It fell flat. 'I'll be out in a moment.'

'Okay!' Elliot ran back outside and gave chase to Jude and Josie, both of whom had been loitering by the top step at the back door.

Felan sighed. He couldn't exactly just head back upstairs and ignore the kids forever, even if he wanted to. Something niggled at the back of his mind that the kids were trying harder than he was, that the kids were trying to get to know him, and yet all Felan did was hide away in his room and pretend they didn't exist. Apart from Gemma. He couldn't stay away from the kid if he tried.

It wasn't the kids' fault he was miserable. It wasn't the kids' fault he was damaged in a way he didn't think he'd ever recover from; too many pieces of himself had been chipped away and were lost forever to the cavity that was his existence.

Trying to school his features into something that wasn't miserable, Felan knocked on Mrs Walters' bedroom door. A ground floor bedroom, of all places.

'Come in,' she called from the other side.

Felan pushed open the door, hating the feeling of trepidation that came with it.

Mrs Walters sat behind her desk in the corner of the room, working her way through endless stacks of paperwork. She glanced up, offering him a smile that Felan was convinced he didn't deserve. 'You've had something to eat?' she asked.

'Yeah,' he said, for some reason unable to meet her eyes. He settled his gaze on a spot just beside her head. 'I'm going outside with the kids. I just thought I'd let you know.'

'Okay. Have fun,' she said kindly. 'You can leave my door open if you like.'

'Sure.'

He left her to it, put on his new, black trainers, zipped up his brown jacket, and wandered down the steps and down the path in the garden. He walked to the treeline and through the opening to where the climbing frame lived.

In one mind, Felan was jealous. He'd never had the kind of childhood that allowed for play, the kind of childhood that allowed for fun. The jealousy sat at the bottom of his stomach, a heavy *thing* which gnawed away at his insides, a persistent ache he feared he'd never be rid of.

In another mind, the kids were innocent. They deserved this.

Felan wasn't. He didn't.

The poppies in the flower bed had taken a bit of a beating due to the heavy rain over the last few days. Their heads hung limp and weak, their red petals drooping and tearing, and he thought that the smallest gust of wind would snap them. Fragile, that's how he felt, like one more hit would shatter him completely into broken pieces that would be impossible to put back together again. Not that he'd ever admit that out loud.

Today was the first sunny day since Blaez had left. He supposed he ought to make the most of it while it lasted. Sunny days never seemed to last long in Weisworth, Mrs Walters had told him, and they were always closely followed by heavy rain for what felt like weeks. But he wasn't complaining. Felan decided that he would never complain again.

Something tugged at his jacket. He looked down and couldn't have stopped himself from smiling if he wanted to. 'Now what can I do for you, Gemma?'

She looked all cute wrapped up in her little bumblebee coat. It might have been sunny, but the air was cold and the wind was bitter. *Just like me*. She pointed up at the monkey bars and pulled her trademark sad face. 'Too small!' she cried, in that forthright way Felan had grown to adore.

'I think I should be able to help with that,' he said.

She grabbed his hand and dragged him over to the climbing frame. He went willingly, glancing up at the other kids as they walked. Elliot, Mary, Jude and Josie were all accounted for.

'Come on then, Gem,' he said, helping her climb up the four rungs of the ladder. 'Arms up.'

'No tickling.'

'Absolutely not,' he said, picking her up. 'Okay, grab onto the bar. Yes, now grab the next one... I won't drop you... then the next, oops, and the next, there you go...'

Bless her – Gemma was indeed far too small to play on the monkey bars, but she gave it a good go. He would never tell her, but he did all the work, holding her off the ground so she could grab the bars. Once at the other end, he set her down and accepted the high five she offered. Fondness blossomed beneath his skin, slowly unfurling like a flower in the sun.

'Awesome!' she cried, jumping up and down.

'We'll make a monkey out of you yet,' he said, ruffling her curls. Somewhere in his heart, he already thought she was quite the cheeky one.

A panicked shout sounded from somewhere behind him. Felan spun around like lightning, zeroing in on Elliot as the boy slipped from the top of the climbing frame – what the hell was he doing all the way up there anyway? Felan covered the short distance in a second, scooped him up before he hit the floor head first, and grunted. The kid wasn't exactly light.

Elliot laughed in delight. 'You're so fast! Like Superman!'

'I wouldn't have had to be if you weren't showing off,' Felan reprimanded. Elliot had the decency to look embarrassed, at least. 'What were you doing all the way at the top? I thought Mrs

Walters spoke to you about it last time.'

Just because he didn't talk to the kids much, it didn't mean that he didn't listen to the conversations that happened around him.

'I just wanted to feel tall,' he mumbled.

As irritating as the kid could sometimes be, Elliot reminded Felan of himself all the time. 'There are other ways of feeling tall that aren't dangerous, Elliot,' he said, setting the boy on his feet. He gave him an awkward pat to his shoulder. The motion felt foreign.

He wasn't cut out for this. He wasn't.

'Sorry, Felan.'

'Just don't do it again.'

Elliot stood up straight and saluted. 'Yes Sir!'

Felan watched, bewildered, as the kid ran off to join the others like nothing had happened. Kids bounced back quickly – or so he'd been told – but Felan wouldn't. He had known that for a long time.

Gemma stomped her crocodile wellies. The wet grass squelched beneath her. 'Again!'

Felan tried for a smile. 'Sure.'

Very soon after, Felan had a queue of small children wanting to cross the monkey bars too. He found he didn't mind – he liked to be useful. If the kids were having fun, then he was finally doing something right... but he couldn't stop the voices in his head that kept saying, *they shouldn't be around me. I'm dangerous. What if I hurt them? What if I forget myself and do something stupid? What if...*

'I'm hungry,' Gemma whined.

'Okay. One more turn each and then we'll head inside for lunch,' he said, keeping the voices in his head at bay. The kids had to believe he was normal, or as normal as Felan could get away with pretending to be.

Gemma giggled and his doubts flew away like an empty sweet wrapper in the wind.

Chapter 3: Weak Links

When Felan and the kids eventually traipsed back inside the house, Mrs Walters had what Felan could only describe as a feast laid out on the kitchen table. The kids took their seats and filled their plates with all kinds of sandwiches and crisps and cut up pieces of fruit and vegetables. Felan saw food he liked, but he hovered by the kitchen sink, unsure. He wanted the kids to eat their fill first.

Mrs Walters walked over and stood next to him. He was pleased to note that she kept a safe distance between them. She nodded in the direction of the table. 'You must be hungry after all of that running around,' she said.

Felan shrugged. 'I'll eat when they finish.'

Well, it wasn't a total lie, but he knew Mrs Walters wouldn't believe him anyway. She was good at seeing right through him. Annoyingly good.

'I was watching you from the kitchen window. It looked like the kids were having fun,' she said. 'And it looked like you were too.'

'Yeah…' he said, staring down at his feet.

'Good.' She asked him to look up at her. He did so without complaint, in the same way a lonely, loyal dog would. 'I'm glad. Now, there's enough food on that table for everyone. Go and sit down, and I want you to eat something.'

Knowing he would be fighting a losing battle if he didn't, he sat down in the chair next to Gemma and picked up the smallest sandwich he could find and took a bite.

There were lots of things he had missed out on because of his less than conventional circumstances, yet despite his world getting bigger now that he was out of Guadalupe, he still felt like he was stuck, like he was waiting for something terrible to happen. He hated waiting. He loathed it.

Out of the corner of his eye, he noticed Mrs Walters watching him. He took another bite of his sandwich and added some carrot sticks and a few grapes to his plate.

Gemma patted his arm. 'Hungry?'

Felan popped a grape in his mouth. 'A little.'

He wasn't, but Gemma didn't need to know that.

The girl sat up in her chair, picked up another sandwich and put it on Felan's plate. It looked like a jam sandwich (Gemma's favourite, judging by the smears all around her mouth), and Felan wanted to put it back on the table for the other kids, but he could never say no to her.

He forced himself to pick up the sandwich and take a bite. 'Thanks, Gem,' he said quietly. She immediately went back to her own plate, everything covered in jam. Even the crisps were covered, and Felan thought that was an achievement in itself.

He managed to eat everything on his plate (which admittedly wasn't much) and Mrs Walters rewarded him with a smile. A warm feeling settled in his chest and he wanted to chase it. He wanted to find out where it led to.

The feeling faded seconds later. It left him floundering.

The kids finished their lunch after Felan did, managing to pack in extortionate amounts of food. Especially Jude. According to Josie, Jude was like a hoover and he often ate everyone's leftovers. Josie also exaggerated a lot, according to Jude.

Felan wasn't sure what to think.

When given the all-clear, the kids took off in the direction of the living room. Felan immediately got to work in the kitchen, working in silence with Mrs Walters while the sound of the kids' voices travelled down the hallway. She cleared away the table and wrapped up any leftovers for later while Felan washed the dishes and wiped down the surfaces, and when he was finished, he rewarded himself with a glass of water. He wondered how he'd managed years of sneaking drips of water from the rusted bath tap while his father was asleep (until the water stopped flowing altogether, that was), and how he'd happily drank from the broken shower head at the Warehouse. A working tap was so much more convenient, he thought.

Life seemed so simple now, yet it was harder than it had ever been before.

'You're thinking again,' Mrs Walters said. When he didn't respond, she continued, 'I just want you to know that I'm proud of you.' She walked off, back in the direction of her bedroom, and Felan finished his water in silence, wondering why she'd say something like that when she had no reason to.

He spent the rest of the day in his room, pen in hand, a blank page in front of him. Ever since his revelation, he hadn't written a single word. He'd thought about it plenty, but writing it down? The words were there, in his head, and yet he couldn't bring himself to put them down on paper. He thought it was because it might make what happened to him real. Being so far away from the city that ruined him made it seem like an awful nightmare he had finally woken up from. He wished it were only a nightmare, but the scars on his body proved otherwise.

So many scars.

***

'How's your room? Still got four walls?' Blaez teased when she called him later that evening.

'It does. Thank you for your concern.'

'What have you been up to on this fine Sunday, then?'

'I played outside with the kids.' He told her all about the monkey bars, and Elliot falling off. About lunch.

'I told you they were good kids,' she said.

The childlike joy he felt lingered in his chest, even if he didn't want it to. 'I'm glad Elliot asked me. I would've just spent the day in my room. I like that they're starting to be comfortable around me now.'

He did like it. He *adored* it, in fact, adored it so much that Felan would do anything to keep them safe from harm… and so, in equal measure, he wanted to push them away because Felan was dangerous and the kids deserved better. The kids deserved to be safe. Bitterness crawled up from his stomach and lodged itself firmly in Felan's throat, stealing his voice, and wasn't that the crux of the problem?

'That's because you've spent time with them,' Blaez said. 'They won't get used to you if you stay locked in your room all the time – and this is the part where you tell me I'm right.'

'Actually, I think this is the part where I tell you goodnight.'

'Such a killjoy,' she said fondly. He could imagine the smile on her face. 'Goodnight, Felan. Don't spend every day shut inside your room, okay? Even if it's just to walk around the garden. Fresh air will do you good.'

He liked that she cared so much, but she should worry about herself. He wanted to tell her so. He wanted to tell her he missed her, and that she should hurry it up and come back. He wanted to tell her that he regretted letting her go. She shouldn't be in Guadalupe. She should be safe in Weisworth.

 With him.

'Be safe,' was all he managed.

'I always am!'

It took Felan a long time to fall asleep.

Nightmares woke him up not long after. He checked his phone. It had just gone three in the morning.

He wrote down the first few words in his notebook.

Will it ever stop?

Entry 1 – 5:27am

How do I start this?

~~I don't know what I'm supposed to write down?~~

This is stupid.

It's a stupid notebook. It's just a stupid notebook. How is this helping? If anything, it's making me more frustrated and angrier. It's making everything worse. I can't sleep as it is. ~~Why~~ How is getting worked up going to help me sleep?

I don't know what I expected when I decided on writing, but it wasn't this.

I don't get how anything is supposed to help me now.

Chapter 4: Co-dependency

The kids didn't protest when Mrs Walters bundled four of them into the minivan to take to school on Monday morning. In fact, they looked almost excited to be going.

Felan was confused. He hated school and he didn't have a single happy memory of his time there. There had been too many bullies, and too many teachers turning a blind eye to what he had endured.

'I'll be back in half an hour,' Mrs Walters said.

Felan and Gemma waved from the front step. Only when the minivan was no longer in sight did Felan close and lock the door. Just in case. He looked down at the kid that was still holding his hand, taking comfort in the contact. He shook off the uneasy feeling that had nestled in the gaps between his ribs. Gemma didn't need to think that anything was amiss. He wanted to keep things as normal as he could for her.

'Are we working on your numbers this morning?'

'Yep. I can count to ten now,' she said proudly, puffing out her stomach.

He crouched down and poked her belly. 'Do you think you can show me?'

'I'm a big girl now.'

Felan didn't have the heart to remind her that only yesterday she was too small to do the monkey bars by herself. They sat at the table in the living room and counted until Mrs Walters got back from the school drop-off.

Gemma wouldn't start school properly until September, and Felan had no idea what his plans were yet. Sometimes, he needed someone to pester him (he didn't want anyone to tell Blaez that though), and he hoped Mrs Walters would be that person.

He guessed it was what a parent did, pester their child and

help them make important decisions. He wouldn't know; one got hit by a car before he could make any real decisions, and the other beat him up if he so much as breathed the wrong way.

Christ. He was a real joy to be around lately.

'Gem – have you tried counting to fifteen yet?'

A look of uncertainty crossed her face. 'It's hard after ten,' she whispered, as if telling him some big secret. He was impressed with the length of her sentences today. He assumed she must've heard it before somewhere because normally she only spoke two or three words at a time.

'You're absolutely right, but you're a big girl – I think you can handle it.'

'I am. Show me,' she demanded.

By the time Mrs Walters came back, Gemma could proudly count to ten without her fingers, and with help she could get to twelve.

'Good girl,' Mrs Walters praised. 'Felan and I are just going to have a little chat. Do you want to get your colouring book out, and we'll do some more numbers later?'

'Okay!' Gemma hopped off her chair and raced up to her room. She came back thirty seconds later with two books and her pencil case. Felan followed Mrs Walters to the sofas and tried to make himself comfortable. He failed miserably.

A part of him was telling him to run.

It was always telling him to run.

'Have I… did I do something wrong?' he asked softly.

He was brought back to a time with Harvey in one of the many boardrooms at the Warehouse. Harvey had been there for him when no one else had. The man's heart had been in the right place, and Felan hadn't seen it.

He'd been ten feet down his whole life and now that he was beginning to climb out of that hole, the climbing terrified him. Would he ever reach the top? And on the off chance that he did make it, what would he find when he got there? *Who* would he find?

Mrs Walters' eyebrows furrowed. 'Why would you think that?'

'It always happens, sooner or later.'

'Well, I can assure you, you've done nothing wrong,' she said kindly. She leant forward. 'I wanted to talk to you about your plans. Have you come to a decision about what you're going to do this year?'

Ah. *That* decision. Last year, he was worrying about his dad and people finding out, how they'd think he was weak and an easy target (they already thought that, but confirming it would hurt even more). Earlier in the year, he was in a constant state of panic about Nick and Blaez and his friends. Now? Now he had a choice of what to panic over. So, naturally, he chose everything.

The real question was this: school or work?

'I don't think I can handle school. Authority figures...' Felan shook his head. An authority figure would always remind him of Nick or his father. 'I don't like feeling like I'm not in control.'

'It would be the same if you were to get a job,' she said.

'Well, it's different,' Felan argued.

With a job, he could quit if he didn't like it. School? Not an option. Besides, if he got himself a job he could start paying Tristan and Mr Bailey back, and Mrs Walters. All three of them had willingly spent money on him. A runaway. A criminal. A murderer.

He bit his lip. He wondered how he could explain it to her without sounding like a lunatic.

'I haven't been to school for a long time. My dad pulled me out when I was fourteen so that, uh...' he broke off. 'Anyway... I just don't think I'd be welcome. School was never for someone like me anyway.'

Because of his dad (and to a degree, the bullies that had tormented him), Felan had missed out on getting a proper education, and that simple fact set him apart from every other teenager in the world. He was the outlier to society, the strange kid, *the freak*, the oddity who had no chance at a normal future because of events that were out of his control.

'You know, if you wanted to go back to school, but not physically go into one, you can study from here. We can get you a tutor,' she suggested. 'That's something we can do for you.'

Mrs Walters was giving him an out. She was trying. She was really trying. Felan couldn't find it in himself to do the same.

She studied him for a long time. 'Like I said before, you don't have to give me your answer now, but you need to have made your mind up by September.'

He glanced over at the calendar hung on the living room wall, already full up with the other kids' activities and appointments and days out with their friends from school. He tried to ignore that Zac's name was still there. So was April's, and so was Amelia's. He averted his gaze to the side of the big calendar. It was June, so he had a little under three months to sort something out.

'I can tell you now, I won't be physically going to school.'

Mrs Walters wrote something in her notebook. 'We can work with that.'

'May I ask… what's Blaez doing? Has she decided yet?'

'She's not given me a straight answer either,' she said carefully.

'Okay. Cool. Thank you,' he said. Without warning, unease settled inside him and he felt like he was seven all over again, feeling his father's strike that first time, and the shock and the disbelief and the betrayal that immediately followed. He folded his hands in his lap, twisting his fingers together. His knee bounced in tandem with his racing heart.

'You're allowed to feel sad, Felan,' Mrs Walters reminded him. 'You didn't deserve what happened to you.'

She kept telling him that lately. He didn't know why. He wasn't sad. He didn't feel sad. He didn't feel anything. He told her as much, and it was probably the most honest thing he'd said to her in days.

'I think you do,' she said.

He leapt to his feet. 'I'm going upstairs.'

Mrs Walters nodded her head, as if expecting the sudden announcement. 'Okay. You know where we are.'

He left Gemma in Mrs Walters' capable hands and sat in his room. He wasn't sulking. No. He didn't sulk. Felan wasn't one to sulk. He had no reason to. There was no way in hell he was sulking.

He just hadn't heard from Blaez today – it set him off-kilter. Besides, Blaez would be able to help him make a decision about what to do regarding his future. She knew what he was good at. She knew him better than anyone. She knew him better than he knew himself and he couldn't make the decision without her.

That was another question. What *was* he good at? To be honest, he hadn't tried a lot of things (for obvious reasons) so he had yet to discover anything, however, when he took the time to try, he was actually good with kids. They listened to him… sometimes, even if he wished they wouldn't. He had taught Gemma some of her numbers. He was good at cleaning too. He washed up the dishes most nights. Maybe he could go to one of the few cafés around town and wash up. Or maybe he could do an online course from his room. Sure, he'd need to earn enough to buy himself a computer first, but…

A computer. If he managed to get access to a computer, he could hack into the cameras at the underground base and see what was going on. He could catch a glimpse of Accalia, and of Edward. He could help Tristan and Mr Bailey stop Nick for good.

The thought was only fleeting, yet the lump that formed in his throat lingered for what felt like hours.

He knew Tristan had someone watching the cameras around the clock. Felan wouldn't be giving them any new information, and… and if he *did* hack into them, he was terrified of what he might see, terrified of what he might uncover, if there was anyone else, if there was anyone new.

If there were any more innocent, helpless kids.

Felan lay on his bed and shut his eyes when an ache began to blossom behind them. The dark sometimes helped – it took some of the pain away – but still it lingered. He didn't know when exactly it changed, but all he knew was that the dark was no longer safe. The dark didn't hide his thoughts anymore – it only served to amplify them.

He was still in bed when Blaez called him an hour later.

'Done already?' he asked. 'It's barely ten.'

'Quick day,' she said. 'Mirriam asked about you.'

Mirriam was the judge who Blaez was speaking to. A judge who, according to Blaez, wasn't exactly fair.

'Yeah?' He traced the squares and the circles on his duvet. The designs were a bit young for a sixteen-year-old, but Felan knew they had been intended for a kid, not him. Not someone dangerous. Not a criminal.

The room had been Zac's, he remembered bitterly. The kid had probably chosen everything in this room before he left. (He had. He'd chosen the duvet himself. Wasn't that what Elliot had said?) It didn't feel right for Felan to swoop in and take his place so quickly. It felt like he was hopping into a freshly dug grave. Shivers shot down his spine.

'I miss you, Felan.'

'I miss you too.'

A particularly loud shriek from outside had him on his feet, his nosed pressed to the windowpane. It was just the young kids in the house opposite again. It was fine. Everything was fine.

'Why haven't you been replying to their texts?'

Felan collapsed back onto his bed. The glow-in-the-dark stars weren't quite so spectacular in the daytime. 'You know why.'

'Yeah, I do,' she said. 'And they know too – they're just worried about you.'

'I don't know what to say to them. Tristan and Mr Bailey saw me when I was... The thought of them brings back those memories, and I don't want that.'

He wasn't sulking, he wasn't avoiding them, and he wasn't avoiding... *it*. Before. Everything was Before now. Before, Before, Before. Felan wanted to finally feel safe in the After, an After that would have no more Afters.

'Being back here – it's worse than I thought. I'm safe, don't worry about that,' she added hastily. 'Every alley and street I see – I did something on them, something I'm not proud of, in the name of someone who wanted to hurt me. It's hard, but I'm getting through it, day by day. Talking helps. Of course, I've only been talking for a few days now, but it helps. Speaking to different people helps. It makes the pain of what I did, the pain of what I was made to do, easier to live with.'

Felan knew exactly where Blaez was going with this. 'I don't want to talk to anyone. I just want to be left alone.'

'Then that's your burden to bear, Felan.'

He wished it were dark so the stars on the ceiling would glow. In the daytime, they looked mishappen and out of place. 'All I wanted was a family,' he began. 'And now I wish I didn't have to face anyone ever again.'

It was the first time he'd said that out loud. It sounded childish, but he just didn't want people to look at him and know exactly what he did. Sometimes, all he wanted to do was disappear.

Sometimes, when I fall asleep, I wish I never wake up.

'You're taking great care of Gemma, you know,' Blaez said. 'She loves you.'

'Yeah, well, I don't know why.'

They talked until Mrs Walters called for him. He wandered downstairs, his headache still in place but not quite so bad, and followed her into the garden. She took him all the way to the other side, past her tiny herb planter beneath the kitchen window (in his first week in Weisworth, Felan had learned all of the different uses for basil, thyme, sage and parsley) and far away from the climbing frame and the monkey bars.

'I was hoping you'd be able to help me,' she said.

Felan flinched.

'I want to make a vegetable patch,' she explained. 'It needs to be dug, and the seeds bought and planted, and obviously weeded and watered. I want the kids to be able to help grow them, so we can work on something together as a group.'

'I can go to the shop to get some seeds,' he offered. Sure, he'd be looking over his shoulder every five seconds in case Nick showed up, but he could feign bravery. 'What did you want to plant?'

'Just simple things. Carrots. Parsnips. Potatoes. Things we use all the time. I think it would do us all some good to focus on a project, and it gets us outside every day.'

Felan decided he was going to try. 'I think that's a great idea.'

***

He headed into town after lunch using the money Mrs Walters had given him to get what he needed at the local garden centre. He peered into the pond there and marvelled at the size of some of the fish (they were almost as long as his arm!), before he went back inside and chose the packets of seeds and the handfuls of both seed potatoes and onion sets. Luckily, they already had trowels and watering cans in the shed at the bottom of the garden.

It wasn't until later that evening, after a loud dinner with all of the kids, that Felan ducked out into the garden with the trowels and started digging. It was oddly therapeutic, in a way, to make the same motion over and over. He guessed it was why he enjoyed washing up so much. He tossed the weeds into the hedge beside him and continued to sift the soil until it was loose.

He heard footsteps a short while later.

'What are you doing?' Jude asked.

'Making a vegetable patch,' he said. 'Would you like to help? There's a spare trowel.'

The kid didn't say no, so Felan showed him how to weed, and how to dig, and they settled into their work. They found solace in the silence.

Entry 2 – 00:41am

The one person I can rely on isn't here.

The one person whose touch I can tolerate without my skin crawling, I can't touch. I want to be loved, but I don't remember what that feels like. Blaez started to remind me, but she's gone now.

I know I'm isolating myself. I know it's not normal. I know I'm not normal, but... I don't know what else to do. For years I've relied upon myself. I learned to not ask for help because I would never get it. I had never gotten it until now and I don't know how to deal with it. I don't know how to deal with change. I've been ignored and neglected and abused my entire life. Being at peace isn't normal. Being at peace shouldn't happen to someone like me.

I still don't see how writing this down is helping.

Chapter 5: Quaking

'What do we say to Mrs Walters?' Felan reminded the kids while they all carried their dirty plates to the worktop beside the sink. He squirted washing-up liquid into the bowl and ran the hot water until it was scalding. He plunged his hands straight in, choosing to forgo the gloves on this occasion.

'Thank you!' they chorused.

'You're all very welcome,' Mrs Walters said warmly. 'Felan and I are going to wash up. Why don't you all head into the living room and watch the TV? Remember, it's Josie's turn to pick tonight.'

The kids ran out of the kitchen, little Gemma taking up the rear, giggling as she tried to keep up with their much larger steps.

'You're really good with the kids, you know?' Mrs Walters began. 'I'll admit, when Tristan first got in contact with me about you and Blaez, I wasn't sure how it was going to work – you were both so much older than the kids I already had, but… it turns out I didn't need to worry at all.'

Oh, she had every reason to worry. She should still be worried.

'They're smaller than I thought they would be,' Felan admitted.

He knew how small Edward had been at twelve, and all of the kids were younger than him. The thought of any of the kids going through what Felan had…

And I left Edward behind.

'Sorry, Mrs Walters. Do you mind if I do the clean-up on my own?'

She searched him for something before she settled a gentle hand on his shoulder, choosing to ignore the way he flinched away. 'If you need anything, just shout. We're only down the hall.' Mrs Walters left the room, and the shouting from the living room gradually quietened.

Felan let out a sigh of relief. Some peace and quiet, if only for a moment.

He looked down at the steam rising from the bowl. The water wasn't hot enough for what he wanted to do.

God, what the *hell* was he doing here?

He thought of little Edward who should be in Weisworth instead. Felan should have been the one to stay behind, he knew. It would have been the better outcome. Besides, maybe Felan could have found...

Who was he kidding? He wouldn't have found anywhere better to stay. That's why he was in Weisworth in the first place – no one else had wanted him, so last-resort orphanage hundreds of miles away it was. Out of sight, out of mind.

The orphanages in Guadalupe had to have been dreadful. He remembered how Caleb had once described them: 'overwhelmed and underfunded.' That wasn't the case in Weisworth. Mrs Walters had assured him on multiple occasions that they had enough money to go around, and that there was plenty of space for everyone. Correction: there was plenty of space now that April and Amelia had moved elsewhere.

A loud crash from upstairs startled Felan, and he lost his grip on the plate he'd been drying. It hit the tiled floor with a smash, sending pieces flying in all directions. He gaped at the mess in shock, all the while the echo of slaps and gunshots rattled around in his head like a broken record. The bullet sank into his arm all over again. The bombs exploded once more in the crowded streets of Guadalupe. Crying sounded in earnest. He saw everything. He wished he didn't.

He wished he didn't have to see anything ever again.

'Felan?' He blinked. Mrs Walters stood a safe distance from him, concern pulling her face taut. 'Are you alright?' she asked. She glanced down at the mess on the floor.

Felan couldn't tell if she was angry or not. 'I'm sorry,' he said. 'I'll clean it up. I'm sorry.' He stepped back, his eyes wet in the corners.

'Don't move,' she said. Felan stopped immediately, waiting in what felt like purgatory for what came next. 'You're not the first person to break a plate in this house. There's no harm done.'

There was always harm done when it came to Felan – then it registered in his brain what she'd said.

Oh.

Oh.

Mrs Walters dodged the shards and grabbed the brush from the cupboard. She swept the shattered remains into a pile far away from Felan.

'I have a habit of breaking things,' he eventually said, still unsure of where the line was, of where exactly the new boundaries ended.

'Nonsense. It's just a plate.' Mrs Walters swept the pile into the dustpan and Felan shuffled over to hold the bin open; he thought it best to make himself useful, just in case she changed her mind. 'Thank you,' she said, and tipped the pieces inside. They made another crash as they hit the bottom.

'What was that noise? Before?' Felan asked.

Mrs Walters made herself busy putting away the dustpan and brush. 'Some of the kids were running around upstairs and slammed a door.'

Felan hung his head and pinched the bridge of his nose. It had been nothing. He had gotten himself so worked up over nothing. How pathetic. He should be over it. It had been weeks.

'Felan…'

'It's not their fault,' he said. 'I don't blame them. I promise you I don't blame them.'

He didn't argue when Mrs Walters started helping with what was left of the washing-up. Felan avoided the knives like the plague. He ALWAYS avoided the knives. 'I'll buy another plate,' he said. 'I'll replace it.'

She shook her head. 'There are plenty of spares up in the loft somewhere. Tell you what, you can help me clear it out tomorrow if you like.'

'Sure.'

'And besides, accidents happen in a house full of children,' she said with a laugh.

In response, Felan feigned a laugh, though he wondered how much money he had taken away from the kids since his arrival. He wondered how much he'd deprived the kids of by taking a spot he didn't deserve.

He wondered how much longer he'd be allowed to stay somewhere everyone knew he didn't belong.

Entry 3 – 1:14am

I had another nightmare.

It... it felt so real. I really thought Blaez was back with Nick. I really thought he'd hurt her again. She had a black eye and her mascara was running and she was bleeding.

Then Nick loomed over her with a knife, the same knife that cut me so many times before. Blaez opened her mouth to scream.

That's when I woke up. I called Blaez straight away. She's fine. She was asleep and I woke her up. I shouldn't have called, but she reassured me that it was fine, that I could call her any time, but she fell asleep after five minutes and left me on my own again and now I can't stop thinking.

No one ever told me how hard it was going to be to adapt to a new environment.

I have a hard time convincing myself that I'm actually safe here with the kids, with Mrs Walters. I still don't fully believe it.

I keep waiting for the day when Nick comes waltzing through those doors and takes me back. I'm still waiting, and I don't know why. I thought I was over with the whole waiting thing.

But waiting for the past to return is so much easier than striding forward into an unknown future.

Chapter 6: A Welcome Distraction

The following day, Felan and Mrs Walters took advantage of the empty house and followed through with her suggestion to clear out the loft.

He had been a little apprehensive when Mrs Walters pulled open the hatch in the ceiling upstairs and a ladder came down after it. Once it was secure, she climbed up. He tentatively climbed after her.

'It's a little dusty up here,' she warned.

Dusty was an understatement. He felt it hit his face, and when he looked up he thought there must have been some loose tiles because he could see daylight in multiple places, and where the light filtered through it left a trail of dusty swirls in the air. They would have been cool if Felan hadn't practically inhaled one upon entry. He coughed into his arm.

It reminded Felan of the underground base. It reminded him of staying underground for days on end without any natural light. It reminded him of being stuck in the dark without any hope of escape.

Felan wiped a cobweb from his face and shuddered.

They spent the morning and a good chunk of the afternoon sorting through the boxes that were piled up in the loft. It was hot and hard work, but Felan found that he enjoyed the constant moving about. He helped find the spare plates and the bowls and the cutlery, and he volunteered to manoeuvre them all the way down to the kitchen table to sort out later.

'If you need a break at any point, you let me know,' Mrs Walters said when he climbed back up the ladder for the next lot.

'Sure.'

Felan found a box of board games for the kids to play, and Mrs Walters discovered multiple sets of spare duvets and clothes in another. She pulled out a grey duvet set, complete with a sheet and two pillowcases.

'I think this might suit your needs better than your current set,' she said. 'I'll put it in the wash.'

'Okay.'

Man, his one-word responses must have been getting tiresome. Luckily, Mrs Walters thought nothing of it and continued sorting through boxes, humming a tune Felan had never heard before.

He sat down in front of a box, no longer bothered by the dust and the dirt that covered his clothes, and opened it. He looked down at the contents and tugged at the wool he found inside. 'What's this?' he asked, picking one of them up. Beneath it he found some odd-looking plastic sticks with hooks on the ends.

Mrs Walters glanced around. 'Oh, that's my old knitting kit. There should be some books in there too. Have it, if you like. I think you'll take to it quite well.'

Felan shrugged and closed the box again. 'Thank you,' he said. He took it straight down to his room to look at later before climbing back up the ladder for a third time, however he soon lost count of the number of times he made that particular climb. So that Mrs Walters didn't have to, Felan carried the heavier boxes downstairs to the playroom to join the other boxes of spare clothes and spare everythings. From there, they worked in silence, unpacking games and pens and pads of paper, and washing up the new kitchenware.

Just before three in the afternoon Mrs Walters left to pick up the kids, leaving Felan alone in the big house. At a loss as to what to do to amuse himself, Felan began chopping up the carrots for dinner. It would be less work for Mrs Walters when she got home, he knew, so at least there was that.

He tried his best to ignore that he was holding a sharp knife.

With the first chop, he half expected blood to pour from the vegetable, but it was simply that, a vegetable. He was being ridiculous.

Josie liked carrots. He could do this for Josie. He *was* doing this for Josie. *But it would be so easy to pretend the knife slipped.* He froze mid chop and tilted the knife to examine it. It was serrated, so it would be easy to…

The minivan rolled to a stop outside, and Felan began chopping the carrots again in earnest. Nothing happened. He was fine. Everything was fine.

The kids came in, took off their shoes and hung up their coats, running upstairs to get changed without so much as a hello to Felan. He didn't mind. He deserved it.

'Don't forget to put your socks in the laundry basket!' Mrs Walters shouted after them, before noticing Felan's efforts. 'Thank you for this. You've been working so hard all day. You didn't have to do this too.'

Felan dropped the knife onto the chopping board with a clatter. 'It's only some carrots,' he mumbled, as if trying to convince himself of the fact. He clenched and unclenched his hands, hating how they trembled in plain sight.

Mrs Walters reached out and encased his hands with her own. 'It's more than that,' she said. 'You remembered Josie likes them. You did it because you knew it would help me and… and it's the first time I've seen you touch a sharp knife since you arrived,' she finished quietly.

Felan bit his lip. No way was he going to admit to what he'd thought before they all came back. 'Still.'

Mrs Walters gave his hands a squeeze. 'Don't ever make excuses for your wins, Felan. No matter how small they are.'

The kids saved Felan from responding by charging into the kitchen. Mrs Walters dropped his hands and Felan backed away, suddenly breathless. The kids said their hellos as they ran through and out of the back door, before heading down to the climbing frame, a daily ritual when the weather was nice.

Felan marvelled at their endless, bounding energy. He was sure he had been like that once, but at the moment, everything just felt so *heavy*, like something invisible was sat atop his chest, preventing him from taking a full breath, like his lungs were incapable of inflating properly.

'I'll finish up the carrots, shall I?' Mrs Walters asked.

He nodded mutely.

'Felan, it's *okay*.'

'I'll lay the table,' he decided out loud.

'I think you've done more than your fair share today.'

'I'll lay the table,' he said again, harsher than he intended.

Mrs Walters carried on chopping up the carrots and moved them into the top two tiers of the steamer. 'Thank you, Felan. That's very helpful.'

Sometimes, Felan wished she would just hit him to get it over with. He wished she would hit him hard enough so that he could feel it, hard enough so that he could feel something other than *heavy*.

***

It was a simple dinner: fish fingers, chips, carrots and peas, though Josie didn't have the latter. Throughout the meal, Felan was content to sit in silence and listen to the kids and Mrs Walters talk, the kids going on endless tangents about what they had learned at school, or in Gemma's case nursery, that day. Some of the topics piqued his interest, but he stayed quiet. Secretly, he hoped that one of them would bring him into the conversation, into any conversation, really.

They didn't.

Resentment bubbled inside his body, an emotion that Felan didn't know what to do with, so when everyone was finished eating, he helped with the clean-up once again, because what else was he good for? He'd feel terrible if he ate their food and then left Mrs Walters to tidy up on her own. That wasn't how things worked.

Every time he got something, he had to give something, or do something, in return.

And now he was overthinking again. Great.

He requested to spend the evening alone, and Mrs Walters smiled in that understanding way of hers. 'You know where I am,' she said. The kids had bolted back outside to play while the days were still long.

When he was back in the safety of his room, Felan breathed deeply for a few minutes. He tugged on his hair until his hands stopped trembling. Then he saw the box sat in the middle of his room.

He got down on his knees and laid out the contents on the bedroom floor, taking his time to look over everything. True to Mrs Walters' word, Felan found the books buried at the bottom beneath bundles of wool. He breezed through the books pretty fast, and then set his gaze upon the needles. That's what they were called. He picked them up, chose some yellow wool (maybe by some miracle, it would cheer him up), and did his best to follow the book's instructions. It was slow progress, and when his knees protested from being knelt on for so long, he migrated to his bed. He was so invested that he didn't notice the time whizzing by until Mrs Walters popped her head in to say goodnight.

'Huh?' Felan said. He turned to look at the clock on his bedside table, the clock that sat behind his brooch, the brooch which, every time Felan looked at it, filled him with warmth at the memory of his best friend. 'Oh my God.'

'Time flies when you're having fun,' she said with a gentle smile.

'Huh. Yeah, I suppose so.' Felan set down his project. 'Thanks for today, and I'm sorry about earlier.'

'I should be thanking you,' she said. 'And don't worry about it. New places take some time to get used to, after all.' Mrs Walters shut the door.

Felan waited five minutes. He made his way to the bathroom to clean up and change before he headed back to bed. He curled up, but his thoughts kept going back to the project sat on his desk. When he still couldn't get to sleep an hour later, he got up, switched on his desk lamp and carried on knitting until he couldn't keep his eyes open. Only then did he return to his bed. Fighting to stay awake, he stared up at the glow-in-the-dark stars on his ceiling, and he prayed.

He prayed everything worked out this time around, yet he couldn't help but be enticed by the big black hole he could feel coming his way.

He couldn't help but beg it to hurry up.

Entry 4 – 4:57am

I'm forgetting her face. I'm forgetting her voice. I'm forgetting everything about her.

The one thing I will not forget, ever, is how safe and comforted she made me feel. I will never forget the joy she brought into my life. Even if I forget everything else, I will never forget her warmth.

I just wish I saw more of her in me.

All I see when I look in the mirror is Dad. There are pieces of her in me, in how I look, but I'm the spitting image of him. I wonder if that ever upset her. I wonder if she regretted me. I wonder if she hated me so much that she wanted me gone.

I regret that I look like Dad. I regret a lot of things. Like father like son, right? Isn't that how the saying goes?

It definitely isn't like mother like son. I'm nothing like Mum. She was good, and she was kind. I'm the complete opposite. I'm everything she isn't. I am an amalgamation (I learned that word from Jude the other day. He's a really smart kid) of every bad thing in this world. I bring danger. I cause pain. All I do is hurt people.

I don't like hurting people. I don't want to hurt people.

I just want to be normal.

Is that too much to ask?

Chapter 7: Rift

Sometimes, late at night when the shadows were too human in form, sharp pinpricks of pain flared from his bullet wound scar. The residual pain was never as bad as it had been when he'd been shot, but it hurt enough to bring tears to his eyes, it hurt enough to send him into a state of panic, a state of panic bad enough to text Blaez.

It hurt even more when his texts remained unseen and unanswered for hours, or even days, at a time.

On the days he didn't hear from her, he'd finally text back Tristan with a simple, *Is she safe?* He'd get an affirmative within the hour, but it never helped. He trusted Tristan, but it wasn't the same as Blaez confirming it herself. It wasn't the same as hearing her voice.

He wondered how long it would take, this whole thing with Mirriam. He wanted Blaez here. He wanted Blaez here so they could make their decision about the coming year together, like they always did. What would happen to them, to their friendship, if Blaez stayed in Guadalupe any longer? She'd only been gone for a week or so and already Felan could feel the cracks forming, could already feel the bottomless fissures filling with lava and spitting in the new space between them.

What else could there possibly be to talk about?

'Blaez?'

'Hmm?'

The phone call was an early one… he thought it had been two in the morning when his phone had vibrated by his head. As usual, he had been wide awake.

'When do you think you'll come back?'

Silence had never sounded so loud.

'I… I really don't know,' Blaez began. 'There's a lot of stuff going on here at the moment. There's still so much to talk about. We haven't even started looking at train tickets yet.'

Felan's stomach dropped. She hadn't booked a train back. She'd booked a one-way ticket to get as far away from him as possible. 'Oh.'

'I hope it's soon,' she said. 'It's weird being apart from you for so long.'

'Well… I'll be here,' he said lamely. He couldn't believe it. There he was, anticipating a return within the next week or so when in reality Blaez hadn't even thought about it, hadn't even thought about *him*.

'Felan,' she implored. 'Talk to me.'

'I miss you, Blaez. I'm… I'm lonely.'

Even he could hear how pathetic he sounded saying that out loud.

'You've got the kids. You've got Mrs Walters.'

'It's not the same. They're not… you. They don't understand me.'

'Then talk to them.' She sounded so tired. She sounded so miserable. 'Make them understand.'

But Felan was miserable too. 'I don't want to.'

'Then stop putting this all on me!'

Felan flinched away from his phone. The first time he'd upset her, he'd sworn it would be the last, that he'd do whatever it took to keep her happy.

Still failing.

'No, I didn't mean… I'm sorry, Blaez,' Felan said, his body entombed by the familiar feelings of misery and guilt, so familiar that they had made a home within him. 'I didn't mean to put all of this on you.'

'Then why did you?'

'I don't know.'

She made a frustrated noise down the phone. 'I can offer you advice, but I can't do everything for you.'

'I'm not asking you to.' The words tasted bitter as soon as he said them. They left a sour, rancid taste in his mouth, like he hadn't brushed his teeth for a month.

He remembered that taste well.

'Then stop putting down every suggestion I make. I'm trying to help you, but I can't do that if you refuse to help yourself.' She huffed. He could practically see the little scowl she was undoubtedly wearing.

The guilt dissipated, and all of the anger he had kept at bay for the last however long broke free. 'Don't you dare, Blaez. Don't pretend like you know what I'm feeling. You don't have any idea – none of you do!' Felan seethed. He didn't know why, because it wasn't Blaez he was angry at. 'It felt like I was on my own. For *so long*. And then you came along and…'

'And what, Felan!' she yelled. 'What did I do?'

'Nothing! You did nothing!'

Wrong, he wanted to say. *You did nothing wrong*. But he couldn't find it in him to correct himself. His burning anger refused to die down, a forest fire raging out of control.

Blaez wasn't coming back.

She gasped a little down the line. 'I tried. I tried so hard to be a good person to you when no one else would.'

Her words? Yeah, they stung. They stung more than he thought they would. 'You pitied me,' he said.

'How could I not?'

'So what, our friendship was based upon *pity*?'

'No, Felan, I just –'

'I don't want your pity.'

'Then what is it you want from me?'

The fights. The aggression. The anger. That's what he *didn't* want, yet he couldn't for the life of him articulate what he meant. Things might have been different if he had learned to say the truth and not a half-truth.

When Felan didn't answer, Blaez continued. 'Are you saying you never wanted… what, honesty?'

'You're putting words in my mouth now. That's not fair.'

'None of this is fair! What else has to happen before you realise that? It wasn't *fair* that Randi and Caleb died! It wasn't *fair* that Harvey died! It wasn't *fair* that I was…' Blaez choked back a sob. 'None of this is fair!'

'Stop yelling at me!'

'No, you started this! We're arguing now because of *you*! Because *you* stayed behind and let me come back here on my own!'

'You *left*. Don't make me the bad guy here,' Felan cried. 'You're all I have left! And what use are you if I can't tell you how I feel?'

'What use am I? What use are *you*, Felan?'

Felan's head spun, a meteorite hurtling down towards the Earth. What use *was* he?

'We were always moving at full speed in different directions and there was never any time to stop and now that I've stopped I don't know what to do! I was the only one…'

'You were not the only one,' Blaez said darkly. 'Yes, you are a victim, and I'm sorry, but you are not the only victim. Don't you *dare* speak to me like that again, do you hear me? I know we're both hurting, but I don't like your tone.'

'I don't know what else to do! I just feel so… so…'

Broken.

Empty.

Helpless.

Alone.

So, so alone.

'I don't know what else to do either, but speaking to each other the way we just did? It won't get us anywhere.' She paused for a moment, held the frayed line steady while she waited for the fish to bite.

And bite Felan did. He always did. It was one of his many flaws. 'Then what are we going to do? Hang up and pretend that this conversation never happened? Never talk to each other again?'

'It's always about *you*,' she said. He could almost feel her anger through the phone. 'We always have conversations about *you* – but what about *me*?'

For an unknown amount of time, Felan breathed heavily down the phone in an attempt to calm himself down so he didn't hurt Blaez any more than he already had done. For someone who claimed to hate hurting people, he did a fantastic job of doing so. Every time.

'I can't have this conversation with you right now,' Blaez said suddenly.

'So your solution is to leave me on my own? Again?' Felan asked, incredulous.

'Whatever. I have to go. It's late enough as it is, and I have to be up early in the morning. *To make use of myself.*'

'Don't...'

The phone beeped twice, and Felan looked at the screen in disbelief. Blaez had never hung up on him before.

In a fit of anger, he slammed his phone down hard on the bed, rolled over and covered his face with his pillow. He couldn't believe he had gotten so worked up so fast. Of all people, he had blown up at Blaez.

It was unnecessary.

It was uncalled for.

He was a disgrace.

He shouldn't exist.

It would be better if he didn't exist.

I don't want to be here anymore.

Felan rolled back slightly so he was lying on his side. He curled up beneath his new, grey covers and stared at nothing, chewing the skin on the inside of his lip. Had he really meant what he said to Blaez?

Yes.

Well, he had accepted that he wasn't okay, but he had known that anyway. He had known that a long time ago, even before his mother had died. He had known he wasn't *normal*. What he'd also known was that he was an oddity. Something to ogle at. Something to laugh at. Something to hit. Something to break.

His father had known it, and maybe his mother had too. Had she seen it? *Had she known?*

Blaez was all he had left, and now she was seeing him, *in pieces*, and all he could see was the same mistake he kept on making, time and time again. In hindsight, it was no wonder she'd rather be in Guadalupe than be with him.

His heart thudded painfully. He curled up some more and willed the phantom pain in his arm to fade.

It throbbed all night long.

***

Maybe he should just run away – it would be better for everyone. Blaez wouldn't have to deal with him anymore. Mrs Walters could focus on the kids without wasting her time on him, and the kids would grow up untainted and undamaged without him around.

Yeah. He'd run away – but where would he go?

Well, he snarked himself, *that was the point.* To go somewhere else, to get as far away as possible, to be literally anywhere else where no one knew him.

But what if someone worse than Nick found him?

His phone beeped a while later, long after he'd given up on sleep. He rolled over to check his messages.

I'm still unbelievably angry with you, but I just wanted to remind you that I love you. Please don't forget that.

Guilt ate away at his insides, gnawing away on the softest parts of him. Blaez was still awake because of him. He'd kept her up because of his temper. He'd upset her. Again.

When would it end?

He typed out a response and hit send: *I'm sorry it escalated so fast. I haven't been myself lately… and for what it's worth, I love you too.*

In the hours that followed, Blaez never responded – and at four in the morning, when he couldn't shut his brain off, Felan sat at his desk and began to write.

Entry 5 – 4:04am

I really messed up this time, didn't I?

I never say what I really mean. I said things that I knew would hurt you because I don't know how to express myself. I lashed out. I should have stayed silent. Your current situation is stressful enough without me adding baggage and even more stress. You don't need me being selfish right now.

You don't need me, full stop.

I forget how young we are. I forget how young you were when you were first introduced to violence, when you were first introduced to Nick and the others. I forget how much longer you were stuck with them. I forget how much more you've suffered than me, and yet I'm the one in pieces.

My problem? I never know how to talk about my feelings. I talk to myself about my life and how I feel in my head all of the time. I explain it so well to myself, but getting it to come out of my mouth is so hard. It's like there's something choking me whenever I try to talk, like there's a cold hand clamping down hard on my throat.

Maybe that's where my writing comes in. It's just me in my head, and no one is reading, no one is listening. But maybe that's also the problem.

I want to be seen, I want to be heard, but I don't want anyone to see the dark side of me. I don't want anyone to know how badly I'm hurting.

I'd rather a hole in the floor swallow me up so I don't have to explain anything to anyone ever again, but it's different with you, Blaez.

I guess I'd hoped you changed your mind about going back. I guess I'd hoped you'd stay here with me. It was completely unfair for me to try to get you to change your mind. I don't know what you want, but I know, right now, it isn't me. I can't stop thinking that you left to get away from me.

I wouldn't blame you if you did.

I wish I could get away from me too.

I want you to be happier, Blaez, whether that's with or without me.

Chapter 8: Slipping

He let the freezing rain pound onto his back; it was cold, and hard, and everything he deserved.

After a few hours of broken sleep, Felan had woken up and heard the rain. He'd felt the urge to scratch the itch that had been growing inside him for weeks, and had run as fast as he could around the quiet town at the crack of dawn. For a moment he was back in Guadalupe, running away all over again in the pouring rain.

His pyjamas were soaked through by the time the house came back into view.

He traipsed back in, and Mrs Walters looked like she had had a heart attack when she saw him shivering and nearly blue. Well, that was what she had told him after. She asked what the hell he'd been doing, and when he didn't respond, she had sent him for a scalding shower. Normally, a shower would declutter his thoughts and allow him to make sense of them, ordering everything into neat, little rows. Today it did no such thing. His thoughts were as loud as ever, overlapping and snapping at his heels like a starving, rabid dog that foamed at the mouth. He shut the hot water off the moment he stopped shivering and wiped away the condensation on the bathroom mirror.

His father's cold eyes stared back.

Felan spent the rest of the day sat at his desk, notebook open, staring out of the window. He revelled in how it felt to be hit again; familiar, painful, and his way of life.

***

The second time he ran in the rain, it was for a completely different reason.

For the past few months (it started long before Felan and

Blaez moved in), Jude had been going out for mornings and evenings at the weekends with a lovely couple who lived just outside of Weisworth. It had looked promising, Jude coming back every time with a smile that lasted a whole week. In every other universe, it would have worked out. It was a perfect match.

At least, it should have been.

Felan peered through the living room window as the grey truck pulled up into the driveway. 'He's back!' he called. Rain hammered down hard, harder than it had done all day.

Mrs Walters joined him. 'Is it another smile?'

The back door of the truck flew open, and Jude bolted down the street. Chris and Penny ran after him. They stopped at the end of the drive.

'No,' Felan whispered. No… they were going to adopt Jude, right? They wouldn't say no. Not after all of that.

Not bothering with a jacket, he hurried outside, hot on Mrs Walters' heels. Tears streamed down Penny's cheeks (though at first it was hard to tell in the rain), and the familiar expression of guilt pulled Chris's face taut.

Felan knew that look well. It greeted him every time he looked in the mirror.

'What happened?' Mrs Walters demanded, an air of urgency to her voice.

'He heard us talking…'

Felan bolted down the driveway and took off in the direction he'd seen Jude heading in. He wasn't going to fail the kid like Chris and Penny had done. He was going to find the kid and bring him home.

Part of him wondered when he started to care so much – but then, part of him knew what it was like to have no one. The rest of him wished he had someone running after him all that time ago.

'Jude!' he shouted. Rain lashed his face. The street, normally bright and clear, was dark and dismal, the black clouds hovering low overhead. He splashed through puddle after puddle. Water soaked his new trainers. He swallowed a rather large lump in his throat.

Despair didn't ride in on a white horse. In fact, it crashed in with the thunder clouds, struck devoted hearts like lightning bolts, devouring everything in its path.

And it was enough to send a little kid running into the pouring rain, because if there was no hope, what did he have left?

'Jude!'

The rain drowned out his voice. It was hopeless. Shouting at the rain would get him nowhere, especially at a time like this. Where would Jude go? He talked to the kid, right? Where was the kid's favourite place?

The further he ran, the more he hated Chris and Penny. They did this. They caused the kid to run off in the rain, lost, alone and hurting.

Felan knew how hurt someone had to be to consider running. He knew the pain that came along with it; he never wanted another kid to feel the way he had felt. No kid deserved to feel that way.

It just wasn't good enough.

Felan found Jude huddled beneath the peeling, red slide on the other side of Weisworth. It was a small town, but it was a good fifteen-minute run from one side to the other. He recognised the park as the same one Chris and Penny had brought Jude to numerous times on sunny days, the poor kid.

Felan didn't hide his arrival. He splashed through murky puddles and kicked loose stones so the kid could hear him coming. Jude glared at him through red-rimmed eyes. A knot tugged in Felan's stomach. Chris and Penny had made Jude cry.

He sat down beside the kid, who immediately shuffled away. Felan tried not to take it too personally. He did the same thing himself, didn't he? He'd done the same thing ever since he arrived in Weisworth. He lashed out at the people who cared because he didn't want to admit his feelings.

He promised himself he would never lash out again.

'Why did you follow me?' the kid asked, hostile in a way that reminded Felan of Guadalupe, that reminded Felan of dangerous street corners and dark back alleys. He sounded bitter and wrong, and not at all like Jude.

'I was worried about you,' Felan said, and he realised that, somehow, he had begun to care for the kids. He didn't know when it happened, but at some point, the kids shifted from being kids to being people he cared about, and goddam was Felan going to do his best to protect them from harm, even if that meant protecting them from himself.

'No, you weren't! You're just like the others! You pretend to care, and then you leave. You always leave!'

'I care, Jude,' Felan said. 'I'm sorry if I've never shown it before, but I promise I do.' He would go to the ends of the Earth for the kids if a higher power allowed it. 'Now why don't you tell me what happened? It must've been bad for you to run away so fast.'

Before he knew it, the kid was crying beside him. It hurt his soul more than he thought he could bear. He was proud to be this person for Jude, but he ached knowing he never had this himself. He *ached*.

'They don't want me, okay? I overheard them talking when they thought I wasn't listening,' Jude sobbed.

Felan's heart constricted painfully behind his ribcage. He drew the boy in for a hug and held him tight. 'I'm sorry. I know how much you wanted it to work out.'

Jude punched Felan in the chest. 'You don't know anything! You're older than me and you still ended up here!'

Felan almost begged Jude to hit him harder. He felt the familiar tingle in his blood, and Felan nearly fell right back into the pit.

As of today, it was the longest Felan had gone without being in physical pain, and... and a terrible part of him missed it. He missed the ache that came with it, the nagging, gnawing feeling that itched. At some point, pain had become normal. Pain had become part of his everyday routine. Now, there was no physical pain. No running. No violence.

He wanted Jude to hit him harder, he wanted to *hurt*, but he couldn't do that to the kid. The thought of Jude hitting someone else made Felan think of Edward, little Edward who he had left behind, little Edward who might've already gotten his tattoo, little Edward who might've picked up a knife and used it and…

Instead, Felan chose to do what he wished someone had done for him.

'You don't hit people,' Felan scolded. 'And Jude… I think you did like them. You're upset that they don't want you.' Jude sniffled and stared at the floor. 'You thought you were finally going to have a home.'

And when Jude burst into tears again, Felan held him tight once more.

Small hands twisted themselves into Felan's jumper and pulled. 'Why does no one want me?'

'Why does everyone I love keep secrets from me?'

Beneath the peeling, red slide, in the pouring rain, Felan held Jude close and said nothing. He said nothing while the kid cried, just rubbed his shoulder, patted his arm, and rejoiced in the euphoria he felt at being needed.

The rain stopped a short while later, and Jude held Felan's hand the whole way home.

Chapter 9: Proposals

'I don't suppose you've given this coming year any more thought?' Mrs Walters asked while she boiled the kettle.

The kids were fast asleep, especially Jude, the poor kid. He had been sent to bed with a stern talking to about running off and a warm hug from Mrs Walters.

Felan had watched the interaction between Jude and Mrs Walters with jealousy, despite his best efforts to shut it out.

Every kid deserved comfort, so why did Felan loathe seeing it?

'I think I want to work,' he said. 'There're a few cafés in town looking for part-time workers – I was thinking of washing up over lunch hours a few days a week, just to start with. And then I was thinking about taking an online course, something to do with nature, or plants, that sort of thing. I don't really know.'

'In any case, I'm glad you've given it some thought, and that you've been proactive in looking.' She set down a mug of hot chocolate and a plate of biscuits in front of him. 'I'd be more than happy to help you write your CV.'

He took a sip. Velvety warmth filled his mouth. 'I think I'd like that.'

'And I never properly thanked you for earlier,' Mrs Walters said. 'When you went after Jude.'

He reached for a biscuit. 'You don't need to thank me, Mrs Walters. Really.' After he got past the initial fear, a longing settled itself in his chest when she grasped his hand; longing for a world in which he had someone like Mrs Walters in his life all along.

She squeezed his hand. 'You've been so good to the kids here, and to me. They look up to you, Felan.'

Oddly enough, that didn't unsettle him. In fact, he revelled in it, the feeling of being needed. The kids liked him (despite his best efforts to push them away), and asked him questions, and wanted him to play. He liked how he could focus solely on them – it was easy to forget about his problems when he did that. Running after Jude… it did that for him. He focused on the running, and Jude, and he forgot (for a moment) that anything even happened to him in the first place.

'They're good kids,' he whispered, squeezing her hand back. Her touch grounded him somewhat, he realised, in the same way Blaez's touch had always grounded him. Mrs Walters touch gathered all of his broken pieces, and she waited like a shepherd overlooking her flock while he pulled himself back together.

It hurt him to know that, if he did disappear, she'd always be waiting. She'd always be waiting for someone who wasn't coming home, waiting for that last sheep to return to its flock.

'And so are you.'

Felan didn't want to ruin the moment by disagreeing, so he settled for an in-between.

'I'm trying to be.'

If only she knew.

Entry 6 – 11:45pm

I know that I'm going to have to deal with the things that I'm writing about. I know that.

It's just... it's just hard at the moment. It's easier to ignore those things and pretend everything's fine. It's always easier to play pretend.

Mum and I used to play pretend in Oakley Park every weekend. We pretended that we were adventurers discovering the park for the very first time, and we explored until the sky turned dark.

I stopped playing pretend the day Mum died, but I never stopped pretending. For a long time, I pretended Mum was still alive, that she was just away for work. It was easier to deal with the kids at school if I said that. They would mock me either way, so it was best to pretend and hide the truth from them.

When I found the little boy in the park, I played pretend for the first time in years. I pretended that he was okay. I pretended that he just needed some food and some water and some sleep. I pretended that nothing was really wrong.

Instead, I slept beside a dead body for hours because I was too scared to accept that the boy was a lost cause.

I'm scared that I'm never going to move past what happened. I'm scared that I'm going to be controlled by that city forever.

I am forever tainted, and I fear that I will never be clean again.

Chapter 10: Rumination

The next afternoon, as a way of keeping up appearances, Felan walked into town with copies of his brand-new CV.

The first café he visited was nice enough, but the man behind the counter said nothing when he took the CV. Felan didn't get his hopes up. He walked out pretty defeated, though he didn't know why he cared. He didn't plan to be around for much longer anyway.

Still, the second café was perfect. An older lady waved at him from behind the coffee machine, a kind smile on her face.

'Hi, I'm looking for a part-time job,' he said.

'Hello! It's lovely to meet you – my name's Lisa. I've worked here longer than you've been alive, I'd wager!'

'Nice to meet you, too. I'm Felan,' he said. 'It's a wonderful place you've got here.'

Comfy sofas looked out over the floor-to-ceiling windows, and simple tables and chairs randomly littered the hard floor, some tables larger than others. An array of paintings and photographs lined the dusty, pink walls. A magazine stand stood by the front door. A little old woman hobbled over and picked one up before she sat back down on one of the sofas, flipped through the pages and sipped on her chosen hot drink. Felan noted the slice of cake beside her cup. It was quiet, but he could manage quiet.

A lie.

'Oh, it's not my place. It's Mark's,' Lisa explained, taking his CV. 'I'll make sure he gets this first thing in the morning – either way we'll be in touch.'

'Thank you. Have a lovely day.'

'And you, Felan. I hope to see you around.'

As he left, a pit opened up in Felan's chest, and he mourned the reality in which he stayed here.

***

Felan woke up gasping, a scream caught in his throat, and Randi's name never made it past his lips. Sweating profusely, he checked every corner of his room for something out of place in the dark, for a glimpse of a humanoid shadow.

He slumped back down when he was sure nothing was in the room with him. He rubbed his face and tried to settle his breathing enough to get back to sleep. He couldn't. He couldn't quite catch his breath, and despite knowing he was alone in the room, he kept stealing glances at the corners and praying there was nothing lurking beneath his bed.

Every time he closed his eyes, he saw Randi die over and over; he watched Nick slit Harvey's throat; he saw his mother's body on the road, listless and bleeding; he saw the man he killed, and Tristan, the man he shot. He saw himself in the centre of the chaos, a bridge between two worlds he didn't want connecting. There had been nothing he could do to stop it and then Nick came waltzing through the front door of the orphanage and killed all of the kids, one by one, smiling the entire time until Felan was the only one left.

Felan sat up abruptly, a hand on his chest, trying to remember how to breathe, his vision foggy. *Not now*, he begged. *Please not now*. If he had a panic attack it would only end if he passed out.

Slowly, his vision returned to normal, and as quietly as he could Felan checked on all of the kids. He peeked his head through their open doors, his heart thudding violently, a prisoner wailing on the bars of their prison cell, begging for escape, begging for *release*.

The kids were okay. They were all alive, and there was no Nick in sight. Once in his room, he laid back onto his bed, his eyes burning with unshed tears.

He should never have come to Weisworth.

On his bedside table, next to where his brooch lived, his phone quietly rang. He answered after two rings. There was only one person who'd call so late at night. 'Hi.'

'Hi,' Blaez said. 'It's really good to hear your voice.'

Felan let a tear fall down his cheek. 'Likewise.'

He thought that she probably had a nightmare too. He hated the idea of her suffering. She didn't deserve to suffer. But he did. He got people killed.

'Felan, I... I hate this distance between us,' Blaez said.

'I do too.' And yet he couldn't shake the feeling that she'd be safer away, far away, from him.

'I had a nightmare.'

He choked on a sob. 'I had one too.'

'I was running. It was really dark and someone caught me. I couldn't...' she trailed off.

'I keep seeing everyone die,' he croaked. 'I see *their* deaths, over and over. Then Nick comes waltzing through the front door and hurts the kids. I don't...' His breath shook. He was sure Blaez could hear it down the line. 'Blaez, I don't know what to do.'

'I wish I knew how to help.'

'I see the life leave their eyes,' he said. 'My friends. *Our* friends. And the guy I killed... I see my hands moving and fog clouds his eyes. They're unfocused and they just stare at me, through me, up to the sky. I did that, Blaez. I made that happen.'

'I love you,' she whispered.

Her heartfelt words weren't enough to shake him. He doubted anything would be enough ever again.

'Sometimes it's all I can think about.' Felan shuddered. 'Do you ever think about dying?' It was silent for a moment, and he didn't think she was going to answer. 'Blaez?'

'I used to, when I was younger,' she eventually said. 'Not so much now though.'

Silent tears ran down Felan's cheeks. Everything was fine. He was fine.

'Felan?'

He tried to calm the racing of his heart that came with being known by people. He tried to calm himself by counting the stars glowing on the ceiling. Tears continued to run, one lonely trail at a time.

'Felan? Are you still there?'

Barely, he thought. *I don't want to be.*

'You're scaring me,' Blaez whispered. 'Is everything okay?'

No. No, it wasn't. Nothing was okay. It never would be okay again. 'I don't like scaring people,' he said. 'I promised myself I'd never scare anyone ever again. I'm so sorry.'

'No, don't apologise. I'm just worried about you.'

'I'm fine.' Even he could hear how fake he sounded. If he heard it, then so did Blaez. Damn it all. He got up and paced his bedroom, blood pounding in his ears.

'Where are you right now?'

'In my room.'

'Are you safe?' God, she sounded terrified. 'Have you, I mean… have you done anything?'

'I've done lots of things, Blaez. I've done lots of terrible things.' He sniffled, praying it would put an end to his crying. His voice wavered against his will. 'I don't want to think about it anymore.'

Blaez let out a sound Felan could only describe as wounded, a starving puppy whimpering on a street corner. 'Okay. It's okay, Felan. Everything's going to be okay. Just… just sit down for a bit, yeah? Just sit down.' Her voice wavered too. It even broke at one point.

I'm good at breaking things, he thought, lying flat on his back.

He knew what had to be done, he knew what he needed to do, so why was he crying?

'What are you thinking about?' Blaez asked.

Felan shrugged. When he remembered she couldn't see him he said, 'Everything. All of the bad things.'

'How do they make you feel?'

He curled in on himself. Blaez didn't need this right now. She needed comfort of her own and yet here he was, taking everything for himself like he always did. Blaez didn't need to therapize him. In fact, she probably needed therapy herself. She needed to talk to someone and he wasn't allowing her that. He never allowed her anything. He took and he took and he never gave anything in return. 'Like I want it to stop,' he whispered.

'I don't, I…' Blaez fell silent. 'I don't know what that means.'

And God, Felan loathed explaining himself. He loathed it, but he figured he owed it to her. An explanation was the least he could do after everything he'd done, after all the times he'd failed his best friend.

'I'm here, right? In Weisworth. I'm here in Weisworth, not in Guadalupe, but now that I'm here all I can think about is *there*, Before, and I don't want to think about it anymore. I want it all to stop.' Felan sniffled. 'I want everything to stop. If life stopped, the bad things wouldn't follow me around. Nothing bad would happen ever again.' He would be free. He could see his mum again. He wouldn't have to *do* anything ever again.

Blaez's breath came in short and sharp bursts. 'If life stopped?'

'Yeah.'

'And you've thought about life stopping before? Your… your life stopping?'

He tangled his fingers in his hair, regretting opening his stupid mouth. He shouldn't have asked her the question in the first place. He should have kept quiet, just like his father had always told him.

Muffled sobs sounded down the phone. 'I'm scared, Felan,' Blaez whispered in a broken voice.

Felan uncurled himself and stared up at the ceiling. The carpeted floor was oddly comfortable. 'I'm sorry, Blaez. I'm really sorry.'

'No, no, just… please, keep talking to me,' she begged.

He wanted nothing more than to be silenced forever. 'Why?'

'Just so I know you're still there,' she said. 'Please keep talking to me.'

But he didn't know what to say. He had nothing *to* say.

Blaez's cries grew progressively louder. He thought about hanging up. His finger twitched nearer to his phone, hovering over the screen.

'Please don't hang up on me,' she said suddenly. 'Please don't leave me alone like this.'

Deep down, Felan realised she wasn't just talking about the phone call. He smacked the back of his head on the carpeted floor.

It didn't have the desired effect.

'Tell me anything. I just need to hear your voice for a while. I need to know that you're still here.'

I've thought about it multiple times. The first time was while I was still with Dad. The second time was atop the Warehouse roof after Harvey. I thought of you, and I stopped myself. I stepped back, I sat down, and I waited. You showed up, and I thought I was passed it. I thought I was getting better.

I was never getting better. I was always getting worse.

'There's nothing to worry about,' he said. 'I'm fine, Blaez. Everything's fine. Just a blip from the nightmare. I'm fine.'

'You're not. I know you're not.'

Felan got up off the floor, laid down on his bed and curled up beneath his covers. He wanted to hide. He didn't want to see anyone ever again. 'Can you talk to me instead?' he asked. 'Just until I fall asleep?'

'Of course I can.' She sounded resigned, and yet she talked. She talked nonstop, quietly, about the drawings she'd been doing while she was in Tristan's flat, about the rock painting she'd gotten really into and, 'Felan, I'm bringing my favourite ones back with me so that we can hide them in the woods for other people to find,' and 'Tristan's been lovely. I forgot how nice he was when I met him the first time. He truly wants to help us, Felan. That's all he's ever wanted. Mr Bailey too. They just want to help us, and kids like us, have better lives.'

And all Felan had done since he'd arrived in Weisworth was ignore their texts, was dodge their calls, was forget they even existed because any memory of them was now tainted.

'What's wrong with me, Blaez?' he asked suddenly when she paused for breath.

He scratched at his arm. It didn't help. He kept scratching. Blaez couldn't see him. It was fine. He was fine. No one needed to know.

'There's nothing wrong with you,' she said. 'You're responding to what's happened to you.'

'I wish you were here.'

And there it was again. The elephant that refused to leave the room.

'I wish I was there too.'

They murmured to each other until the early hours of the morning, trying to provide as much comfort as they could whilst not waking their respective housemates. He didn't remember falling asleep, but when he jolted awake it was still dark. He found his phone beside him on the bed and an unread text from Blaez: *Sleep well <3 xx*

Felan groaned quietly. Blaez had called him for comfort, and all he had done was scare her beyond belief – and then he had the audacity to fall asleep on her while she was talking.

He replied: *Thanks. You too <3 xx*

As if that would make everything better.

Every time he thought he was making progress, Nick waltzed right back in with his trademark smirk and a bloody knife in his hand. Everywhere Felan turned, Nick was there, waiting for him, ready to strike.

If you don't kill me, I'll do it myself.

He knew he was capable of such an action. His hands had caused death in the past. His hands were cursed. At the back of his mind, he heard Nick laughing.

Felan sat at his desk and began to write scattered thoughts in his notebook.

Entry 7 – 2:17am

If you didn't get to live, why do I? What gives me the right to life when yours was so cruelly ripped from you?

I tried to save him. I promise. I tried to get him to come back. I'm sorry I lied. I never wanted to lie but I thought I was keeping you both safe. I hate lies. I've always, always hated lies.

I'm sorry I shut you out. ~~I didn't know what to say to you after~~

~~Why did you go off with them? What were you thinking? What did you think was going to happen?~~

I know I took Blaez away from you. I was so excited to finally have a friend that I didn't think of the consequences it would bring to you.

Caleb... I can't remember the last time I spoke to you. I don't remember when our last conversation was, or what we talked about. I'm ashamed to admit I didn't give it any thought until now.

Don't blame Randi. He was just trying to keep you safe. He wanted you to live, more than anything. Please don't blame him for loving you. In fact, you should blame me. I kept Randi's whereabouts a secret from you, but I promise you, wherever you are, I tried to help. I cared about both of you, and yet you're gone, and I'm still here. It just doesn't seem right. You should be here. You should both be here. Not me. I'm so sorry.

I'm so, so sorry.

Entry 8 – 2:29am

Why didn't you come back with me? You might still be alive if you didn't run.

~~I just wanted to help.~~

I cared about you – about both of you – and I'm sorry things ended the way they did.

I didn't think for a moment that you'd die. I didn't think for a moment that I'd lose both of you. I can't even begin to imagine how the girls are feeling. They knew you. ~~Looking back on it, I didn't know you at all.~~

I didn't know you for long, but I hope I made a difference to your lives. I hope I wasn't only a bad omen. I hope you don't hate me, but a sinister part of me hopes you do. You should be here, not me.

It should never have been me.

I should never have been rewarded for a failure as terrible as mine.

Wherever you are, Randi... be safe.

I hope Caleb's there with you. I hope you've sorted everything out.

I wanted you to live. I wanted both of you to live.

I'm sorry.

Entry 9 – 2:41am

I'm sorry, first and foremost. I'm so, so sorry for leaving you behind with them. I know you hate me. I know you hate me so much for leaving you alone, and I know you hate me for getting your friends killed. I don't deserve to be safe when you aren't. I don't deserve any of the good things I've been given when you're stuck.

I hope things get better for you. I hope you're not plagued by as many nightmares as I've been plagued with.

I can't apologise enough, Accalia.

And I'm sorry we didn't get to say goodbye. If there was something you deserved, it was a goodbye.

Entry 10 – 2:48am

I'm sorry you've been dragged into this. You shouldn't be there. You should be here, in my place. I should have stayed and looked after you. I should have gotten you out of there. I'm so sorry I didn't.

Accalia's good. So is Tala, I think. At least, that's what Blaez tells me. They'll protect you. I hope they'll do what's right and get you somewhere safe, or at least stop Nick and the others from hurting you.

I don't know you, but I know them. I hope you never have to do the things I did.

I hope you're still you, Edward.

I really hope you're still you.

Entry 11 – 3:01am

I can't sleep.

I keep going over everything that happened and
I can't stop thinking.

I can't stop the what ifs and the if onlys.

I can't stop thinking.

I just want everything to stop.

I want it to STOP.

I want everything to stop.

Entry 12 – 3:04am

75

I think I'm going insane, going over everything again and again and I don't know how to fix it.

I don't know how to fix myself.

I'm terrified because I don't know if I deserve to be fixed.

Entry 13 – 3:09am

I didn't stop trying because I didn't want ~~any more of my friends to die~~ Blaez to die. I didn't want Blaez to get hurt. I didn't want anyone else to get hurt because of me.

I didn't want to die because there were still people around me to protect, but here there are no dangers to protect the kids from. There's no threat. There's nothing.

Nothing except me.

I pray that something terrible happens to me because of all the terrible things that I did before.

This new life isn't going to work. I may have been hopeful to escape, but I'm too damaged. I'm too bent out of shape and too misguided to change my own life.

Entry 14 – 3:13am

I don't tell people how I feel because other people have it worse. My suffering pales in comparison to some of the stories I've heard over the years.

I told Blaez. Now she's worrying. This is why I stay quiet. I don't want to worry people, and I most certainly don't want to scare people.

There's never a right moment to say something as big as this. There is no right moment to say the things that have been on my mind.

What if no one understands?

Entry 15 – 3:33am

I'm fine.

~~I'm not fine.~~

I'm fine.

That's what I keep telling anyone who asks. I don't think they believe me, but they haven't asked me if I'm sure. If they really cared, that's what they'd do, right? Instead, they've left me alone. I shouldn't be annoyed about that because that's exactly what I wanted them to do. It's exactly what I hoped they'd do so I don't have to talk about it, so I don't have to talk about anything.

~~Why am I so hypocritical?~~

I'm falling apart.

I'm falling apart and I don't know how to make it stop. I just want it to stop.

No one knows how close to the edge I really am. I didn't realise there was an edge, but I sure as hell have found it.

No one knows.

Well, Blaez knows.

Maybe I'll slip before she tells anyone.

Maybe I'll be long gone before I have to face her again. I don't want to have to face her after what I admitted to her.

I don't want to deal with the aftermath.

Entry 16 – 3:48am

If the other kids from school could see me now, they'd be laughing. They'd be heckling and spitting in my face and telling me I've failed.

I know I've failed.

I've been failing my entire life.

If the other kids could see me now, they'd tell me I'm still just as weird now as I was back then. If the kids down the hall saw what I was truly capable of, saw what I had done, they'd be kicking and screaming and running for the hills. I don't know why they haven't already. One day I'm going to have to tell them the truth and it's going to kill me to see the horror and the disappointment on their faces.

If I don't kill myself first.

I think I've felt like this before, many times, but I never allowed myself time to stop and think about it. The closest I got to thinking about it was sat atop the warehouse roof after Harvey was killed, and after that moment I swore I'd never stop long enough to think about it again. Now I'm in Weisworth, with all the time in the world, and I've thought about it. I've thought about it a lot. I think about it every day. I think of how I'd do it. I think of all the reasons why. Then I think of all the people I'd be leaving behind.

They'd be better off without me. Mrs Walters can focus on the kids, and Blaez can focus on herself. Having me around?

It was an accident waiting to happen.

Entry 17 – 4:09am

It'll be so much easier for you if I disappear. That way, you won't have the constant reminder of what we did. If I disappear, I know for sure I can't hurt you again. I've hurt you enough already. I couldn't live with myself if something terrible happened to you because of me. Not again.

You deserve so much better than me. You deserve peace. You can't achieve that with me around.

You helped me when no one else could, or would, and you saved me more often than I could save you. I owe you my life, and that's exactly why I have to do this. It's why I have to leave you all behind. I can't live with this constant reminder of what I did to get us here, Blaez.

Maybe I should have jumped off the warehouse roof when I had the chance. Maybe I should've let the cops catch me; they might've put a bullet in me somewhere it could never heal.

If I leave, you won't have to burden yourself with me anymore. You can focus entirely on yourself and be all the things you want to be. That life isn't possible for someone like me.

I love you, Blaez.

And I'm sorry.

Entry 18 – 4:27am

You took advantage of me. You knew I was out there, alone, scared, and you preyed on me. You gave me hope in my darkest moment, and then you destroyed it.

You abused me.

You manipulated me.

You exploited me.

You gave me scars. You gave me so many scars that will never heal and you feel no remorse for it.

I know you're still out there, so why haven't you found me yet? I'm waiting for you. I'm right here.

Just please don't hurt the kids. I'll go willingly. If it means the kids are safe, then I'll do whatever you want me to do. I'll do anything.

Come and take me back. I can't deal with all of this waiting around for bad things to happen again.

I can't do this. I don't know safety, but I do know violence.

You won, okay? You won, so please come and get me.

Please, Nick. I'm begging you.

Chapter 11: Crescendo

He could feel the pit tugging on him, one muscle at a time. He could feel the void of himself shrivel up and contort into a shape only intangible feelings and volatile thoughts could create.

He'd never been this close to the edge before.

With feverish hands, Felan reached into the wardrobe and removed the backpack he'd stashed away, packed and ready to go at a moment's notice, ready for the day he decided to do it.

It. He was terrified of *it*. It frightened him how normal it was to think about it. It. He should just say it as it was, shouldn't he?

It. Suicide. Offing himself. Ending his life.

It wasn't the act he sought, but the aftermath. It was knowing that, if all went right, he wouldn't have to think or remember or see or do anything ever again. The only thing was... he didn't exactly have a plan.

He set the backpack at the foot of the bed and stepped back, daring it to move.

He was scared it wouldn't work, whatever it was, whatever he ended up doing. He was scared that he'd change his mind. He was scared that he'd already changed his mind and would try to stop himself. He was scared that he would die scared and regretting everything.

Maybe he could go to the kitchen and get a sharp knife. That would certainly do the job, though Felan feared he wouldn't be able to go through with it. It was too violent an act. He'd had enough of violent acts to last a lifetime.

The thought crossed his mind and before he knew it he was stood on the edge of the Warehouse roof, looking down at the gravel path below, wondering how long the fall would be, and how much it would hurt when he finally reached it.

He snapped out of it at the sound of birdsong in the forest ahead. He blinked rapidly, taking a large step back. No. He couldn't do it. If he did it, who would look after Blaez? Who would watch over her, and the others?

Who would stop Nick?

Felan muttered to himself and paced his room again. He was certain he'd wear the carpet out. It was still dark outside, and it wouldn't be long before it started to lighten up. He prayed he was long gone by then... but how?

He had backed away from the Warehouse roof, and, in the end, Blaez had been the only one he had protected. Randi and Caleb had died, and he'd left the others behind. More and more often, he thought back to the Warehouse roof and what would have happened had he simply just jumped when he had the chance.

He was going to do *something*. He was sure of it. He had to do something. He had to.

Quietly, Felan made his bed. He left his brooch and his phone on the bedside table, and slinging on his backpack, Felan left the room and crept downstairs. He kept his gaze straight ahead, and resisted glancing at the doors of the kids' bedrooms, resisted detouring in for one last look at the sleeping children he'd grown to adore.

He wasn't sure if he'd be able to go through with it if he did that.

He took extra care when he walked past Mrs Walters' bedroom door, shutting himself in the kitchen. The door closed with a quiet *click*.

Besides the hum of the fridge and the freezer, gentle and somewhat soothing, the kitchen was quiet. It made his thoughts louder. If they had been frantic and running on a merry-go-round in his bedroom, they were being thrown this way and that by a raging hurricane down in the kitchen. Needing some light, Felan flicked on the one above the back door and although only small, it lit the room enough for him to find what he was looking for. His heart pounded in his chest, so loud he felt it in his ears, when he reached out for the knife he used to chop up the carrots, *Josie's carrots*, he thought absentmindedly.

Felan pulled up the sleeve of his jumper, revealing a criss-cross of bumpy, red and white lines along his arm. He gripped the knife tight and pressed the blade against his skin. He'd heard that people harmed themselves to regain some semblance of control in their lives – what was one more scar when he already had so many?

You deserve this, his thoughts told him. *Just do it already.*

He took a breath. He took another. He found himself getting frustrated. *Do it.* All he had to do was give himself a tiny scratch, a tiny cut on the wrist, and then he could leave, then he'd *know.*

He couldn't. The fear of pain stopped him. The fear of what might happen when he drew blood stopped him. Could he face the sight of blood after all this time? Sure, he'd seen it in his dreams and in his nightmares but he hadn't seen it in person for weeks, he hadn't… *felt* it for weeks, and it was the longest he'd ever gone without feeling the *warmth*, the *wetness*, the *redness* of it all over him.

He'd… missed it. It revolted him. It enticed him. *One little cut and everything will be okay again.*

He gritted his teeth and pressed. It hurt, but it didn't break the skin. 'Come on,' he muttered to himself. 'It's not difficult. Just do it.'

You've killed someone before. This is easy.

He pressed the knife down for a second time, and then he remembered; he remembered Gemma's laughter, remembered how the sound had sat in his heart for days after he'd first heard it, remembered *all* of their laughter echoing down the hall. He remembered running with his friends in the clearing, back in Guadalupe. He remembered running in the woods with Blaez. He remembered Blaez, and the bright light in her eyes whenever he made a stupid joke.

He clutched the knife tighter.

Who would help Mrs Walters look after the kids? What would happen to the kids? What would happen to Blaez?

What would happen to me?

For the first time in his life, Felan stopped and he thought of the consequences.

If their roles were reversed, Felan would be crushed and heartbroken forever if he had learned Blaez had taken her own life. He knew she'd be just as crushed and heartbroken if he went through with it now.

She would be on her own again.

He couldn't allow that.

He dropped the knife. It clattered onto the countertop and he backed away, his hands shaking.

He couldn't believe it. He couldn't believe that he'd almost done it. He ran a hand through his hair, his long hair that he hadn't properly brushed for days, too overcome by the sheer *weight* of existence.

Felan wanted to leave the knife where it was but Mrs Walters would question it, and if the kids managed to get a hold of it and one of them had an accident...

He put the knife back in the wooden block, flicked off the light, and crept back upstairs. Mrs Walters didn't stir. Coldness seeped into his skin, seeped all the way down to his bones like he'd been rained on for days on end in the middle of winter – and still he sweated. His jumper clung to him in all of the wrong places, warm and wet and uncomfortable, a stark contrast to the cold that resided inside of him.

The first thing he did when he shut himself in his room was sling his backpack into the back of his wardrobe. He forced the doors closed, stepped back into the middle of the room, and breathed. He threw his jumper off and it landed out of sight in the shadows. The spot on his wrist where he'd tried to cut himself stung. It wouldn't leave a mark. It would heal and no one would be any the wiser to what he'd tried to do.

One of the kids snored from somewhere down the hall.

That was all it took.

He collapsed to his knees on the carpeted floor, on the floor of the room, on the floor of *his* room. His room. His. All his. Tears streamed down his cheeks in floods. He couldn't stop shaking.

He'd almost –

He'd wanted to –

He'd tried to –

What are you doing, you idiot?

Chapter 12: Solstice

In the painfully long day that followed, Felan spent his time trying (and failing) to write in his notebook, still shell-shocked from what he'd almost done.

'How's your writing going?' Mrs Walters asked two hours after his almost attempt. She had poked her head in to find Felan hunched over his desk after a sleepless night, his pen held firmly in his hand.

'Some days are better than others,' he said. He wasn't being completely honest, but nobody needed to know that. No one needed to know that he'd had a complete and utter shocker of a morning. He'd get over it. He'd move past it like he always did.

But what if there was a next time? What if, when the next time came, he couldn't stop himself?

Mrs Walters gave him a long look, like she didn't quite believe him but didn't want to argue, and left the room.

Felan almost called after her – his voice died in his throat.

He crossed out another angry, disjointed sentence. He hadn't realised he had so many thoughts that needed to come out. Dark thoughts. The sheer number, and the sheer violence of them, terrified him. They weren't anywhere near as bad as they had been just hours earlier, but they were still bad. A cause for concern, some would say.

The fact that Mrs Walters had come in… he didn't blame Blaez. Not one bit. He'd do the same if he thought Blaez was going to…

There was another knock on his bedroom door. He slammed his notebook closed. 'Yeah?'

Mrs Walters appeared again, this time determined. 'Do you mind if we have a chat?'

Felan shrugged from his desk. Gemma was at nursery, and the rest of the kids were at school. It was fine – no little people were about to eavesdrop or walk in.

She sat on his bed and patted the space beside her. An invitation. Felan moved over without question (still he remained that lonely, loyal dog going wherever whenever he was called). He didn't know when it happened, but he trusted Mrs Walters. At least, he trusted her a bit. He understood that she truly cared about him, and he understood that she wasn't pretending like most people did, like Nick had done, like Nick had done in the months Felan was with him.

Like Nick had done to everyone else who had fallen for his act.

'Tristan called me,' Mrs Walters said, her voice both cautious and assertive. 'Apparently Blaez shared a few... *concerns* with him that he thought should be shared with me.'

Anxiety crept up his throat, like a slug (or something worse) cutting off his airway and choking him. Taking deep breaths didn't ease the discomfort at all. The anxiety took root in the depths of his lungs and resided there, polluting the oxygen all around him.

'We both know what was discussed, Mrs Walters,' he said, playing with his hands, twisting and locking his fingers between each other. It helped him somewhat. It also didn't.

'I just want to be certain that we're on the same page here.'

Felan's mind raced. He missed the freedom of living on the streets. He missed the running even more. He missed the constant movement, the constant purpose. He feared he was too comfortable with Mrs Walters. With her, it was constant anxiety about his place and his purpose, and the fear of not knowing what was to come each day. At least in Guadalupe, Felan knew what was expected of him. He knew what he had to do to get through each day. He knew what he had to do to get to the other side.

However, in Weisworth, he dreaded the endless hours of boredom and quiet. He dreaded the thoughts that he couldn't stop, that came unbidden and out of nowhere like freak storms, and he feared that the fleeting moments of boredom would make him do something stupid.

He didn't want to relapse into that life, the life he had led in Guadalupe, but part of him, the sadistic part of him, missed the danger, and it also missed the pain. It was why, late at night when he couldn't sleep, Felan would hold his hands beneath boiling hot water until it became unbearable, or he pinched himself hard enough to leave a tiny bruise, the smallest bruise he'd ever seen on his body, so small nobody would see if they weren't actively looking for it.

He missed the pain more than anything.

But how could he express all of that without sounding completely mad?

Felan sat on the edge of his bed with his head in his hands.

There was no going back now.

'What's going on in that head of yours?' Mrs Walters asked gently.

Too much. Too much is going on and I want it to stop.

'Please don't make me say it.'

'Felan. What you've been through – it's unimaginable. You've lost people, including your friends. Caleb, was it? And Randi? I remember you mentioning them before.'

An overwhelming feeling he couldn't identify rose in him. She remembered their names? He told her something. She remembered. And then he did too, for the second time in one morning.

He missed them more than he thought he would. They had been friends, but they hadn't really known each other at all; he could say the same about Blaez. After everything was said and done, how well did he really know the girl? How well did Blaez really know him?

He lifted his head. 'Maybe, but they weren't mine to lose,' Felan said, staring at his pale and scrawny hands. He twisted and locked them and pulled at them again because he couldn't find it in himself to stop the harsh motion. In fact, he welcomed it. Harsh was familiar, and familiar was good. 'They weren't my friends. Not really. They were Blaez's. They were Accalia's. They were only nice to me because of Blaez.'

'Do you really believe that?'

If he closed his eyes, he could almost pretend he was with

them. Would they welcome him with open arms, or would they hate him?

'You can still grieve for them, Felan.'

'That's for Blaez. For their *real* friends. I was just there, and they took pity on me.'

And then I went and got them both killed.

Mrs Walters took his hands into her own and squeezed. 'They meant something to you,' she said. 'I know they did.'

Funny. He didn't realise she knew him better than he knew himself. 'They should be here, in this house. Not me. It should never have been me. They were innocent.'

'So are you. Please don't forget that.'

'No!' He tore his hands away. 'They should still be alive! Not me.'

'Felan...'

'I don't deserve to live!' he yelled, his voice breaking on the last word. 'Not after what I did.' And then it all came pouring out, like something had struck a hole in a crumbling dam and nothing, *nothing*, could prevent the flow from ravaging the ancient town situated below. 'I tried to, I wanted to... I just wanted to disappear. I didn't realise, I didn't know – I don't know why I...' Felan hunched over. 'I don't want to be here anymore,' he said in a broken whisper. 'I've had enough. It's too much. I'm feeling too much and it's all... it's all just too much.' His hands twitched in his lap. His vision swam. He wiped at his eyes but more tears took their place, and finally Mrs Walters pulled him in for a hug.

Felan collapsed into her arms and cried.

He remembered sitting atop the Warehouse roof for days after Harvey was killed, after he thought Harvey had betrayed him, after he thought another adult had let him down. He'd sat on the edge and he had done his best to avoid looking down, instead focusing on the forest in front of him, on the wildlife that teemed all around them.

He looked down. Of course he did. How could he not after everything that had happened?

He had contemplated the drop more than once until he'd

realised what he was doing and stepped back. He hadn't thought about it again. He pretended it didn't happen. He kept going for Blaez. He had to keep her safe, and for that he had to be breathing.

But Blaez was safe, and he couldn't pretend any more.

He remembered all of the times he was in danger himself. He remembered the jolts of fear, and he remembered the flickers of relief when he thought it might be it – only he'd made it through to the other side and another part of him had died because he was still stuck.

So many parts of him had died, so many parts of him had been chipped off by his time in the city, and Felan didn't know how much of himself was left to carry on living.

He sobbed into Mrs Walters' shoulder, aware that she was saying something, but not aware enough to listen.

When he finally got a grip of himself, he pulled away from the embrace and kept a short distance between them. He looked down at the carpeted floor, awfully glad that his tears were slowing. Crying was embarrassing, even if it shouldn't be.

'I'm sorry,' he said hoarsely. 'I never wanted to burden you with all of this. It's not fair on you.'

'Look at me, Felan,' she said softly. Her hazel eyes looked sad, like his mother's had been. 'You should never have had to deal with this in the first place.' She cupped his cheek. Felan leaned into the touch, revelling in the contact, revelling in its warmth. 'You did a very brave thing by telling me this.'

If he was going to tell her the truth, he supposed he might as well go all-in. 'I feel guilty for being alive. I don't feel like I'm allowed to move on.' His lip wobbled. 'I shouldn't be here.'

They made eye contact, her seemingly searching for something, for something specific, in his eyes. He thought she must have found what she was looking for. 'Tell me one thing every day,' she said. She dropped her hand back into her lap. 'Tell me one thing that happened to you.'

Dark thoughts were always at the front of his mind so he didn't have to think for long. 'I was always running, from one thing to another.'

'Thank you.'

It hit him, then and there, that he had begun to settle. He had promised himself he wouldn't, because every time he did get comfortable somewhere, he was sent away, and if he wasn't sent away then he'd run, because after everything he'd done to get to where he was, he didn't deserve anything good. He didn't deserve atonement, but if it took his entire life to do so, he'd atone for his mistakes. Maybe, in his next life, things would be better.

'It's just... slow, here,' he said. 'It gives me too much time to think. I keep going over everything in my head, to see if there was something I could've done differently.'

And what Felan discovered was that there were lots of things he could've done differently, however he feared that no matter what, the outcome would have always remained the same.

'If you do that, you'll be making matters a whole lot worse.'

'I always do.'

'That's the city talking for you, and all of the people that did you harm. That isn't you talking. You were surviving,' Mrs Walters said. 'Your story is different to a lot of the other kids that come through these doors, but there's nothing wrong with just surviving.'

But at what cost?

'You know, some of the kids see someone once a month. A professional. We can sort that out for you too, if you like. It's nothing to be ashamed of.'

'No.'

'Felan...'

'I'm sick and tired of adults telling me how to feel. Only I know what I'm feeling.'

Mrs Walters sat as calm as ever beside him, silent. Felan averted his gaze to the window in time to see a startled starling take flight.

'Okay,' Mrs Walters said. 'You have your notebook, and you have the daily thing to tell me. I think that'll be a good start.'

Felan couldn't stop himself from spiralling. He hated himself, and that was no secret. Nick had known it, Blaez knew it, Tristan knew it, and now Mrs Walters knew it too. He hated the person he saw whenever he looked in the mirror, yet underneath, he could see the little boy staring back, the little boy he had failed to protect.

Himself.

'What if I can't be fixed?'

It was the question that kept him up at night, the reason why he'd ended up in the kitchen with a knife held to his wrist and a backpack slung over his shoulders.

'You aren't on your own anymore, Felan. You have people around you who want to help. Do you understand that?'

He bit his lip. The kids seemed to always seek him out, and some days it was his approval they sought above Mrs Walters. He loved the kids, *his kids*, he realised with some degree of shock, and to think of his kids going through what he was going through... No kid should feel like that, ever, and he thought that maybe, just maybe, he deserved to be happy and supported too.

After everything he had been through, if there was one thing he deserved, it was to feel safe, and to feel at home – whether that was some place or someone. For now, he was glad that someone had finally seen him for who he was. A child. An innocent child caught up in a life he didn't choose, caught up in a life he had no chance of escaping from.

'I think I'm starting to,' he said, feeling a dim spark of hope ignite inside of him.

'Good lad.' She ruffled his hair. 'It's going to get better. I promise.'

Chapter 13: Permutation

'Is Josie not going to school?' Felan asked, suddenly aware of the nine-year-old girl sitting patiently on the stairs. He could have sworn the kids had all gotten into the minivan earlier.

'Mental health day,' Mrs Walters explained. 'She's having the day off.'

'That's a thing?'

'It might not be a thing in some places, but in this house I make a point to get the kids to use them.' She turned to Josie. 'Are you ready to go?'

'Just gotta get my jumper!' The kid bounded up the stairs two at a time.

Felan crossed his arms, struggling to understand. He guessed he must have made a strange face because Mrs Walters raised her eyebrows at him. According to Blaez, he had a habit of making strange faces whenever he was confused.

'Every one of my kids is allowed a mental health day when they need one – including you, Felan – and if they want a haircut to feel more like themselves again, than a haircut is what they'll get.'

Josie thundered back down, her favourite brown jumper in hand. She quickly pulled it on and bounced up and down. 'Can we go now?'

Mrs Walters put a steadying hand on Josie's shoulder. 'We'll be back in about an hour, Felan,' she said, looking pointedly at him. 'I'll check in with you while we're out, if that's okay with you.'

Felan wrapped his arms tighter around himself. 'Actually, if you don't mind, could I – I… could I come?'

Josie's face lit up. 'Are you getting a haircut too?'

Felan glanced from the kid to Mrs Walters. 'If that's not too much trouble?'

'Of course it's not. Tell you what, we'll even stop for a hot chocolate on the way back. How does that sound?'

'Thank you,' Josie squealed.

Mrs Walters looked down fondly at the young girl. Felan swallowed the lump in his throat. 'You don't need to thank me. Now let's go.'

***

The three of them made the short walk into town together, Josie chattering away to Mrs Walters while Felan stayed quiet, his hands resting inside his jumper pockets. It was nice to be outside for once, to have a change of scenery. He'd forgotten how calming fresh air could be, how gentle the breeze on his cheeks could be.

Every now and then Mrs Walters looked over to him and said, 'All good?'

Felan smiled back every time. 'All good.' *Tell me one thing every day.* 'Actually, can I say the one thing now?'

'Of course you can.'

'I used to cut my own hair.' It wasn't the worst thing he'd ever done in the city, but it was still embarrassing. He didn't have a choice – if it got too long, it would get in the way, and if it got in the way, people could sneak up on him, and if people could sneak up on him…

'You won't have to anymore,' Mrs Walters promised. 'Thank you for telling me.' And that was that.

Easy.

If only.

There were a few people milling about in town when they arrived and Felan kept a careful eye on each and every one of them. It didn't hurt to be aware of his surroundings. He wasn't paranoid. He wasn't.

They approached a blue building halfway up the street, the outside adorned with a hanging basket, and a fake pair of scissors hung down just above the door. Mrs Walters walked inside first, closely followed by Josie. Felan closed the door gently behind him and glanced around at the interior. Other than a short lady behind the counter, and two actual hairdressers (a man and a woman), the building was empty. The floor was hard beneath his feet, his new trainers squeaking a little with every step. He made sure to tread lighter after that. In front of the large windows sat cushioned benches – for those who were waiting, Felan assumed. Mirrors lined one wall (with hundreds of little lights surrounding each mirror), and four chairs sat in front of them. Before he could catch a glimpse of himself in one of the many mirrors, he looked over to where Josie had rushed over to the white counter.

'Good morning, Josie. Mrs Walters!' the lady behind the counter exclaimed. She smiled warmly at Felan. 'And who might you be?'

Felan sent a panicked look to Mrs Walters, unsure of how to proceed. Whenever he met new people in Guadalupe, they didn't want his name. All they had wanted was what he was carrying, stashed away inside a satchel.

'This is Felan,' Mrs Walters said, coming to his rescue. 'He's one of mine.'

The lady behind the counter winked at him. 'You can call me Tracey.'

Felan managed a half smile. Thankfully, Josie distracted everyone. She was great at distractions. 'Hi,' Josie said. 'How's your cat?'

'Mr Biggles is all better now, Josie. He had a bad tooth which the vets had to remove. He's as right as rain.'

'Good. I don't like it when animals are hurting.'

'Neither do I.' Tracey pointed over to the other woman. 'Scarlet is ready for you.'

'Cool. Thanks!'

Without missing a beat, Josie walked right up to Scarlet and hopped onto the chair in front of the mirror, talking about something or other. Scarlet listened intently. The lady had light blue streaks in her blonde hair – Felan thought Blaez might like to try that style one day. He thought it would suit her.

'I don't suppose you can fit Felan in last minute?' Mrs Walters asked. 'If not, we're happy to come back another time.'

Tracey pointed over to the man. 'Lloyd's free.' She turned to Felan. 'If that's okay with you, Honey?'

Felan eyed Lloyd up without making it obvious he was doing so: he was taller than Felan, with blond dreadlocks tied back into a sort-of bun, and tattoos danced along one arm. He looked like he could really hurt Felan if he wanted to. Felan had had enough of being hurt. He almost turned and bolted from the building there and then.

But he saw Lloyd's face. It was gentle. He had a kind smile. He reminded Felan of Larry, a stranger who had been resigned, but had also only been patient and kind.

'Sure.'

Lloyd gestured for him to follow. Felan hesitated before he moved his feet. Mrs Walters patted his arm as he walked by. He jumped back a little, still very much on high alert. 'I'll be here the whole time, just over there,' she said, pointing to the benches Felan had seen when he'd first walked in the building.

'Okay.' He willed the nervousness to fade. It didn't. Felan approached Lloyd slowly. 'Hi,' he said.

'Hello – Felan, is it?' Felan nodded. He was glad when the man didn't reach out for a handshake. Felan didn't think he was capable of that right now. 'My name's Lloyd. Take a seat when you're ready and we'll get started.' He gave Felan a winning smile before he walked away and disappeared into the back room.

Felan sat down on the chair a few spaces down from Josie and stared at the floor. He point-blank refused to look in the mirror. He didn't want to see his dad staring back. He prayed he would never see his dad ever again.

Lloyd made plenty of noise when he returned, and Felan wondered if he'd dealt with jumpy customers before. The man brandished what looked like a black cape. 'I'm going to lay this over you so that it catches your hair instead of it getting stuck in your clothes.'

'Okay.'

Felan sat stock still while Lloyd fastened it. He twisted his hands together underneath the cape, glad that no one could see the anxious motion.

'Have you any ideas of what you might like done?'

'I just don't want to hide anymore.'

'Sure thing. I can work with that,' Lloyd said. 'I'll start off with wetting your hair a little, and then brushing it with a comb. After that, I'll switch to scissors.'

Felan liked Lloyd, he decided. The man did exactly what he said he would, and if he was going to do something else he hadn't already warned Felan about, he would ask if it was okay. To some people it might seem overboard, but Felan appreciated the gesture. Not everyone was so accommodating. Not everyone was so patient.

As Lloyd started to cut his hair, he asked Felan to tilt his head down. He was more than happy to obey. Felan followed the little clumps of hair as they slid down the cape and fell to the floor, and focused on how tiny, brown piles formed at his feet.

Part of him wanted to look in the mirror to see exactly what Lloyd was doing, to see what his hair looked like, but he didn't want to see his dad. He didn't want to see how terrible he looked. He didn't want to look in the eyes of the person he'd almost killed.

He would stay looking at the floor, thank you very much.

'Look straight ahead for me?' Lloyd asked.

Felan tensed. Christ, he hadn't anticipated this. He took a breath, closed his eyes, and lifted his head. He didn't want to see. He knew he should look. He knew he had to look at some point, but he didn't want to. He didn't think he'd be able to bear it.

'If you want to stop at any point, just let me know,' Lloyd said. 'I'm in no rush.'

Out of view, Felan's hands trembled in his lap. 'I'm fine.'

Lloyd carried on cutting Felan's hair and Felan thought he did a good job of not flinching every time Lloyd's fingers brushed his head. In actual fact, the touch was oddly grounding, soothing almost, and for a moment a memory of his mother stroking his hair hit him like a bullet train. (It was his mother. For a moment it was his mother.) But the smell of strong aftershave felt like a physical slap to the face, sending him crashing back down to reality.

His mother had always smelled of lemons.

Two chairs down, Felan listened in to Josie and Scarlet's conversation as a way of distraction.

'Is there any reason for the short hair, or did you just fancy a change?' Scarlet asked.

'I used to have long hair, like, really long hair. It came all the way down to my waist! But my older brothers used to pull it all the time and I didn't like it. It hurt whenever they did that. Now I have it short. Just in case.'

Felan stiffened. Her brothers had done what? He'd have given anything to have a younger sibling like her, and her brothers had taken advantage.

'That wasn't nice of them,' Scarlet said.

'It's okay! I like having short hair anyway. It doesn't take as long to dry when it's short.'

'That's very true – it's why I like having short hair too. I have friends with hair all the way down to their bottoms!'

Josie giggled, and Felan relaxed a little. She was okay. The audacity of her brothers... Felan opened his eyes and looked at the mirror, over to where Josie was sat without moving his head. As if sensing he was looking, Josie gave him a cheeky grin in the mirror before she stuck her tongue out. Felan stuck his tongue out in return. Josie grinned for a second time, and the war began. They were a few minutes into a silly face war when Lloyd said, 'There we go. What do you think?'

Completely distracted, Felan looked straight ahead in the mirror. The first thing he saw was his eyes – the same cold, grey eyes that had stared down at him in anger for years. He saw the bruise-like circles beneath them and sagged a little in the chair. Not a great start. He eventually managed to drag his gaze away from his face and focused on his hair. It was still on the shaggier side, but it was short enough that it didn't hang in his eyes like it had done before. Lloyd had trimmed the bottom and shaped it nicely. Some of the weight had been taken out, and Felan felt lighter.

It didn't feel like he was trying to hide any more.

'It's perfect,' Felan said after a moment of pleasant surprise. 'Thank you.'

Lloyd removed the cape and Felan stood up. He joined Mrs Walters by the benches, taking the spot next to her. She gave him a warm smile and shuffled a little closer to him. 'Your hair looks great,' she complimented.

Felan ducked his head. His cheeks reddened. 'Thanks.'

After Josie was finished and Mrs Walters had paid, the three of them left the building. Felan walked behind Josie and Mrs Walters down the street, replying with a simple 'yes, please' when she asked if he still wanted a hot chocolate. She bought them from a stall and they drank them on the way home. The drink warmed his insides and reminded him of Blaez, of Tristan, of the man's flat, of their few days of refuge there huddled together on the sofa. That had been the start.

Cars of all sizes trundled down the road next to them.

It would be a real shame if one of them ran off the road and I just happened to be in the way.

Felan flinched away. Mrs Walters gave him a questioning look but he waved her away. It was nothing she needed to concern herself with.

He was fine.

He was always fine.

Entry 19 – 11:47pm

How had Convel known about the abuse? How had he known about my dad? How had he known about what happened to Mum?

It's only speculation of course, but I've come to the conclusion that Nick had been watching me for a long time. Nick must have known of my situation and told everyone else. How else could Convel have known?

It had to have been Nick. It had to be, which begs the question... did Harvey know too?

On another note: Nick had known the Protrudes were encroaching in on their territory from the start.

From the day I was saved, all the way until I discovered their existence, Nick had known. Nick had known the whole time.

Had my 'save' been orchestrated from the very start?

What about Harvey? What had Harvey's part been in all of this?

I was blind to miss it. I was blind to miss everything. Nick used me, Nick toyed with me, and he played me like a fiddle. Nick exploited my fears and my dreams and he turned them into phobias and nightmares that won't leave me alone. Nick was a master of manipulation, and I was his latest pawn.

Chapter 14: Dead Ringer

The next day, Felan went to the shop with Mrs Walters for the first time.

'We'll go now, and then we can pick Gemma up from nursery on the way home,' Mrs Walters said.

It wasn't the size of the shop that shocked him; it was the prices. It was the realisation of how much money was spent on food each week. When he expressed this to Mrs Walters, all she said in return was, 'Don't you worry yourself. We have enough money.'

Felan wasn't convinced.

People stopped and talked to Mrs Walters the whole way round the shop, while Felan stood there awkwardly, listening but trying not to eavesdrop at the same time. He smiled when they laughed, and at one point he made awkward eye contact with a lady who wouldn't stop talking.

The second person (an older man with his wife) asked Mrs Walters how the kids were getting on.

'Really well,' she said, grabbing something from the shelf beside her and putting in the trolley. 'Actually, this is one of mine.' Mrs Walters looked at Felan with so much love in her eyes that he almost went weak at the knees. That was twice. That was twice in a matter of days that she'd introduced him as such.

He couldn't believe he'd wanted to throw it all away.

'This is Felan – he's one of my latest, along with his friend. He's been a wonderful addition to the house.'

The third person they spoke to wasn't quite so welcoming. It was another older man; Felan's skin crawled. He looked so much like Nick that Felan almost passed out when he saw those black, black eyes of his, black like space without any stars or planets. Just a black, empty void. He was ready to bolt... but then he saw the unblemished face and, upon closer inspection, the man had all of his fingers. A good likeness, but not the real thing. Felan searched Mrs Walters' face the entire time for any discomfort. He didn't find any, but exasperation was there clear as day.

'Is he one of yours?' a gruff voice asked.

Felan lifted his head. He met the man's gaze defiantly.

'He is.' Mrs Walters rested a hand on Felan's back and gently tapped her fingers along his spine. He wondered if she had noticed his internal struggle.

'In any case, look after yourself.' With that, the man sauntered off and disappeared into the crowds of people.

'Come on,' Mrs Walters said, pushing Felan gently forward.

'Another friend from school?' He tried to sound calm, but even he could hear how tense he was.

'He isn't a threat, Felan,' she said. 'He's a little... scary, but he's no threat. I promise you.'

'He just reminded me of someone, that's all.'

'I thought he must have done. You went very pale for a moment there.'

'Nick,' Felan choked out. 'He reminded me of Nick.'

God, there were so many people in the shop. Anyone could...

Mrs Walters picked a few things off another shelf – the kids' favourite snacks, he vaguely recalled – before she turned to him. 'Do you want to pick something?'

He blinked owlishly. 'Huh?'

Two hands grasped his, firm but gentle. 'Don't worry, Felan. You had a bit of a scare and now you're on edge. It's a natural reaction to trauma.'

Trauma. He and Blaez often joked that they were trauma bonded, and that's why they were friends in the first place.

He was born into the world innocent and oblivious, and he left the city of Guadalupe with enough trauma to carry into his next life. He didn't remember much of the situation before his mother died, but things definitely got worse after. He liked to think that, had she survived, his father would never have done what he did to him. Had she survived, the Wolves would never have found him.

But what about Blaez? Where would that have left her? What would have happened to her if Nick had never found him?

'I'm sorry,' he mumbled.

'It's okay,' she said. 'I promise you it's okay. Now, would you like some sweets? I find they always make me feel better.'

'Sweets. For me?' He was confused.

Mrs Walters squeezed his hands. 'Of course.'

'Are you sure, though? I know there's a lot of food to pay for already and I don't want to put you out of pocket. I can pay for them myself.' He let go of Mrs Walters' hands and rummaged around in his trouser pocket. Coins jingled somewhere inside. 'I have a bit of money on me.'

'Felan.' He looked up. 'I wouldn't ask you to choose something and then make you pay for it. I promise it's fine. Pick whichever bag you like.'

God, he was such a mess. Red in the face, he picked some sweets he'd seen Gemma eating the other day and put them in the trolley. He could share them with her. She deserved a treat more than he did anyway.

'Is there anything else you'd like?'

'No, I'm good. Thanks though.'

'Come on, then – let's go pay for all of this, and we'll go collect Gemma.'

Felan was glad. He didn't want to bump into anyone else.

He'd had enough of large crowds for one day.

Chapter 15: Being Seen

'You know a lot of people,' Felan commented once they were back in the safety of the minivan.

'It's a small town. You get the odd unkind one, but for the most part, Weisworth is a friendly place.'

'That's why Blaez and I were moved here, wasn't it?'

'It was one of the reasons,' she said, 'but not the only one.'

In all honesty, the slightly ambiguous answer stumped him. He bit his lip, thinking of all the reasons why she would accept someone like him into her home, her home that was full of little kids. 'What was your reasoning? If you don't mind me asking.'

He wanted to know, out of all of the other kids out there who needed help, why Mrs Walters had chosen him, and why she had chosen Blaez.

'You needed a place to stay, and I had space,' she said simply.

'And you're sure you made the right decision?'

'I *know* I made the right decision.' Mrs Walters turned off into the sideroad that led to Gemma's nursery. 'You're one of my kids, Felan. I'm not letting you go.'

The child inside of Felan wanted to cry. 'I just wanted to be wanted,' he said.

'I want you. The kids want you. Blaez wants you. We all want you here.' Mrs Walters spared a glance over at him before she focused back on the road. 'I don't know what we'd do if anything happened to you.'

Shame crept up his throat. He swallowed it down. 'It feels surreal to hear someone say it out loud.'

'I will say it however many times it takes for you to believe it.'

They rolled to a stop outside of the nursery. It was a small, bright building on the corner of the street. The fences that separated the street from the nursery were an array of yellows and blues, and the gate was pastel pink. It certainly was a clash of colours, but it stood out. It was different. Felan rather liked it.

'Can I go and get her?' he asked.

'I think she'd love that.'

Felan walked through the gate and up the woodchip path alone, Mrs Walters happily sitting in the minivan with the window rolled all the way down. He looked back twice and felt a bit better knowing he was in her line of sight the whole time.

He either didn't think it through, or he forgot, but as he approached the building, he realised he was surrounded by other parents. He gave out a few tentative smiles and a quiet hello to the nearest mums and dads and guardians, but he mostly stayed out of everyone's way.

He saw Gemma stood in the doorway to the nursery, and he waved when he was sure she'd seen him. She waved back excitedly, flapping her hands and jumping up and down. It was cuteness overload.

She was really going to be the death of him.

One of the younger women (Felan thought she must be in her early twenties) walked over to him. Felan did that awkward thing where he looked anywhere but her until she stopped right in front of him. He offered her a hesitant smile. 'Hi,' he said, not sure if he was going to freeze or run.

'Hello. I haven't seen you around here before.'

Oh. She was just making sure he wasn't a weirdo, loitering in the vicinity of young children. 'I've only recently moved here,' he said in a way of explanation.

'Oh,' she said in mild surprise. 'Are you picking up?'

'Yeah, I'm here for my…' and he realised he didn't know what Gemma was to him. Well, he knew, but he hadn't said it out loud yet. He wasn't sure if he'd be welcome.

The door opened and Gemma ran full sprint in his direction. She tackled his legs and hugged them with her tiny arms. Felan laughed, staggering back a little, but managed to stay on his feet. He crouched down and hugged her in return. She nestled in further. Warmth blossomed in his heart, and he swore the tendrils of it spread all the way to his fingertips.

The young woman smiled down at them. 'Your sister?'

'Yeah,' he said, smiling back. 'My sister.' It felt good to finally say it out loud. It felt right. He'd always wanted a sibling, and now the universe had blessed him with multiple.

Gemma pulled away and grinned cheekily up at him. 'Hi!'

He ruffled her hair. 'Did you have a good time?'

'Yes! It's better now you are here!'

He was proud to note how much better her sentences were becoming. Then he realised what she'd said and he flushed at the comment. Her green eyes sparkled with mischief.

The young woman laughed. 'I'll leave you to it. It was lovely to meet you.' She went to walk away.

'Wait!' Felan called, back to standing instantly.

She turned back around, a question on her face. She didn't look annoyed in the slightest.

'I, um. Thank you,' he said. He squeezed Gemma's shoulder. The kid didn't seem to mind. 'Thank you for saying hello.'

'It was my pleasure.'

Felan didn't catch her name, but he was okay with that. A win was a win, after all, and if he froze at the approach of a rather tall man, Felan prayed he hid it well.

The man held out his hand. 'I'm James – I run the nursery. You must be Felan.' His words were gentle and soft, and Felan could instantly see why he worked with children.

Felan shook James's hand. The man had a firm grasp. 'Yeah. Good to meet you.'

James smiled down at the kid that was trying to force her way through Felan's legs. 'This little lady has told me all about you.'

Gemma giggled. Felan lifted his leg a little and tickled her neck when she squeezed through the gap. She giggled again.

'Quite the chatterbox, I'm sure,' Felan joked. It was something he'd heard Mrs Walters say about all of the kids on numerous occasions. He doubted he would ever be called one, but Blaez on the other hand...

'She's told everyone here about her new, big brother,'

James said. 'In fact, you've been the talk of the town for a few weeks now.'

Felan flushed. 'I, uh, well… um…' Gemma couldn't stop giggling as she swung around Felan's legs. The sound of her laughter melted his heart.

'It's alright. I know it's a lot to take in.' James looked at something behind Felan and waved. Felan glanced around to see Mrs Walters waving from the minivan. He hoped she wasn't angry about him taking too long. 'I'll let you guys get on,' James said, as if he could read Felan's thoughts. 'And welcome to Weisworth, Felan. I really hope it works out for you.'

He walked off to speak to another set of parents before Felan found an answer. He hoped James didn't think he had been rude.

The mothers that had gathered by the door swooned over James, whispering among themselves and fanning their faces. It reminded Felan of the Slum. 'Poor guy,' Felan muttered. Something tugged on his hand. He looked down.

'Are you okay?' Gemma asked, no longer swinging, curious, if not a little alarmed.

Felan felt the guilt creep back in. She couldn't even be a kid around him without his intrusive thoughts ruining everything. 'Yeah,' he said. He stooped down to grab Gemma's bag before he took her hand. 'Let's get you home, kiddo.'

Chapter 16: New Attachments

After they got home and unpacked the shopping (Gemma tried to help but it ended up taking twice as long when she kept putting frozen items in the cupboards), Felan took her outside into the garden to play.

He shared his packet of sweets with her, and it was so worth it to see her giggling again, and her shiny eyes. He had always noticed it, but he forgot how much her eyes sparkled when she was happy. Felan wondered, as he sat on the grass with Gemma eating sweets, if he ever had the sparkly eyes too. He wondered if he'd ever get them back.

'I'm heading out to get the kids!' Mrs Walters shouted from the back door. 'I'll be back soon.'

'Bye!' Felan and Gemma chorused.

They finished the sweets a few minutes later. Felan shoved the crumpled-up packet into his pocket.

'My favourite,' Gemma said, a smile broadening across her face. 'Yummy.'

Felan poked her cheek. 'Why do you think I chose them?'

She giggled.

His heart swelled with affection, and he imagined that this was how his mother had felt about him. She must have done, otherwise why else would she have pushed him out of the way of the car all that time ago?

Despite being a beautiful thing, love was dangerous.

'But it's our secret.' Felan held a finger to his lips. 'Otherwise the others will get jealous that they didn't get any sweets. We can't have that now, can we?'

She nodded her head solemnly. 'Jealous.' She made a motion of zipping her lips shut. 'Zipped.'

They talked some more about their favourite foods and the

flowers in the garden. Gemma liked red flowers, apparently. Felan could work with that. He remembered seeing lots of red flowers at the nursery earlier.

'Do you like James? The man at the nursery?'

'Yes! Yes!' She clapped her hands together. 'He reads with funny voices. He does the people.'

'The characters?'

'Yeah!'

'And what book is he reading to you at the moment?'

Gemma explained the premise of multiple stories, and Felan was content to let her blabber on about different books and how nice James and the other kids at nursery were until Mrs Walters returned with the others in tow.

It was absolute carnage.

Elliot was louder than normal, Felan noted instantly on arrival, and the others buzzed with a restless energy that came hand in hand with being at school all day while the sun was out.

Felan and Gemma walked through the back door and into the kitchen. 'I'll take them outside,' he offered to Mrs Walters.

She pulled things out of the fridge and the freezer and switched the oven on in one fluid movement. 'Could you? Thank you, Felan. Food will be an hour, two at most.'

'Yeah, they're no trouble,' he said. 'Just send them outside when they finish getting changed.' He quickly glanced around. Taking advantage of the empty kitchen, Felan tossed the empty packet of sweets into the bin and covered it with a tissue. There. The other kids would never know.

Mrs Walters winked at him. She began to deftly chop up carrots for dinner. 'I'll be sure to pass them over to you.'

He found two buckets and two large stones when he went back outside with Gemma. With her help, he put one item in each corner of the bottom of the garden and waited by the monkey bars for the kids to arrive. Felan ended up helping Gemma across twice before the other kids came running out, racing each other down the garden and through the gap in the treeline. Elliot jumped around like something possessed.

He did a quick headcount before he started. 'Because you're all incredibly hyper, we're going to do some laps of the garden.'

As expected, the kids groaned and began to complain immediately. 'It's not our fault we have to sit down all day doing nothing,' Elliot whined.

'I know it isn't, but it's also not fair to shout and scream at the top of your lungs while Mrs Walters is driving, or while she's cooking your dinner.' He raised an eyebrow at the kids. They had the decency to look guilty. 'We'll set off together.'

Elliot looked confused. 'You're running too?'

'Why wouldn't I?'

Felan hadn't run anywhere in weeks, and he found that he missed it. It was something he should do more often, but the one thing he lacked at the moment was the motivation and the determination to do, well, anything. He lacked drive. He lacked consistency. He lacked commitment.

He hoped he found it soon. He hoped he found it *all* soon.

'I've marked out our course with buckets and large stones – please go *around* them,' he looked pointedly to Jude, who scowled. The kid hated rules of any kind when it came to games. If there was a loophole, the kid would find it; he would find it and feign ignorance.

'I don't know how far I'll be able to run,' Mary said quietly.

Felan smiled down at her. 'I'll be happy with any distance, okay?' She nodded. 'Good. Let's go.'

If he was being honest with himself, running hurt him. It was something he had done all the time in Guadalupe – yet it wasn't the constant running away from trouble that hurt him.

It was the memories.

He remembered running with Blaez, Accalia, Caleb, Randi… he remembered running with all of them, and the training session. That had been the first time, in a long time, that he felt like he had people around him who cared. He was happy that day, after that race, yet ever since that day, things just got worse.

Whatever. Now was not the time for such thoughts. He was supposed to be watching the kids. He glanced down beside him at

Mary and Gemma. Elliot had zoomed ahead within seconds, Jude and Josie at his heels. 'Are you okay?' he asked the girls, slowing down a little to match their pace.

They were both red in the face and breathing heavily. 'I'm getting to four laps,' Mary puffed.

'Okay.' He turned to his other side. 'Do you need to sit down, Gem?'

'Nuh uh.'

'Let me know when you want to stop,' he said.

Weeks ago, when Mrs Walters had asked what Felan wanted to do about his education, about what he wanted to work towards, he hadn't a clue. At the time, he hadn't seen a future for himself, anywhere. All he had seen was a dark, empty void and the faces of the people he couldn't save. He knew better now.

If something with nature didn't work out, he wanted to do something with children.

He liked being around them and perhaps in the future he could be a teacher of some kind. Maybe he could volunteer at Gemma's nursery.

For once, he didn't want to cry when he pictured his future. It no longer consisted of dark alleyways and knife wounds and awful people. Instead, he envisioned happy children and a bright room full of laughter.

Most importantly, he saw himself. He had never seen himself in his future before. He didn't realise how sad that was until now. He didn't realise just how sad he had been. He was proud to admit that getting up in the morning wasn't so much of a chore now.

Ahead, Josie and Elliot raced each other (Jude was happy running alone between the two groups), laughing and joking and shrieking at the top of their lungs. They breezed by Felan and the others again, slipped a little on the corner, but carried on like nothing happened. He'd have to have a word with Mrs Walters about getting the pair of them signed up to a running club – or maybe Felan could take them out for runs in the evenings when it wasn't raining. After all, the evenings were still light. It would help the kids get rid of their endless bounds of energy before bed, and it would help Felan settle his own thoughts. He was already mapping out potential routes through the park and along the river. He imagined Blaez coming with them when she came home.

Mary and Gemma called it quits after another lap and sat on the swings. Mary pushed Gemma gently while the others ran, and when Felan noticed how close Jude was to dropping, he called it quits for everyone. 'Okay!' Felan called. 'That's enough for now.'

Jude gave him a grateful smile and went straight over to the climbing frame with Elliot where they began a game about pirates, and there was something about a dinosaur. He wasn't sure about the logistics but they seemed content enough so Felan let them be and headed over to the girls. 'All okay?' he asked.

Gemma giggled. 'Yep!'

Josie suddenly appeared beside them. 'Have you ever made a daisy chain before, Felan?'

'I can't say that I have.'

'Can I teach you?' she asked shyly.

Mary perked up. 'Oh, can we?'

'Sure you can.'

The girls cheered. They led him a short distance away and sat down on the grass, daisies blooming all around them. Gemma joined them, and while the older girls gave Felan a lesson in the intricate craft of daisy chains, Gemma picked daisies and dandelions and decorated Felan's hair with them. Eventually she got bored and quickly became fascinated by the woodlice and the lady bugs that crawled about in the grass.

Following the girls' strict instructions, and with major struggles, Felan completed his first ever daisy chain. The girls wore their perfect chains atop their heads, so Felan copied their actions with his own misshapen chain. Josie and Mary giggled. That was enough for Felan to know that he'd made the right decision. He posed and pulled a face. 'How do I look?'

'You're so silly,' Mary giggled.

Josie smiled. 'Like a princess!'

'Good,' Felan said. 'That's exactly what I was aiming for.'

And then moments later, Mrs Walter's voice called from the

house: 'Dinner's ready!'

While the rest of the kids trudged back to the house, Elliot ran over to Felan and skidded to a stop by his side, full of energy despite the running.

It was going to be a long night.

'That was really good,' Felan said to him

Elliot beamed. 'Can we do that again sometime?'

'Sure we can,' Felan said. 'I'll speak to Mrs Walters at some point.'

'Thanks!'

Chapter 17: Security

Elliot was the first at the table (after quickly washing his hands) and began scarfing down his food. Seven bowls of what Felan knew to be chicken stew sat on the table, and plates of buttered bread lined the centre of it.

'Elliot!' Mrs Walters reprimanded. 'We wait for everyone to sit down before eating, remember?'

He swallowed the food in his mouth and looked down. 'Sorry. I was hungry. I'll remember for tomorrow.'

She ruffled his hair. 'Make sure that you do.' She poured Gemma her juice from the large jug in the middle of the table. The rest of them were old enough to pour their own.

While she did that, Felan helped Gemma wash her hands in the sink before he led her to her seat at the table. He took his usual seat beside her. 'Thank you, Mrs Walters,' he said. 'It smells delicious.' The other kids chorused their thank yous and tucked in.

If Mrs Walters noticed the daisy chains, she said nothing.

Maybe it was the running, but the absence of Blaez ached more than it usually did, like a painful bruise he didn't remember the cause of.

Felan kept an eye on Gemma throughout dinner to make sure she didn't faceplant in her plate. She had done that before, bless her, and it was always when she was eating something with ketchup or gravy; she'd ruined more than one white top in that way. She blinked slowly the whole time, and Felan was all but ready to leap into action if she passed out, but she managed to eat all of her food before she leaned back against her chair and promptly fell asleep.

Felan hadn't eaten a great deal, but he'd had enough to not feel hungry. He set his spoon back in the bowl of his stew and stood up.

'No, you finish your food,' Mrs Walters said, setting her stuff down.

'I've got her,' Felan said easily. He leaned down, picked up the sleeping girl and left the room before Mrs Walters could insist. She had made the stew, so the least he could do was make sure she ate it. He knew she didn't like it when he helped her too much, but this was something he knew how to do. This was something he could do without messing anything up.

Gemma made a tired noise against his shoulder.

'Wake up, sleepy head,' he mumbled, stroking her cheek. 'Just for a bit. You can't sleep in these clothes. And you need to brush your teeth. You don't want to wake up with smelly breath, do you?'

She wasn't very happy about it, but she woke up enough to change into her pyjamas, and to let Felan help her brush her teeth. He would have suggested a bath, but she was way too tired and he didn't feel like he was prepared to assist her.

With gentle hands, he laid her down in her bed and pulled the covers up to her chin. She was asleep again in seconds. He kissed her on the forehead and went to leave the room, however as he was about to close the door he changed his mind. He stood, leaning against the doorframe, watching her sleep.

She was innocent. She was so blissfully unaware of the horrors of life, despite what she might have already seen.

Felan didn't remember a time like that. He had been old enough to remember most things. Sometimes he wished he didn't, but at least he had answers. At least he knew the truth. Other kids weren't so lucky.

It hit him, stood in the doorway, that he was jealous. He was jealous of a four-year-old because she could sleep and he couldn't. But it wasn't Gemma's fault he had issues. He couldn't take it out on her.

He wouldn't.

Footsteps trailed up the stairs and into the hallway, heading in his direction. 'I'll be down to clear up in a bit,' he said quietly, suddenly remembering that he never went back down to help clean up.

'Don't even think about it,' Mrs Walters scolded him. 'I've put the rest of your dinner in a tub for you to reheat later,' she said.

'Thank you.'

The stairs creaked again. Felan glanced down the hallway to see all of the kids traipsing to their respective rooms, ready to wind down for the evening. It was early, but the kids were tired from running – even Elliot now. He seemed to have finally reached his limit.

Felan counted that as a win.

Both of the upstairs showers turned on. The old boiler hummed to life in the cupboard down the hall. Felan looked back into Gemma's room. She hadn't even stirred.

He couldn't imagine being so carefree as to not be scared to close his eyes. Even now he struggled. His sleep was always interrupted sooner or later by nightmares and memories he would rather forget. He had tried so hard to convince himself that it hadn't really happened, that it was just another nightmare, yet there were times when he couldn't quite convince himself. There were times when he didn't trust his memory, when he didn't trust his account of what had happened back in Guadalupe.

What if he *was* going mad?

'It's going to get easier, Felan,' Mrs Walters said. She rested a hand on his back like she had done in the shop earlier. He couldn't believe that had been today. It felt like it had been weeks. 'You're safe here,' she said. 'There's nothing here that can harm you.'

I can.

I can harm myself.

Gemma rolled over beneath the covers. She didn't wake. 'I just wanted a home,' he said. He couldn't take his eyes off her, innocent and undisturbed, sleeping peacefully.

'You never have to worry about finding a home ever again.' He sniffled. 'We want you here. Blaez too, when she comes home for good. We want you here. *Both of you.* You're both a part of our family now.' She glanced at the top of his head, a small smile on her face. 'Daisy chains and all.'

Felan ducked his head to hide his blush. 'Apparently it suits me.'

She ruffled his hair gently, taking care not to damage his new headwear. 'Always be you, Felan,' she said. With that she bid him goodnight and left him pondering in Gemma's doorway.

Entry 20 – 1:37am

I can't believe I thought it was him.

How could I have been so stupid?

He's far away from here, and I know deep down that I'll never see him again, that he'll never find me or Blaez, but I'm scared that one day soon he's just going to appear and ruin everything. I'm not scared. I'm *terrified*. I'm terrified for that day, because I realised today, picking Gemma up from nursery, that I really love these kids. Now that I've spent more time with them, I'm realising just how great they are. I've always wanted siblings, and they were right in front of me this whole time.

I can't believe that I wanted nothing to do with them, that I wanted to end it all... I can't believe that I would have allowed that to happen, that I almost affected their lives forever.

But what I'm slowly learning is that it isn't my fault. Both Blaez and Mrs Walters have told me that I'm just reacting to what's happened.

I like Mrs Walters. She's kind. She's patient.

My attempt scared me more than I care to admit. Not that it was an attempt, but... yeah. I know it's something I should probably speak to Mrs Walters about. I know I should tell her more about what I tried to do, and how I tried to do it, and what my stupid plans for that stupid stunt were, but...

It's a conversation for another day.

On another note, I have a job! I haven't started yet but I will soon. I have to go in for a proper chat with Mark in a few days, but hopefully I get the all-clear.

I'm nervous. I'm nervous if I mess up, because what will happen to me then? What if people realise they don't like me once they get to know me? What if Mark decides he's made a mistake with me? What if it all goes wrong?

But despite the nerves, I'm excited. I realised that today too. I'll finally have plans. There'll finally be something next to my name on the calendar in the living room. It feels like progress.

I've never felt like that before.

Chapter 18: Adjusting

A girl was standing behind the counter making coffees when Felan walked into the café. Her long, brown hair was tied back into two plaits; Felan recognised it as Mary's favourite hairstyle.

'Hi, what can I get for you?' the girl asked.

'Oh, I'm actually here to speak with Mark. My name's Felan.'

'Hannah. I'll go and let him know you're here.' She walked over to a door, popped her head around it, and came back. 'He'll be out in a few minutes.'

'Thanks.'

Within seconds, she was telling him all about her life. She rambled on while she made coffees before she disappeared to deliver them. The side door opened, and a man walked out to greet him. *Mark.* He wasn't scary like Felan had anticipated. He was soft spoken and calming, and Felan really liked him. He was nothing like Nick, which was a good start. If anything, he reminded Felan of James, the man who ran Gemma's nursery.

Mark walked Felan through what he would be doing if he accepted the position (washing up in the back for a few hours four days a week), and when Felan accepted it, Mark handed him over a few work t-shirts. Felan forced out a smile and walked home carrying them in his arms, panicking about how he would have to wear short sleeves.

People would see his arms. People would see his shame.

He didn't want anyone else to see that side of him (after having spoken to Mrs Walters about the t-shirts, she had come back with three black, long-sleeved tops for him).

His first shift had been on a quiet Tuesday. He worked with Hannah, a twenty-one-year-old who loved life, and she didn't question his long-sleeved top beneath his t-shirt. Instead, she had told Felan within five minutes of him clocking in that she was saving up to travel the world. When he had asked who she was going with, she laughed, pulled out her phone, and showed him a picture of a little blue campervan. 'Just me and my pride and joy,' she said.

Felan wished he had that kind of bravery.

'I'm just looking after myself,' Hannah went on to explain. 'It's called self-care, and I rather like the idea of building a life that I don't need to escape from. I want to build a life that I actively enjoy, not passively hate.'

Felan thought he understood, but how could someone just wake up one day and want to change their life? How did someone get the courage and the bravery to do something like that?

In place of asking, he stood quietly and listened to her talk. She seemed very insightful. He thought Blaez would really like her.

***

As his first few shifts were relatively quiet, he had been sent home early, but he thought it was going well. In the café, they sold hot drinks, cold drinks, and cakes and biscuits. Felan was even given a share of tips when the customers were generous enough to leave them.

And when he wasn't working, Felan spent a lot of time sat on the doorstep basking in the sun like a cat.

It was something he and Blaez had come up with weeks ago: get ten minutes of fresh air a day, even if it was just sitting on the doorstep and watching the clouds go by. Often, one of the neighbour's cats came running up to see him and curled up on his lap. He couldn't help but smile and lazily stroke the top of its head.

But despite everything, something niggled away at the back of his mind that it would all collapse. Blaez had gone, therefore everything would soon follow. He tried to convince himself that he was being unrealistic. He tried to convince himself that he had something permanent now, but it was safe to say he failed. He never had been good at convincing himself about the good stuff. For a long time, good stuff hadn't existed. Good stuff was foreign to him.

Felan wasn't going to do anything stupid again, but it didn't prevent the dark thoughts from intruding where they weren't welcome. He had tried not to think about it, because if he thought about it, if he thought about what he had tried to do, then it made it real.

So he thought about forgetting. He wanted to forget about Nick, he wanted to forget about the city of Guadalupe altogether, but Nick, and Guadalupe, had been a part of his life for so long that it wasn't quite as easy as simply forgetting.

His phone buzzed in his pocket.

His ten minutes were up.

Chapter 19: Role Model

With the help of the kids, Felan looked after the vegetable patch, though everything had yet to sprout. He instructed Josie and Gemma on how to water it once a day, and when to leave it be. He tried to teach Elliot how to weed a few times, but the kid was far too interested in flying the trowel like a spaceship. Mary joined in on her twin's antics shortly after so Felan had called that particular venture a day.

Then Elliot asked why they couldn't get a dog. Felan thought back to Guadalupe, where strays of all kinds lay in the streets, emaciated and defeated.

Mary piped up and asked if they could get some bird feeders instead. Mrs Walters warmed to that idea, and Felan was keen too. It would encourage more wildlife into their garden, and the kids could be in charge of keeping the feeders filled with birdseed. There was already a bird's nest in the tree at the bottom of the garden, which the kids had been delighted about when Felan had pointed it out to them, so it made sense.

'It'll be like having a dog, but not,' Mary said to her twin.

The bewildered look on Elliot's face was priceless.

*****

Weeding became Jude and Felan's job.

Felan wouldn't force a conversation, and Jude would only speak when he wanted to. It worked out perfectly, if he didn't say so himself.

It all changed when Jude came home from school early one Thursday morning with a bruise on his cheek and a stern talking to from Mrs Walters. Felan stayed out of the way, digging in the garden, but inside he seethed. Someone had laid a hand on Jude.

Someone had hit him hard enough to leave a mark.

Felan saw the red knuckles on the boy's hand when Jude came out to help with the weeding and he understood immediately. 'You know, fighting doesn't make anything better.'

Jude rolled his eyes. 'Not you as well,' he muttered. 'I already got a telling off from Mrs Walters.'

'I'm not telling you off,' Felan said. 'I just want to talk about it, if you like.'

Jude scowled and started weeding in silence. Felan managed to count to five before the kid exploded. 'They found out about Chris and Penny, okay?' He threw a particularly large weed to the ground and huffed.

Felan decided to carry on like nothing happened. 'That's nothing to be ashamed of.' He spared Jude a brief glance. 'You're allowed to be upset.'

'They kept making horrible jokes, and saying mean things.' His bottom lip quivered. 'I got angry, and I hit them first. I started the fight.' The kid dipped his head down. 'I didn't mean to start it. I just got angry.'

'I was bullied at school, you know,' Felan said. Though he hadn't said it to Mrs Walters, he wondered if it counted as his one thing for the day. Perhaps he and Jude were more alike than he had originally realised. 'They called me all sorts of horrid things, and they liked to hit me. They broke my things too.'

Jude looked up. 'Is that why you didn't want to go back to school?'

Felan mulled it over, thinking of the best way to explain it without overwhelming the kid. 'It wasn't the only reason. My point is, before I came here… I got into a lot of fights and I lost nearly every single one. The people I was fighting were bigger and scarier than me, and I never stood a chance.' When he was sure he had the boy's undivided attention, Felan pulled up the sleeves of his jumper and showed off the hideous red and white lines he'd grown to hate, the scars he was yet to share with any of the kids.

The red and white lines he had just shared with Jude.

Jude sat on the floor, cross-legged, staring at the scars on Felan's arms with wide eyes. 'Then why did you fight them?'

'I didn't have a choice,' Felan said. 'I never started them, but if I wanted to go home, I had to fight back. I had to put up a fight, even though it meant I would lose, but you have a choice, Jude. You can choose not to fight. You can choose to talk to this person. You can choose whatever action you want.'

'I get to choose?' He sounded so unsure and Felan vowed to never let Jude feel that way again.

Felan nodded. 'Yeah.'

Jude took a moment to let everything sink in. He looked away, back to the pile of weeds, but his eyes kept flickering back to Felan's arms. 'I'm going to choose to be good,' he finally said, getting back to his knees and pulling up weeds again.

Felan did the same. 'I'm glad.'

Chapter 20: Regression

It rained for two days, and Felan couldn't bring himself to get out of bed.

Something intangible held him down, something with sharp claws that clung to him like fog over the hills, and it took hours for Felan to realise what it was.

Exhaustion.

It was the exhaustion that came hand in hand with living, the exhaustion that had made a home within the confines of his body ever since he was a boy grieving his mother's death. So he laid there, *exhausted*, exhausted despite doing nothing, like there was someone, somewhere, holding the remote to Felan's life, their finger pressed down firmly on the PAUSE button.

He had never been more thankful that the café didn't require his services for a few days.

Beside his head, his phone buzzed, the familiar text tone sounding quietly in the room. Felan drowned out the noise with his duvet. The text tone still sent a spark of fear shooting down his spine as he remembered his drop-offs, and the constant influx of texts that wouldn't stop unless he showed up with his satchel.

Since his arrival in Weisworth, Felan had considered changing his text tone to something less triggering; he couldn't quite bring himself to.

It was familiar, and familiar was good.

Three more texts came in quick succession, vibrating by his head.

Felan peeled back the covers.

Another text.

And another.

No. No. No, not again. He wouldn't do it. He wasn't going out on drop-offs again. He hated them. He hated selling drugs to people. He hated it when the customers took advantage of him. He hated it when said customers got violent.

Another text.

Felan threw his phone across the room and squeezed himself inside the small gap between the wall and his chest of drawers, his knees bent to his chest, his head in his hands. He found he couldn't quite remember how to breathe. Was his chest supposed to hurt so much? Why couldn't he just *breathe?*

His phone buzzed into the carpet.

He never wanted to do the drop-offs in the first place. He never wanted any of it. He sold drugs on street corners to give money to a man who wanted him for his youth.

All Felan had ever wanted to do was help.

'Felan?'

Mrs Walters. No. She couldn't see. He tried to reply but he still couldn't breathe right. He sucked in a breath. He expelled it too fast and choked, his lungs feeling two sizes too small for his body.

A knock on his door. 'Felan – dinner's ready.'

No. No, she couldn't see him. Not like that. She wouldn't look at him the same way ever again.

The door opened. He wanted to run away, so far away. He wished the floor would open up and swallow him, chew him, grind him up, hide him down below, *anything* to take him away from his current predicament.

'Oh, Felan.'

He looked away. He hated pity, he hated sorrow, and he hated it most when it was directed at him.

The floor in front of him creaked.

'Don't touch me,' he choked out.

'I won't,' she said. 'What happened?'

He simply stared at Mrs Walters, stared into her hazel eyes that flashed with sorrow, knowing panic was written plainly across his face. He'd watched himself break down in the mirror more than once, and every time he hated what he saw. He hated how ugly and animalistic he looked in those rare moments he was brave enough to actually *look*. He was ashamed of the person who lived beneath his skin; despite the few good things he'd done since arriving in Weisworth, he was still ashamed.

'It's okay,' Mrs Walters soothed in that gentle voice of hers. 'You're safe here. It's just us. You're *safe*.'

He nodded. He knew that, he really did, but at the same time, every little thing reminded him of the person he used to be, of all the things that person used to do. Every time he closed his eyes, darkness lingered in his dreams, and in the times it spilled into his waking hours, he heard Nick's voice, his whispers, his promises and his threats.

Things wouldn't hurt if you behaved.

Every day it hurt to look into the mirror and see the eyes of the person he hated most.

'Listen to me,' Mrs Walters said firmly. 'Breathe in, hold it, and let it go.' Felan did as he was told. He behaved. That was all he could do now. Behave and hope for the best, since he was too far gone down the rabbit hole that was his life. 'Well done – keep doing it until you've calmed down.'

After a few minutes, and with Mrs Walters' soft encouragement, with her steadfast presence in front of him, he breathed normally again. He slumped down, red in the face – both in embarrassment and from lack of breath. He looked her in the eye; she gave nothing away.

'What set you off?'

There was no use in hiding it. 'My phone,' he muttered. 'It kept pinging – I thought for a moment I was back with Nick doing drop-offs. I thought…' He stared down at his arms in disgust; red and white lines and messy scar tissue. He winced as a memory of a particularly nasty cut latched onto him. He breathed out. The memory faded.

'That's understandable,' she said.

'No, it isn't!' he exploded. 'How can Blaez be okay with being back *there*, and I can't even… and I can't even receive a text without panicking?'

Mrs Walters thought for a moment. 'Have you considered changing the text tone?' Felan nodded. 'Did you want me to help you with it, or is it something you want to do on your own?'

'On my own,' he said. He couldn't handle Mrs Walters seeing him break down again. It was bad enough that she'd walked in on him having a full-blown panic attack. It was bad enough that she knew how terrible he was feeling, that she knew one of his darkest secrets.

He didn't like being known. Being known in Guadalupe was a death sentence, but being known in Weisworth? He had yet to figure that out.

'I know it seems hopeless now, but it will get easier, Felan.'

That was what Blaez had always said. She had told him that from the very beginning, yet he didn't believe it. Life was better, sure, but himself? He was not better, and he knew it. He was a long way from being better, and anyone who didn't see that was a fool.

'You need to eat something.'

He scratched at his arms with blunt fingernails. 'I'm not hungry.'

She patted the top of his hands firmly. He stilled his movements immediately. 'Take it easy – if you decide you're hungry later, go and make yourself some food. Okay?'

He nodded.

Felan stayed in the gap long after Mrs Walters left. He stretched his legs out in front of him, shuddering. Something about the enclosed space meant safety. He could see if anyone came into his room, and the walls were warm – it was like a hug. His phone buzzed once more, but he made no move to check it. It was probably Blaez anyway, and she wouldn't care if he didn't reply straight away. He knew he should check, just to make sure, but he… he couldn't. It was too soon after…

'Fee?' A four-year-old walked into his room, her little face twisted into the beginnings of a frown (no matter how many times he corrected her, she still couldn't quite say his name. He let her have it after a while, and, truth be told, Felan rather liked the nickname). 'Fee, why are you on the floor?'

He tried his best to make his smile convincing. 'I just needed some quiet for a while.'

Gemma shrugged and, as oblivious as ever, squeezed herself into the gap and sat on his lap. He wrapped an arm around her and let her play with his hands, something she liked to do every now and then. He rested his chin atop her head, atop her curls, and held her close. She wouldn't judge him, he knew.

He was also very aware that his bare arms were on full display.

'Marks,' she said, surprised. 'Your arms have marks.'

Hmm. Perhaps she wasn't as oblivious as he had initially thought. Some days, she acted so much younger than her age, and other days, she seemed more mature than all of the other kids combined.

'Poorly. Poorly arms,' she mumbled. 'Are they...' Gemma paused, her little mind turning. 'Are they poorly now?'

'No,' he said. He thought about how he could explain it to a child as young as Gemma and still get her to understand. 'Remembering hurts. Remembering makes me poorly.'

Apparently, that was enough to satisfy her curiosity. She leaned back against his chest and made herself comfortable. Smiling to himself, he told her a made-up story about fairies in a faraway forest. She fell asleep with a quiet snore, and when he was sure she was completely gone, he stood up and carried her to bed. It was early, probably too early for her to be sleeping, but she clearly needed the rest if she was tired enough to fall asleep so fast. He tucked her beneath her fairy covers, left her bedroom door slightly ajar, and walked downstairs to help with the after-dinner clean-up.

It was the first productive thing he'd done all day.

'You're really good to her, Felan,' Mrs Walters said, when he told her where Gemma was.

He picked up a tea towel and began drying the clean plates. 'I just know what it's like to have no one. I don't want that for her.' Gemma deserved a loving family with a massive house and all the cuddles and hugs she could ever want, and maybe, just maybe, that was what he deserved too.

'Maybe you'll be the person to change things for kids like her.'

'What can one kid do against the whole world?' he asked bitterly.

'You'd be surprised.'

Entry 21 – 12:08am

Every time I think back on what happened in Guadalupe, it hurts me on the inside. It's like there's this glass ball inside of me, and it's now shattered, and its pieces are stabbing everywhere. I don't recall when this ball shattered, or when it first formed, but its pieces have been stabbing me for a long time – for as long as I can remember. As I told Gemma earlier, remembering hurts. Remembering will always hurt, but it will be easier to bear. It won't hurt as much as time passes.

Every memory I have of Guadalupe is a punishment for the decisions I have made, and I somehow need to accept that.

Chapter 21: Safekeeping

Although the uniform left a lot to be desired (a burnt-orange t-shirt – and now a long-sleeved top), Felan's job at the café was perfect.

He was on washing-up duty in the back, as well as cleaning down tables ready for the next customers. The customers in question called him sweet and polite – especially the older ladies that visited daily – and their compliments always left him red in the face and jittery.

Though Felan could still be a bit jumpy around customers, especially when someone snuck up on him, he wasn't quite so nervous anymore.

'Felan?' Lisa called.

'In here,' he said, loading a series of cups and saucers into the dishwasher.

Her head popped through the door. 'I'm so sorry to ask at such short notice – Hannah can't make her shift this afternoon, and Matt is already out of town. Do you think you can work until closing?'

Judging by the panicked look on her face, and the amount of dishes piling up, Felan knew they were swamped. He couldn't leave Lisa on her own without help. Besides, it wasn't like he had any plans for the afternoon (other than rotting in his bed).

'Of course – do you mind if I call someone to let them know I'll be home a bit later?'

'Thank you, lad. Thank you so much. Of course. You're a life saver.' With that, Lisa ran from the room.

Felan sighed. He would have liked to go home on time, but he liked helping people too much. And he rather liked washing up. He called Mrs Walters to tell her the situation – he found it a bit strange that someone wanted to know his movements because they cared about his wellbeing, as opposed to them wanting him to sell more drugs to make them more money. He supposed he liked that Mrs Walters cared, even if he didn't quite understand why she did.

With that thought in mind, he headed out into the fray. Doing a quick survey, there weren't many tables to clean down, though Lisa had a queue at the till that went almost to the front door. He doubted the heavy rain was helping matters.

He had to be brave. He couldn't hide in the back for the rest of his life, even if that was the only place he wanted to be, even if that was the only place he felt *safe*.

He walked over to Lisa, very aware of the queue of customers watching his every move. 'Would you like a hand over here?'

She looked like she could hug him to death. 'I'd love a hand. I know you haven't had any front-of-house training, but we'll muddle through it together.'

Felan put on a brave smile and stood on the till while Lisa busied herself with the seven orders already waiting to go out. 'Hi,' Felan said to an elderly couple next in line. 'I'm so sorry about the wait – what can we get for you?'

And on and on it went. He made some mistakes, but they were fixable, as Lisa kept telling him when he felt himself get worked up over them. Once he'd gotten rid of the queue, he helped Lisa make the hot drinks. She showed him the correct way to make a latte, how a cappuccino should look, and the perfect amount of powder to use to make the tastiest hot chocolate. The coffee machine itself was foreign to him, with all its knobs and switches and gauges, though he got the hang of it fast enough.

I wonder what would happen if I burned myself on the coffee machine.

Lisa distracted him before he could panic by showing him where to find the sachets of sugar and the packets of biscuits and the cakes (if they had been ordered) and how to lay the tray before delivering it to the correct table. He apologised to every customer he dealt with. 'I don't normally do front of house,' he said, hoping it would help appease the customers who had been waiting a little while to receive their drinks.

'Don't worry about it at all, lad,' a lovely lady said with a smile. 'You can't help being busy. I think you're both doing an amazing job.'

He walked back over to the till with a generous tip and a red face. Lisa showed him where the tip jar was – it was safe to say that the tips were more generous than usual.

The last two hours flew by. Felan wasn't the biggest fan of strangers, but he thought he did an okay job. He hadn't spoken to so many people in such a short space of time – ever! It was a little unsettling. Actually, it was more than unsettling. He tapped his collar bone once or twice when he felt the unease build in his stomach. He tapped harder when it rose to the back of his throat.

If she saw, Lisa didn't acknowledge how red and wet his eyes were for the remainder of the shift, and when he was sure she could cope on her own with front of house, Felan retreated back to the dishwasher with mountains of cups and spoons and saucers.

I wonder if it's possible for someone to drown themselves in an industrial dishwasher.

Felan flinched.

Somewhere, out on the floor, Lisa walked around, and the sound of the sign clattering against the window jolted him back to reality. He hastily rolled up his long sleeves and got to work. Lisa always helped him after the last customer had left, after she'd turned the *open* sign around to say *closed*.

'I'm sorry for throwing you in at the deep end,' Lisa said. 'I'm so grateful for your help.'

Felan carried on washing up and, out of the corner of his eye, he could see Lisa eyeing up his scars. His shoulders tensed. 'You're welcome.'

'So what happened there?' she asked, pointing to his arms.

He focused on a particularly tough coffee stain. 'I was involved with the wrong people.'

'You're safe now, lad,' she said, drying up the plates and saucers while he reloaded the dishwasher. The job was always quicker with two people, but Felan often liked the solitude that came with washing up. He didn't have to *be* anything. He didn't have to put on a show. He could just exist.

'Yeah,' Felan said. 'I'm in a better place now.' He blinked a few times. 'I just made a lot of mistakes. I made all the wrong choices.' He was very much aware of Lisa staring at him.

They finished the job in silence, and when it was all done, Lisa said, 'May I hug you?'

Immediately Felan recoiled. He put a safe distance between himself and Lisa, and thought of all the things that could go wrong, and what that might mean for his future at the café.

Until, without warning, his tears spilled over and he nodded.

Lisa held him tight in a strong, warm hug. He hadn't realised how badly he'd needed it. In fact, he hadn't realised how much he trusted the older lady. It was nice to have someone outside of the house who he could rely on.

Felan pulled away and wiped at his eyes, thoroughly embarrassed.

Lisa watched him with a fond look. 'I don't know what happened, or what you went through before now, but it's all going to be okay.'

That was all anyone ever said to him nowadays. 'I –' He cut himself off, and he thought. He had been going to argue (a frustrating default of his), but perhaps she was right. Nothing bad had happened to him since he had arrived at Weisworth. No one had physically harmed him. No one had said anything horrible to him. It had been almost like the way it should have been.

He settled with, 'I really hope it's better this time around.'

'There's a good lad. Now, let's finish up here, and then I'll drop you home. It's pouring outside.'

'No, I can walk. It's only down the road.'

Lisa gave him a look reminiscent of Mrs Walters. 'Nonsense. You agreed to stay on longer to help me out, so the least I can do is drop you home. You'll just have to tell me where I'm going.'

If Felan had learned anything working at the café over the last few weeks, it was that there was no arguing with Lisa. He agreed to her suggestion with a quiet thanks. They finished the end-of-day jobs and before he knew it Felan was sat in the passenger seat of Lisa's car giving her directions.

'Just in there,' Felan said. He pointed to the massive house that was now his home. His home. *His*.

Lisa stopped the car and patted Felan on the shoulder. He thought he did a great job of not flinching. 'You know where I am if you need to talk,' she said.

'Yeah, I do.'

'This is a good place,' Lisa said, nodding in the direction of the orphanage. 'Mrs Walters is amazing. I'm glad you managed to get here.'

'Me too,' he said, and he realised he meant it. He discovered he was meaning a lot of the things he said at the moment.

'Goodbye, Felan. We'll see you on Thursday.'

'Yeah, see you Thursday.'

Felan made the dash across the road to the house after checking it was safe to do so. Mrs Walters waited with an umbrella at the end of the driveway – Felan's insides preened at the sight. Behind him, Lisa honked her horn. He turned around and waved as she drove off.

'Who was that?' Mrs Walters asked, pulling Felan further under the umbrella.

'Lisa – I work with her.'

'I know Lisa – she's an angel.'

The memory of her hugging him felt like being wrapped up inside a fluffy blanket. 'Yeah. She is.'

They walked arm in arm back to the house, hurrying to the door. He followed Mrs Walters inside, shaking his jacket a little before he hung it on the coat rack. Then he remembered something he'd been meaning to ask her for days. 'The daily telling thing… does it only apply to you, or can it be used on other people?'

She shook off the umbrella and let it stand in the bucket by the front door. 'Is this your way of telling me you've been talking to other people about things?'

He stood awkwardly in the entrance hall. 'Is that okay?'

She noted his stance and walked right on over, setting her

hands down gently atop his shoulders. 'Felan, it's more than okay. You can tell whoever you like, whoever you're comfortable telling. I only asked that you tell me because I didn't think you'd be open to talking about it with others so soon.'

He guessed that made sense. 'I talked to Jude a little the other day, and just now I talked to Lisa.'

Mrs Walters squeezed his shoulders and released him. 'I'm proud of you.' He flushed horribly. 'And you're still enjoying it at the café?'

'I am,' Felan said. 'It gives me something else to focus on. It takes my mind off everything.'

'As long as you don't hide from it, that's absolutely fine.'

'I know.'

'Good. Now go and clean up – I've got a plate warming up in the oven for you.'

'You didn't have to.'

'Nonsense. I'll have it on the table in ten minutes.'

'Thank you.'

She smiled as he made for the stairs. 'You're always welcome.'

Felan started to think he might be.

Chapter 22: Nurture

'I saved Randi's life,' Felan said one evening after the kids had all gone to bed. It was just himself and Mrs Walters sat in the front room with the TV on low. It wasn't showing anything exciting, just the same old soaps that always played, but background noise helped him to talk.

'Your friend?'

Felan nodded. 'He got shot. I carried him back to the Warehouse after the others had left him for dead... It wasn't enough. It just made him even more of a target to Nick.'

'You tried,' she said. 'You did the right thing.'

'Maybe, but it wasn't enough,' he repeated. 'Nick just sent him right back out into danger. I couldn't... If I'd just convinced him to come back with me...'

Mrs Walters watched him carefully. 'He might've suffered an even worse fate had he come back with you. I need you to understand that.'

'He was murdered in front of an audience like some sort of circus act, and Caleb screamed. For *so long*. Nick laughed. He laughed and so did the others and I just stood there and...'

Felan drew back, suddenly aware of how much he had said, of how easy it had been to talk out of nowhere. 'I don't want to say any more.'

'That's okay,' Mrs Walters placated. 'Thank you for sharing that with me.'

He hurried up the stairs to his bedroom.

It took an age for him to fall asleep.

***

He woke up to a nightmare shortly after. As of late, they were about Caleb and Randi, the boys he couldn't save. They blamed him; he watched them die; they attacked him.

Not necessarily in that order.

He wrote about it in his notebook while the images were still fresh, while the words they'd said to him were at the forefront of his mind.

'We're dead because of you! This is all your fault.'

Felan didn't try to sleep after that.

Hours later, the kids roused, and the house was once again busy with movement. On a good day, the domestic sounds calmed Felan down. On a good day, he felt at ease enough to join them.

Today wasn't a good day, so Felan waited until the house was empty before he left the safety of his room.

He wrapped himself up in an oversized jumper and made the arduous journey down to the kitchen. He found an apple in the fruit bowl and took a small bite. And another. His stomach rolled over once and Felan supressed a gag. Tossing the remains in the food waste, he stood at the sink, staring out the window and into the back garden, waiting for Mrs Walters to come back from the school run.

What is this?

What am I doing?

She arrived back in record time, poured herself a glass of water and stood beside him. 'How are you feeling today?'

He didn't feel much like talking so he shrugged.

'You weren't sleeping this morning,' she said, not at all fazed by his lack of verbal response.

He shook his head.

'Nightmares?'

'Something like that,' he muttered. He rubbed at his eyes. He always hated how itchy they felt when he hadn't slept. 'I've been writing. In my notebook.'

'Oh,' she said, in a surprised tone. 'Good. That's really good.'

Felan clenched his fists. 'I don't want anyone to read it.'

'No, no that's… that was never the goal of your notebook,' she reassured. 'Those are your words, and they will stay that way until you're ready to share them. Or not. That's fine too.'

He let out a little sigh of relief. 'Okay.'

***

Friday night was a killer.

He dreamed of the day his mother was killed, and the endless, gnawing grief he'd lived with since he was seven years old (the grief he'd birthed when Felan realised that his mother was never coming home) flared like a wildfire once more. Her absence dangled above Felan's head like a lure, like the esca from those anglerfish he'd read about once, and the sadness that came hand in hand with her loss riddled his body like a volatile disease.

He'd spent the rest of the night staring up at his ceiling. He had thought of writing about her, but he was too distraught to put her down on paper. He was too distraught about how the sound of his mother's voice was fading from his memory. He tried to picture her face in his mind – even that image was fading too.

Saturday morning, Mrs Walters ushered the kids into the front room and pulled Felan into the kitchen, concern etched into her face. 'Talk to me, Felan,' she said. She kept her distance, and for that Felan was grateful.

'I had a dream.'

'About Guadalupe?'

'About the day my mum died.'

He failed to mention it was his birthday. He had decided years ago that he would never celebrate it again, even if he had just turned seventeen overnight. Why would he want to celebrate the day his mother had died? Others would throw parties. Felan would rather throw something through a window. He supposed throwing something out of one was better than throwing *himself* out of one.

Baby steps.

Mrs Walters motioned in the direction of the back garden. 'Let's take this outside, shall we?'

'What about the kids?'

'They'll be okay. We won't be going far.' She headed on out and took a seat on one of the concrete steps leading further down into the garden. Felan waited a beat before he followed her. And then he talked.

'I don't know who was behind the wheel of the car that day. Looking back on it now, I assume it was a drunk driver. And you know the worst part? Nothing came from it. I don't think there was even an investigation – if there was, I didn't know about it.' Somewhere, at the end of the garden, a bird sang. 'My mother was killed and it was glossed over like it wasn't important.' His hands trembled. He balled them into fists. 'When I was older, I tried to find out what happened.'

Nothing had come from his late-night search at the library. Nothing ever did.

'What was she like?' Mrs Walters asked.

'She was beautiful, and kind.' Even if he was forgetting what she looked like and how she sounded. 'She kept me safe when it mattered. She… she made the ultimate sacrifice for me that day.' He looked down. 'She saved my life. I know she loved me, because why else would she do that?'

He remembered how sad she had always looked, and it broke his heart for that to be the main thing he remembered about her. He hadn't noticed it much at the time, but now that he looked back on it… it was painfully obvious to him now just how much pain she had been in.

'I know it wasn't intentional,' he continued. 'I know she wanted me to be safe, but she also left me on my own. Everything changed after that moment.' Felan twisted his fingers together, another recent habit of his. 'I still see her sometimes. In the bluebells. They were her favourites. They were all over the woodlands and the parks in Guadalupe.' He looked over at the flowerbed that was full of poppies, sunflowers and pink and white cornflowers. Maybe…

'We can get bluebells for the garden,' she said, as if following his train of thought. 'We can plant them in the flowerbeds. Of course, they won't flower until next year, but that's something we can do.'

'Really?'

'I want this house to feel like your home too, Felan.'

Smiling to himself, he found a stick beside him and drew a circle in a patch of dirt at his feet. 'Does this house feel like your home, Mrs Walters?'

'It's been my home for a long time,' she said.

'If you don't mind me asking, where's your family?'

He noticed that she never went away anywhere, and that she never spoke to anyone outside of the people she knew around town when she went to the shops. That didn't count. It wasn't the same as making plans. It was something else his mother had never done. She had never left him on his own until the day she died.

'To be honest with you, Felan, I don't know,' she said.

He had learned a new word the other day. Dysfunctional. Many of the kids that walked through Mrs Walters' front door had come from severely dysfunctional families, and that was putting it kindly.

A small ball of anger formed in his gut at Mrs Walters' admission. That didn't sit right with Felan at all. What was the point in a family if they never saw each other? What kind of a family was that?

He studied Mrs Walters' face. 'What happened?'

'We had different views of the world,' she said. 'We all wanted different things, and by staying in contact we were hurting each other.'

'How so?'

'My parents didn't think I was being fair to myself, working here. Living here,' she corrected. 'They thought I was setting myself up for heartbreak after heartbreak. They didn't want that for me, and yet they refused to listen to me, to what I wanted.'

A group of birds flew overheard. 'I bet it's hard when the kids move on, huh?'

'I try not to get attached,' she said. 'Every new kid that comes through my doors, I promise myself I'll keep my distance.' Felan glanced her way when she paused. Her face fell, the mask she wore around Felan slipping down to reveal something helpless. 'I never can,' she finished quietly.

Sorrow for Mrs Walters nestled at the bottom of his heart, however, deep down, Felan was glad she didn't keep her distance from him, even if at the start he had wanted her to. 'Was it hard when April and Amelia left?'

'Yes, and no. They were only here for a few weeks, but a few weeks is enough time to get attached. It's enough time to get to know someone. It's enough time to create memories.'

Then he asked something that had plagued Felan ever since the girls had left. 'Why did they move on?'

'The girls came to me one night and told me they didn't like living with lots of people,' she explained. 'They said it was too loud and they found it hard to settle, so I made some phone calls, and the next day foster parents arrived to take them in.'

'As quick as that?'

'Quicker than you might think.' Mrs Walters sighed. 'As much as I want every child who walks through my doors to love this house, a place like this isn't suited to every child, and I have to respect that. April and Amelia weren't happy here, and I had the power and the resources to get them moved somewhere else, so I did. There are so many wonderful, trustworthy foster parents here in Weisworth, ready to drop everything at a moment's notice to help a child in need.' Mrs Walters smiled. 'I know that the girls are happier where they are now. I know that they're being looked after.'

'Do you hear from kids that have moved on from here?'

'I'm still in contact with kids I housed over ten years ago, though they're not kids any more. They're almost adults now, I suppose,' she said ruefully. 'So many kids have walked through my doors, and I remember every single one of them, whether they stayed for one night, or for many years. Zac stayed under my care for six months before he got adopted. The kids were all upset to see him go, as was I.' She paused. 'See, Felan, some kids never leave the system, and some are only in it for a matter of months. It just depends on the child, and the availability of parents looking to adopt.'

As sad as it was, Felan was content knowing he'd one day outgrow the system. 'Are you happy?' he asked.

'I always wish I had a bigger place so that I could house more kids, but it doesn't work like that. I'm sure you can remember – we were overpopulated by two when you and Blaez arrived, and that is not your fault,' she said firmly. 'You and Blaez needed your separate rooms, so the twins ended up sharing a room, and so did April and Amelia. But there wasn't enough space at the dinner table, and no one really wanted to share. It just so happened that the girls moving on was the perfect plan for having enough space for you and Blaez. The twins could have their privacy from each other, and suddenly everyone could fit at the dinner table again.'

'I prefer it when the table is full,' Felan admitted. 'I don't like the empty seat where Blaez is supposed to be.'

'And that's exactly why I'm happy with what I've got, with *who* I've got. My kitchen table is full – or it will be when Blaez comes home – and I have a house filled with wonderful, bright children. My house is filled with love. That's all I ever wanted.'

Felan thought about what his future might look like now that he was guaranteed a fighting chance of a good one. Maybe he'd move in somewhere with Blaez when they were old enough (if she wasn't sick of him by then). He'd definitely keep in touch with Mrs Walters and the kids, and he'd be damned if he didn't visit them often. He'd like to work more hours at the café, and maybe even branch out somewhere else. He wanted a garden with plenty of space for growing vegetables and flowers. Then, he'd go halves on a car with Blaez. She had been constantly going on about learning to drive the minute they'd arrived in Weisworth. *'Then we can go anywhere!'*

For Felan? He would forever be content in the passenger seat. Perhaps one day he'd learn how to drive – probably not – but he agreed with Blaez: they could go anywhere. He wanted to explore new places. He liked the idea of travelling and he knew that Blaez did too. They could explore the world on their own terms. Together.

'Of course, my parents were right,' Mrs Walters carried on,

bringing Felan out of his thoughts. 'Every time a kid waves goodbye from the backseat of a car it breaks my heart, but in a good way. I'm heartbroken I won't be able to see them every day, but I'm so relieved they managed to find a new home.'

'And that's why your parents are the way they are?'

Mrs Walters nodded. 'I have no bad blood with them. Perhaps one day we can work things out, but for now,' she said, grasping Felan's hand, 'I'm content with the family I have.'

'Don't leave it too late.' Felan said. 'Not everyone is guaranteed a tomorrow.'

She smiled, but Felan knew deep down that it was no use. He knew that look in her eye.

Resignation.

Entry 22 – 9:36pm

I was six years old the last time I walked through the front door of the library.

I was ten when I found a way to sneak in at night through the broken window on the ground floor.

The library itself wasn't anything special. It was just a run-down building with computers that blinked on and off all the time. And books. So many old books. So many words. So many stories. I remember feeling sad because I knew I wasn't going to be able to read them all.

I taught myself a number of things on those computers, and I learned a number of other things too. I learned about the war. ~~I learned about dangerous people~~ I learned more about dangerous people. I snuck out late at night if Dad was in one of his moods. I snuck out late at night every day to complete my homework as I got older. I did my homework at the back of the library using the flickering light of the computer screens.

A few weeks after the first time I snuck inside, I found a candle and a box of matches at my designated spot.

The lady who owned it must have known about me sneaking in. It was there that I learned about security cameras. It was there that I tried my hand at the city cameras and watched.

After that, I lit the candle and it gave me enough light. My handwriting improved. My eyes didn't hurt as much. Every Friday night I found a cookie beside the candle, and when winter came, two blankets were waiting for me. I never spoke to the lady who owned the library, but I left written thank yous behind. I photocopied the first homework assignment I got 100% on and left it on the desk with a little *thank you* scrawled in the top corner.

In between homework assignments I searched for news about Mum. I never found anything. I learned about missing kids. I learned about things that might've gotten me in trouble if anyone ever cared to ask, if anyone ever cared to follow, if anyone ever cared to look. The run-down building on the corner of the street became my saving grace, and my only escape.

Everything changed when I went to the hospital. Everything changed when Dad went too far. I didn't go back to the library for a long time. Nick came into my life, and he ruined me.

I didn't think I could be ruined any more than I already had been, but Nick had found a way.

***

I was pulled from school at fourteen years old, yet I continued to sneak out every night to teach myself about the world.

It was all I had.

Dad had had enough of the notes through the door and the taunts and insults from the other kids, and of the teacher who wanted to know why I'd gotten into another fight. Only there never was a fight. Dad had hit me in the face and the teacher had assumed I was to blame. After all, I was the strange kid that had no friends who was always involved in fights.

As a result, Dad never let me go back to school. I wasn't allowed anywhere without his permission; he never knew of my excursions to the library, and the teachers never knew of his abuse. No one questioned why I was suddenly being pulled out of school and no one came to the flat to check on me. It was like I didn't exist. It was like I didn't matter.

During my time with Nick, I ended up going back to the library. I managed to sneak out of the warehouse one night and I made my way there. The broken window had been fixed, but it had been left on the latch. I lifted it and climbed inside like I had done so many times before.

There was no sense of déjà vu. The candle was gone. The blankets were gone. Despite it being a Friday, there was no cookie waiting for me next to the old keyboard. Even the librarian had given up on me.

I searched my name.

I was dead, only I wasn't. I was breathing and reading the article with eyes that could see, and taking the information in with a brain that still worked. 'Article' was generous for what I was reading. In reality, it was two sentences of text at the bottom of page 17, an offhand comment that no one would ever see. Most people got bored of the paper by page 2, bored of the same monotonous tone, of the same stories being told week after week.

It hit me then, what that meant. No one was looking for me. No one cared about me. No one was waiting for me to come home. No one. Not a single person in the entire city cared about me.

The city had given up on me, and I was afraid. I was covered in bruises and cuts and I had a tattoo and I was terrified of what I might be made to do next.

I know I can't take it back, but I can move forward, I think. I'm going to try my best to move forward.

That's all I can do now.

Keep.

Moving.

Forward.

Chapter 23: Quiet Moments

With his hands balled into fists, ready to swing should one of them approach him, Felan quickened his step and breezed by the group of teenagers who were drinking and smoking on the corner of the street.

He wrinkled his nose at the smell of alcohol, and the sickly scent that certainly wasn't cigarettes. They laughed and jeered amongst each other, and thankfully paid Felan no attention.

For some stupid reason, he didn't think there would be any of *that* up in Weisworth. He thought he was far enough away to never see it again. A big city, yes, but a rural town somewhere up north?

It felt like his past was following him.

What if something else followed him, or someone?

Felan hurried the rest of the way home, only relaxing when he stepped through the front door and said his hellos. He unclenched his fist and sighed. So much for progress. So much for getting better.

What if I never get better?

In the back garden, the soil around the poppies and the sunflowers had been disturbed. 'I planted the bluebell bulbs,' Mrs Walters explained when she followed him out to find him staring at the mess in the flowerbed.

'Thank you,' he said softly, all of the tension bleeding out of his body.

Out of everything in the world, bluebells were the only tie he had left to his mother. He could have easily been depressed about that fact, but instead he chose to love it. He loved the fact that the only tie he had left to his mother was life itself, and that was beautiful.

One of the many holes in his heart slowly began to heal.

***

While debating his new purpose in Weisworth, Felan came up with the following things:

His purpose was to wake up in the morning.

His purpose was to get out of bed.

His purpose was to go outside and see the plants.

His purpose was to breathe.

Despite everything, his purpose was to *live*.

Humming to himself, Felan grabbed the tub of birdseed from beneath the sink and headed for the back door. The birds had completely ransacked the food Felan had put out there only days ago, the different species taking it in turns to swoop down. He didn't blame them. If he were back in Guadalupe, he'd kill for something to eat.

You killed for less than that.

'Are you feeding the birds?'

Felan jumped in fright. Jude stood awkwardly by the kitchen table, worry on his young face, and Felan could practically see the unease rippling across his small body in waves. The kid had been quieter than usual the last few days. It didn't sit right with Felan at all. 'I am. Do you want to help?'

'Okay.'

Although he got on well with the kid now, it was still more awkward than not. Felan thought perhaps they were too similar, and that was why conversation between them (sometimes) felt forced and stinted; Felan was going to try his damned hardest to rectify the situation. 'Come on, then.'

They walked down the garden in silence and made short work of refilling the bird feeders. Felan half expected Jude to say something, to tell him about the latest drawing he'd been working on. He didn't. It was the most un-Jude-like the kid had ever been since Felan had arrived in Weisworth.

Gone was the outgoing boy Felan was jealous of. Instead, a withdrawn child had taken his place.

Walking back towards the house with Jude beside him,

still restless and not at all himself, Felan made a decision. 'Sit with me?'

The kid sat down on the top step without answering. Felan sat down beside him, the tub of birdseed hidden behind them by the back door. Down the path, little birds already dove in multiples to get to the food. Jude watched their movements intently, his elbows resting on his knees, but he was distracted. He appeared to be looking through the birds, not at them, like he was seeing something that wasn't really there. Jude's body physically deflated and Felan decided he couldn't put it off any longer.

'What's going on? You're very quiet.'

'I just don't have much to say at the moment.'

'That's okay. You're allowed to be quiet for a while, if you like.'

He gave Felan a pointed look. 'People don't like it when I'm quiet.'

In return, Felan pulled a guilty face. 'It's not that I don't like it... in fact, I'm probably the biggest advocate for extended silences every now and then.'

Jude's face crinkled in confusion. 'Advocate?'

'It means to support something,' Felan explained. 'Sometimes, noise gets too loud and I need a bit of quiet.'

'It gets loud for you too?'

Felan nodded. 'You never have to be afraid of wanting some quiet, and you never have to be afraid to get it from me.'

'Okay.'

Now, that could have easily been the end of the conversation. Weeks ago, Felan may have left it at that and moved on – however Felan liked to think that he'd grown a little bit more aware over the last few weeks, aware enough to notice that something else was bothering Jude. The bruise on the kid's face had almost faded, though he kept catching the kid rubbing the area.

'What's going on with the person at school?' Felan asked.

Jude shrugged. 'He keeps coming over to me but I walk away. I don't know what to tell him. I don't want to get into another argument. I don't want to start another fight.'

Good. That was progress. 'Then maybe you should tell him that.'

In lieu of a reply, Jude shuffled closer and leaned into Felan's side, squeezing his arms around Felan's middle. Felan froze for a moment, completely caught off guard before he relaxed into Jude's touch. He wrapped an arm around the kid's shoulders and pulled him closer.

'Thanks,' Jude said.

Felan rested his head atop Jude's. 'Any time.'

Chapter 24: An Open Exchange

She picked up on the sixth ring.

'Hey, Felan,' she said tentatively.

The moment he heard her voice down the phone, the guilt that had been festering in his stomach hit him tenfold. 'Hi,' he said, a lump firmly lodged in his throat.

Silence.

All his fault.

'I'm sorry for not calling,' she blurted out suddenly. 'I just… I didn't know if I was welcome anymore. I wasn't sure if you were angry at me for telling someone and… are you angry with me?'

He should have taken his own advice sooner. He shouldn't have let it go on for as long as it had done. He'd been getting better, and Blaez had been thinking the worst ever since, worrying over nothing.

'No. Never,' Felan said. 'Blaez… I will always make space for you. You know that. No matter what.'

Silence again.

This time it wasn't awkward, or charged with wild emotion. It wasn't damning.

It was a silence born from relief.

All his life he prayed that he didn't mess up, he prayed that he did everything right, because if he did everything right, then nothing could ever go wrong – however, he'd grown up believing that *he* was wrong, convinced for so long that *he* was the problem. Thankfully, he'd met some pretty incredible people that had helped him convince himself otherwise. Blaez was one of them, and no way was he letting her feel how he'd felt. Never again.

'I'm calling to say thank you… and to say I'm sorry,' Felan said. 'You called me for comfort that night and instead I… You didn't deserve that. I made it all about myself, as usual. I never realised just how selfish I could be.' Felan clenched his jaw, shame crawling through his veins like a parasite.

'No. No, you're not selfish. You've been putting yourself first for once… as have I. It doesn't make you a bad person for doing right by yourself. If anyone deserves to put themselves first it's you, Felan.'

He didn't quite know what to say to that.

'I should have called more myself but I didn't,' Blaez continued. 'Don't think yourself selfish because you didn't call – I didn't call either. It… it goes both ways, but I do appreciate the apology.'

'I get that, but… but it feels like I've really messed up with you, Blaez.'

'You haven't. It's okay. I was more concerned about you.' He really wished she wouldn't worry about him so much. He was fine. 'I know it was bad in Guadalupe, and I know it was especially bad for you, but I didn't realise just how *much* you were struggling. And then we called *that* night and you sounded so, so… *wrong*, and I was worried that I was never going to see you again. It was terrifying. I was terrified,' she finished in a whisper.

Felan shivered. 'But it's not an excuse for abandoning you in the way I did,' he said. 'I should have cared more, and I'm sorry. I didn't mean to scare you. I didn't mean to leave you alone.'

'I promise you it's fine,' Blaez reassured. 'I'm just glad you're okay.'

Felan hesitated. How could he explain to her how he was feeling without worrying her even more? That was the last thing he wanted to do with this phone call. The whole point of the call was to reassure her so that she'd *stop* worrying. 'I'm getting there,' he admitted after a few moments of deliberation. 'I have my moments, but… I think I'm getting there.'

'Did you… did you try to do something?'

He couldn't lie to her. Not about this. Not about something as serious and important as this. 'I was going to,' he said. 'But I stopped myself, I… I don't exactly know what the turning point was, or why my brain decided to walk down that particular path, but I promise you I'm working everything out. I promise.' Felan relaxed atop his bed, sinking into his covers. 'Anyway – tell me everything.'

She did, and Felan listened. He listened to her well into the night until she'd caught him up to date with everything that was going on in Guadalupe... however he got the distinct impression that she'd omitted a few key points of her story, that she'd missed out a few important details about her life. He didn't bring it up. They would have time for a proper in-depth catch-up when she came home, and anyway, it was her choice if she wanted to tell him or not.

She was allowed her secrets, after all.

As was he.

'You know, I think it was after our fight that I realised something wasn't... right, with you,' Blaez said, 'and I think we were both stressed, and we were both hurting, and we weren't thinking about each other in the moment. What we should have done was just not talk altogether.' She took a breath. 'I want you to promise me that if, at any point, you need a break from me, from our friendship, you'll tell me. I won't be offended. Even best friends need space from each other every now and then, no matter how much we love each other.'

Felan smiled, staring adoringly up at the ceiling. He focused on one little star in particular, directly atop his bed, away from the other miniature constellations he and Blaez had made months ago. It was Blaez's star. It was semi-isolated, but it burned so bright. It was the brightest star he'd ever seen.

'Only if you do the same with me,' he said. 'I can't fight with you again. I can't go through that again.'

'Me neither,' she said. 'Deal?'

'Deal,' he said. 'And we thought we were smart.'

She laughed, and the sound warmed his insides. Felan would go to the ends of the earth to hear it forever. He'd bottle it, if he could.

He closed his eyes, and it was as if she was right beside him again. It was as if she had never left. Soft snores poured through the phone and Felan ended the call with one final whispered, 'Goodnight, Blaez.'

He prayed he had given her some peace.

Entry 23 – 12:24am

You probably had a family. You probably had children that will be forever waiting for you to come home.

I'm sorry.

There was no justification for my actions that day. I was scared. I wanted to prove myself. I said yes to people who I should've run from.

You died as a result.

His name was Harvey, the man who killed you. I trusted him to do the right thing and he put a bullet through your head like it was nothing.

You have to know I had no idea what was going to happen. I didn't think he was being serious. I thought we were stealing and running. I didn't realise we were capable of killing too. I didn't realise I was capable of killing.

Almost immediately after we left your shop, I ran into a homeless man and killed him.

He was going to kill me if I didn't.

I didn't even think. I remembered I had a knife and I struck. Maybe I thought he was my dad for a split second. Maybe I even heard my dad's voice too, in my head, but the homeless man was coming at me with a knife and I did the only thing I could think of.

Two dead in a matter of hours, maybe even minutes.

I didn't want to be a killer.

Every day it plays on my mind about how things could have been different – but if it hadn't been me, it would have been someone else.

I will bear that burden for the rest of my life at the expense of another kid bearing it for me.

Chapter 25: Preparing

Another week passed, and Felan was out of the door before Mrs Walters and the kids woke up.

It was a warm but mizzly Saturday morning, and with his new waterproof coat on, Felan walked into town – not before leaving a note on the kitchen table and making sure he had locked the front door with his key. That had been a new development. It showed the trust Mrs Walters placed in him, trust Felan didn't think he deserved.

He appreciated it all the same, though.

Mrs Walters had planned to take everyone out to the Weisworth Woodland Walk, a local woodland hidden on the outskirts of the town, so Felan had taken it upon himself to buy some walking boots, walking socks and walking trousers for the excursion. Upon entering the outdoor shop, the woman behind the till directed him to the right areas and helped him choose the right things. He paid with his bank card for the first time, which was another new experience.

Mrs Walters, with the help of Tristan, had helped him set up a bank account where he could keep his money from his job. He had paid in a majority of his cash, though he kept a small sum back in case of emergencies, and he stored the card in his wallet; Mark now paid Felan's wages directly into the bank.

Next, Felan ventured into the toy shop and bought five cheap, plastic magnifying glasses for the kids. They liked nature and he was sure they'd love the opportunity to get a closer look at it. He'd put together a little activity sheet for them while they had watched a documentary the other night and he couldn't wait for them to see it. His handwriting still wasn't the best, but at least it was legible now. All that writing in his notebooks was paying off.

The sun appeared from behind grey clouds. There was

something about walking in the early morning rays that put a spring in his step, like a flat battery slowly recharging.

The front door was already unlocked when he got back, and he found Mrs Walters and Jude sat at the kitchen table with a giant stack of toast between them. An army of jams and spreads stood beside it.

'Morning,' Felan said. He shucked his shoes and jacket and set down his new purchases before he joined them at the table.

'Good morning,' Mrs Walters said brightly. 'Have you eaten yet?'

'No.'

'Help yourself. And thank you for the note.'

Felan nabbed a small piece of toast and ate it dry, much to Jude's chagrin. He was the biggest advocate for butter and apricot jam on toast. 'I had some things to do, and I didn't want to wake you up.' He appeased the kid by spreading a thin layer of butter atop the next piece.

'I appreciate that. Now eat up before the others wake up, then you guys can have first dibs on the bathrooms.'

Jude took Mrs Walters' words to heart and dashed away from the table with a quiet 'thank you'.

Felan watched him go with a smile. 'I take it he's excited for today?'

'I think they all are,' Mrs Walters said. 'They couldn't stop talking about all of the things they were going to see.'

Felan took his plate to the sink and poured himself a glass of water. He drank generously. 'I'm going to get ready now and then I'll help with the kids.' He paused. 'I have a surprise for them.'

'Is that what you were working on last night?'

'Maybe.'

She laughed to herself and made a start on another round of toast for the other kids. 'You never cease to amaze me, Felan.'

His cheeks grew warm, touched to hear her say that.

Setting down his now empty glass, Felan made a beeline for the stairs. 'I'll see you in a bit.' He picked up his new purchases and headed straight to his room.

He swapped his jeans for his new walking trousers. They were dusty brown in colour with lots of pockets, and even had zip-off trouser legs. In warmer weather, he could wear them as shorts too. That was an added bonus, and so it should be with the price he had paid for them.

He put on his new walking socks, immediately liking the weight of them. He pulled on his jacket over his t-shirt. Rain hadn't been forecast for the rest of the day, but he could always pack his waterproof coat in his rucksack with the stuff for the kids. Speaking of which...

He tucked their magnifying glasses inside his rucksack with the activity sheets, remembering the pencils at the last minute.

He didn't know about anyone else, but Felan thought he made quite a good babysitter.

Due to the excitement of the day ahead, it took a grand total of one hour and seventeen minutes to get all the kids fed, dressed and buckled up in the minivan. While the gaggle of kids pulled on their wellie boots, and while Mrs Walters helped Gemma zip up her coat and pop her buttons, Felan packed some snacks and fruit into his bag. Gemma might think she was an independent kid, but the simplest things still seemed to evade her. Mrs Walters worried about her a lot, but she had come to the conclusion that every kid was different; Gemma would pick things up in her own time, and if she didn't, they'd deal with it as it came.

Once everyone was buckled up inside the minivan, it roared to life. Felan tapped his feet in the footwell, his new walking boots making the sound louder than normal.

'I assume that's where you went this morning?' Mrs Walters asked, nodding at his new attire.

'I got a few extra things too,' he said. He patted the rucksack sat at his feet, a smile gracing his lips. He was looking forward to seeing the woods again. It seemed to be an age since Felan and Blaez had run rampant in the woods in Guadalupe. Despite everything, he missed it.

'If I didn't know you any better, I'd say you're as excited as the kids are.'

'I know forests and woodlands quite well, but this one's new,' he said. 'It's exciting. Things are different.'

'I haven't seen you this excited for something before,' she said. Felan didn't reply. Mrs Walters hummed to herself while she merged into traffic. 'Well, I for one am excited about what you've got in store for us. If it's okay with you, I'll let you take the lead today.'

'Really?'

'Absolutely. I'm still going to be with you to help.' She spared him a glance. 'Only if you're happy with that, of course.'

'I am,' he said. 'Thank you.'

'You've got this, Felan. I have faith in you.'

Felan stayed quiet for the rest of the ride, content with staring out of the window and listening to the kids behind him chatter incessantly amongst themselves. It was nice to be able to relax a little. Of course, he still held onto the handle above his head, just in case, but he allowed himself that one small mercy. He'd be shocked if he ever felt comfortable in a moving vehicle after what happened to his mother.

Felan leant his head back against the headrest and closed his eyes. He focused on Gemma's giggling, on the twins bickering, on Josie and Jude talking to each other about the nature documentary they had watched the night before.

If she was watching him, he thought his mother might have been proud of him.

Chapter 26: Exploration

Felan was the first one out of the vehicle. He slung his rucksack on and opened the sliding door for the kids. 'Head to the boot and Mrs Walters will wait for you there,' he instructed.

Elliot, Josie and Jude rushed out in record time, while Mary and Gemma took things at their own pace. Felan closed the door and followed them round.

'I know it's only a woodland, but no running off,' Mrs Walters said. She gave Elliot a long look. 'You stay in sight of Felan and I at all times. Now, there will be lots of dogs on walks today.' Gemma let out a squeal of excitement. 'No touching unless you ask their owners first. Some dogs don't like being touched, and they might lash out. Do you all understand?'

'Yes, Mrs Walters,' the kids chorused.

'Good. Felan is going to be taking the lead today. Listen to what he says, and please be respectful.'

The kids all turned to him in excitement. Elliot gave him a thumbs-up and a big smile.

'Come on, then,' Felan said. He pointed to the start of the trail, or where he assumed the start was. 'Follow me.'

He led the kids down the path, glancing over his shoulder every few steps to make sure all five kids and Mrs Walters were still in one piece. With his heart beating a little faster than normal, he scanned the scenery ahead for people and for potential danger.

The anxiety, and his thoughts, quietened down when he saw the first patch of cornflowers, when he saw the exposed snowdrop bulbs beside them where a rodent had obviously been foraging.

He could do this.

Felan stopped and crouched down, beckoning the kids closer. He reached a hand out to gently touch the little bulbs peeking through the soil. 'Does anybody know what these are?' He received a sea of blank stares. 'These are snowdrop bulbs. They've finished flowering now, but when they finish, the foliage – the leaves – turn yellow and die. The bulb will then lie dormant through the rest of summer and winter until next spring.'

'Dormant?' Elliot questioned.

'Asleep,' Felan said. 'The bulbs are tired after growing flowers all spring, so they sleep until next year.'

'Cool!' Elliot exclaimed.

'Does anyone know what a snowdrop looks like?'

'They look like snow,' Josie said.

'Pretty,' Gemma said.

Felan smiled. 'Exactly. And a fun fact about snowdrops – they were named after earrings, and not drops of snow.' He rifled around in his rucksack and handed out the activity sheets and magnifying glasses. 'I've put together a little sheet for everyone. I want us to work together to try to find as many of the things on the sheet as possible, and maybe some extra things too. The snowdrop bulbs can be the first extra sighting, can't they?'

The kids got to work, Mrs Walters helping Gemma with hers. Occasionally they asked Felan to explain something, or to repeat something he had already said, their faces forged with rapt attention, and when the kids had finished examining the bulbs with their hands and through their magnifying glasses, Felan covered the visible bulbs with more dirt before he got back to his feet.

'Let's leave them to sleep and move on, shall we?'

Shortly after setting off again, Felan pointed out ivy, moss and brambles.

'How are you so smart?' Elliot whined.

'Before I came here, I spent a lot of time in the forest,' Felan explained. 'I learned a thing or two.'

In all honesty, he wasn't that smart. It was just familiar. Listing off different leaves and trees and berries and flowers and fungi was familiar – he just hadn't done it all with a group of engaged, excitable kids before.

Felan pointed out deer tracks in the mud and encouraged the kids to draw a picture on their sheets. He taught them rabbit tracks too, and which song belonged to which species of bird (the ones he knew, anyway), and flowers. Oh how he loved the flowers. Mrs Walters gave him a supportive smile while she helped Gemma copy down a set of deer tracks on her activity sheet.

Further down the path he found a rather large piece of bracket fungus. He beckoned the kids over. They were amazed to see woodlice and all sorts of insects crawling over it, taking it in turns to take a closer look with their magnifying glasses. 'Everything in the woods is either a home or food for something else,' Felan said. Mary and the boys watched the woodlice explore the fungus in wonder. Gemma tried to pick one up. 'Be gentle,' he said. 'And remember to put them back after.'

Josie wasn't so keen and kept her distance.

He led them over to a tree stump he had spied across the path and he showed them more moss and explained what lived inside it and why it grew. He then went on to explain how people could determine how old trees were by the number of rings on the stump. The kids counted the rings together while Felan took a step back, content with letting them be.

He didn't think he was doing an awful job. The kids seemed to be enjoying themselves, and Mrs Walters had yet to intervene. He had thought that, if he had been doing a terrible job, she would have taken the lead from him a while ago.

A branch snapped somewhere to his left.

Felan whirled around on instinct, looking left and right to check for movement. A bush in his immediate eyesight rustled. The branches beside it shifted. He swallowed. Maybe it was just the breeze.

While Mrs Walters and the kids were distracted, Felan slowly crept his way over. He took slow, deep breaths, a hand out in front of him, ready to fight off a potential attacker. Twigs snapped underfoot and, when he pushed the branch out of the way, his heart stopped. He approached with cautious steps, letting the branch fall back into its natural position.

He hadn't seen one since the Warehouse, hadn't seen one since he had found it trampled and broken. He remembered telling

Blaez all about them. He was taken back to late nights with his mother while they researched all things fungi for his school project; he just hadn't had the heart to tell his mother how badly received his fascination with nature had been.

Felan gathered the kids' attention and gave them the same rundown he'd given Blaez back in Guadalupe, just in a more child-friendly way. He sent a photo of the fairy ring to Blaez, captioned, *I think it's going to be better this time around*. She replied instantly with a heart and a smiley face.

Another twig snapped.

Felan hurried everyone along. He led the way and occasionally took them off the path to get a closer look at something – they found ruins of what appeared to be an old house from hundreds of years ago. Felan took a photo, muttered a quick prayer under his breath, and moved on. It was best to not disturb anything, no matter how long ago it had been laid to rest.

Glancing out into the fields beyond the trees, Felan stopped abruptly. 'Quiet,' he said stern, but calm. The kids shut up in an instant. He beckoned them closer. 'Come here – quiet now – to the edge. Stand here.' When the kids were all in position, he crouched down and pointed out into the field. 'There. Straight ahead,' he said.

They let out a collective gasp at the sight of a brown deer munching on the tall grass. The grass a few feet away ruffled. A fawn stumbled out into the open in the direction of its mother. Gemma squealed. Felan settled a hand on her shoulder and squeezed gently.

'I know,' he whispered. 'Hush now.'

She managed to contain herself for an entire five seconds until a second fawn stumbled over. She let out the loudest squeal Felan had ever heard from her and jumped up and down. Her little face collapsed when the three animals bolted, disappearing once more into the grass.

'Was I too loud?' she asked, crestfallen.

Felan moved so that he was in front of the girl and redid some of her coat poppers that had come undone. 'A little, but you didn't do anything wrong. They're easily startled. It's normal.'

Gemma was pretty upset for the rest of the walk, but she perked up whenever she saw dogs. Felan was proud to note that the kids were all respectful and polite, just as Mrs Walters had requested, and always asked the owners before petting them – until a rather large dog with a blue jacket approached. The dog looked uneasy, as did the young lady walking it. Elliot and Jude ran on ahead, eager to stroke it, totally oblivious to the animal's unease. The dog froze, before pulling back and whining.

'Elliot. Jude. Come back here please,' Mrs Walters called out, and they did so without complaint. 'It's a service dog. That means it's at work, looking after the young lady who's walking it. You can't touch them. Now come over here and out of the way so they can get through.'

'Oh, b-bless you,' the young lady stammered as she got closer. 'I've had a few encounters today and they weren't as accommodating as you've been.'

'It's nothing,' Mrs Walters said with a smile.

A bad dog bite could do some serious damage. What would happen if I antagonised it?

The kids asked endless questions about the service dog, and Felan zoned out. He hadn't even known that service dogs were a thing. He thought back to the dying dog he had come across on the streets in Guadalupe, foaming at the mouth with its ribcage crushed. Felan had left it behind because there had been nothing he could do to save it.

Another twig snapped.

He guessed he must have made a face, because Mrs Walters took one look at him and ushered the kids along again.

Felan found some wild garlic not long after. He stooped down to break off a leaf, letting the kids sniff it. They were absolutely flabbergasted. Next, he showed them wild mushrooms. 'Just be careful. They look like the ones you can buy in the shop, but a majority of the wild ones are poisonous. That means dangerous, okay?'

The kids nodded and agreed. Gemma looked confused.

'What's pois-nous?'

'Pois-on-ous,' Mrs Walters said while Felan carried on leading the kids around. 'They're bad. They can make you really sick. Really poorly.'

'Pois-nous,' she said again. 'Bad. Mushrooms are bad.'

'Not all mushrooms are bad, Gem,' Mrs Walters corrected. 'Just don't go eating any you find in the garden, okay?'

'Only ones you or Fee cook,' she agreed.

'Good girl,' Mrs Walters said, winking at Felan.

They carried on exploring until Felan stumbled upon a rope swing. Well, 'swing' was a generous term for a length of rope attached to a thick tree branch. A small plank of wood was tied to the bottom. Excited, the kids took it in turns to have a go, letting out exclamations of glee when Felan pushed them higher and higher.

Everyone except for Josie.

It was in the woods that Felan discovered she had a fear of heights. Not that it was a long drop beneath the swing, but when it got going, there was a considerable distance from the swing to the ground. It was nothing dangerous, but for someone afraid of heights... He didn't want to force the kid if she didn't want to, but she had looked so miserable watching the others have a go and Felan didn't want her to miss out.

'Do you want to have a go with me?' he asked gently, holding the swing steady.

She still looked nervous, though she approached him warily. 'What if I fall?'

'I won't let you,' Felan said. He sat down on the swing, his feet firmly planted on the floor. He held out a hand to the girl. 'I promise.'

A promise from Felan was all it took, apparently. When she voiced her consent, he picked her up and sat her on his lap, an arm around her middle to keep her steady. She held onto the rope with both hands. 'Ready, Josie?'

'I think so,' she squeaked.

He picked up his feet and they swung forward. Josie squeaked again and leaned back against Felan's chest. He held her a little tighter. 'You're safe,' he said. 'I promise I won't let you fall.'

A few swings later, she laughed in delight, her previous fear gone. Elliot and Jude pushed them, and Felan's heart burst when Josie shouted that she wanted to go higher.

I love these kids. I love these kids so much.

Chapter 27: Two Steps Back

They paused for a food break shortly after.

Felan had found a little clearing through a break in the bushes and the trees, consisting of a handful of benches and tree stumps. They took up two of the benches, and once everyone was sat down, Felan unzipped his bag and handed out the variety of snacks he'd packed inside earlier that morning. It was safe to say the kids devoured everything in sight (namely Jude), and before long the kids were clamouring to carry on exploring.

'You can play in the clearing for a while,' Mrs Walters said. 'Just stay where we can see you, and no running off.'

'Okay!'

Apart from Gemma, all of the kids ran off and chased each other. There was a break in the trees above them and sunlight glittered down, making the grass sparkle like hundreds of tiny diamonds. The kids giggled and laughed like they always did, running circles around each other.

Felan felt exhausted just watching them. 'I didn't think they'd have so much energy,' he said, breaking off a piece of his banana and handing it to Gemma when he caught her eyeing it up for the third time. In return she gave him her signature cheeky grin and held out her bag of crisps. Felan took one and said, 'Thanks, Gem.'

'They're young. They're excited,' Mrs Walters said. She raised an eyebrow. 'I can't believe you managed to get Josie to go on the swing.'

Felan shrugged.

'She's been under my care for three years, you know?' Mrs Walters began. 'She can quite happily tear around and do anything as long as both of her feet are planted firmly on the ground, but the minute there's a tiny bit of height? That's a no go. She becomes a nervous wreck and refuses every time.'

'Really?'

'Yeah.' Mrs Walters smiled. 'You're a good influence on the kids. I truly hope you know that.'

Before he could stutter out a response, a tiny hand grabbed his arm. Felan looked to the side. 'You make me happy,' Gemma said simply, her green eyes glittering.

Felan tugged gently on her princess curls. 'You make me happy too.'

She clapped her hands together before she went back to eating her packet of crisps.

His soul all warm, Felan looked over to where the kids were playing, all three of them chasing each other and sliding over the wet grass, all three of them laughing –

Three? No, there were four of them. There should be four of them. It was scary how quickly his blood ran cold. Felan did a quick head count and shot to his feet. 'Mary,' he said, looking all around. 'Where's Mary?'

Alarmed, Mrs Walters jumped to her feet too. 'Mary?'

The other kids stopped playing. Elliot looked all around. 'She was just here! I swear she was right behind me!'

Mrs Walters beckoned Felan away from Gemma, just a few paces.

'She's a smart kid,' Felan reassured, despite his heart pounding hard and fast in his body. 'She won't have gone far.'

'She isn't one to run off in the first place,' Mrs Walters said quietly, so quietly that Gemma couldn't hear.

And Felan remembered. 'The twigs,' he muttered under his breath.

'The what?'

'The twigs. I've been hearing twigs snapping every so often, in the bushes. I figured it was just an animal or something, but what if it wasn't? What if…'

What if someone had taken Mary?

'Elliot! Josie! Jude! Over here now!' Mrs Walters instructed.

The kids ran over without complaint, and even Gemma got to her feet, seemingly understanding that something wasn't quite right. Mrs Walters took her hand firmly and, as a group, they walked around the edge of the little clearing, calling Mary's name.

Nothing.

Not even another twig snapping.

It was like Mary had vanished into thin air. She'd been there, and then she wasn't.

'Mary?' Felan called again, praying the kids didn't hear the break in his voice, or the fear that laced it.

Still nothing. There was nothing for so long that Felan thought maybe…

A scream echoed from the woods. It was close.

'Mary,' Mrs Walters said, her face paler than Felan had ever seen.

He met Mrs Walter's gaze, his mouth dry, a hundred thoughts running through his head.

Someone needs to go to Mary. Someone needs to stay with the kids. If it's bad, the kids can't see. If it's bad, I've had practice. If it's dangerous, I can fight.

He steeled himself, knowing what he had to do.

'Stay here,' Felan said.

Then he ran in the direction of the scream, oblivious to the kids' panic, and oblivious to Mrs Walters' frantic shouts for him to come back.

He would deal with the consequences of his decision later. Mary was in trouble, and he had to find her. He wouldn't be able to live with himself if something happened to her because he wasn't paying attention. He looked away for *one moment…*

'Mary!' he shouted, crashing through the undergrowth, looking for a sign, any sign. What had she been wearing? What colour was her jumper? Was she wearing a coat? When he couldn't come up with a definitive answer Felan felt like crumpling to the woodland floor in despair. How could he not know the answer? How could he not remember?

He was so focused on berating himself he almost missed the yellow coat running up ahead, the yellow coat he suddenly remembered Mary had been wearing. Mary. She was safe.

And then he saw the person chasing her.

'Mary!' Felan shouted.

The kid looked up, sheer terror on her little face, and Felan leapt into action. He ran forward at speed, ducked under low-hanging branches and reached the kid first. He skidded to a stop and put his back to Mary, shielding her body with his own, and stared down the person who dared to harm his little sister.

It was a woman, he realised. Twigs and leaves were tangled in her hair, resembling a bird's nest. Her clothes were torn in places and covered in dirt. She was practically the spitting image of Felan before Nick had found him on the streets in Guadalupe; dirty, alone and desperate.

'Stay away from her,' Felan growled when the woman kept advancing. He bent his knees a little, one foot slightly forward in case he needed to fight her off.

The woman smiled, that same predatory smile he'd seen so many times on Nick, and she lunged towards them.

Felan reacted instantaneously. He shoved Mary away, hard enough for her to hit the floor with a dull thud, hard enough to cut her off midscream. The guilt he felt was astronomical – he didn't want to hurt her, he didn't – but the guilt faded away to panic when he felt a cold, bony hand clamp down hard on his arm.

His heart faltered. He was breathless for a moment. His skin crawled at the unwanted contact.

He hadn't been grabbed since...

Not since...

A rogue hand shot out and pinned Felan to the wall.

Bruce punched him hard, so hard Felan's head slammed into the wall, again and again. Black tinted his vision...

'Get off me!'

Felan swung his fist blindly. It collided with the side of the woman's head, hard enough to send her stumbling back, dazed, stumbling so fast she let go of Felan's arm in the process. The back of her head collided solidly with a tree, so loud that Felan gasped, an invisible hand clamping around his throat, a heavy weight pressing down on his ribcage, squeezing his lungs.

She collapsed to the floor in a tangle of dirty limbs and ragged clothes. She didn't move.

No.

Felan looked back and forth between his hands and the unconscious woman. His knees wobbled. His heart raced so fast he feared it would burst out from the confines of his chest and take off through the woods.

He'd done it again.

He'd hurt someone.

He'd hurt someone in front of Mary.

Mary.

Oh God, Mary.

Felan staggered over to the woman and collapsed to his knees. He bent his head over her mouth and listened. She was still breathing, thank God. Felan grabbed her wrist and checked her pulse. It was steady and strong.

'Mary,' he said shakily, bile burning in his mouth. 'Mary, go and get Mrs Walters.'

He glanced back to where Mary had been lying on the forest floor, scared and frightened after he'd pushed her down. A yellow coat sprinted away from him, back the way he'd come, back to Mrs Walters and the rest of the kids.

He'd done it this time. The kids would know how dangerous he was. Mrs Walters would want him out of the house for good.

I ruined it. I've ruined everything.

Hot tears spilled down his cheeks, unbidden and messy. He didn't mean to. He'd panicked when she'd grabbed him. He'd swung without thinking. He hadn't meant to hurt her.

But she was chasing Mary. She deserved it.

Felan kept a finger on the woman's wrist, finding comfort in the steady pulse of her heartbeat, trying his best to remember how to breathe.

He was dangerous.

He was a failure.

Still failing.

Chapter 28: An Honest Account

The woman was still unconscious when the paramedics arrived.

Felan stammered out an account of what happened, moving out the way so they could tend to her. 'Is she going to be okay?' he asked.

'We'll look after her,' one of them promised.

A hand settled on Felan's arm. He flinched, breathless, until he saw who it belonged to.

'Come on, Felan,' Mrs Walters said gently. 'Let's leave them to do their job.' She helped Felan to his feet and walked him a short distance away.

'Where are the kids?' he asked, suddenly realising that the kids were nowhere to be seen.

'They're with the police. They need to have a chat with you at some point.'

Great. Just great. 'Am I in trouble?'

'Not with me,' Mrs Walters promised. 'And it was self-defence. You were protecting Mary. You were protecting yourself.'

Felan sat down with his back against a tree, hugging his knees to his chest. 'It keeps following me,' he said, feeling like a child who had just lost his mother all over again. 'No matter where I go or what I do, violence keeps following me.'

Mrs Walters crouched in front of him, her hands on his knees. 'There's nothing wrong with protecting yourself.'

'I panicked,' he said, his voice cracking. 'No one's grabbed me like that since...'

'Breathe, Felan,' Mrs Walters said. 'Just breathe.'

Felan tried. He really did.

'What if she's really hurt?'

What if I've caused permanent damage? What if she never wakes up?

'Then we'll deal with it when it comes, but right now I just need you to breathe, okay? Breathe with me.'

Twigs snapped under heavy footfalls, the footfalls themselves growing louder, getting closer. Felan tensed and refused to look up, hiding his face in the crook of his elbow. It was childish logic, but if he didn't look at it, it wasn't real. It couldn't hurt him.

It was a shame the same logic never applied to his father.

'How are we doing over here?' a man's voice asked.

'Still a little shaken up, I think,' Mrs Walters said. 'Can we have a few more minutes?'

'Certainly. Just give me a shout when you're ready.' The footsteps petered out. Felan relaxed back against the tree and lifted his head enough to watch the police officer walk away.

'He's the constable,' Mrs Walters explained. 'Mr Hatch. He's kind, and he'll hear you out.'

'Mr Bailey was my only positive experience with the police,' he admitted quietly. Mr Bailey had been the only one to treat him with compassion, like he was a human being. He had been the only cop who, at first meeting, hadn't pulled a gun on him.

'Just tell him exactly what happened. I'll be with you the whole time.' Mrs Walters squeezed his knees supportively. 'If you need a break, just tell me. We'll go at your own pace.'

Together, they got to their feet and walked over to where Mr Hatch was waiting. 'All good?' the constable asked.

Felan nodded wordlessly.

'Where would you feel most comfortable having this chat? It's nothing to worry about. We just need an account of the incident for our records.'

He'd be more comfortable if he could see the kids. He needed to be sure that the kids were okay. 'By the benches?'

'Sure,' Mr Hatch said, leading the way, Mrs Walters and Felan following close behind. Across the small clearing, the other officer was still amusing the kids, the kids who were all accounted for – the kids who were safe. The kids were okay. Mary was okay.

She almost wasn't.

He sighed to himself, sitting down on one of the benches, Mrs

Walters beside him. Mr Hatch sat opposite him, a notepad and a pen in hand, fiddling with a camera attached to his vest. Mrs Walters ran her hand up and down Felan's back while he talked.

'Mary was missing,' Felan started. His hands clutched at the wooden tabletop. 'She's my little sister. Well, she's not actually my sister but… anyway, um, she was missing. I heard her scream. We all did.' He glanced over at Mrs Walters who nodded in agreement. 'So I ran into the woods to find her. I found her really fast, but she was being chased by that woman.'

Felan shuddered.

'And then what happened?' Mr Hatch said, taking notes.

'I managed to get between them,' he said, 'but she lunged for me… for us. I pushed Mary out of the way. The woman grabbed my arm. I, I panicked, and I swung, and… I didn't mean to hurt her, I really didn't. She let go of me and fell back and hit her head on a tree…' Felan clutched the table harder, so hard his hands hurt. 'I didn't mean to hit her so hard, I swear.'

'Breathe, Felan,' Mrs Walters murmured.

Mr Hatch carried on. 'Did you recognise the woman at all?'

Felan shook his head. 'I've never seen her before.'

'Did she say anything to you? Did she give any indication as to why she might have gone for you?'

Felan shut his eyes. Nick's knowing smirk was waiting for him. He wrenched them back open. 'She just smiled at me, like she was going to get what she wanted.'

'Were you aware of her presence before the incident?'

'Not her specifically, but I thought that maybe someone was following us,' Felan said, thinking for a moment.

The constable frowned. 'What makes you say that?'

'I kept hearing twigs snapping. At first I thought it was an animal, but it was always just out of sight. Do you… do you think she was following us, to get one of us alone?'

'I'm afraid we won't know until she wakes up.'

If she wakes up.

'Now, you aren't in any trouble, Felan,' Mr Hatch reassured. 'From what you and your family have told me, it was entirely self-defence. She threatened you, and therefore you tried to protect yourself.'

'I hurt her,' Felan said numbly. The numbness infected his flesh and seeped all the way into his bones. His skin tingled uncomfortably. 'I hurt someone.'

I hurt someone again.

'It was an accident,' the officer said kindly.

He asked a few more questions before him and his partner left the woodland walk, leaving their ragtag group behind in the small clearing.

Felan opted to stay seated on the bench while Mrs Walters saw to the kids. He leaned forwards with his elbows on the wooden table and rested his head in his hands with a groan.

Of all the days...

He hated bitterness, hated how it had made a home in his soul. It had ruled his life, and on more than one occasion it had forced him to make some questionable decisions; only, he thought he was past it now. He thought he'd outgrown the bitterness – but how could he outgrow something that was now a part of him?

It might have been self-defence, but part of him wanted to do it. Part of him had been prepared to kill that woman if it meant Mary was safe. He would have given up everything, as long as she was okay.

And now Mary had seen the violent side to him, the side of him he'd kept separate from her, from all of them.

Still failing.

'Felan?'

He sat up. Mrs Walters was back, the kids approaching slowly. She bustled over and pulled him in for a hug. 'You're okay,' she muttered. Felan didn't think he was supposed to hear it. 'Right,' she said, pulling away. 'We're going home. I'm so sorry today ended on a bad note. I know you spent ages planning this.'

He didn't care. He just wanted to leave. 'It's fine. We can come back another time.'

'Of course we can.'

Felan stood up from the bench and made to walk over to the

kids, just to be sure. Mrs Walters stopped him. 'What?'

'Are you okay?'

No. 'I'm all good. It's the kids I'm more worried about.'

She raised an eyebrow. 'Right now, I'm more concerned about you.'

Felan opened his mouth and closed it again. He made a frustrated noise before he finally settled with, 'I'm fine... or, I will be.'

Mrs Walters looked like she wanted to say something else, looked like she wanted to argue; eventually, she gave him a smile and patted his arm.

Before he could take another step, Mary ran over and launched herself at Felan. 'I'm sorry for wandering off,' she cried, hugging him tight around his middle.

'Just make sure you don't make a habit of it,' Felan said. He wrapped his arms around her shoulders and held her close. 'And besides, that woman shouldn't have chased you like that.'

'You saved me.'

'I won't ever let anything bad happen to you.' Felan glanced around at the rest of the kids. 'To any of you.'

'Are you okay?' Jude asked quietly.

Felan reached a hand out to ruffle his hair, Mary still glued to his side. 'All good. I promise.'

He'd assaulted a woman. He'd hit her hard enough to knock her out. He'd thrown Mary to the ground.

Other than that, he was doing just fine.

Still failing.

Chapter 29: Dominoes

All of the kids (except for Mary) were playing outside in the garden.

Mary was huddled up on the sofa beside Felan watching a documentary about dinosaurs, and every now and then Felan caught her eyes closing, her head sinking down to her chest, before she snapped awake. After the fifth time, she stayed asleep, emitting quiet snores, so Felan turned the volume of the TV down in case a loud noise startled her. She'd had a trying day and a big scare. She needed to relax. She needed to rest.

As for Felan? He was due in the café today, and he thought it was about time he got ready for work. Sighing quietly, he got up off the sofa and made his way upstairs, getting changed into his uniform. He would have liked to stay home, but he refused to let Hannah down – she couldn't cover the shift alone. It was the busiest day of the week, after all, and Felan wasn't dead weight.

He wasn't.

After coming back downstairs and slipping on his shoes, he found Mrs Walters stationed at the kitchen table filling out more paperwork.

She's probably writing up what happened today, Felan thought guiltily. His hand ached from where he'd thrown his punch. He ached all over from his failure.

'All okay?' she asked.

'Yeah. Mary's asleep on the sofa,' he said. 'And I'm heading out now, so I'll see you later.' Felan turned to leave the kitchen.

'Where are you going?'

Felan turned back around. 'To work. It's Saturday.'

Mrs Walters set her pen down and stood up, shaking her head. 'No. You're not going, not after what happened today.'

Felan's stomach dropped. Mrs Walters had never said no to him before, not like that. She'd always been supportive of his choices, of his decisions.

She doesn't trust me anymore, he thought.

'You can't stop me,' he said, harsher than he intended it to sound.

Mrs Walters didn't bat an eyelid. 'Maybe so, but you've had an ordeal today, Felan. I think it's for the best that you stay home and relax.'

He liked Mrs Walters, but right now she was making it very, very difficult to stay calm. 'All people have done my whole life is tell me how I should feel, and what I should do.'

'I understand,' she said, 'but I just want what's best for you. That's all I want.'

I just want what's best for you.

No one had ever said that to him before, no one had ever cared about him that much before, and yet... 'Don't you think I should be making those decisions for myself?'

She raised a single eyebrow, a skill the kids found hilarious. She looked like she was going to press the issue further; Felan waited with bated breath for her to snap, waited for her to finally raise a hand and unleash her frustrations out on him.

Mrs Walters simply walked over and pulled him in for a hug, one of her hands cradling the back of his head, her fingers stroking the short hair at the nape of his neck. 'I understand,' she repeated. 'Just remember that there is no shame in taking some time for yourself, especially after a scare like earlier. There's no shame at all.'

'I just want things to go back to normal,' he mumbled.

'Okay. Okay,' she said. She let him go and Felan immediately missed the contact. 'But if there are any problems, if there's any trouble, you call me. Is that understood?'

He nodded. 'I'm sorry. I didn't mean to snap or anything.'

'I know,' she said. 'I appreciate the apology though.'

He offered her a smile. 'I'll see you later.'

'Have fun.'

'Always do.'

***

Felan walked to work with cold air on his face, the sun glowing in the sky. He marvelled at the feeling. It had always been hot in Guadalupe. It had always been stifling, even when he had been stood in the shadows cast by tall buildings, and yet in Weisworth, tall buildings didn't exist – except the big clock atop the town hall smack bang in the middle of town. All of the houses were well kept, and their gardens were even more so. In general, everyone was happy and positive, and always strived to help each other.

He waved to Old John from across the street, a keen gardener, and no matter the weather, he could be found in his front garden trimming his shrubs. Last week, he had shaped them into large footballs. Today, they looked more like squares.

Felan arrived at the café with a few minutes to spare. He clocked in and headed straight for Hannah who was stuck at the till with a queue nearly out the door.

'My hero,' Hannah said, laughing, when he began making the orders.

'I try.'

He spent the next hour making coffees, and it got so busy they had to call in Lisa for backup. Within minutes of her arriving, they found a rhythm. Lisa stayed on the till and set the trays up with cakes and biscuits if they were required, Hannah stayed on the coffee machine (out of the three of them, she was the fastest), and Felan ran the drinks to tables and took away the empties in-between loading and unloading the dishwasher.

It was by far the busiest shift Felan had worked to date, and so far, he was loving every moment of it. He was so busy that he didn't have time to think about...

'Boy, over here!'

Felan turned to the man who had been demanding his attention for the past minute or so. His hands clutched the tray of coffees tighter. 'I'll be with you in a minute. My hands are quite full,' he joked, smiling, in an attempt to appease the man. Felan didn't wait for a response. He carried on walking over to the group of ladies sat down a few tables away. The man's eyes burned into the back of his skull, but there wasn't a lot he could do about it.

It was rare, but they got the odd horrid customer from time to time. Lisa was a firm believer in 'just kill them with kindness. Just keep smiling.'

He tried. He swore that he tried.

'I said, over here!'

A hand grabbed his elbow, and Felan flinched. He whirled around, breathless, and yanked his arm away – he was being grabbed again, *he was being grabbed again* – but in the process he sent the tray of hot drinks flying everywhere.

He watched them fall in slow motion. They hit the café floor with a loud smash, sending china, glass and coffee in all directions.

The entire room went quiet. The only thing he could hear was the coffee machine screeching away by the counter, and his heart pounding in his ears.

Every eye was on him, on the mess he'd made. He stood rooted to the spot, unsure of how to proceed.

'Watch it, boy!' the man exploded. 'You nearly chucked that all over me!'

If Felan hadn't already been having a bad day, he would have apologised… but he was having a terrible day, and he didn't have any patience left. His usual long fuse was non-existent when dealing with such rude people.

'It wouldn't have happened if you hadn't grabbed me! I told you I'd be with you in a minute!' Felan yelled back, angry. Fear crept up his spine, pooling on the back of his neck within seconds of the outburst.

He'd just shouted at a customer. He'd just shouted at a complete stranger.

He was absolutely mortified.

The man had a face like thunder, his face pulled taut in anger. 'What did you just say to me?'

Felan's blood ran cold. He'd done it again.

Still failing.

Before Felan could stutter out a response, the man raised a large hand, murder on his face. He looked just like his father, just like Nick, before they used to…

Felan cowered away, shielding his face with his arms and waited. He waited for the strike that would inevitably follow, his pale hands trembling with anticipation, with fear. *Not again. Please, not again.*

'Don't you *dare* lay another hand on him!'

Angry footsteps stormed over. Felan risked a peek and saw Lisa stood in front of him, shielding him from the man – the same thing Felan had done for Mary in the woods only hours before.

'He nearly burned me, throwing those drinks around like that!'

'Because you came up behind him and grabbed him!'

'Says who?'

'Says me,' Lisa said. 'Says everyone else in this room who saw you being rude to him a moment ago.'

A chorus of agreement rang around the café. Felan dropped his arms a little and backed up.

Lisa turned to Felan, not touching him, her hands out where he could see them. 'I'll handle this,' she said, gentle, soothing.

All Felan could do was nod. With his cheeks burning in embarrassment, he hurried away and locked himself in the staff bathroom before he slid down to the floor, his back against the door. He closed his eyes and tried to remember the breathing techniques Mrs Walters had taught him the last time he'd struggled for breath after a sudden shock. A panic attack, he remembered. He was having a panic attack.

Why was it that every time he thought he was making progress, something happened to make him take even more steps back?

Felan gasped out a breath. He tried to hold in his next one.

He thought he'd gotten a hold of his anger. He thought he'd finally wrestled a collar on it and tied it up with a leash.

It turned out that he hadn't. It turned out that his anger was as wild and feral as ever.

He was fine. He was fine.

His eyes filled with frustrated tears.

He wasn't fine.

How could he go back out there? How could he face all those people again?

Mrs Walters was right. He should have stayed at home today. He never should have tried.

The door to the staff bathroom opened, and someone rapped gently on the stall door. 'He's gone, Felan, and he won't ever be coming back.'

Lisa.

He sniffled. Tears burned their way down his cheeks like acid.

'No one's upset with you,' she said. 'Not a single person out there believes you were at fault. They all saw the way he was treating you, and they all saw him grab you. You were well within your rights to stand up for yourself.'

Felan sat up, leaned the back of his head against the stall door, and breathed. *In through the nose, hold it for four seconds, and out through the mouth.*

'There are people in this world who always seem to seek out trouble,' Lisa continued. 'They live to cause arguments, and they go looking for them. It was just a shame he chose our café today.' The sound of her voice grounded him enough to stop the tears from falling. 'Do you need me to call someone to pick you up?'

He shook his head, but when he remembered she couldn't see him, he said hollowly, 'No, I'm fine. I'm fine.'

'I must say I disagree with you.'

He banged the back of his head on the door. 'I'm fine.'

If you hit your head harder, you might fall unconscious. That's what happened to the woman you assaulted.

'Can you unlock the door?'

He knew it would be obvious that he'd been crying, but there wasn't anything he could do about it. Quickly rubbing at his cheeks, Felan unlocked the door and he briefly met Lisa's concerned gaze before he stared down at the floor.

'Is it okay if I touch you?' she asked.

He nodded.

'A verbal answer, please.'

'Yes,' he whispered.

She approached slowly and took his hands into her own. 'It's okay if you want to go home,' she said. 'It's not a nice situation to be placed in, and no one blames you.'

Felan squeezed her hands and looked up. 'I'll be okay,' he decided. He wasn't going to let anyone ruin his life anymore. He was going to take back control. 'If I go home early, they'll ask questions. I don't want to answer any questions right now.'

Lisa searched his eyes intently, much like Mrs Walters often did, before she nodded. 'Okay. Take a few more minutes though. Hannah and I can cope.'

He was already shaking his head by the time Lisa had finished her sentence. 'No, I'll come now.'

'Felan…'

'Please,' he said. 'If I leave it any longer, I'll never come back out.'

If I leave it any longer, then they win. I want to be the winner for a change. I want to be in control.

'If you're sure,' she said. 'Remember: you have nothing to prove. To anyone.'

'I know,' he said.

But I do. I do have something to prove.

To myself.

***

After he'd wiped all evidence of tears from his face, Felan headed back out into the café.

He hesitated in the doorway, glancing around. The mess he'd made on the floor had been cleared, and there were a few less customers than before. Felan looked over to *that* seat and saw that Lisa had been true to her word – the man was long gone.

Felan made a beeline for the empty tables and cleared away all of the dirty cups and saucers, avoiding any and all customers as best he could.

He couldn't look them in the eyes, not even the regulars he

knew by name. They'd seen him. They'd seen his reaction to the threat of a strike. They'd seen him shout at another customer. They'd seen his terror.

To cut a long story short, he was embarrassed.

For the next half an hour, Felan shuffled between empty tables to the dishwasher, loading and unloading and drying. Hannah tried to make conversation when Felan stacked clean cups and saucers and spoons by the machine, but all Felan did was offer her a timid smile before he scurried back to the dishwasher, hiding once more.

Although he hated to admit it, the events of the day had really knocked his confidence – and he was ashamed. He'd been making progress. The café had been a safe space, and now…

At four o'clock on the dot, Lisa turned the metal sign around to *closed* and locked the door. Felan exhaled shakily – it was like he had been subconsciously holding his breath the entire time, waiting for the next incident to happen, and now he could breathe again.

When the empty cups blurred in front of him, Felan clenched his fists so hard they shook. No. He wouldn't cry. Not again. He'd cried enough for one day.

The sound of approaching footsteps startled him. He whirled around.

Lisa walked over with her hands out in front of her. 'It's only me,' she said. 'It's just me, you and Hannah in here now.'

Felan nodded, cursing himself. He knew that. Of course he'd known that – yet his heart still raced, beating faster than usual, and the fear he'd thought he'd gotten a grip of reared its ugly head once more.

'He was quite a scary bloke,' Lisa commented. 'The three ladies sat behind him said he was scary too.'

Felan's arms itched in a way they hadn't itched for weeks, and he tugged at his long sleeves. 'You don't have to take care of me like this. I'm not fragile.'

'I never said you were, lad,' she said. 'But what that man did was unacceptable.'

Tears filled his eyes again, unbidden, and he met Lisa's warm ones in panic. 'I thought he was going to, I thought...'

And when Lisa held out her arms, Felan rushed forward and sank into them, pressing his face into her shoulder. She hugged him, rubbing a hand up and down his back. 'I know,' she said. 'I know.'

Felan was very much aware of Hannah quietly cleaning up around them.

'I've just had a bit of a day today,' Felan blurted out. 'Everything seems to be going wrong.'

I keep doing everything wrong.

Lisa hummed in acknowledgement. 'You coming back out like nothing happened was probably one of the bravest things I've ever seen anyone do.'

Felan pulled away, rolling his eyes, but managed a chuckle. 'You're just saying that.'

'She doesn't say things she doesn't mean!' Hannah called over from where she was cleaning down the coffee machine.

That really made Felan laugh.

'Let's put it this way,' Lisa said. 'Had it been me, I would have run home crying and never shown my face again. The fact that you got straight back to work speaks volumes of the person you are.'

'And what person is that?'

God, things had been *so good*. He'd been getting better. He'd been getting so much better... and in a single second he'd resorted back to violence, back to his Guadalupe state of mind.

High alert.

Ready to strike.

Ready to run.

A coward.

'A brave, determined, wonderful young man.'

All of the fear and adrenaline that had accumulated inside of him over the past few hours fizzled out into an eerie calm.

'I know that you haven't had the best start to life,' she said. 'I know that you've been through a lot before you came here. I know you've suffered.' Felan looked down. 'But you're going to do something *amazing*. You're going to achieve something most people can only dream about. I can feel it.'

Felan wasn't so sure. 'But… I'm just me.'

'And that is the only person you ever need to be.'

Entry 24 – 1:53am

I didn't tell Mrs Walters about the incident at the café.

I don't want her to know that I failed, that I was wrong, that I wasn't okay.

And now I've had another nightmare.

It was about the woman in the woods. In the dream, when she grabbed me, I hit her once, then twice, and I kept hitting her until she went down.

I killed her. I killed her and Mary ran from me, from my bloody hands, and I was alone on the forest floor, a dead body beside me.

'You are not welcome in my home anymore,' Mrs Walters had said. She left with the kids in tow and called the police.

I called Blaez. 'Don't ever call me again.'

When I looked up at the sound of footsteps, it was Nick walking towards me, a pitying look on his face.

It disgusted me that I felt relief at the sight of him.

He stopped just in front of me and tutted three times. *'Come with me,'* he had offered, holding out his hand.

I woke up before I could take it.

I woke up feeling sick to my stomach, covered in a cold sweat.

I've just done a quick lap of the kids' bedrooms to make sure they're all safe (they are, thank goodness) and now I'm writing this because I'm terrified to go back to sleep.

I don't want to hurt anyone else.

Chapter 30: Unwanted Recollection

The beginnings of summer approached, as did the first sprouts of the various vegetables Felan had planted weeks ago. It was nothing special, a few tiny tufts of green poking through the soil, but it was a start.

Felan rallied the kids before school to show them the progress. They were just as excited as he was.

'How long until we can pick something?' Mary asked.

Ever since the incident in the woods, she'd been a little more reserved than normal, and Felan was pleased to note that she was slowly coming back into herself.

As for him? He was still a work in progress.

'Not for a few more months – they still need to grow some more,' Felan explained. The girl looked crestfallen. 'We'll be eating our own vegetables before you know it, you'll see.'

Growth was growth. Felan had managed to cultivate and grow something from seed. He was doing *something*.

He said goodbye to the kids with a smile on his face, and a high five to each of them. It was only three more days until the kids were off for six weeks over the summer. Blaez had expressed multiple times over the phone that she was upset to miss the summer holidays, gutted to miss the kids being home all day. 'They're gremlins, and they'll be feral within days,' Felan had joked.

As excited as he was to see the kids more, he was dreading the number of books he'd have to read to a certain four-year-old about princes and princesses.

Jude hung back while the other kids jumped in the minivan. 'I talked to the other boy yesterday,' he said, shuffling his feet. 'We aren't going to talk to each other anymore because we don't want to hurt each other for no reason.'

Felan pulled him in for a one-armed hug. 'I'm so proud of you.'

Jude hugged him back quickly before he scampered into the minivan after the others. The kid held his head higher than he normally did, and something warm filled Felan's chest.

Gemma came running up to his side. They waved from the doorstep while the minivan turned the corner, honking twice as it went. Felan looked down at Gemma, pulling a face. 'Numbers?' he asked.

'Numbers,' she said, nodding in agreement.

He ran through numbers with Gemma, and when Mrs Walters returned a short while later, he felt so uncharacteristically positive that he replied to Tristan for the first time in over three weeks to schedule a call after lunch. A bubble of worry formed in his gut. Felan hadn't spoken to the man since, well… since he'd tried to make himself disappear. There, he said it. The memory of that night still made him shiver, still made him feel so incredibly guilty. He'd almost thrown everything away because of, what, a single moment of sheer desperation?

'We won't disturb you,' Mrs Walters said when Felan told her that he was expecting a call.

He shut his bedroom door and paced until the phone rang. 'Hi,' he said to the man on the other end of the phone. He sat down at his desk and stared out of his bedroom window, watching the branches of the tree just outside sway in the breeze.

'Felan.' Instantly, the tension broke and he leant back in his desk chair. 'It's good to hear your voice,' Tristan said.

'You too.'

'So, how are you settling in? What have you been up to?'

Felan liked how Tristan didn't mention his lack of replies. He liked how Tristan didn't judge him. 'I'm settling in well – better than I thought I would, actually. The kids are great. They're really good kids. And I have a job,' he said. 'I like it here.'

'I'm glad to hear it.'

'I feel… safer. And I feel better.' Well, not completely, especially not after the horror show that had been *that* Saturday, but Tristan didn't need to know about that.

'That's really good.'

Felan bit his lip when the conversation lulled. That was why he hadn't responded. How did you talk to someone after they saved your life? How did you talk to someone after they had seen you at your worst? At your lowest? He didn't want to be ungrateful, but what did Tristan get out of it?

'So… what did you want to talk about?' Felan asked, his mouth dry. Did Tristan know about what happened? Had news of the assault reached Guadalupe, and now Felan was to be moved elsewhere?

Despite Mrs Walters having reassured him that he was in Weisworth to stay, part of him feared the worst. Part of him feared he'd be sent away. It was *that* part of the story. It was the part where they said they had made a mistake in placing him there.

It was the part where it all fell apart.

'At the station, I know you said you wanted to leave the past in the past, but… I want to arrest your father.'

Oh.

Oh.

That hadn't been what he'd expected to hear. The overwhelming smell of cigarettes and cheap beer came back to him, unwanted and most definitely unwelcome. He'd done a pretty good job over the last few days of trying not to think about it.

'I was going to bring it up before we sent you to Mrs Walters, but you were in no fit state to make that decision at the time. I think you are now.' If Felan was in a fit state, it was news to him. 'I think it would do you good to get some closure from that particular wound.'

Felan sat there, stunned. 'I… I don't know.'

'It's okay. You don't have to decide right away – it's just something to think about.'

Felan didn't know what he wanted, no more than the next person did, however he'd rather like to leave the past in the past.

And yet… having his father arrested might help him settle some more. Obviously, getting Nick arrested would help his situation tremendously, but his father had been an open wound for far too long. Before he could overthink his decision, he gave Tristan the address he had run away from, and his father's name.

'He might've already moved on, but I'd be surprised,' Felan said, tapping his fingertips atop his desk.

Something rustled down the line. He thought that maybe Tristan was making notes. 'That was very brave of you, Felan.'

'You'll call me when you get him?'

'Of course. I'll be in touch.'

Entry 25 – 3:16pm

Talking to Jude this morning brought up memories of my school bullies.

Their taunts and jeers and punches came back all at once.

The teachers turning a blind eye.

The teachers ignoring the bruises on my face.

The teachers who mocked my awful handwriting.

Insults from peers I've never forgotten.

I never told anyone what they called me, not even Blaez. I thought she'd get upset if she heard, and she'd be upset for good reason. They insulted people like her, and I suppose people like me, though I don't know for sure. I've never really given it much thought.

In all honesty, I don't care what I am. I just want to do things that make me happy, and if I meet someone along the way, then that's an added bonus, only... only I don't know if I have the capacity to let someone in. I don't know if I can allow myself the luxury of another person in my life. I'm not cut out for this.

I'm just grateful for what, and who, I have right now.

And I'm proud of Jude for making that decision. I'm proud of him for talking to this person. I'm proud of them for being mature enough to stop it.

I wish the bullies had been mature enough to stop what they were doing to me.

If you're not like them, you're different. That's what the rulebook says. If you display any signs of oddities, you were different. You were not the same.

I'll never be the same again.

Chapter 31: Ingrained Reaction

For five days, Felan heard nothing. Five, very long days.

The kids, now officially on their summer holiday, did a pretty good job of distracting him, however no matter the distraction, his thoughts always drifted back to *that* Saturday. Constable Hatch called up a few days after the assault. '*She's fine,*' he'd told Felan over the phone. '*It was just a knock to the head and she's already over the concussion. She's getting the help she needs and she'll never harm you again.*'

His thoughts also drifted back to Tristan. He felt too awkward to text or call the man for an update, so instead he waited.

Had they not been able to find his dad? Were they waiting for something? Or had Tristan simply forgotten to call?

Felan walked back home after another busy shift at the café on the fifth day, slower than he normally would, mulling everything over.

What if something bad had happened?

He pushed open the front door, said his hellos to Mrs Walters and the kids before he took the stairs two at a time. Still lost in thought, he walked into his bedroom, confused at the sight before him. At the end of his bed stood Elliot, trembling, and he held a Ziploc bag of what looked like purple-coloured wood chippings.

'Elliot?'

The kid snapped his head up. 'Felan!'

If Felan didn't know better, he would have said the kid looked guilty about something. 'What have you got there?' he asked, setting down his bag behind the door.

'I'm really sorry – it was an accident!' He held the Ziploc bag out to Felan. 'I was just having a look, I swear! I must've knocked it off and trod on it... I'm really sorry.'

Felan took it. The kid looked far too traumatized for

something as small as an accident. He was going to give the kid a hug, and tell him it was okay, that everything would be fine, that no accident was going to come with consequences, or with bad repercussions – until Felan recognised the shade of purple in the Ziploc bag. He looked over to the spot on his bedside table where the brooch had been sitting for weeks.

Gone.

Had he been thinking straight, Felan wouldn't be upset. Felan would understand. Accidents happened after all, and it wasn't a big deal.

Felan wasn't thinking straight. His hands began to tremble. 'Is this my brooch?'

'I'm really sorry,' the kid squeaked. 'I'm really, really sorry.'

Felan took a breath. And another. He knew he should approach the situation differently, with understanding and forgiveness, but all he could think about was anger. Despair. Blaez's brooch, his first gift in years. Broken. In pieces. All because a stupid kid went snooping in his bedroom.

'Why were you even in here in the first place, Elliot?' Felan demanded. He shoved the remnants of the brooch in his jumper pocket. 'You know you're not supposed to be in here!'

'I know I'm not,' he cried. 'I forgot you were working and came to find you, but…'

'Do you have any idea what you've done!' Felan took a step closer to the kid. 'You broke something that wasn't yours to break! This was important to me, Elliot!'

The boy quivered, tears rolling down his cheeks. 'I'm sorry, Felan. I'm really sorry. I won't do it again.'

'Damn right you…'

Felan's hand at his waist came up empty, and when he realised what exactly it was he had been reaching for, he bolted, a sick feeling growing in his stomach. He thought he'd heard Mrs Walters shouting after him, but he was gone, full sprint down the street, *away*, away from the kids, away from Elliot, and away from the people he could harm, because that was who he was. Terrible. Horrible. Selfish. *Dangerous*.

First it had been the woman in the woods, then it was Elliot. Who would be next?

His breath came in short and sharp bursts, the sick feeling rising to the back of his throat. He hunched over on the side of the road and vomited. Nothing much came up, and he gasped, wiping his mouth on his sleeve, the bitter taste settling on his tongue far too fast for his liking. Before the smell could make him vomit again, he took off once more. He rounded a corner. If only a car would completely total him and wipe him clean from existence. That would be nice right about now.

Someone called to him across the street. He thought it might have been a customer from the café though he couldn't tell through his watery eyes and his frantic mantra that beat in tandem with his racing heart.

Run. Just run. Keep running. Don't stop.

He sprinted by Old John's place without waving like he usually would. He sprinted by lots of places without taking note of where he was going. His stomach churned horribly for a second time and he gave in, too weak to fight it. Felan stopped at the corner of a street he didn't recognise and vomited into the bushes beside him, once, twice, three times.

The purple brooch from Blaez was in pieces, lots of tiny, *tiny* pieces that Felan knew, deep down, would never fit together again.

And yet, through it all, a bell rung somewhere in his vicinity. It wasn't one of those little above-the-door bells that rung whenever someone walked inside a small shop. It was one of those heavy church bells designed to be heard from miles away. The loud ringing cut through the panic that sat heavy in his chest.

There was a church nearby. There had to be. He was an idiot to think there wouldn't be a church in a town like Weisworth.

The bell rang again. Felan followed the sound like a duckling following its mother. He looked about for signs on the side of the road but came back empty-handed. Felan crossed the quiet side road and hurried further along.

Where is it? Where?

Felan rounded another corner.

And there it was, in all its glory, stood at the end of the lane. He approached quickly – it wasn't a walk, but it wasn't quite a run either, just that awkward in-between people often did when others held a door open for them and they were just a little too far away.

Weisworth Community Church, he read at the gate, with its soaring bell tower. It wasn't blue-topped like Oakley Church had been. It was completely white, barring the stained-glass windows. It was clean. It wasn't falling apart.

Most days, Felan felt like he was.

He pushed the gate open. It creaked a little, but once he was inside it swung back slowly with barely a sound. Walking up the stone path, his shoes tapped along beneath him. All around him, the headstones were clean and the grass was cut. A variety of fresh flowers lay atop a majority of the mounds: tulips, roses, cornflowers and sunflowers, to name a few.

The white bricks of the church shone in the sun like a beacon.

He breathed. He breathed through the lingering taste of vomit at the back of his throat. He breathed in the air, the same, warm air that brushed against his skin.

His mum would've loved it, he knew, and Felan wondered if he'd ever be brave enough to go back to Guadalupe to get her a headstone, to give her a proper, final resting place that wasn't beneath an overgrown bramble bush. His heart ached terribly. It felt like something was crawling up from his stomach, something heavy, something with sharp claws – every breath he took sent waves of pain shooting down his body. He could have sworn they reached all the way down to his toes.

Voices. Voices sounded close by and after a quick look around he couldn't see who they belonged to. Felan thought they were people visiting loved ones, but he kept an eye out in case they weren't as friendly as he'd imagined them to be.

He glanced back to the church.

Surrounding the building and its grounds was a wall. It was crumbling in places and moss grew in the cracks, yet it suited the area perfectly. Visible over the top were brick houses with large gardens and red roofs. Felan saw trees too. Lots and lots of trees.

The white edifice wasn't entombed by a city that thrived on corruption. It wasn't haunted by sirens. It wasn't a home for forgotten people, for forgotten stories, for heartbreak after heartbreak.

It was a home for those held dearest. It was peaceful. It was slow. It was reflective. Felan had never liked the idea of slowness until Weisworth Community Church. He hadn't liked reflective much either.

Blaez told him that his mindset would change now that he was away from Guadalupe, now that he was away from Nick, away from danger and the constant threats against his life. She said that he'd think things through differently because his fight or flight response wouldn't be in action, because his body wasn't running at a hundred miles an hour.

She was right, of course. She had always been right.

'I really think you would have liked her, Mum,' Felan said, glancing up at the bell tower. 'And I really think Blaez would have liked you too.'

A tender breeze stroked his cheeks, so gentle he momentarily mistook it for his mother's dainty fingers. Her touch was nothing more than a distant memory, a distant memory that was slowly being forgotten. He turned his head to chase the feeling. She was here. She was listening. She was guiding him.

He knew it.

***

Felan thought he should probably text Mrs Walters, or call her, to say he was okay.

That was the least he could do after running off like that (it was the least he could do after upsetting Elliot). Reaching into his trouser pocket, Felan discovered that he didn't actually have his phone on him, meaning that he couldn't call Mrs Walters to try to explain, to reassure her, to try to persuade her to reason with him. He was completely on his own.

'As I should be,' he muttered bitterly.

The thing inside him crawled a little bit higher. It nestled at the back of his throat and laid in wait, its claws pressing against his oesophagus. He swallowed again. It didn't budge. Fantastic.

With nothing else to do he wandered up and down the rows of graves, wondering what kind of people they had been before they died. While it felt wrong to encroach on private resting places, the rooted panic inside of him slowly faded as he read the names and the messages that were forever etched into stone, and Felan realised something.

It wasn't just him.

He wasn't the only person in the world to lose someone. Other people had suffered loss, some even greater than his. He'd been so wrapped up in his own losses that he failed to comprehend those of others.

The thing still sat at the back of his throat, but that was the thing. It wasn't just a *thing*. It had never been just a *thing*.

It was sadness.

It was shame.

It was complete and utter humiliation.

All because he'd panicked. All because he felt threatened by an eight-year-old.

It was an accident, he told himself. Over and over. It had been an accident. Elliot hadn't meant to break his brooch. It was just a stupid accident and it didn't mean anything.

But the brooch meant so much to him. It meant so much, and now it was broken.

He hadn't lost it with the kids before, and he couldn't believe that it had been the brooch that had triggered it. He couldn't believe that he'd reached for a knife that wasn't there. He couldn't believe that such a movement was so ingrained in him – to reach for his knife at the first sign of a threat.

Elliot hadn't deserved Felan's anger. He hadn't deserved any of the stuff that had happened to him. Instead, Felan had made everything worse, and now Elliot's home was no longer safe.

Mrs Walters probably hated him. He doubted she even wanted him back. He felt sick just thinking about it. After finally deciding to get his life back, had he just destroyed his only chance?

He could go back, he realised. It wasn't too late. He had walked back to Nick after something had gone wrong, so what was so different about running back to Mrs Walters with his tail between his legs?

Felan knew the answer immediately.

With Nick, he knew he was going to get hurt either way. Nick was always going to hurt him, and he'd grown used to it. Pain had become part of his daily routine.

With Mrs Walters? He didn't know what to expect when he got back. He didn't know what was waiting for him. The unknown terrified him because he was so used to punishment. The unknown terrified him because he had no idea what was coming… but why should it be terrifying? Why should he continue to let the unknown be an all-powerful, omniscient being that dictated every decision he made?

Muttering a quick prayer under his breath, Felan left the church. He knew what he had to do.

Chapter 32: Crashing Down

Felan wandered around until he found a street he recognised, and headed in the direction of the repair shop in town.

After realising he'd left his wallet at home too, Felan remembered he had some tip money in the pocket of his jeans. Hopefully that would cover the cost of what he needed to do.

'It's old, this thing,' the man behind the counter said. 'It's not worth the money it would cost to get it fixed, *if* it can be fixed. It's done its time, lad.'

'But it's important to me,' Felan said desperately. 'Is there not anything you can do?'

The man pushed the Ziploc bag back. 'I'm sorry.'

Felan left the shop with tears threatening to spill over. He didn't let them. He refused. Elliot was allowed to cry, not him. Not after the way he'd treated the kid earlier.

He crossed the road to get to the bookstore and enlisted one of the worker's help in finding a specific book. The kid liked reading, and he had already spent his monthly allowance, so Felan chose the book the kid kept going on and on about. He paid with the cash in his pocket, went to the corner shop for some chewing gum to get the taste of vomit out of his mouth, and walked home.

Judging by the screeches and the peals of laughter, he figured the kids were playing in the back garden. He crept inside the house, checked that the kids were in fact safe outside and in one piece, before he took his shoes off and climbed the stairs. He had a very good idea of where both Elliot and Mrs Walters would be. The kid's bedroom door was open. He peeked his head through and the *thing* wriggled in Felan's throat uncomfortably. On the bed, Elliot was in tears, his eyes red and puffy, while Mrs Walters hugged him.

The floorboards creaked beneath him, signalling his approach. Mrs Walters glanced up and gave him a look, a look so stern

Felan wanted to cower away, but there was visible relief in her gaze too. The sick feeling in his stomach worsened. The *thing* was stabbing now, repeatedly, over and over, its claws retracting and unsheathing before they stabbed once more. He refused to throw up again.

He could do this. He *had* to do it.

He knelt down in front of them. 'I'm sorry, buddy,' Felan said. 'I didn't mean to get so angry. I promise, I *promise* you it will never happen again.'

Elliot sat up, wearing his tears like a badge of honour. 'Are you still angry?'

'No. No, not at all. It was just a spur of the moment thing. I overreacted.'

'You looked really angry.' Elliot's bottom lip wobbled. 'You looked really scary.'

He'd scared him. He'd made the kid cry. He was also aware of Mrs Walters watching this conversation play out right in front him. 'I'm sorry for scaring you.' Felan rummaged in his bag for the book. He hoped it was enough for Elliot to forgive him. 'I got you something.'

He didn't blame the kid one bit for the apprehensive look that followed. 'What is it?'

Felan withdrew the book and placed it in Elliot's lap. 'I know you were excited for this one.'

The kid picked it up, his eyes wide. 'For me?'

'For you,' Felan confirmed. 'It's an apology, a promise, and a gift. All in one.'

'This is the special edition,' Elliot gasped out.

'It's signed, too.'

Elliot stared at the book in shock. Felan held his breath and prayed.

And then the kid threw himself at him, squeezed him tight around his middle, his new book abandoned on the bed. Felan hugged him back just as tight and pressed his lips to the top of Elliot's head. 'I'm really sorry, Elliot,' Felan said. 'Can you forgive me?'

'Only if you forgive me too,' Elliot said.

Mrs Walters watched on with a smile on her face. Felan glanced down at the kid, pulling away a little.

Elliot sniffled. 'I really didn't mean to break it.'

'I know, and there's nothing to forgive.' He ruffled the kid's hair and helped him to his feet. 'It was an old thing anyway. It didn't have much time left,' he said, echoing what the repair man had told him earlier.

Elliot looked down. 'It really was an accident.'

'I know it was, buddy.' Felan frowned when Elliot didn't lift his head. 'Hey, look at me,' he said gently. 'I promise it's okay. I promise I'm not mad at you. I promise I won't ever get angry like that at you again. *I promise.*'

Elliot smiled, and everything was right with the world. 'Will you read it with me?' Elliot asked. He picked up the book and flicked through the pages until he reached what Felan assumed was chapter one.

Felan glanced at Mrs Walters. She nodded her approval.

'I'd love to.'

Mrs Walters stood up and gave Felan another look before she squeezed Elliot's shoulder. 'I'll leave you boys to it.' She shut the door behind her.

'Come on,' Elliot called. He patted the space beside him on his bed. 'I've been waiting for this book for *ages* and I don't want to wait anymore!'

'Okay, okay,' Felan said, laughing. 'I'm coming.' He sat beside Elliot and the kid started to read, his voice excited and loud.

Felan smiled to himself.

A win was a win.

***

Elliot fell asleep just as he'd begun reading chapter three.

Without waking him, Felan eased the book from the kid's hands, placed the bookmark inside, and set the book quietly on the bedside table. Grabbing the blanket from the foot of his bed, he pulled it up and over Elliot's sleeping body, just in case he got cold, and left the room, pulling the door closed.

Felan found Mrs Walters sat at the kitchen table with a cup of coffee, deep in thought.

'Hi,' he said sheepishly, sitting in the chair across from her. She must hate him. She'd probably put on an act in front of Elliot, and now she was going to say she wanted him out. He was dangerous. She didn't want him anywhere near the kids again.

Felan wrung his hands together. The thought of leaving the kids broke his heart. The thought of leaving Weisworth broke his heart too. Weisworth was his home.

If he didn't have Weisworth anymore, what would he have left?

'I tried to call you,' she said, watching him, an eyebrow raised. 'Why didn't you answer the phone?'

He swallowed. The *thing* still sat there, unfazed. Cold and stern were words he'd never associated with Mrs Walters before, but now she was the epitome of them.

Epitome. He'd learned that word from Jude the other day. He really was a smart kid.

'I left it here, I think,' he said. His voice shook. He was in trouble. He knew it. 'I didn't pick it up when I ran off.' Felan rubbed the back of his neck, waiting.

This was it. This was the part where she changed her mind about him and wanted him gone.

'Thank you for coming back,' Mrs Walters said quietly. Felan looked up, confused. She looked older than he'd ever seen her. Gone was cold and stern, and weary was the only word that came to mind when he saw her now. 'When you bolted, I thought for a moment that you'd…' She sighed. 'Never mind. It doesn't matter. You're home. You're *safe*, and that's all that matters now.'

Okay, maybe he wasn't in as much trouble as he'd initially thought, but still the sick feeling didn't fade. First, he had scared Blaez on the phone *that* night, then he had scared Mary in the woods, earlier he had scared Elliot, and now he had scared Mrs Walters by bolting.

He sucked at keeping promises.

Mrs Walters leaned closer to the table. 'You aren't in any trouble. I just want to know what happened.'

He huffed out a sigh of relief, still uncomfortable, his heart still racing a hundred miles an hour. 'It was stupid,' he said. 'The brooch. It was a gift from Blaez, from Guadalupe. It meant a lot to me, and I know it was an accident. I just got too angry too fast and I shouted at him.' Felan cringed. 'I wish I hadn't reacted like that. He looked terrified. Of me. He looked like Mary did after I...'

Mrs Walters reached across the table and took one his hands in her own. 'Breathe,' she reminded him. Felan did as he was told. 'Thank you for apologising to him. I know it meant a lot. To both of you.'

'I'm sorry for overreacting.'

She squeezed his hand again. She let go and grabbed her coffee, taking a sip. 'Can I trust that you won't shout at any of the kids again?'

'Yeah, one hundred per cent. I just got overwhelmed and... I felt threatened?' Felan curled in on himself a little, curled his hands onto his lap. 'And it was like I was back *there* again, so I did the only thing I knew how.'

'Can I also trust that you won't run off again?'

Felan lowered his gaze. He trembled in his seat. 'I promise.'

'Look at me,' she said softly. Felan waited until the trembling stopped before he did as she asked. 'Thank you for telling me the truth.'

'I'm not lying any more,' he said, determined. 'I won't lie ever again.' He waited a beat. 'I ended up at the church.'

Now it was Mrs Walters' turn to look confused. 'I didn't know you were religious.'

'I'm not,' Felan said. 'I don't think so, anyway. I mean, I pray often, but it isn't to God, or to any God in particular, just... it's just to whoever's listening. *If* anyone's listening.'

With a gentle smile gracing her lips, she asked, 'And how was the church?'

He thought for a moment. 'Peaceful. And... and it was like I was with Mum again,' he said. 'I know it sounds crazy, but it's the same thing with the bluebells. I can feel her there. I *felt* her there.'

'It's not crazy in the slightest,' she said. 'It's how you feel.'

Felan fisted his hands into his jumper until the motion hurt. 'I thought you'd be angry with me,' he admitted. 'I thought...'

Mrs Walters looked like she was a thousand miles away. 'You thought I'd want you gone.'

He looked toward the kitchen window. It blurred in his vision. 'Maybe.'

'This is your home,' she said. 'This is your home for as long as you need it. No matter the arguments, or the disagreements, or God forbid, the fighting. Even if you shout at me. Even if you make a mistake. Even if you're not hungry when dinner is ready. Even if you need some time to be alone.' The fridge hummed from across the room. The kitchen light flickered overhead. 'This is your home,' she repeated. 'I am not letting you go that easily. You have my word.'

The *thing* thrashed at the back of his throat. Before he could stop them, the tears were falling hot and fast down his cheeks. 'I'm sorry,' he said.

He couldn't believe he'd thought her capable of throwing him out.

How could he think so low of such an incredible person?

'Never apologise for feeling emotion, Felan. It takes a strong person to recognise it, and it takes an even stronger one to feel it.' Felan looked back. She was smiling. 'Never be afraid to simply let yourself *feel*.'

Chapter 33: The Verdict

It wasn't until he was back in the relative safety of his bedroom with the door closed that he checked his phone. He ignored the missed calls from Mrs Walters; his eyes were still wet from crying, from *feeling*, as Mrs Walters had put it.

When he'd woken up that morning, crying hadn't been on his bingo card.

Neither had upsetting Elliot.

He also hadn't bet on Tristan getting in touch, either. His phone didn't lie. There were three missed calls from the man, all within ten minutes of each other. Felan went to call him back immediately, but his finger hovered over the call icon. Felan was terrified of what he might find out. He couldn't take another hit. Not today. It couldn't be so important that it couldn't wait until tomorrow, right?

Screw it. He hit the button and waited while it rang, and rang, and rang.

Tristan's voice greeted him seconds later. 'Felan?'

'Well?' he asked, in a higher pitch than normal. 'Did you get him?'

The silence that followed told Felan everything he needed to know.

'I'm sorry, Felan.'

His eyes burned and disappointment rippled through him in waves that threatened to drag him under. He had been treading water for so long, swallowing the occasional mouthful of water, and a single phone call made the water rise to eye level. He was drowning. He was drowning all over again and he couldn't stop.

'He'd been dead a long time by the time we'd got there.'

Felan remembered seeing a dead rabbit in the forest while he walked back to the Warehouse with Blaez. He remembered how the flies had swarmed to the decaying matter, remembered how the rabbit had festered out in the open. He wondered if the flies had swarmed to his father too. And Harvey. And Randi. And Caleb. And...

'What killed him?' Felan asked.

'It's hard to say – an overdose? Alcohol poisoning? We can't be sure until the autopsy comes back.'

What did he say? What *could* he say? He had envisioned a very different conversation in his head. No, he had *hoped* for a very different conversation, and instead he was left with *that*?

'Right.'

'Felan,' Tristan implored. 'I know how much you wanted him held accountable.'

It wasn't even about that anymore. 'There's no use in crying over spilled milk.'

'No, Felan. This is so much more than that,' Tristan said. 'This is the man that abused you – and now he'll never get what he deserves.'

He couldn't exactly argue with Tristan on that one. It was *exactly* how he was feeling, and also it wasn't.

Yes, he was upset, he was angry, and Felan did hate his father; it was the disappointment that rattled him. He didn't know how to let it out. He was used to being a disappointment, and he was used to being angry – he was used to being the punching bag for people to let their frustrations out on – but being disappointed *with* someone hadn't happened in a long time. It wasn't Tristan's fault, but the man had gotten Felan's hopes up. He had told Felan that they would arrest his father.

He didn't give Felan the one thing he so desperately wanted.

'Thank you for trying,' he said.

He hung up before Tristan could say anything else. He instantly called Blaez. There was no answer, and for a moment, just a moment, he thought he had been left behind all over again, stuck in the in-between, alone, cold, and full to the brim with guilt and shame and despair. It was like being back on the streets again, before Nick. He was alone. He was on his own again, lost in the world without a single person who cared.

His phone slipped through his fingers and hit the carpeted floor with a thud. Felan followed soon after it. The impact hurt his knees, but he'd felt worse, he'd overcome worse pain than that – he'd just never felt so much turmoil and so much *aching* in his heart before.

His father, the man supposed to love and raise him, dead, after hurting him for so long.

He had never felt like a son to him, but a burden, just an intruder in someone else's home.

His father, a terrible, terrible man, never getting what he deserved, and Felan never being able to ask him why.

He laid on his bed, clutched his pillow to his chest, and cried.

Still failing.

Entry 26 – 6:32pm

What did I do? What did I do that made you hate me so much?

You blame me for what happened to Mum. I know you do. We were never close, but you tolerated me, and when Mum died you... you snapped.

Now you're dead and you will never face the consequences of your actions.

I hate you. Part of me always will. This is your fault. You had no right to do what you did. No right at all.

~~You weren't~~

~~Why~~

You never once laid a hand on me while Mum was still alive. Maybe that's because you were taking it out on her and I didn't see, but at the start, you left me alone. Sure, you shouted, and you got angry, but Mum was always there to calm you down. Mum was always there to get me out of the way. I hate myself for not knowing if you did anything to her, but you must have done, right? She must have taken the brunt of your anger and your aggression to protect me, but then my seventh birthday happened and she was no longer the shield between us. I was within arm's reach of you, and you damn well made sure I knew it.

I was in the waiting room with Tristan for hours, crying and confused, because although I knew what had happened, I didn't understand. He was there, and you were nowhere to be found. I fell asleep, like all kids do when they're exhausted, and when I woke up Tristan was gone, and you still hadn't shown. I was alone.

It took another three hours for you to come and pick your son up from the hospital after a horrific accident had killed your wife. My mum.

You were drunk. I didn't realise it at the time. I was seven. I didn't know anything. When you eventually showed up, I ran to you and hugged you. I cried. You didn't react. I thought that maybe you were just as upset as I was. I thought you were hiding your emotions for my sake.

Like father like son.

But you grabbed me by the arm and marched me to the car. You rarely drove. In fact, you never drove. I was too scared to get in after what happened with Mum. You opened the back door and shoved me inside. I cried the entire drive back to the flat.

You blamed me for what happened. I ran off to my room and stayed there.

I never saw that blue car again.

***

You were scary.

You were terrifying.

I was terrified of you and what you would do to me.

Even the idea of you scared me, and the kids at school knew that too. When I was eleven they started posting notes through the letterbox and somehow you would always find them first. You never told me what the notes said, but I had a pretty good idea. It was the names they called me at school all the time.

Fairy Boy.

Strange.

Freak.

Worse things were said too, but I don't want to write them down here. I hated them. I still hate them.

You hated them too, didn't you? But it wasn't the words you hated – it was your association with them. It was your association with *me*. Instead of defending me, you defended yourself, isn't that right, Dad? You defended yourself against me in the middle of the night. You tried to assault me every time you saw me – if you were awake and not passed out on the sofa, that was.

I think you would have killed me if you didn't have quite so much fun hurting me.

More than once, I wished you would.

I wished you would snap my neck when you strangled me.

I wished you would hit my head a little too hard, too hard for me to come back from.

I wished you would cut me that little bit deeper.

But you didn't cut me that night, did you? You just beat me to hell and left me in a daze in the hallway. You kicked me and punched me and you slammed my head into the wall over and over and over again.

All I remember after was pain. It was vivid, and pulsing, and I could see it, the colours of it, in my head. I don't know how, but I dragged myself out of the flat and stumbled to the hospital. I saw the doors. I fell through them and I collapsed. I woke up in a hospital bed. The lights were bright. Everything hurt.

I knew you were going to notice me missing at some point. Or not.

I never gave the hospital my name. Well — they never asked. They didn't ask me anything, really. I stayed until the pain was manageable, until my head stopped spinning, and then I ran.

I ran because I remembered. I remembered what you'd done, and I remembered that you failed. I couldn't even die properly. Despite wanting everything to be over, part of me had fought myself and carried me to the hospital. I had fought myself to save myself.

And so I ran.

Nick found me.

The cycle started again.

Chapter 34: Orbiting

Mrs Walters shouted up to say that dinner was ready.

Felan ignored the call. He ignored pretty much everything, really. He couldn't bring himself to change out of his work clothes, even though his sleeve still smelled of vomit, and although the chewing gum had warded off the worst of the bitter taste, it still lingered.

Someone knocked on his bedroom door.

'There's some food downstairs for you if you get hungry later.' It was Mrs Walters, because of course it was. 'Tristan called. I know what's happened,' she said through the closed door. 'I'm not going to force you to come out, and I'm not going to force you to talk, but we're here, okay? We're all here for you when you're ready.' Another wave of tears ran down his cheeks and he curled up as much as possible beneath his covers. 'I'll come and check on you later.'

With that, she walked away, and Felan cried some more.

He cried so much that a pain he'd never felt before latched onto his throat, a deep, burning pain, so hot and so sharp that it stole all the air from his lungs. He let the feeling take him. He let everything take him. He didn't want to think any more. Not today. He didn't want to think about anything ever again... But he had to. He'd promised Blaez that he'd think about things. He'd promised Blaez that he wasn't going to be a danger to himself anymore. He'd promised her he'd be safe. He promised her everything – so why couldn't he ever give it to her?

An indeterminate amount of time later, a four-year-old crawled into his bed, planting her head right next to his. Felan didn't have the energy to hide from her. She frowned. 'You have sad eyes.'

'Sad eyes?'

Darkness swirled around in her green eyes, and it spread

across her face, twisting it in all the wrong places; far too much darkness and hurt for someone so young. 'Mummy had sad eyes. She went away. Are you going to go away too?'

That had been the longest sentence (or rather sentences) Gemma had ever uttered in a row, by far the most challenging, and Felan thought his heart might've broken in that moment.

He had debated running away. He had planned something stupid for weeks, and he had thought about it subconsciously every day whilst he lay in bed, unable to do anything else, unable to fathom why people cared about him.

Then there was Gemma, four years old but so much older, who asked him something so simple, and he thought: *If I succeeded, if I had gone through with it, what exactly would I have been leaving behind?*

'I promise I'm not going anywhere.'

'Good – I want you to stay.' She grinned and pressed a sloppy kiss on his cheek.

Stunned, Felan rubbed the spot where she had kissed him. The last person to kiss him had been Blaez, and then his mother, oh so achingly long ago. 'You really want me to stay?'

Gemma cuddled into his side. Small hands clutched his jumper. 'My big brother.'

Felan didn't know what to say. Before, Blaez had been his go-to cuddler, but since she had gone back to Guadalupe, Gemma had taken over that role, and the other kids were beginning to ask for hugs every now and then. Felan was always more than happy to oblige, even if he didn't really understand why they wanted to touch someone as tainted and damaged as him, especially after what he'd done to the woman in the woods.

The little girl carried on talking like Felan wasn't in the middle of having an existential crisis. 'What was your mummy like?' she asked, her eyes round and open and always watching.

'My mummy loved me lots,' he said. 'She looked after me until she went away. What about yours?'

'She read me stories! They had ma-magic aminals.' He didn't correct her mispronunciation. He didn't have it in him to correct her today. Then she frowned again and Felan wished she wouldn't. 'She was sad. She cried. She didn't wake up.'

'My mummy was sad too, Gem,' he said. 'She was really sad.'

Gemma wiped away the tears that dribbled down his cheeks with not so gentle fingers, to the point where it felt like she was poking his eyes out, but Felan appreciated the sentiment all the same. 'I like that you are here,' she said.

He didn't know what it was about little kids, but he found it was easier to open up to them. Perhaps it was the idea of no judgement. Perhaps it was the idea that they understood all too well how he was feeling most days. He liked that he finally felt like he belonged somewhere, even if he hated the thought of the kids understanding his feelings in any capacity.

'I like that I'm here too,' he whispered.

She wiggled closer. 'I love you.'

Felan wrapped his arms around her and held her tight. 'I love you too.' A beat. 'I love you so much.'

She fell asleep remarkably fast for someone who had just changed Felan's life in the span of two minutes. He shifted a little on his bed, did his best to not wake her up, and protectively curled around her.

No one would ever hurt her again.

*****

He didn't remember falling asleep.

Gemma was still passed out when he woke, pressed against his chest, and he had two messages from Blaez. It was an image, followed by a heart emoji.

Mrs Walters must have come in to check on him again, because as he stared at a photo of him and Gemma asleep, it stoked the fire inside his body, warming him all over. He texted Blaez a smiley face, everything forgiven, and kissed Gemma's forehead.

The orphanage was more than a house to place unwanted children. It was a home. It was a family. Felan's family. Nothing, and no one, would ever take that away from him again.

Entry 27 – 1:43am

I'm sorry.

I was hungry. I swiped a punnet of grapes from the edge of your stall and no one noticed. Maybe you did but if you saw you never called after me. Maybe you knew. Maybe you didn't.

I don't know.

I'm sorry I stole from you.

I hope you can forgive me.

Entry 28 – 1:51am

222

Thank you for the bread roll and for the water. And to answer your question properly this time, I am going to save the world. I'm going to save my own world and I'm going to do it my own way.

My own world, my own way.

Entry 29 – 2:01am

223

A note to the universe:

I'm taking my life back.

Chapter 35: Temporary Setback

The headache hit him first.

He let out a low groan, his hands automatically untangling themselves from the covers and rubbing circles into his temples. He blinked. Fog filled the room, and Felan struggled to see clearly.

The chill hit him next. Every muscle in his body ached something chronic. He swallowed and it felt like he was trying to choke down sandpaper.

Maybe a glass of water would help the situation.

It took a good few minutes for Felan to peel back his covers, and when he stood up, the room spun so much he almost immediately fell back down. He hacked a cough, and for God's sake, why did everything hurt so much?

He managed to check the time on his phone – he'd woken much earlier than he normally would (on the rare occasion that he actually slept through the night). No one would be up for a while yet, he knew, so he'd have the house to himself.

Good. I don't want anyone to see me like this.

It had taken a few choice curse words and ten minutes to wobble his way down to the kitchen, holding onto everything he could get his trembling hands to latch onto, and another two minutes to collapse at the kitchen table with a glass of water, sweating and shivering and, Christ, had the spinning gotten worse? Despite managing to choke down a few sips of water, a sick feeling brewed in the confines of his stomach. He sloshed a fair bit of water over the table before he managed to set the glass back down.

Perhaps it had been a mistake to get out of bed after all.

He laid his head on the table with a groan and drifted. He startled when a gentle hand shook his shoulder sometime later.

'You should've stayed in bed,' someone tutted. 'You should have called me.'

Felan wrapped a shaky arm around his stomach. Even *that* was starting to hurt. 'I'm fine,' he mumbled. His voice didn't sound like his at all. 'Just gotta ignore it.'

Mrs Walters tutted again. 'You're going straight back to bed.'

'No.' He stifled back another groan. 'I have work later.'

'Not today you don't. I'll call them once you're back in bed. *Resting*. You're ill, Felan. I'm just surprised it's taken so long to catch up to you.'

Felan squinted up at Mrs Walters through half-lidded eyes. It was a mistake. His vision swam and his head pounded. He clutched the table until everything stabilised. 'How do you mean?'

'It's a combination of stress, emotional turmoil, overthinking… and I know you haven't been sleeping well,' she said. She felt his forehead with the back of her hand. 'After a while, these things pile up. I doubt the news of your father's passing helped.'

Felan waited until the spinning had stopped before he replied, 'I haven't been ill like this… ever.'

'You've stopped,' she said, not unkindly. 'You're processing. You're coming to terms with things. It happens to us all. Now, up you get. You're going straight back to bed.'

He didn't argue a second time. He was far too tired and far too drained for that.

Mrs Walters held him steady while they made the arduous journey upstairs, and when they reached his bedroom Felan collapsed back into bed, struggling to pull the covers over himself. He whined pitifully and kicked his legs. If he had been with it, he would have been ashamed of how childish he was acting.

It felt like he was moving in slow motion.

'Hush,' Mrs Walters soothed. She untangled the covers and draped them over him, tucking him in, and patted his leg through the duvet. 'I'll be back in a moment.'

Felan sniffled and buried his face into the covers. His mouth tasted stale and his stomach did the occasional summersault – he didn't think he was going to be sick, though. He thought it might just be an anxiety thing.

The floorboards beneath his carpet creaked. 'I need you to

sit up for me. You'll feel better after a proper drink of water and some paracetamol,' Mrs Walters said. 'I promise.'

He lifted his head. Mrs Walters sat on the edge of his bed, a glass of water in one hand and a small blue box in the other.

'I don't think...' he trailed off, looking at Mrs Walters, pleading for her to understand.

'It's okay, I can hold it for you,' she said.

He flushed in embarrassment.

'They're useful for when the kids are sick,' she explained, having noted the look on his face when he saw the bright green straw sticking out of the glass. 'They don't have to hold anything, and it still feels like they're doing it themselves. They feel like they're still in control.'

Felan had never used a straw before, but he found it to be... different? The water was cool in his mouth and dulled the ache behind his eyes somewhat. His stomach still felt uneasy. Again, anxiety. Not sickness.

He never did have an easy excuse.

Mrs Walters held out a small white pill in the palm of her hand.

Felan eyed it warily, memories of drop-offs hitting him at full force.

'It's just paracetamol,' she said.

Now that she mentioned it, it looked nothing like the substances he had sold on street corners in Guadalupe. He was being stupid. As usual.

Felan sat up with a groan, resting on his elbows, and held out a shaky hand. No way was he letting her feed him like a baby. Mrs Walters gave him an exasperated look but dropped the pill onto his outstretched hand. He popped it in his mouth, swallowing it with a few sips of water.

'Good. Now rest.'

He collapsed back down and curled up on his side, clutching the duvet close to his chest. It didn't do much to ease the discomfort, but he could pretend.

Felan was good at pretending.

He drifted off to gentle fingers caressing his hair, barely conscious, and barely aware.

***

He thought he had heard the kids' voices break through the haze at one point, but the haze was too strong (the waves of tiredness and exhaustion were too strong), and they pulled him back to conscious nothingness.

His bedroom door opened and closed periodically. He didn't see it, but he heard it, the sound poking holes in the haze that enveloped him. *The last time someone had done that*, he thought groggily, *was Harvey*. The computer room, Felan remembered. Harvey was dead now. Randi too. And Caleb. He willingly left Accalia, and Edward, behind.

The only person he'd been able to save was Blaez, but she was gone, back somewhere that Felan could never follow.

He wished his mum was still alive. She would have taken care of him. She would have stayed with him and looked after him while he was sick. She would have stroked his cheek and kissed his forehead and tucked him in.

But she was dead too.

Felan wept exhausted tears into his duvet.

***

His duvet was still wet when Mrs Walters roused him later on. 'I know you want to sleep, but I need you to have some more water. And maybe try for some food.'

Felan managed three sips and a dry cracker before he laid back down. If he so much as raised his head too much the whole world spun like a ship re-entering the atmosphere.

Mrs Walters tucked him in once more, brushing his hair out of his eyes. She was too kind, too pure, too lovely, to be looking after someone like him. 'Just rest.'

Felan wouldn't have been able to stop crying if he tried when she stroked his cheek. She did it so softly, her hand cupping his jaw, stroking with a gentle thumb, slow and grounding, and he cried silent tears that ran rivers down his cheeks. Mrs Walters brushed them away with the same thumb, the same, gentle thumb. He trembled when she kissed his forehead.

'It'll pass,' she whispered.

She left. Felan cried again. She was too kind, too pure, too lovely. He didn't want to taint her, or damage her, by being around her all the time.

He drifted back off to sleep.

Chapter 36: Paralysed

Felan startled awake.

At first, he hadn't been sure what had woken him. Nothing seemed amiss upon waking, but something felt… *off*. Something didn't feel right, like there was a memory lingering just out of reach.

Then he heard the tapping, a deadly tapping he hadn't heard since his first few nights in Weisworth, a deadly tapping that had come from outside the house. Only this time, the tapping seemed to be coming from the *inside*.

His heart thudded painfully in his chest, thudding so loud he felt it in his ears.

The tapping grew louder, so loud that even the kids must have heard it by now.

The tapping stopped.

He waited.

He waited some more.

Nothing.

He debated going back to sleep but what if it wasn't nothing? What if it was *someone*?

He slipped out from beneath his covers and checked the garden from his bedroom window first. Even in the dark, he could make out the blue slide on the climbing frame peeking through the treeline.

Felan jumped at the echo of a single tap. He turned away from the window and made his way to the door. He entered the dark hallway slowly, doing his best to avoid the creaky floorboards. There was no point in alerting the potential intruder downstairs that he was on the move, that someone in the house was awake.

The absence of the tapping left Felan on edge. Sweat formed on his forehead and a single bead dripped down the side of his face.

Something had gone horribly wrong.

He just didn't know what.

He crept a few more steps and reached Gemma's room. He closed the door behind him, glad to see her fairy lights flickering faintly in the corner.

He hated the dark.

'Gemma?' he called quietly. It might be deemed odd, but the kid loved to curl up beneath her duvet at the foot of the bed. He approached the mound of duvet and tickled the top. 'Gemma,' he tried again.

Nothing.

He tickled harder.

He froze.

'Gem?'

He lifted the duvet.

His heart thudded in his chest once more, threatening to burst out of his ribcage.

She wasn't there.

He ripped open her cupboard door, dragged everything out, but there was no sign of her. He fell to his hands and knees and checked beneath her bed, threw her duvet to the floor, knocked the pillows off, just in case, but there was still no sign of the four-year-old that had wormed her way into his heart. If not asleep in her bed, where could she be?

A sleepover, he decided quickly. She was asleep in one of the other rooms. The kids did that sometimes if they'd had a particularly bad day. The twins were notorious for climbing into each other's beds in the middle of the night.

He checked Josie's room next: her duvet was slung on the floor, and the window was wide open. Empty. He checked Jude's room: it was the same story, and still no sign. And when he found the twins' rooms empty, and in the same state of disarray, he whimpered, the terrified sound escaping him before he had a chance to think.

All of their beds had been disturbed, and there was no sign of them anywhere. Upon a frantic check, he noted that even

Blaez's room had been disturbed. That was odd. Blaez was still in Guadalupe, wasn't she? Who had been snooping in her room while she wasn't home? Who had been snooping, and how had no one noticed, or heard, the intrusion? And where was Mrs Walters?

A sound echoed downstairs. It was different to the tapping, but still oh so terrifying. The hairs along Felan's arms stood on end. Footsteps. He could hear footsteps coming from downstairs. Large footsteps. Too heavy to be the kids, or Mrs Walters. Too loud for a thief.

This person wanted to be heard.

He grasped the candlestick he had sworn Mrs Walters had moved to the front room a month ago and slowly made his way down, one stair at a time, the candlestick raised, gripped by two pale, trembling hands. He'd swing if he had to. He'd hurt someone if it meant the kids were safe.

Halfway down the stairs, the footsteps stopped.

Felan paused for what felt like an eternity, one foot raised a centimetre above the stair below, willing his knees to hold, and waited to hear from the intruder.

Nothing.

Unless they'd heard him coming. If that was the case, he had to get somewhere safe. Fast.

He successfully navigated his way to Mrs Walters' room on the ground floor in the dark without making a sound. In place of knocking, he slipped inside and shut the door. He hurried straight over and flicked on her bedside lamp.

'Mrs Walters,' he gasped out, breathless. 'I think there's some…'

He couldn't believe it. Her bed had been disturbed too, and after searching the whole room feverishly, he concluded that there was no sign of the woman who had taken him in.

The panic clung to him again, but he didn't have the time to let it take hold. He had to find everyone. Perhaps they were having a sleepover in the front room. They'd done that before too. More than once, Felan had woken up with Gemma curled up on his lap and Elliot pressed against his side, the credits rolling quietly from whatever film they had watched that night (more than once, he had woken up warm and happy and at peace, surrounded by all of the people he loved. Well, almost all of them). A pang of hurt blossomed when he realised that, if it were the case, if the kids really were having a sleepover, he hadn't been invited.

But he knew that wasn't the case at all. Something was wrong. The kids always made their beds, and so did Mrs Walters, and she wouldn't arrange anything or take anyone out of the house without telling him beforehand where they were going. She would have left a note.

The childish part of him wanted to curl up in Mrs Walters' bed and wait for sunrise. The childish part of him wanted to hide at the back of the closet and pretend nothing was wrong.

The terrified part of him knew he had to keep searching. He had to be sure that they weren't in the house before he called for help.

Holding up the candlestick again, he walked back out into the darkness. He crept around the downstairs of the house, looking over his shoulder every few seconds and praying he didn't see a scarred face bearing down upon him. He couldn't hear any footsteps, though that didn't mean the intruder wasn't lying in wait.

He pushed open the door to the playroom. The room was completely empty, bar the sofa and chairs, but the boxes himself and Mrs Walters had dumped inside were nowhere to be found. That wasn't right. He was sure Mrs Walters had taken the chairs to the dump weeks ago. The boxes, as far as he was aware, should still be in a state of disarray in the corner of the room.

They weren't.

Maybe he was going insane after all.

The window, however, was a completely different story again. It hadn't just fallen out of alignment this time.

It was completely smashed in.

Glass littered the floor, glittering in the moonlight like thousands of crushed, little stars, and the frame had completely detached itself from the wall. The curtains were torn, one of them hanging from the loose rail, and the other in a heap on the floor.

Was that the noise he heard? Had he just imagined the footsteps? The tapping? Had the tapping come from the curtain rail, or from...

The tapping started up again, louder than before. Footsteps followed soon after. His knees shook and he collapsed to the floor, feeling oddly feverish and warm and not at all like himself. There *was* an intruder! They'd taken the kids and Mrs Walters. They'd forced their way inside and... and...

As if some higher power had flicked a switch in Felan's body, he climbed back to his feet and followed the sounds of the tapping, and the footsteps, to the living room, the candlestick raised, ready to swing.

His chest stuttered for breath. His heart jackhammered wildly. Felan pushed open the door to the living room, and whatever air was left in his lungs rushed out.

Nick stood in the middle of the living room, his clothes torn and covered in blood, a large knife in his hand. Something trickled down the sharp blade and dripped to the floor, glinting beneath the light. Felan followed the drip down. At Nick's feet laid the kids, and Blaez, and Mrs Walters, motionless, bloodied and sprawled out in unnatural angles.

Felan dropped the candlestick. It hit the floor with a clatter.

With the same, predatory smile he always used to wear, Nick made his way over to Felan, stepping over the bodies on the floor. 'You thought you could escape me?'

Felan didn't think he'd ever have to look the man in the eye again. It was over. They were dead. Everyone was dead. They were gone. It was over. It was all over.

'You thought you were going to get away with it, didn't you?'

He couldn't move. He couldn't run. What would running achieve? There was no one left for him to run to. There was no one left to defend him. If he ran, Nick would just chase him to the next place, and the next, and death and destruction would follow Felan wherever he went.

The kids... the kids were gone. They were all gone.

Tears fell in floods, a narrow river bursting its banks. He

collapsed to his knees again. He couldn't look away from Gemma, with her neck all twisted and her eyes, her innocent, green eyes, open wide in fear. Gemma. His little girl. Gone. Wearing her favourite pink nightie now stained red. Gone. He stared in disbelief. Gone.

Gone. They're all gone.

What have I done?

'They called for you, you know.' Nick came to a stop beside Felan and laid a hand on the boy's shoulder. Felan shook harder. He couldn't look away. 'They *screamed*. They *begged* for you. And you. Didn't. Come. You betrayed them. Just like you betrayed me.'

Felan bowed his head and cried harder. It wasn't a nightmare. It was real. Nick had come for him, for them, as he said he would. 'Please,' he whimpered. He hadn't heard the kids shout. He hadn't heard them scream. He couldn't have saved them if he didn't know they were in danger in the first place... and yet he should have been aware of the danger. He should have saved them.

He was a stone in someone's shoe. He was a thorn in someone's side. He was gone-off milk in the fridge. He was raw meat festering in the burning sun and riddled with parasites. He was infection. He was sickness. He was death.

'Please, what?'

'Felan!'

Someone shouted his name, a familiar voice, but it couldn't be. She was dead. She was dead right in front of him. No one alive was anywhere close to him.

'That's right,' Nick taunted. 'No one is going to come looking. By the time you're all found, it will be too late, and I will be far, far away from here.'

'Felan!'

He had to be hallucinating. He had to be. The woman who the voice belonged to was lying in a pool of her own blood a few feet in front of him, her neck sliced open and her fingers gnarled and crushed.

Nick crouched down beside Felan and held out the knife,

the same knife that had marked Felan so often before, the same knife that had killed Harvey, that had killed Randi, that had killed countless others.

'Take it,' Nick whispered. Felan did so with bated breath. It felt familiar. It felt *normal*, despite how much time had passed. It felt *right*. 'Good boy.'

A fresh wave of tears ran down his cheeks. 'What do you want from me?'

'I want you to take the fall. I want them to find this knife in your hands. You were always dangerous, *malicious*. You lacked control.'

Felan couldn't stop the sobs that escaped him.

'They'll find the knife in your cold, dead, hands, and they'll know exactly what happened here. You had one of your rages. You had one of your... *episodes*. The people of this town believe you to have violent tendencies. You killed the inhabitants of this house, and when you realised what you'd done, you took your own life because you didn't want to face the consequences of your actions.'

Felan swallowed bile. He continued to sob. Everything hurt. He needed help but no one was coming. He was on his own. He was on his own all over again... And yet he was confused. People in Weisworth didn't like him? Lisa liked him, didn't she? Hannah liked him. The customers and his neighbours liked him.

Had everyone been lying to him this whole time?

A loud, keening sound filled the room. 'Was it my fault?' he sobbed, clutching the knife tighter. He felt the familiarity of blood slicking his fingers, hated how it calmed that wilder side of him.

'What was your fault, dear boy?'

'Everything. Did I get everyone killed? Was it my fault?'

Nick cupped Felan's cheek with a blood-stained hand and sighed. Felan leaned into the touch. He had never been more disgusted with himself.

'You were never going to be free of your past,' he said. 'No matter how far away you run, I will always find you.'

'Answer me!' Felan cried.

And Nick smiled. *That* smile. The same smile that haunted Felan's dreams, that lingered in the shadows. He moved like lightning, grabbing a handful of Felan's hair and pulling it back, exposing his neck. Felan stared right up at the ceiling, staring in horror at the blood splatters that he found there, at the flies hovering in the vicinity, ready to feast.

Nick took Felan's hand and brought the blade to Felan's neck.

'You, were always, *always*, to blame.' The knife dug in deeper. Felan choked on his breath. Everything blurred. The world around him grew distorted and dark. 'You deserve this. You've deserved this for a very long time.'

But...

But...

He didn't want to die. Not anymore. There was a time when he wanted to, but that time had passed. That minor setback in his life was over... or so he thought. He'd finally started to live again, and now his past had come back to haunt him.

Just as he'd always feared it would.

'I'm sorry,' was all he managed to get out.

Something blocked Felan's view of the ceiling, and he realised in horror that it was Nick. It was the only thing that appeared clear in his staticky vision. The man stared Felan down with those black, black eyes of his, so black it was like staring into a dark abyss. Even the scar on his face looked wrong; it looked aggravated, it looked bigger, and if Felan squinted, if he blinked through the haze and the fog and the tears that overcame him, he thought he could see something *wriggling* beneath the surface.

Nick smiled wider, and it pulled the scar taut. 'I'm not.'

Felan closed his eyes. He ignored the way the sharp blade pressed against his throat, pressing deeper and deeper. He ignored the warmth that trickled down his neck. It didn't even hurt. The terrifying part was that it didn't hurt.

Nothing could hurt him ever again.

That was all he'd ever wanted.

Chapter 37: Reality

'Felan!'

He wrenched his eyes open, taking in as much of the darkness as possible. Everything was still fuzzy and distorted, but Nick wasn't there. Nick wasn't anywhere in the vicinity. His body shook. He panted. He brought a trembling hand up to his neck and pressed down. There was no cut. There was nothing but the tears than ran down his cheeks.

He was alive.

He was still alive.

Why did the realisation fill him with so much sadness?

'The kids,' he muttered to himself, his glow-in-the-dark stars breaking through the fog. 'Blaez. Mrs Walters.'

'I'm here,' someone said. 'The kids are safe. They're all asleep in their beds. Blaez is safe too.'

Felan cowered away. He had failed to noticed Mrs Walters crouched beside his bed in her pyjamas, her hair tousled and unbrushed – and very much alive. She reached for him. He flinched away and clawed at his arms. When the pads of his fingers weren't enough, he used his nails instead.

It wasn't enough. It was never enough.

Two hands settled firmly atop his own, stopping the self-destructive motion. 'Stop. You're safe.'

It had been a slaughter, a bloodbath. He had held a knife. He had felt blood on his hands. Nick had come for him, like he had always said he would.

But it wasn't real. Mrs Walters was in front of him, alive and breathing. It had been a dream, a nightmare. It had been a figment of his sick, twisted imagination.

No matter how hard he begged himself to stop crying, to calm down, the tears continued to fall. Feeling like his lungs were two sizes too small for his body, he struggled to breathe, the air around him not moving, trapped in the confines of his scratchy throat.

He was vaguely aware of Mrs Walters talking to him. She sounded miles away. He was too tired to focus, too lost in the haze of terror and despair that raged about him.

As a boy, Felan had never been afraid of the monsters beneath his bed. He had never been afraid of the dark, or of strange noises, or of large animals hunting him down. There had never been a reason to fear such things because his mother had always promised to be there, had always promised to protect him from harm.

She left him.

She lied.

Instead, he had become terrified of the drunk, angry man in the room next door. He had become dependent on the shadows in his room to keep him company, to keep him safe. He remembered crying once, and wished that, if there *were* monsters beneath his bed, they'd take him away because the monsters would be kinder to him, wouldn't they? The monsters would look after him.

The real monster had been related to him, a carbon copy. The real monster had easy access to him. Felan had been afraid of monsters like that ever since. He was terrified of the monsters who prowled the streets for prey, for the small, for the weak, for the vulnerable, and worse, he was terrified of the monster who lived inside his body, ready to take control at a moment's notice.

Felan shuddered. The involuntary motion brought him back and Mrs Walters didn't sound quite so far away anymore.

'I think you've gone into shock. It's okay.' She settled her hands atop his once again. 'Are you with me?'

Felan blearily met her gaze. 'I'm sorry. I didn't mean to.'

'You have nothing to apologise for,' she said, giving his hands a squeeze. 'Would a hot chocolate help?'

'No,' he choked out. The thought of consuming anything after what he'd just seen, after what he'd just felt…

'Okay. Hush now. *Breathe.* You just have to breathe.'

He clutched Mrs Walters' hand to his chest and did exactly that.

He didn't remember falling asleep.

***

He woke intermittently.

He heard their laughter down the hallway. He heard their footsteps patter down the stairs. He heard the front door open and close shortly after. He heard the keys rattle. He heard the minivan come back. He wasn't aware of how much time had passed.

Then he remembered.

He remembered the familiar feeling of a knife in his hands. He remembered Nick slitting his throat. He remembered the blood. Felan brought a hand up to his neck to remind himself that he was still alive, that it had in fact been a nightmare. He remembered his panic.

Remnants of that same panic lingered in the deep cavities of his chest. He tapped away on his collarbone until it dispersed.

The kids were alive. They weren't cold and unmoving on the living room floor. Gemma's tiny neck wasn't twisted. She hadn't died scared.

Mrs Walters came back into his room and, despite knowing, he still had to ask. 'Where are the kids?'

'There's an art class running in town today. I thought it best to get them out of the house for a while,' Mrs Walters said.

'I thought I heard them,' he mumbled into his pillow.

'This morning, probably. You've been resting today.'

And with that, he drifted off to sleep.

***

Mrs Walters bustled into his room and opened his bedroom window. 'Some fresh air will do you good,' she said.

'Where's Blaez?' he croaked.

Mrs Walters took a seat on the edge of his bed. 'With Tristan. She's safe.' She laid a hand on his forehead. 'I double-checked,' she added gently.

He relaxed back into his pillow at her confirmation. He yawned. 'Tristan's nice.'

She smoothed back Felan's hair from his eyes. 'He is nice,' Mrs Walters agreed.

'He saved me.' Then he frowned. 'He's too nice. Too nice for me. Like you.'

'Oh, no, Felan. We do this because we want to.'

And then for no reason, he began to cry. 'I miss Blaez. I miss my best friend.'

Mrs Walters brushed the pad of her thumb along his jaw. 'She misses you too. But she'll be home soon. I promise.' She left the room.

She left him.

She lied.

Chapter 38: Clandestine

Felan wished he'd brought a jacket.

The weather in Guadalupe was always temperamental at the best of times. He guessed he hadn't anticipated being out for so long, a lesson he probably should have learnt by now. He crossed his arms in an attempt to fend off the cold, his thin jumper not doing much to protect him from the elements.

Felan didn't bother to avoid the cracks in the pavement (like all the kids at school had done) as he walked – it was a luxury gifted to him gratis. In fact, the car had broken more than his mother's back.

Felan scowled, remembering the earlier events. Nick had cornered him first thing and told him to head out into the city. 'Information gathering,' he had said, whilst playing with his knife. Felan didn't need to be told twice. He tried to find Blaez on his way out, but apparently, she was already engaged. He didn't think much of it. Maybe he'd run into her at some point. Or not. After all, Guadalupe was massive, and he had yet to run into (or find) Randi. The boy was still MIA and no one had heard a peep. Not even Caleb.

For the most part, no one paid any attention to Felan while he wandered around the city. He slipped in and out of shops and market stalls in the Fringe, through crowds of people, lingering in the shadows on busy street corners. He heard a conversation about Ivory at one point, how someone was about to get a huge shipment, and a lot of money. 'A fortune', the guy with a big beard and a Hawaiian shirt said. That was definitely worth passing on to Nick. It might even be enough to prevent another punishment.

A bell dinged somewhere across the street. Upon further investigation, he located a rustic pottery shop; well-crafted pots and cups and saucers lined the windows, although the windows themselves had cracks and a few holes. The door had bits of wood nailed to it, the edges splintering and pointing in all directions.

A miniature teapot caught his eye – his mother had owned something similar, but a larger version. His dad had chucked it at Felan's head two weeks after his seventh birthday and Felan had watched the pieces fall to the floor all around him, another one of his mother's things broken.

The teapot was a distant memory now, as was his mother.

The same bell dinged once more.

Time to go.

Felan slipped through a crowd and ignored the heavenly smell of the hotdog stand a few feet away from him. He hadn't eaten in days, only managing to gulp down water from his shower head, and it was unlikely he'd be able to scrounge money off anyone, let alone beg for free food. He'd gone longer without food living with his dad. Heck, he was sure he'd find something edible in the bins, but not while there were so many people about to witness it. He hated the judgement the most.

He could wait a while longer.

However, by the time darkness fell, there were still too many people hanging around for him to even try to scrounge some food. His stomach rumbled. A restaurant owner locking up ignored him. Great. On a good day, he got at least one pitiful look from someone and some stale bread, or even a mouldy slice of cheese. Not today though.

He was sure they would have something back at the Warehouse – even if it was out of date. He'd make do with that.

On the plus side, he had something to offer Nick. He'd eavesdropped on a few decent conversations worthy of the man's attention. Maybe that would be enough to get back in his good books, although judging by the look on Nick's face earlier, he wasn't getting out of his punishment that easily.

Felan slipped into the shadows once again, taking the back alleys he knew by heart. Months ago, he would have questioned such knowledge. Months ago, he would never have dreamed of taking those dark paths alone. They were a blessing now –

anything to avoid being seen by the wrong people, anything to avoid being seen in general. His knife hung at his hip, tucked snuggly into his trousers. The thought of using it after…

Felan squeezed through the hole in the metal gate, shuffled by panes of glass and broken chairs, grabbed the familiar handhold halfway up the wall and climbed. He dropped down to the other side.

His hand found his knife in an instant. Blocking his exit stood a silhouette, holding what Felan knew to be a very large knife. He gulped.

'Who's looking for me, boy?' the voice growled.

'No – no one,' Felan stammered out.

His knife didn't calm him like it used to. He couldn't get the image of the homeless man out of his head. He let go of his weapon and fought the urge to toss it away – anything to get the memory of another man's blood on his hands gone – but if he did that, he would have nothing to protect himself with.

'I don't play games.' He lumbered closer. Felan didn't move. 'Now talk.'

But he couldn't. He didn't know what the guy wanted from him. He'd never met him before, heck, he'd never even seen him before.

The guy wore a dirty, white shirt and black trousers, like he'd been to a job interview and gotten into a scuffle enroute. He remembered his mum going to one of those once.

Felan could feel the guy's sour breath on him and, with a sneer, the guy tore Felan's sleeve. He shoved the boy beneath the scattered moonlight. His tattoo was on full display.

'What does Nick want?'

'Nothing. Nothing,' Felan stuttered, backing away, tugging his torn sleeve back down the best he could.

Without so much as a warning, the guy lunged at him. Felan cried out in surprise. He threw his arms up in front of him to shield his face and his neck.

At first, the guy only attacked him with his fists, raining blow after blow at the boy. Felan held back his grunts of pain; if he learnt anything in his sixteen years, it was to never let anyone have the satisfaction of knowing they hurt you.

He managed to get a hit or two in himself, but it was like hitting a brick wall.

Futile and painful.

Then the guy lunged with his knife.

Felan evaded the first strike, his arms still up, protecting his face. He slapped at the guy's hand, hoping he'd drop the weapon. The guy only swung harder and faster. Tearing ensued, and Felan's arm exploded in pain, tears flooding his vision. He blinked them away furiously.

He would not cry. He would not beg. He would take it, and he would move on like he always did.

If he could somehow get the guy on the floor…

Felan took two more cuts before he tried to kick the guy's legs out from beneath him. His foot hit the side of the guy's knee perfectly and Felan nearly cheered – his attacker didn't falter. If anything, it only served to make him angrier. A hollow victory.

A barrage of strikes swiftly followed and Felan collapsed to the floor, making damn sure to keep his face protected. He didn't care about the state of his arms. There were too many scars littering them already – he could hide those with long sleeves and no one would be any the wiser when he got back to the Warehouse.

If he got back to the Warehouse.

'Stop!' he cried out.

His attacker simply laughed and slashed with his knife over and over. Blood flowed freely down Felan's arms, all over him, everywhere, seeping into his clothes. He wanted to be sick.

No one was coming to save him. Not this time. 'Stop! Just stop it!' His lungs throbbed, his chest ached, and his trembling arms had been torn to ribbons.

As quickly as it had begun, the onslaught stopped. The man collapsed on top of Felan. Dead? Out cold? Felan didn't know. He didn't wait around to find out.

Not daring to believe his luck, he scrabbled out from beneath the guy and, once he was a safe distance away, his stomach heaved. Nothing came up of course. His stomach was empty, and the hunger from earlier dissipated to nausea, not helped at all by the vile feeling of warm blood spilling over his skin. His arms shook with the effort of keeping himself upright, aching something tremendous.

He flinched at the sound of approaching footsteps.

'I thought I told you to be careful.'

He snapped his head in the direction of the voice, but he couldn't see through his tears. He wiped his eyes with a bit of torn fabric. His arms burned. His throat threatened to close.

'Thank you,' he gasped. 'Thank you.'

Blaez collapsed to her knees with a barely concealed wince and brought Felan's arms in for closer inspection. 'Don't mention it.' Her touch, soft and gentle, calmed him somewhat.

'How did you find me?'

'I heard you.'

What must she think of him, not even able to defend himself against one man? He was weak, just as his father had always said. He wasn't strong. He would never be strong.

'No one deserves that,' Blaez said. 'No one deserves to feel like no one's coming to save them.'

Felan looked at Blaez, properly looked at her, and if he didn't know any better, he'd say Blaez was trying hard not to cry. He'd seen that face in the mirror more than once. He looked harder, squinting through the last of his tears; strands of her choppy hair lay plastered to her forehead; her face pale and sweating more than it should be; her clothes all rumpled and torn in places; bleeding.

'Blaez,' he murmured. A single drop of blood trickled down from the corner of her eye.

'What?' she snapped.

'You're bleeding.'

'No, I think you're the one that's bleeding.' She coughed into her elbow. 'Quite badly, I might add.'

A second drop joined the first. Barely noticeable, hiding in the crease of her eye, was a cut.

'Here, let me.' He rose a hand to wipe it away, focusing his efforts on keeping his hand steady.

She slapped him. 'Get your hands off me!'

Felan blanched, dropping his hand back down. 'Blaez?'

She blinked in what he could only describe as pure anger. She rather aggressively tore his jumper into thin strips and wrapped his wounds.

He wanted to say something, but his voice was stolen by her shaky breaths, by the lingering panic that had made a home in her watery eyes. What had scared Blaez so much? What had happened?

'Christ, Felan, I leave you alone for one day...'

She sounded different; her voice was rough, not its normal cadence, and slightly hysterical. Maybe she was ill.

'Hey, it wasn't your fault,' he said.

'If I'd been with you, none of this would have happened!' With the way her hands trembled, Felan got the feeling she wasn't just talking about him. Her fingers gripped him a little too tight. 'That should hold until we get you back to the Warehouse.'

'Are we going now?'

'Your stupidity pains me,' she said with a roll of her eyes. 'Yes, you moron, we're going now.' With more strength than he remembered, Blaez helped him to his feet. 'You good?'

'Perfect.' He turned his head and stared down at the prone figure of his attacker, lying face down on the floor. 'What do we do with him?'

'Leave him. Unfortunately, scum like that survive in a city like this.' The disgust in her voice rattled him more than he thought it would.

Blaez was everything Felan strived to be: brave, strong and hopeful. Every time, she managed to pull him out of whatever dark place she found him in with gentle hands, coaxing him back out into the light. She made him smile. She gave him a purpose again.

And Felan couldn't return the favour. He didn't know how to help, or where to start, and the guilt and hatred of himself overtook any hope he had of giving Blaez the solace she deserved. Because she deserved the world, not this. She never deserved this.

Felan brushed his hand against hers.

She pulled away immediately, almost as if she'd been burned. 'Let's go,' she snapped. On their way out of the alley, Blaez made sure to tread rather harshly on the guy's hand. Felan happily did the same.

This time, a smaller silhouette blocked their exit. It walked towards them. Both Blaez and Felan paused midstride, their knives in hand, ready to fight.

Ready to run.

'I didn't realise you two were working together,' a familiar voice called.

Felan sheathed his knife and raised an eyebrow. 'I didn't realise you were out here at all.'

It wasn't the first time Felan caught him out when he wasn't supposed to be.

Caleb glared; the dark circles beneath his eyes only made the expression more pitiful. 'I was looking for Randi.'

'Still no word?' Blaez asked.

'No,' he said. 'Anyway, what happened to you guys?'

'I got jumped.' Felan raised his arms. Blood oozed beneath the makeshift bandages. The cuts themselves stung like crazy and Felan knew they'd continue to bleed for hours. 'And get this for information – the man who jumped me knew Nick, somehow. He wanted to know why I was following him. He wanted to know what Nick wanted... I literally ran into him by accident. I've never seen him before in my life.' Felan tried to shake the remnants of fear that held him captive. 'I'll tell you what, there really are lunatics about, especially at night.' He glanced at Blaez. 'She saved my life,' he said.

'Yeah, she's good at that.' Caleb gave Blaez a once over. 'Why do you look like you just lost a fight?'

If not for the thunder on Blaez's face, Felan would have poked fun. There. Just another reason why Blaez deserved better friends.

'I was being followed and I tripped, okay?' She turned away.

'You never trip,' Felan mumbled, mostly to himself.

'You wouldn't just trip over,' Caleb argued, frowning in Blaez's direction. 'Not unless something got in your way. Or someone.'

She whirled around, the broken moonlight beaming down upon her, highlighting everything Felan didn't see before: the smudge to her eyeliner, the scary, dark patch below her eye that definitely wasn't there yesterday; her cargo trousers, torn at the knees, and a thin trail of blood dripping steadily down the side of her angry face.

'I tripped, alright? Now shut up and get moving.'

And when he slipped into bed hours later, his arms burning, his entire existence bursting into flames, Felan pretended he couldn't hear her muffled sobs from her bedroom across the hall all night long.

Entry 30 – 3:47pm

I owe her so much.

I owe her far more than I can give her. Mrs Walters didn't have to, but she's taken care of me anyway. Despite how nice it is, it also reminds me of my failed attempt to help the little boy I'd found practically frozen in the park. I'd tried to take care of him. I failed.

He was the second person I'd touched who had ended up dead.

She's like a mum, and I guess I've started to see her as one – as mine.

I know she doesn't want anything in return. I know that. I just... I don't... I just don't know how to accept it. Is that crazy? My whole life, people have always wanted something in return. Nothing was ever done out of kindness. There was always an ulterior motive when it came to me.

In Weisworth? 100% kindness, and no ulterior motives. It's new. It's a far cry from what I'd grown up with, and a far cry from what Blaez had grown up with too.

Blaez...

After the night of the attack, she'd been

jumpy and distracted and she looked so far away whenever she zoned out... and zoned out she did, more than I remembered her doing before. She'd been snappy too, and short-tempered. Well, more short-tempered than normal. I didn't know what to do so I left it alone. Maybe I made the wrong choice by doing that; I'm good at making those.

The scars that man left on my arms are in varying shades of colour. While a majority of my scars are pale, white lines, there are others that are red and pink and dark and ugly and I don't like them. I don't like the way they sit on my body. I don't like the bumpiness, or the rawness. Sometimes they really hurt. Sometimes it feels like I've been cut to ribbons all over again.

I'm scared that they'll always hurt. I'm scared that they'll always remind me of that night, and of the friend I failed to comfort when she needed me most.

Chapter 39: Restoring

As quick as it had come, Felan's illness disappeared, like a freak storm barraging an unprepared town.

He was no longer feverish or trembling, and his lingering headache no longer pulsated behind his eyes. Despite being exhausted, he felt more like himself than he'd done in a long time.

He found Mrs Walters in the kitchen, paperwork spread out across the tabletop, slowly writing on one of the many sheets of paper.

'Admin day?' Felan asked, putting two slices of bread into the toaster.

'I'm afraid so,' she said. She set down the pen and stood up, walking over to him. 'You're looking better.' She placed her hand on his forehead. He didn't bother fighting it. In fact, he'd grown to appreciate the gentle touch. 'Still a little warm,' she mused.

'I feel better.'

She smiled. 'Good.' She moved on past him and made a beeline for the coffee.

'Where are the kids?'

'Another club.'

He sighed in relief. It was safe to say that the nightmare had rattled him, and he feared he'd be dealing with the aftermath for weeks.

They were dead. They were covered in blood. Their bodies were twisted and stiffening.

Eventually, after opening and closing his mouth multiple times, Felan found the courage to say what had been on his mind for days while he buttered his toast. He always found it easier to talk when he wasn't looking at the person, or when the person was looking elsewhere. When the recipient looked at him, he found he had a tendency to stutter, and to not say exactly what he needed to.

The joys of being a people-pleaser.

'Thank you,' he said quietly.

'There's no need to thank me.'

Felan set his buttered toast onto a plate and carried it over to the table, sitting down at the end with the least amount of paperwork. Mrs Walters joined him with a cup of coffee, a question on her face. She looked tired, he thought guiltily.

'No one's ever, I mean… that's the first time that…' he trailed off, rubbing the back of his neck. 'That was the first time, in a really long time, that someone's taken care of me like that. I was left to my own devices, or I ignored it completely. I… I've never been allowed to just *be* ill.'

Her expression softened into something sad. 'There's nothing wrong with resting. Our bodies need it.' Then she raised an eyebrow at him. 'There will never be any repercussions for being unwell in this house.'

He focused back on his toast and nibbled on the crust.

'You never have to be afraid to tell me that you don't feel well.' She gave his shoulder a gentle squeeze before she got up and retook her seat at the head of table, surrounded by paperwork once more.

Felan finished his toast in silence, washed up his plate and the knife he'd used, and headed into the back garden. He sighed the moment the cool air hit his face. The tension trapped in his shoulders released, and he felt a million times lighter than he had done over the last few days. It was amazing what going outside did for the soul. He promised himself that he would never take the outside for granted again.

He amused himself by watering the plants, by watching the sunflowers sway gently in the wind, and by filling up the bird feeders at the bottom of the garden. Within minutes, small birds swooped down, chittering and tweeting and singing, perched onto the feeders and ate their fill. It had been a great suggestion on Mary's part to get the bird feeders. It had been an even better suggestion of Jude's to attach them to the trees in the treeline, instead of the lone tree off to the side by the back of the house.

Behind him, the climbing frame and the swings sat neglected.

He sat himself down on one of the swings and kicked gently, losing himself in the motion. While he swung, the birds came and went in groups, and every time he looked back at the house just beyond the treeline, he could make out Mrs Walters at the kitchen table, coffee off to one side, furiously writing away.

Entry 31 – 3:41am

You sacrificed your life to help kids like me, kids like Blaez... kids like us. You gave up a life of freedom for a life of pain and danger to try to put a stop to it all. I didn't give you enough credit at the time. I thought you were just another adult who let me down. I barely knew you, but you were kind to me. I guess that was the problem, wasn't it?

And then you killed the shopkeeper. I never wanted to trust you again. I lost all faith in you.

It wasn't until after I got out that I thought... what else were you made to do to cover your tracks? What else did you have to do in order to stay under the radar? Not just with Nick, but also with Maddison.

You killing the shopkeeper wasn't a last resort – mine was. If I didn't kill the homeless man, he would have killed me. You don't have that excuse.

Nothing gives you the right to take a life, Harvey. Nothing.

How many lives did you ruin in the name of protecting children?

How many kids did you actually manage to save before Nick killed you?

I hope it was worth it.

For your sake, I really hope it was worth it.

Chapter 40: Back to Normality

One day later, when Mrs Walters *finally* let him leave the vicinity of the house, Felan went back to work. He bid her farewell and started the short walk into town, a spring in his step. He was calling Blaez before he reached the end of the driveway.

'You're alive!' she exclaimed upon answering.

'Just about,' he joked. 'I wanted to hear your voice. How is everything with you?'

And so Blaez rambled about Tristan and Mr Bailey and the judge, and all of the places she'd visited outside of the city and Felan had listened with a smile on his face. He would never bore of the sound of her voice; it was like the sweetest honey and Felan couldn't get enough of it. In fact, he could listen to her talk for hours on end – yet he still couldn't shake the feeling that there was something she wasn't saying.

He didn't argue. He didn't make a big deal out of it.

She would tell him when she was ready.

Felan pushed open the door to the café and waved to Lisa, who stood behind the till, fiddling with the coffee machine. She waved back, rolling her eyes playfully when she saw the phone held to his ear. It was good-natured. He'd missed her a lot.

'I've gotta go, Blaez,' Felan said apologetically, heading for his locker in the kitchen. 'I start work in a few minutes.'

'I won't keep you,' she said. 'Thanks for calling. It was good to hear your voice.'

'And yours.'

'I love you.'

Felan's heart burst with happiness. 'I love you too.' He felt Lisa's gaze on him from across the room, but he didn't care. Nothing could take away the feeling of warmth that blossomed inside of him every time Blaez said those words.

He put his bag and his phone inside his locker, tucked the tiny key into his trouser pocket, and made his way over to Lisa. 'Sorry about that,' he said sheepishly.

Normally, he would have said goodbye to Blaez before he came in, but he had decided to indulge in her company today, even if it was just for a few more seconds.

'Nonsense.' Lisa pulled him in for a hug and gave him a once-over. 'Now, you're sure you're feeling better?'

'Positive.'

'Good.' She let him go and winked. 'Who was that on the phone? If you don't mind me asking.'

Felan groaned internally. He could already see where this conversation was going. He'd had it too many times to count with the kids. 'My best friend. She isn't home right now.'

'What's her name?'

'Blaez.'

'That's a lovely name.' Lisa said it with a weird intonation, and wiggled her eyebrows.

Right, time to change the subject. 'Yeah. Anyway, where do you want me today?'

Thankfully Lisa relented, drumming her fingers atop the counter. 'Are you up for some front of house?'

'Absolutely.'

'Excellent. Let's get started.'

They had a busy rush with people ordering takeaway coffees, and Felan lost count of the number of cappuccinos and double espressos he made. Lisa was beside him the whole time by way of moral support, and to lend a hand when something came up that he still wasn't sure of.

A little old man who Lisa was friendly with came in for a cup of tea and a slice of cake, and then two ladies walked in for hot chocolate and biscuits, occupying the comfy seats by the window. Within half an hour both tables had left, leaving Lisa and Felan with an empty café for the remainder of lunch. To pass the time, they sat on one of the many empty tables with a hot chocolate (topped with whipped cream and marshmallows) and a coffee.

They shared a slice of creamy carrot cake.

The fourth time Felan caught Lisa watching him, he spoke up. 'Have I got something on my face?' He was taken back to the very day he had met Blaez in the clearing, the short girl who had been kind enough to come and say hello, ultimately changing the course of his life forever.

'You didn't look well on your last shift, but I didn't want to intrude,' Lisa said gently. 'You're looking a lot better now.'

He slumped back in the chair. 'I was just overthinking. Everything. As usual.'

'You've found an outlet for it now?'

'Yeah. I'm working on it.'

And when Lisa beamed at him with that smile of hers, Felan knew he was safe with her. She had been nothing but kind to him since his first day. She reminded him so much of Mrs Walters, and Tristan, and Mr Bailey, and all of the adults that had showed him kindness and compassion despite his situation.

'It's really good to have you back, Felan,' she said. 'It's not been the same without you.'

'Thank you,' he said. He used his spoon to eat the cream and marshmallows from the top of his hot chocolate. 'It's good to be back.'

A familiar twinkle sparkled in Lisa's eyes. 'Let's hope it stays that way and we don't scare you off.'

'Nah, I think I'm used to it by now. Besides, who else would put up with all of you if I wasn't here?'

'Cheeky. I like it.' She finished her coffee. 'Hannah will be here at two until closing to cover me while I take my mother shopping. Do you think you can handle her?'

'Oh, I should think so. Do you think you can handle your mother?'

Lisa rolled her eyes. 'Let's hope so.'

Felan finished his hot chocolate just as a few customers walked in. He headed straight over to the till and took their orders while Lisa tidied up the small amount of mess they'd made. She lingered by the till while he made their takeaway coffees and bid them farewell.

At five to two, Hannah breezed through the front door. 'Good afternoon, everybody,' she greeted.

'Right, thanks for your help, Felan, see you soon!' Lisa ran to the door, handbag slung over her arm. 'Tag, you're it!' she shouted, swatting Hannah on the shoulder as she passed.

Hannah let out a noise of mock outrage before she came over. 'Busy morning?'

Felan snorted. 'Not in the slightest.'

In a similar fashion to the first half of the day, the second half was just as quiet. Amidst the few customers they did get, Hannah prattled away about her dreams of travelling the world once she had saved up enough money, and in return he talked about Blaez, his best friend in the entire world, and about his new family. He told her about Mrs Walters and the kids and about how lucky he was to be where he was.

Of course, Hannah knew where he lived, but she had never pried into his past, or his situation. She had accepted him and talked to him like he was normal. He supposed that was because, deep down, he was normal. He liked that about her. He liked that about all of them at the café. He hadn't seen much of Mark lately due to an extortionate number of business meetings, hence their need for extra help, but Mark hadn't pried either. They were good people. Almost like family. Extended family.

'I think as a society we should make an effort to be kind,' Hannah said. 'We should make an effort to say nice things more often. Being kind shouldn't come as a surprise, and being abusive and aggressive and angry shouldn't be considered normal.'

Felan rubbed his arms. 'It would make a change.'

'Mrs Walters is really good, I hear,' Hannah said supportively. 'My little brother is friends with one of the kids there, I think. Or are they in the same class? I don't remember, but he says they're all really polite, and all really nice. A testament to Mrs Walters, I'd wager.'

Felan wondered what Mrs Walters thought about all of the praise she seemed to get from every person in Weisworth.

'I've never met anyone like her before, and I doubt I ever will again,' he said.

He ate his words when Lisa arrived back at the café after closing to drop him home, despite his constant protests that he could walk.

'We've been really impressed with your efforts, Felan,' Lisa said. She pulled up in front of the driveway and turned off the engine. 'Your work ethic is next to none. You've got the hang of everything so fast and we really appreciate all that you've done for us these last few weeks.'

He prayed she hadn't noticed, but even he could feel how hot his cheeks were. 'It was nothing.'

'We're giving you a pay rise.'

His mouth fell open. 'No, I can't...'

'You deserve it, Felan. I discussed it with Mark the other day, though admittedly it wasn't a particularly long conversation.'

'I'm fine with the money I get now.' The money he got already was far too much, especially considering he'd just been off for a week and left them with no cover at short notice.

'Nonsense. Besides, it's already done.' Lisa gave him a look that told Felan there would be no arguing with her.

'Thank you.'

'No,' Lisa said. 'Thank you.'

Mrs Walters greeted him with a warm hug at the front drive, and as one they waved to Lisa while she drove off, honking her horn twice. They walked up the path to the house and immediately Mrs Walter's bombarded him with her two favourite questions while he struggled to kick his shoes off: 'How was work? Did you have a good day?' She led him into the kitchen where she had a plate of food ready on the table.

Felan smiled to himself. He was so lucky to have someone like Mrs Walters in his life. 'Work was fine. It was really quiet so we mostly had a chat. And yeah, I had a good day.' He washed his hands before he sat down at the table. 'I got a pay rise,' he told her, still in shock, still confused at the turn of events. He picked up his knife and fork and stared at them like they were extraterrestrial objects.

'Oh, that's fantastic news!'

He dug into his food. Mrs Walters sat across the table from him and chatted away about the kids' antics, and her plans for future weekend trips that she wanted his input on.

Felan relaxed back into the chair.

He was finally home.

Entry 32 – 5:17am

I guess I never really thought about it before, not until I talked with Blaez the other day about any survivors. I played a vital role in that explosion. I gave out all of the information I could get my hands on so Nick and the others could win.

I had a choice.

I made the wrong one.

I know some of you didn't even get one. I know some of you were in the same boat as me. I know some of you were abducted and taken from the streets under the guise of a better life. I'm sorry I judged you so unfairly.

I'm trying not to judge people anymore, but it's hard. It's hard seeing drunk people in the street and not immediately feel disgusted and unsure. If I see someone who looks remotely like Nick, I panic. I still think the worst of everyone. It's a bad habit I'm trying to break.

Mrs Walters said my first instinct is to think the worst and to expect the worst because then I won't be disappointed when the worst inevitably happens.

I don't think you could have expected your home to be blown to pieces.

Maddison escaped the explosion, unfortunately, and that's the only thing I regret. I regret that she didn't die. I also regret that I didn't kill Nick when I had the chance.

I was too scared to act, just like you were.

Chapter 41: Their Protector

Today was the first day Felan had forgone long sleeves around the house. It was freeing in a way, yet daunting, having his shame on full display. The kids had stopped asking about his scars weeks ago, however he knew having them out in the open would start the questions up once again.

The idea of answering those questions didn't scare Felan as much as it used to.

While Mrs Walters was out shopping, Felan had sent the kids into the front room so that he could do the washing-up. He heard the occasional shout down the hallway, but he trusted them enough to leave them to it. He turned to put the plates in the cupboard when the twins, Elliot and Mary, walked into the kitchen.

'Is everything okay in there?' Felan asked. He shut the cupboard and gave them his full attention. He would hate for the kids to think that he was ignoring them.

'Everything's fine,' Elliot said. Mary nudged him. 'I know, I'm getting to it,' he said to her quietly.

Felan watched the interaction in mild amusement. They got on really well with each other and Felan didn't remember them ever arguing, but every now and then they took the mick out of each other. It reminded Felan of his friendship with Blaez.

'We wanted to talk to you about something,' Elliot blurted out. He reached over and grasped Mary's hand tightly in his own.

Felan gestured to the table. 'Should we sit down?'

'Okay.' They sat down together at the end of the table, and when neither kid spoke, Felan gently prodded, 'What did you want to talk to me about?'

'We thought you might understand,' Elliot said, trying his best to look Felan in the eye and not at Felan's bare arms.

Oh.

Oh.

'We lived with our grandparents before we came here. They were always angry.'

Felan's heart broke in two when Elliot pushed up his sleeve. The scars weren't as extensive as Felan's were, he noted with relief. A single, thin, white line trailed down from Elliot's elbow to his wrist, while Mary had what Felan knew to be a burn scar on the hand Elliot wasn't holding.

Felan had seen their scars before, but he had refused to ask about them. The kids, if they wanted to, and if they felt comfortable enough, would talk to him when they were ready.

'The only vegetable Mary likes is carrots,' Elliot said. Felan hummed in agreement. He always made sure to chop up extra whenever he cooked (until she'd tried broccoli the other day and actually enjoyed it. Mrs Walters had practically collapsed in relief that there was another vegetable she could cook). 'Once, Grandpa didn't cook any when he made dinner so Mary didn't eat her vegetables. He got angry with her and held her hand to the top of the hob.' Mary trembled. Felan trembled for an entirely different reason. 'I tried to stop him and he cut me with a knife. Our neighbours called the police when they heard the screaming. I had to get twenty stitches.'

Elliot said it like it was something to be proud of, but Felan knew better. He leaned closer and reached over, taking each of their hands in his own. They looked at him intently, completely trusting him.

'Thank you for sharing that with me,' Felan said. 'You were both so brave when you shouldn't have had to be. You're safe now. You're safe here with all of us.'

Felan must have said something right (hallelujah) because Elliot smiled up at him like Felan himself had hung the stars in the night sky .

No one had ever looked at him like that before.

Mary squeezed Felan's hand like it was a lifeline. 'How did you get yours?' she asked timidly.

Felan looked down and remembered his lack of sleeves. 'It's

okay to ask,' he said reassuringly when an apologetic look crossed Mary's face, even if his heart pounded away in his chest, pounded so hard and fast he feared it might break his ribs. 'I got mine from lots of horrible people.' He let their hands go and leaned back on the chair, trying to think of the best way to explain. Mary pulled her knees to her chest. Elliot listened with rapt attention. 'It started off as one person, and then the list kept getting longer.'

'Why did so many people want to hurt you?' Mary asked.

'I really don't know, kiddo.' Felan bit back the sob that wanted to spill out of him. 'I was surrounded by bad people, and I was in a really bad place. It wasn't safe.'

Mary bit her lip, deep in thought. 'But you're safe now, right?'

A surge of protectiveness washed over him. Felan got up and hugged the twins tight. 'I'm trying to be.'

Elliot squirmed after a few seconds, resulting in Mary giving him a scolding. 'That's rude, Elliot! When someone initiates a hug, they should be the ones to end it!'

In response, Elliot stuck his tongue out at his sister.

Felan laughed. 'Okay, I'll stop the hug before a fight breaks out.' He stepped back and the twins stood up. 'You're good kids, alright?'

'We know!' They chorused back. Mary smiled up at him. 'Can we knit together later?'

'Of course.'

'And can we draw?' Elliot chimed in.

'Absolutely. Tell you what, if you get your summer work done now, I'll make us some cookies.'

The twins scampered away and when Felan checked on the kids five minutes later, he found all five of them working quietly on their summer work together in the front room. Gemma was colouring to her heart's content. As the oldest of the group, Jude and Josie helped out the others when they got stuck on a question; Felan would have offered his assistance, but he didn't have a clue what they were learning (he'd been a smart kid, but smart in the sense of science and the natural word, not what the government enforced to be taught in schools). Christ, he could barely get by helping Gemma with hers, and she hadn't even started primary school yet. Before long, Gemma would be the one teaching him – but he didn't mind. In fact, he was looking forward to that day.

He slipped out of the room with a smile plastered on his face and got to work on making cookies. It was the first thing Mrs Walters taught him to cook as it was so simple – and a crowd-pleaser. In between measuring out and mixing ingredients, and pouring in an unhealthy amount of chocolate chips, he checked on the kids again. On his third visit, he brought in a jug of orange juice and five plastic cups.

Mrs Walters came home while Felan divided up the cookie dough.

'And how exactly did you do that?' she asked, bemused, setting bags of shopping on the floor and pointing in the direction of the sitting room. 'I haven't seen them that focused on school work for a long time.'

'I said I'd make them cookies.' He picked up one of the pieces of dough and rolled it into a ball. He placed the ball onto a baking tray and pressed down lightly, and then repeated the process until all of the dough was on the baking tray. 'They've exceeded my expectations, that's for sure. I thought there would have been more resistance.'

'Ah. There's nothing wrong with bribery,' she said, beginning to put away the shopping. 'It works a treat, especially when they're as young as they are.'

Felan grinned. 'I learned from the best.'

He put the cookies in the oven at the same time that Mrs Walters finished putting away the shopping. She poured herself a glass of water while Felan set the timer. 'I've got some admin to catch up on in my office. Do you think you'll be okay with them on your own for a while longer?'

'Of course. We're having a group crafting session once they've finished their school work,' he said. 'I think I'll manage.'

'Are you sure?'

'What's the worst that could happen?'

Mrs Walters ruffled his hair. 'Thank you, lad. You know where

I am if there's any trouble.' She shut herself in her office and Felan was alone again.

He didn't mind being alone quite so much anymore.

Humming to himself, he finished the washing-up, and when he checked on the kids to see that they still hadn't finished their summer work, he started to pack their lunches for the morning. They were heading out for a 'wilderness walk' with the school, all ages welcome. It made him feel useful, and it also saved Mrs Walters a job. It must have been a rough admin session because within ten minutes, she came out for a coffee wearing her glasses. She never wore her glasses.

She stopped in her tracks. 'You don't have to keep taking care of other people, Felan. You're allowed to take care of yourself too.'

'I don't know what I'd do with myself otherwise,' he confessed. He cut the sandwiches into triangles and squares (the kids all liked different shapes and fillings and he'd committed their preferences to memory) and bagged them up. 'And I like helping people.' He wrote each kid's name on their respective sandwich so Mrs Walters wouldn't be confused in the morning. 'Even if it's just little things.'

'It's not your job to look after the kids,' she said. 'You need looking after too.'

'I know, but it helps you, and it keeps me from overthinking. I can focus on something else.'

He peeled Josie's satsuma and put it into a tiny container with some green grapes taken off the branch. Jude and Elliot liked an apple, Mary liked a banana, and Gemma would be having lunch at home with Felan and Mrs Walters. Pulling out their lunch bags from the cupboard, he set them on the counter and chucked in their favourite crisps and snacks from the snack drawer. He made sure to put in extra because he wasn't sure how long 'all day' was going to be.

'I'm going to make a guess here, Felan, but… I think that you like taking care of people because it heals the part of you that needed someone to take care of you,' Mrs Walters said, her hazel eyes boring deep into his.

Felan avoided her gaze. 'Like I said, the little things.'

They shared the kitchen in silence until the oven timer beeped.

Gemma came running into the kitchen while he took the cookies out of the oven.

'Careful, Gem. The tray's really hot,' Mrs Walters warned, a mug of coffee in her hand.

The four-year-old stopped a safe distance away and clasped her small hands together. 'They finished,' she said.

Felan set the baking tray down on the oven top and beckoned the little girl closer. 'Oh, so you're the messenger?'

'Mess-e-ger?'

He melted as she tried to sound out the new word. 'A mess-en-ger. It's someone who passes on a message for someone else.'

'I am a mess-e-ger,' she said sweetly, still pronounced wrong, and smiled up at him with that cute, little face of hers. He didn't have the heart to correct her.

'Can you be a messenger again?' he asked. She nodded enthusiastically. He held up his hand, his fingers splayed out. 'Tell them five minutes.'

'Okay!' Then she looked a little sheepish. 'Can I have one?' she asked, pointing up at the tray.

Felan feigned a groan and bent down to pick her up. 'I should think so. Being a messenger is a hard job, isn't it?'

'It is,' she said mournfully, but the sparkle in her eyes was impossible to ignore.

'Pick whichever one you like,' he said. 'Just be careful not to burn your fingers on the tray. It wouldn't do to have a messenger with poorly fingers.'

She swiped the smallest cookie off the tray with a giggle. 'They're warm!'

'They've just come out of the oven,' he said. 'To cook, things need to be hot.'

She took a bite and jumped up and down. 'Yummy!' she said. 'Mummy liked cookies. I don't remember.' Felan stiffened. Gemma finished her cookie and ran off screaming, 'Five minutes!

Art in five!'

What felt like a bucket of ice-cold water was dumped over his head. The ruckus in the other room couldn't shake him, couldn't ward off the cold that had settled into his skin.

'She's okay, Felan,' Mrs Walters said.

'I know, but she gets this look in her eyes sometimes,' Felan said. 'She looks so sad, like she can't remember why.'

'I know. I've seen it too. It worries me, but she's young. She'll bounce back. Kids always do.'

'How long has she been here?' Felan asked. It upset him that he didn't really know that much about her, or the other kids for that matter. He knew their favourite foods, not their stories.

'A little over a year,' Mrs Walters said. 'When she first arrived, she kept asking for her mum.'

'That can't have been easy for her to understand.'

'Little kids… they're a lot more forgiving of the world. They accept things more easily, but it doesn't make it any easier trying to explain to a three-year-old child that their mum was gone.'

Felan knew how long it had taken him to understand what happened to his mother, and he had been seven. He couldn't imagine going through that at the ripe old age of three.

'How did she take it?'

'Too easily. Maybe part of her already knew, as young as she was. It killed me to have that conversation with her every night. She knew her mum wasn't waking up… but I think she's starting to understand now.'

'Do they know what happened? To her mum?'

'She overdosed on sleeping pills,' Mrs Walters said, just above a whisper. 'At first they thought it was an accident, but it became apparent she'd been struggling mentally for some time.'

'Does Gemma know?'

'I didn't have a choice. I couldn't hide it from her, but I refused to sugar-coat it. I told her that her mum took too many pills and that's why she wouldn't wake up.'

'She saw it?' Felan asked numbly. He thought back to the conversation he'd had with Gemma about 'sad eyes' and how she told him that her mum wouldn't wake up. The story had been right there and he hadn't put the pieces together. He blinked. He saw the blue car driving away. He saw his mother's body on the floor. Tristan hadn't let him get close, but he knew what a dead body looked like. The fact that Gemma had seen…

'The neighbours heard her crying,' Mrs Walters said, interrupting Felan's train of thought. 'They raised the alarm when the crying got louder and didn't stop. Gemma had been trying to wake up her mum, but…'

'It's not right,' Felan said, shaking his head. 'None of this is right.'

'It's the way it is, I'm afraid.' She patted his shoulder twice. 'Now there is a group of kids waiting for you in the other room. Go and have some fun.'

Felan stood rooted to the spot long after Mrs Walters had vacated the room. Gemma had already seen too much, and yet she laughed, she played, and she lived. Maybe Felan could do that too.

He made his way to the living room with a plate of warm cookies in his hands, determined.

Chapter 42: A Clean Slate

They spent the rest of the day in the sitting room, knitting and painting and drawing (with a break for dinner in between).

Mrs Walters was met with a chorus of complaints when she came in to announce bedtime, but the kids were good kids and didn't make too much of a fuss. They helped each other tidy away the supplies into the right boxes and drawers and, one by one, the kids filed out of the room until Josie was the only one left.

She had sat by Felan's side for the better part of the evening, asking him quietly for help every now and then. Felan had been more than happy to provide it.

Josie approached him, twiddling her thumbs. He sat on the edge of the sofa as the girl came closer. She tugged the ends of her plaits.

'Are you okay?' he asked.

As soon as the words had left his mouth, Josie dashed over and hugged him tight around his middle. 'I love you,' she whispered.

He hugged her back, shocked by how fast his eyes filled with tears. 'I love you too.'

She scampered off after the others and Felan watched her go, baffled by the admission. He hadn't realised the kids felt that way about him.

'I told you, Felan. They look up to you,' Mrs Walters said. She bustled around him, straightened the cushions on the sofa and tucked the chairs in properly.

'I know you did, I just…'

How could he have even thought of leaving all of this behind? How could he have even considered hurting the kids again? Despite everything, he was still the same despicable boy that had left Guadalupe with Blaez the moment he had a chance with a bag; that very same bag still sat at the back of his wardrobe from where he'd thrown it after his breakdown.

He'd unpack it, he decided. He'd go to bed early and unpack everything and start for real.

Nothing much would have changed, but tomorrow was going to be different. He wasn't going to fail. He was done with failure. No. He would be the author of his own story.

'I'm going to turn in too,' he said, running his fingers along the back of the leather sofa.

Mrs Walters glanced over from where she was packing away the boxes of art supplies in the chest beneath the window. 'Everything okay?'

'Yeah,' he said, standing. He tapped on his collarbone. 'It's just... it's just a lot to take in.'

She smiled in that understanding way of hers. 'Goodnight, Felan. You know where I am if you need anything.'

'Thank you, Mrs Walters. Goodnight.' He made to leave the room. He hesitated at the last minute, his hand resting on the doorframe, turning back.

Mrs Walters watched him with an eyebrow raised. 'Everything okay?' she asked again.

He walked back over to the person who'd taken him in without a second thought and hugged her tight, his face pressed against her shoulder. He sank into her further when she hugged him back, an arm around his middle and a hand resting on the back of his head, holding him. He cried. Crying shouldn't come as a shock to him anymore. He almost laughed at the absurdity of it all.

'Thank you,' he said. 'Thank you for taking a chance on me. On Blaez. Thank you for helping us.'

Mrs Walters hummed. 'You deserve this, Felan. You deserve to feel safe.' He stayed in her embrace for a while longer. 'Get some sleep, lad. We'll all still be here when you wake up.'

He pulled away and wiped at his eyes. 'I know.' He said goodnight to the kids on his way to the bathroom (and even stopped to give both Jude and Elliot a fist bump in the hallway upon their insistence). He peeked into Gemma's bedroom on the way passed. She was fast asleep beneath her covers. He entered her room quietly, pulled the duvet up over her shoulders, smoothed her hair away from her face and kissed her on the temple. She murmured something unintelligible and snuggled deeper into her covers. It was enough to make Felan's heart melt, enough to thaw out the cold from earlier. 'Goodnight, Gem,' he whispered.

He shut himself in his room and looked around.

It was his. All his. It wasn't just the temporary thing he had convinced himself it would be. It wasn't the Warehouse with its makeshift rooms and dangerous inhabitants. It was a home. A family home. He had a home here with Mrs Walters and the kids, and with Blaez. He had a home and people that loved him.

It was a novelty he never thought he'd have again.

***

He stared down at the bag with his hands on his hips for a long time before he dragged it out from the confines of his wardrobe. It had been there ever since his first week.

It had been there since before Blaez had made the decision to return to Guadalupe. Felan hadn't touched the bag since *that* night. He hadn't touched it since he'd slung it back in and slammed the door, lost in the throes of panic.

He knew at some point he'd have to be honest with Mrs Walters about his actions. He knew he'd have to be honest with her about what he had tried to do, what he had *wanted* to do, because the longer he left it the worse the festering of the open wound would become.

Not today. Not tonight. He'd wait a while. After all, he had time.

He sat on the floor beside the bag and unpacked it slowly. He neatly folded all of the clothes he'd slung inside in a moment of hysteria and made a tiny pile on his floor in front of his chest of drawers. In case the rest of the kids were already asleep, he opened the heavy, wooden drawers quietly, placed the clothes inside, and shut them just as softly.

Then he found the letters, the letters he'd stuffed at the bottom, one for every person he cared about. He unfolded the crumpled pieces of paper and tucked them inside his notebook.

He couldn't do it yet, but one day he'd read the words he'd written at his lowest point. No one would ever read them but him.

He was better now. This was his home. He had a family.

When he fell asleep, he was a little more hopeful of the future. He was a little more hopeful of what was to come.

Chapter 43: Bravery

Felan made the second trip to see Dr Sampson alone.

The lady at reception pointed him in the direction of the waiting room and he took a seat in the corner of it. There was only one other person waiting, sitting by the door. It wasn't like the dentist where the room had been filled, everyone sitting in nervous silence. Felan had been absolutely terrified when his name had been called. His mouth had been numb for hours after, and he had one hell of a headache. He swore he still dreamed of the drill rattling around in his mouth to this day.

'Felan. It's good to see you.'

He snapped his head up to see Dr Sampson smiling down at him. 'Hi.'

'Why don't you come on through?' the doctor said kindly. 'It's only a quick appointment today.' Felan let himself be led into the room. 'There's nothing to be scared of. We won't be going over anything new, unless you have anything you want to ask me,' he said, closing the door.

Felan made a noise of acknowledgement. 'I'll let you know if I think of anything.' He removed his long-sleeved shirt before he could talk himself out of it and sat on the examination bed. That was progress in itself. Last time, he had opted to keep his shirt on. Last time, he hadn't wanted anyone else to see.

A long explanation short with terms Felan didn't fully understand, he was making good progress. Apparently. He was still on the lighter side according to Dr Sampson, but he was gaining weight, which was good. As for the scars, they were healing 'very nicely', and the doctor wanted to prescribe Felan some cream. 'It won't make them fade completely, but it'll help to make them less noticeable, if that's what you'd like.'

'Yeah.' Felan drew the doctor's attention to his tattoo, one of the many ways Nick had branded him. 'Is there something you can do for this?'

'I'm afraid not,' the doctor said. 'Although they might seem similar, a tattoo is very different to a scar.'

'It wasn't done in a parlour,' Felan admitted. 'I was taken to someone – the man who did it was nice enough. I don't think it's infected or anything because I've never really had any problems with it, but… can you check it out?'

'Of course.' Dr Sampson pulled up a stool and looked over the tattoo. It was one of Felan's greatest sources of shame. 'Considering the circumstances I imagine it was done under, it's absolutely fine, Felan. It's not infected or anything like that.'

'Okay.'

'I'm assuming it wasn't your choice?' he asked.

'I didn't know where he was taking me,' Felan said. 'It was dark out, and cold, and he led me down these alleyways and then he just… he left me there.' He paused. 'I didn't say no.'

'You're safe now, lad,' Dr Sampson reminded him. 'Nothing will harm you here.'

'I know. I just can't believe how different it is here. How safe it is.' Felan couldn't drag his eyes away from the numerous red and white lines streaked across his forearm, and the mess of aggravated bumps where the bullet had hit him.

He pulled his long-sleeved shirt back on when the memories began to swarm like locusts.

'You got out, Felan. That's all that matters. And you're making great progress.'

'I feel a lot better about everything now,' he said. 'I didn't want to face up to it before. I didn't even want to acknowledge it.'

'Even just coming here alone today is progress in itself. You've matured. You're talking to people… you're talking to me. If I remember correctly, last time you were here you barely said a word.' Felan cast his gaze down. 'And that's nothing to be ashamed of. Is it safe to say that you were still reeling from what happened when you came to see me the first time?'

'I didn't want anyone else to know,' he said. 'And I definitely didn't want anybody to see.'

'There's no shame in that, or that tattoo of yours.'

'Really?'

'No shame at all. Now,' Dr Sampson said, clapping his hands together and peering down at Felan through his glasses, 'you best be getting back. Oh – and wish Mrs Walters a happy birthday for me. It's not until Saturday, but I won't be seeing her for a while.'

'Of course,' Felan said. 'Remind me, what day is it today?'

'It's Thursday. There should be a market in town,' Dr Sampson said with a wink.

'Thank you,' Felan said, smiling. Internally he was panicking. He said goodbye to the doctor and rushed to the market as fast as he could. If he was lucky, maybe he could catch some of the stalls before they dismantled for the day.

He texted Mrs Walters on the way: *Heading into town for a bit, then I'll be home. All good news at the doctors. See you soon x*

***

If Felan had thought the Saturday market at Farley Street had been bustling with people, then the Thursday market in Weisworth was even more so.

This time, instead of swiping a punnet of grapes from the fruit and veg stall, Felan stood in line at the flower stall and paid for the biggest, prettiest summer bouquet he could find. He searched for the perfect card next, and found one on another stall manned by an elderly woman. It would be big enough for all of the kids to sign their names and write any personal messages they wanted.

'I paint these all by hand,' the elderly woman said, putting his chosen card into a brown paper bag.

Felan smiled. 'You're very talented.'

And last but not least, Felan ducked into the photo shop and managed to print out (and get framed) a photo of all of the kids, Felan, Blaez and Mrs Walters that had been taken two weeks after he had arrived in Weisworth.

His family.

He admired the photo the whole way home.

Chapter 44: Celebrations

Felan managed to successfully hide the flowers, the card and the photo from Mrs Walters, and had one by one ushered the kids inside his room to sign the card over the next few days.

'It's a secret,' Felan said. 'It's for Mrs Walters' birthday. You can't tell her about it.'

The kids agreed, especially since they were excited about the prospect of a party. They were even more excited when Felan enlisted their help to make her birthday cake while she went out to run errands for the afternoon.

The kids watched her drive away from the sitting room window, and when the coast was clear, they stampeded into the kitchen. Elliot stopped a few feet from Felan, stood straight and saluted. 'Reporting for duty,' he said.

Felan laughed. 'Come on, then.'

It was, to put it bluntly, complete and utter chaos in the kitchen, but he managed to get everything tidy while the cake – a simple vanilla sponge – was in the oven. He had to bribe Gemma with a chocolate biscuit to clean the flour off her face. Jude had thought it would be funny to blow a small pile all over her. Thankfully, Gemma had thought it was hilarious and demanded he do it again.

Felan put a stop to it soon after.

He sent the kids into the sitting room while the cake cooked and, after taking it out, and when it had cooled down, he ushered the kids back in. They took turns to decorate it: Elliot helped to (rather enthusiastically) make the icing, Mary carefully spread it over the top, Jude added chocolate buttons, Josie added multicoloured sprinkles, and Gemma, after adding fruit jellies, licked the bowl of icing clean.

'Now, remember,' Felan told the kids after he'd hidden the cake in his room with the other presents, 'if Mrs Walters asks what we got up to, we did some drawing, and we watched TV.'

'We know!' they chorused.

Mrs Walters returned home an hour later with two steaming bags of food from the chippy. Felan met her at the door and helped her carry them inside, already having laid the table with plates, cutlery, plastic cups and all of the sauces. Between the two of them, they dished out the food onto the correct plates. 'Dinner's ready!' Mrs Walters called.

What sounded like a herd of elephants stampeded down the hall to the kitchen. 'The food isn't going anywhere,' Mrs Walters said with a laugh. 'Now, wash your hands first.'

The kids did as she asked and sat at the table, digging into their food at warp speed. It was mostly chicken nuggets and chips, and the occasional sausage. Felan and Mrs Walters had battered cod, opting to share a portion of chips. Despite Mrs Walters' best efforts, Felan still hadn't worked up much of an appetite; he doubted that he ever would, but he'd keep trying.

He'd keep trying for the sake of everyone who cared about him.

'Slow down!' Mrs Walters reprimanded the kids.

Felan laughed to himself. They were only eating fast because they wanted to give Mrs Walters the cake. He couldn't fault them for being excited. A party was a party, after all, and a party meant games.

'You'll make yourselves sick if you eat too fast,' Felan said gently. 'Besides, we have plenty of time after dinner to play games.' He gave the kids a look, and when Mrs Walters looked back to her plate, none the wiser, he winked.

Thankfully, the kids slowed down after that – though he marvelled at how much tomato sauce they all continued to add to their plates. Felan liked the stuff, but the kids easily got through a massive bottle within a week and, according to Tristan, Blaez was a fan too.

Felan feared he was surrounded by tomato sauce freaks.

'What did you get up to while I was gone?' Mrs Walters asked, taking the time to look up and down the table at all of the kids.

'Pictures!' Gemma shouted, her mouth stained red. Felan had

to remind himself that it was tomato sauce. 'TV!'

Once he'd extinguished the minor panic, he said, 'We watched a *lot* of TV. I hope you don't mind.'

'I don't mind at all,' she said. 'What pictures did you draw?'

'A little cat,' Mary piped up.

'You mean a kitten,' Elliot ribbed.

'You're a meanie,' she scolded her twin.

Jude looked rather sheepishly at Felan. 'Do you think you could help me draw a dragon later?'

'Of course I can,' Felan said. He felt all warm and fuzzy inside, like he often felt around Blaez whenever she held his hand. 'I would love to.' He doubted he'd be much help, but he'd try his best.

Then, seeing that everyone had almost finished their food, Felan caught Gemma's eye and winked. She yawned once or twice and leaned back in her chair, and her head dipped onto her chest. Felan left it for a moment or two, and just as Mrs Walters noticed, Felan was on his feet and picked the girl up. 'I'll be back in a bit,' he said.

Mrs Walters gave him a grateful look and went back to her food, conversing with the kids some more.

Gemma twitched in his arms, trying hard not to laugh. 'Hush,' he murmured, climbing the stairs. 'Not yet.' The sounds of chatter echoed from the kitchen. The kids were making good on their promise of a distraction. 'Coast is clear, Gem.'

She giggled loudly. 'I was good!'

'Yes, you were, but shh!' he whispered, setting her down. 'We have to be quiet.' Felan ruffled her hair and led her into his room where they'd hidden the cake, the bunch of flowers, the card, and the photo. Gemma made grabby hands at the card and the flowers.

'You've got them?' he asked.

'Yes! They're pretty.'

'They are, aren't they?' Felan mused with a smile. 'Now, let's go and surprise Mrs Walters, shall we?'

The little girl led the way, gingerly stepping to not make any noise, and Felan followed close behind. He carried the cake they'd made earlier (with the photo, now wrapped in silver paper and tied with a red bow, hidden up his baggy sleeve). Having never wrapped a present before, it was safe to say that he'd initially struggled, but a few online videos later, he wasn't at such a loss.

Gemma waited in the hallway, hopping from one foot to the other, and when Felan gave her a thumbs-up, she ran in, Felan walking behind her a moment later.

'Happy birthday!' Gemma squealed. She ran right up to Mrs Walters and thrust the flowers and the card onto her lap.

Mrs Walters sat there, stunned, but gratefully received the gifts. 'I thought you were asleep!'

Gemma giggled. 'We played pretend!'

Felan cleared his throat. 'Are we all ready to sing?'

They were horribly out of tune, but for once he didn't care that it wasn't perfect. Setting the cake down, he saw Mrs Walters' cheeks turn pink.

He was glad that Dr Sampson had told him. He didn't think he'd ever get over the guilt if he hadn't known and they hadn't celebrated her birthday – and he most definitely would never forget the look in her eyes when she'd first seen the bouquet of flowers clutched in Gemma's tiny hands.

'We made it earlier – and we all chipped in, didn't we?' Felan said to the kids. They clamoured to say their piece, and while they told Mrs Walters in more detail what each of them had done to help, Felan cleared away the table – but not until he had hidden the present on his chair. He proceeded to get out smaller plates and a handful of forks for the cake before returning to the table. Mrs Walters happily sliced it up and Felan handed cake-filled plates to all of the kids. When he sat back down on his chair, Felan discreetly moved the present onto his lap to avoid crushing it.

The cake was devoured in what felt like seconds.

'This is delicious,' Mrs Walters said. 'You guys have done a wonderful job!'

'I want to be a baker,' Josie announced. 'I want to own a bakery and sell things.'

She seemed excited by the idea. As for Mrs Walters… she was

intrigued to say the least. 'I think you have the talent for it.'

'Really?'

'Really.'

Mrs Walters opened her card. She read the contents, and when she looked up, Felan swore he had seen tears in her eyes.

'These are lovely messages,' she said. 'Thank you for making my birthday so special.'

The kids ran up and hugged her before they raced into the sitting room. Felan leaned back in his chair, his arms crossed over his stomach. 'I think I may have let them go a little overboard with the icing sugar,' he admitted.

'I think I can let you off. Just this once.' Her fingers brushed the bouquet of flowers. The petals shivered. 'They're beautiful.'

'They were the loveliest ones I could find,' he said. 'And I got you something else.' He grabbed the wrapped photo from his lap and slid it across the table.

'Felan – you shouldn't have!' she exclaimed.

'I'm sorry it isn't much.'

'I don't want to hear any apologies from you today,' she replied. She picked up the present and unwrapped it. Yeah. There were definitely tears in her eyes. 'Oh, Felan,' she said. 'It's perfect. Thank you.'

'It's the least you deserve after everything you've done for us.'

It's the least you deserve after everything you've done for me.

Elliot ran into the kitchen at full speed and skidded on the tiled floor. 'Come on! We've set up Ludo in the other room!' He ran back without waiting for a reply.

Felan got to his feet. 'I've got this,' he said, gesturing to the dirty plates. 'I'll be in as soon as I can.'

Mrs Walters walked over to him and held his arms still. 'Nonsense. We can clear this up later.' He nodded in agreement. 'Good. Now, I'm going to put these beautiful flowers in a vase and then I'll be in.'

He wandered into the other room, noting with relief that everything seemed to be in order, and Mrs Walters followed shortly after with the flowers, now in a vase. She placed them on the windowsill, exactly where Felan had imagined them to sit. She put the photo beside them and brushed her finger along the frame.

Finally. Finally he had done something right.

Splitting into teams of two, they played three rounds of Ludo on the sitting room floor, and Gemma kind of played whenever she wanted to, and when Jude became bored of the first game, he beckoned Felan over to the table.

'Can we draw the dragon now?'

'Sure thing, buddy.'

He wasn't very artistic himself, but Felan helped Jude while the others played a game of cards, though very quickly, and despite all the sugar, Gemma soon fell asleep in Mrs Walters' lap. With a quick glance around, he could tell the other kids were crashing fast too. Felan finished the section of the dragon he had been helping on before he settled a hand over Jude's smaller one. 'We'll finish this another time,' he said. 'I think it's time for bed.'

Jude looked a little crestfallen, but soon agreed when he started yawning. 'Promise?'

'I promise.'

One by one the kids trailed upstairs to bed after wishing Mrs Walters happy birthday and saying their goodnights to Felan. While she followed them up with Gemma in her arms, Felan quietly packed away the games they'd left on the floor. It had been a good day, and Mrs Walters seemed genuinely happy.

He moved into the kitchen next and began to clear the table. He piled the plates and the cutlery up beside the sink and filled it with hot water, squirting in generous amounts of washing-up liquid. He was so lost in the familiar motions that he didn't hear Mrs Walters come back in. He jumped a little when she appeared beside him and began drying up the things left in the drying rack.

'No,' he protested. 'Let me.'

'Nonsense,' she said. 'It'll be quicker with the two of us.'

There was no changing her mind, so Felan decided not to argue. They cleared everything away in peaceful companionship.

'The kids might have helped with the cake, but I know who planned everything,' Mrs Walters said. She hung the tea towel on the oven door and fixed Felan with a stern look.

Oh. He'd overstepped, hadn't he? Damn. He'd just wanted to surprise her with something good – he remembered how she hadn't been in contact with her family for some time and he wanted to do something nice for her for a change. Felan rubbed the back of his neck, his eyes downcast. 'I'm sorry,' he said.

'Whatever for?'

He glanced up. 'I upset you.'

'Quite the opposite – although I am a little surprised how you knew it was my birthday today.'

'Dr Sampson ratted you out. He mentioned it during my check-up.' A sinking feeling settled in his stomach. 'Please don't be mad at him. If anything, be mad at me. I can take it. I didn't know if you wanted to do anything for your birthday so I assumed that you did and I *know* I should have asked but...'

Mrs Walters engulfed him in a tight hug, cutting off his nervous rambling. 'You have nothing, *nothing*, to apologise for. Do you hear me?'

Felan nodded into her shoulder and held on just as tight. He hadn't messed up after all. *Thank God.*

'You are the bravest, kindest, most selfless young man I have ever met.'

Felan shuddered in her arms. She ended the embrace, but kept her hands on his shoulders and looked him in the eyes. He was no longer ashamed of the tears that burned tracks down his cheeks.

'Thank you,' she said. She pressed a kiss to his forehead, and Felan felt safer than he'd ever felt before.

He felt like he was *home*.

Chapter 45: Midnight Promises

Despite it still being her birthday, Mrs Walters decided to catch up on some admin, taking advantage of the kids' early night to fill out the seemingly endless pile of paperwork.

Felan had said his goodnights and was in his room, quietly knitting something for Blaez, listening to some music, headphones half on, half off. He decided that there wasn't much point in trying to sleep when he wasn't tired – whenever he tried, he just got even more frustrated and that helped no one.

Feeling a sudden change in the air, Felan set down his knitting and paused his music, removing his headphones completely. The feeling had been coming and going for the last few minutes, and an uncomfortable weight had settled on his chest. He noticed it when it settled – gentle at first, like freshly fallen snow – but it got heavier and heavier like someone was pressing down firmly, until he could no longer ignore the feeling. He stood up and paced around his room, wondering what the cause could be, for there had been no strange noises, and nothing out of the ordinary had happened. For the most part, everything was fine. Everything was normal.

And yet... something didn't feel right. The last time he had felt like this had been during his nightmare. Felan pinched his arm. He winced. He was definitely awake. It was definitely real.

What the hell was wrong?

Gemma, a voice in his head said. *Check on Gemma.*

Felan left his room. He wasn't one to argue with a gut feeling. Gut feelings were often the body's instinctive reaction to something – he took those reactions as a warning, and he didn't take warnings lightly.

He pushed open Gemma's bedroom door and peeked inside.

The first thing he noticed was that her fairy lights were on, draping down from the ceiling above her bed in the corner of the room, twinkling and slowly changing colours.

The second thing he noticed was that she was huddled at the foot of her bed, atop the covers and clutching her knitted bumble bee. That wasn't anything new (though sometimes she huddled *beneath* the covers too) – Gemma did it quite often. Felan wondered how it could be comfortable, but he would never deny her anything that gave her some semblance of comfort.

The third thing he noticed was that she was crying. He froze in shock, the fond smile falling from his face. Gemma never cried. Ever. It was unsettling to say the least, but her crying wasn't the most unsettling part.

No, the most unsettling part was that she was completely and utterly silent. He couldn't hear a single peep from her, other than little gasps every now and then.

He failed her. He failed that little girl, *his* little girl. Had she cried before and he hadn't heard? Had she cried before and stayed quiet because that's what she had been taught? Making a mental note to speak to Mrs Walters about it in the morning, he rushed inside, having managed to break out of whatever trance he'd gotten lost in, to console the crying child.

'Gemma,' he said, dropping to his knees beside her bed. He set a hand on her shoulder, the urge to provide comfort overcoming any fear he had of scaring her. 'Gemma, it's okay. I promise everything's okay.'

But how could he promise something when he didn't even know what was wrong?

The girl hiccupped. 'Fee?' she questioned, sitting up a little.

'Yeah,' he said, stroking her shoulder. 'It's me.'

She leapt at him and wrapped her little arms around his neck with a quiet cry. He pulled her close and held her there, her little body shuddering against him. His jumper grew damp the longer he held her.

And still she didn't utter a sound.

'You can cry, Gem,' he said. 'Don't ever be afraid to cry.'

Her cries began to sound in earnest, though they were still quieter than they should have been for the amount she was shaking, for the amount she seemed to be *feeling*.

Maybe there was more to Gemma's life with her mother that no one knew about, and how could they know, when Gemma had barely been able to talk when she'd first come to Mrs Walters?

'Fee,' she sobbed. 'Fee, don't go.'

The nickname hit him like a slap to the face. 'I'm not going anywhere,' he reassured her, running a hand up and down her back in what he hoped was a soothing manner. He remembered his mother doing it once, though the memory was weak and hazy. 'We talked about this before, didn't we? I'm staying.'

She hiccupped again. 'You had sad eyes. You kept sleeping. You went away!' she sobbed.

It tugged painfully at the strings that held Felan together, that held him upright, that ensured he functioned correctly, pulling him taut in all directions. Her cries were loud and unfiltered and exhausted. He dreaded to think how long she'd been crying before he went to check on her.

A four-year-old had had a nightmare – all because he didn't know how to talk about his feelings. He didn't realise how much his sadness had affected her. He didn't realise how much his sadness had affected them all.

'I'm sorry,' he mumbled. 'I'm sorry, Gem.'

'Don't sleep,' she begged. 'Don't go away.'

She continued to cry. Her little heart thumped away in her little chest, reminiscent of a string of thunderclouds he'd seen, and seconds later heard, as a child, one steady rumble after another in quick succession. Of course, those thunderclouds eventually dispersed. Gemma's little heart continued to *thump*, *thump*, *thump* away.

Completely at a loss, Felan lowered his face onto her shoulder and cried with her. He didn't realise how much he meant to her. He didn't realise how important he was. He didn't realise Gemma held him to such heights.

Felan had never regretted his frantic decision to try to harm himself more.

He was glad he'd stopped.

He would never have experienced love like this if he didn't.

'I'm here, Sweetheart.' He didn't know where the term of endearment came from, but it felt right to say. 'I'm right here and I'm not going anywhere. I won't leave. I'm not leaving. I'm staying right here.'

The memory was fuzzy and almost forgotten but he heard his mother's voice in his head, clear as a bell. *'It's just a bad dream, Little One. Mummy's here. Sweetheart, Mummy's here and she's never leaving you. Hush now. Hush, Little One. That's it, Sweetheart. I'm not leaving.'*

But she'd left. His mum had left after saying she wouldn't. Felan choked on a sob. 'I'm here, Gem. I'm here and I'm never leaving you. Hush now.'

He'd be better than his mum, and he'd be better than Gemma's. He would be the one to stay. He would be the one to look after her if anything happened. He would be better. He would *do* better.

'It's okay, Gem. Let it out. That's it. Let it all out.'

He would never break another promise. He swore it.

Cheeks wet, and exhausted, Felan kissed Gemma's curls. 'Everything will be okay, you'll see,' he whispered, trailing his fingers up and down her spine. She snuggled closer. 'I'm not leaving you. I promise that I'm not leaving you.' Felan slumped down. 'You'll never be on your own. Never again.'

Never again.

Chapter 46: Remembrance

What Felan loved most about his Sunday shift at the café was Felicity.

Felicity was a charming little lady, well into her eighties, and she came into the café every Sunday morning at eleven on the dot for a small latte and a slice of lemon drizzle cake. Her weekly appearance had begun long before Felan had joined the small team, though upon seeing a new face Felicity had made an effort to talk to him. She always asked after him whenever he wasn't in – especially when she'd heard that Felan had taken ill. She was also the café's most generous tipper. 'He's a lovely lad and he's ever so polite!' he had once heard her say to Lisa.

Felan had flushed, and Lisa had pressed a crisp twenty into his hand.

So, yeah. Felan normally loved his Sundays – only today was the first Sunday shift Felan wasn't loving because Felicity failed to show up.

His gaze flickered between the door and the clock, wondering what was keeping her. He could tell from the furtive glances to the empty chair, the empty chair by the window that Felicity sat in every week for three hours, reading her book – the same book – that Lisa was unnerved too.

It was no secret that Felicity had dementia. It was no secret that she didn't have long left. Some things faded from her memory, yet other things remained. Felan was honoured that his face and his name were two of those things.

It wasn't until two days later, when Felan turned up for his Tuesday shift, that he had discovered the reason why Felicity had never showed.

'She passed away late Saturday night,' Lisa explained gently while Felan had put his stuff in his locker. 'Her son phoned a little while ago. He wanted to thank us for looking after her so well when she came in, and he thanked you by name. Apparently, Felicity raved about you to her family often.'

Felan allowed a sad smile to grace his features. 'Do you think I made a difference?'

'I think you did, Felan. I really think you did.'

It was safe to say that Felan's heart wasn't really in his work that day. Neither was Lisa's, but they shared small smiles and little glances every now and then in a show of silent support to get through it. It was officially the longest shift of Felan's life. It felt like it, anyway.

The bell above the door rung, and a man with a sunhat walked into the café carrying what looked to be a rather large succulent in a terracotta pot. He had a greying beard and he reminded Felan of a wizard from a film the kids had made him watch the other night.

'Hi,' the man said upon seeing Felan cleaning down one of the tables. 'I'm looking for Felan?'

He froze. Had they found him? 'Um…'

'Oh, you must be Jonathan!' Lisa exclaimed, hurrying over. 'I'm so glad you could make it.' She shook Jonathan's hand and rested a supportive hand on Felan's shoulder. 'This is Felicity's son,' Lisa explained to him.

'I'm Felan,' he said, holding out a hand.

Jonathan shook it. 'It's lovely to meet you, though I wish it had been under different circumstances.'

'Me too. I'm really sorry about your mum.'

Dark circles sat beneath the man's eyes, and his face was pale and drawn and decorated with enough lines to draw a map. 'It's been a long time coming,' he said. All Felan could do was nod. Felicity's son held out the succulent. 'She wanted you to have this, Felan,' he said. 'She knew you liked plants, and that you were good at looking after them.'

Felan and Felicity had talked about plants at length, especially the ones that he'd grown in the garden. Felicity had loved nature as much as Felan did.

He accepted the succulent and held the pot close to his chest.

'I'm honoured,' he said hoarsely.

The man then pulled a very familiar, battered copy of a book from his jacket pocket. 'And this.'

Felan felt out of sorts when he took the book, the book that Felicity had read every Sunday. 'I'll cherish it,' he said. He decided that he would read it when he got the chance. He was determined to discover what had drawn her back to the book time and time again; he wanted to know what had been so captivating.

'The funeral is being held at Weisworth Community Church on Friday. It's an open invitation, so you're more than welcome to come.'

'Thank you, Jonathan. We'll keep that in mind,' Lisa said, taking the lead once more.

Jonathan nodded. 'Anyway, I best be off. Thank you again, and good luck.'

'You too,' Felan said.

'Take care!' Lisa called.

Lisa closed the café half an hour early. They made short work of the end of day clean-up, and Lisa dropped Felan home, succulent and book in tow. He had tried for a smile, and, judging by the worry on Lisa's face, he didn't think it had been successful.

When he got inside, he had given Mrs Walters a brief rundown of the day, and why he had a plant in his arms. She kissed him on the forehead and sent him on his way.

'You know where I am,' she said.

The succulent, he decided, would live on his windowsill. There, it would get enough sunlight, and it would always be in full view, a reminder of the amazing, incredible lady Felicity had been.

Her book lived on his bedside table, ready for the day Felan could bring himself to uncover its secrets.

Chapter 47: Permanent Fixture

Desperate to escape his thoughts, Felan had volunteered to watch the kids while Mrs Walters popped out for an hour.

Well, it hadn't been all of the kids: Elliot, Mary and Jude didn't want to go to the shops, while Josie and Gemma were excited for the adventure, which was how Felan found himself sat at the kitchen table, a hot chocolate (now cold) in front of him, with the back door open, three kids running around in the garden.

Despite the events of the day, and the information he'd learned, he was calm, peaceful (just for a moment) and wistful. Felan could tell from Jonathan's visit that Felicity had meant a great deal to him. Without realising it, she had meant a great deal to Felan too.

Felicity might be gone, but he still had Blaez. He would always have Blaez.

God, I miss her.

Elliot ran into the kitchen, his cheeks flushed and his knees bloody, ripping Felan from his musing. He leapt to his feet, his stomach churning at the sight of blood. 'What've you done there?' he asked, a little panicked.

The boy rolled his eyes. 'You're exactly like Mrs Walters. *I'm fine*. I just scraped my knees.'

Felan struggled to keep his panic at bay. It was a scratch. It was nothing life threatening. 'You want me to clean them?'

'Yeah. Mrs Walters always does.'

'Then let's get you cleaned up.'

Now, Felan was no expert in first aid, but he didn't think he had done a terrible job of cleaning away the blood and the grit.

When Randi had been shot, all Felan had done was wrap it up in an attempt to stop the bleeding – he had no idea how Blaez had kept a cool head while she dealt with the bullet stuck in his arm all those months ago. Cleaning scraped knees was harrowing enough. Just seeing Elliot bleeding was harrowing enough. He couldn't imagine pulling a bullet from a friend's arm.

He had to focus. Focus on Elliot. One of the kids. One of *his* kids.

'There,' Felan said, dabbing a damp tissue over the scrape site. He then brushed an antiseptic wipe over it. Elliot winced a little. 'All done.'

'Thanks, Felan.' Elliot didn't jump to his feet like Felan had thought he would. Instead, he stayed sat on the chair, fiddling with the hem of his t-shirt. 'I'm sorry for bringing up Zac.'

Felan watched him closely. 'Why are you sorry?'

'Because… because…' Elliot hung his head. 'Because I didn't realise how much it hurt you.'

'That's…'

'He was my friend. He hadn't even been gone that long before you came and took his room and I got mad, but… but I'm glad you're here,' he said. 'I really like that you're here. You play with us and you look after us. Everyone likes you.' His voice dropped to a mutter. 'I like you.' Elliot averted his gaze to the kitchen window, his cheeks now flushed for a completely different reason.

The beginnings of a smile crept onto Felan's face. 'You don't have to apologise for that. Ever. Zac was your friend.' Felan paused to clear his throat. Elliot turned back to face him. 'It was only natural that you'd be upset when he left. It was only natural that you'd be upset with… well, me.'

'But it wasn't fair to you. It was mean and rude and selfish.'

Felan reached over and ruffled Elliot's hair. 'There's no harm done. I promise.' The kid still looked unsure. 'But I appreciate the apology,' Felan said gently. 'Now go on – outside. I'm sure you've still got an outrageous amount of energy to burn.'

There. That made the kid smile. Felan, bewildered by what had just happened, accepted the fist-bump from Elliot and watched the kid rush back outside as fast as he'd rushed in.

***

Since Elliot's scraped knees, none of the other kids had come running back in for help with anything, so Felan helped Mrs Walters with dinner when she came home, Mary and Gemma running outside to join the others in the garden.

He hadn't known the kids for that long, really, but it felt like forever. It felt like they'd been in his life from the moment he'd first opened his eyes as a baby. They were his family, and he was not going to give them up without a fight.

He grabbed the serrated knife from the block and it wasn't until he'd grasped it firmly, poised for use, that he'd realised what he'd done. He hadn't used that particular knife since *that* night. He'd made a point to avoid it, and now it was in his hands, in his *very* capable hands.

He shook himself. He could do it. He'd done it before. It was just a knife, and it was just a few carrots.

Mrs Walters chattered away somewhere to his right and Felan made the first slice while holding his breath. He made the second, the third, the fourth. It was okay. He could do this. It was easy, really. Slice after slice after slice. There was nothing else to it. It was easy.

In fact, it would be so easy to pretend the knife had just slipped.
Do it. You know you want to. Pretend it slipped.

He dropped the knife onto the chopping board with a clatter and stepped back, breathing heavily.

Behind him, Mrs Walters stopped talking. 'Is everything okay?'

'Yeah,' he managed. He grabbed onto the countertop to keep himself on his feet.

She closed the distance between them, a hand resting on his elbow. 'Are you sure? You've gone very pale,' Mrs Walters commented.

He'd kept the truth from her for as long as he could, and now it was time to come clean. There was no hiding it. 'There's something I never told you.'

'Okay.'

'I tried to, uh… the knife, I mean, I, um…'

'You tried to what?' she prompted.

Felan took a few deep breaths to calm himself. He didn't know if it worked because the anxiety that sat heavy in his chest every day skyrocketed and rose to the tip of his tongue. 'I had a bag packed,' he said. 'I came down one night. I grabbed a knife... that knife.' He nodded to the serrated knife atop the chopping board. 'And, and I tried to... I don't know what I was going to do but I... I wanted to... before I left to...'

Mrs Walters hand on his elbow squeezed harder. 'When was this?'

Felan hung his head. 'The day we talked in my room.'

'This happened sometime after?'

'No,' he said. 'Before. That morning. Really early. I almost...' His voice wavered. 'And then Gemma had that nightmare the other night and it put everything into perspective.' Mrs Walters said nothing. 'I promise I won't do it again. I don't even know what I was thinking. I didn't want to do it, but something inside me convinced me. It tried to make me do it.' He let his head fall lower. He blinked repeatedly, determined not to cry. If he cried then he'd never finish the conversation; despite the panic and the anxiety that coursed through him, Felan wanted to see this conversation through.

'Hey,' Mrs Walters said, suddenly in front of him. 'Are you still with me?'

'Yeah.'

'Look at me.' He did. Her normally warm eyes swam with tears. 'You've been holding that in ever since, haven't you?' His bottom lip quivered. 'And you tried to tell me, didn't you? When you said that you tried, I thought you meant a while ago. I thought it happened while you were still in Guadalupe. I had no idea it was that morning. I had no idea it was *here*. I didn't even think that...' Her tears spilled over, a horrified expression on her face.

Felan had never seen Mrs Walters cry. He hated to be the one to break her. He let go of the countertop and found one of her hands. 'I'm okay,' he pleaded, slightly hysterical. 'Mrs Walters, I promise I'm okay.'

'Have you thought about it since?'

'I try not to, but my thoughts have a mind of their own,' he joked. It fell on deaf ears. 'Just now, cutting up the carrots, I thought about how easy it would be to pretend the knife had slipped... I don't want to hurt myself. I've never wanted to do it. I... I don't want to feel like that again.'

Mrs Walters hugged him for what felt like an eternity. It still wasn't long enough to fix him. He feared nothing would and he'd be existing like this forever, full of love and despair in equal measure, a bridge between worlds he couldn't separate.

She held him at arm's length and looked him over, her face pulled taut by Felan's admission. He'd never seen her so defeated. 'I want you to answer me honestly. Have you ever cut yourself? Have you ever self-harmed in any way?'

Felan shook his head 'No. I couldn't, I... I never self-harmed because other people had always done it for me, and... well, I pinch myself sometimes to check I'm not asleep. I run the water a little too hot. I think about what would happen if a car ran off the road and I happened to be in the way.'

'So you've never...?'

'I've never cut myself,' he confirmed. '*That* morning was the closest I've ever been. I had it, the knife that is, pressed to my wrist. I didn't have a plan but I was going to do *something*, and then I thought of the kids upstairs and I stopped.'

Outside in the garden, the kids shouted. Their voices grew steadily louder.

Mrs Walters came back into herself. She stood tall and held him firmly by the shoulders. 'We're not going to do this now because there are hungry children about to storm the kitchen, but I promise you that tonight I will set some time aside for us to talk about this properly, okay?'

'Please,' he all but begged. He just wanted to get better. He didn't like it when his thoughts had a mind of their own. It was terrifying.

'Okay. Good lad.' Mrs Walters kissed his cheek and patted his shoulders. 'If you could check on what's in the oven, I'll take over the chopping.'

'Thank you.'

'Always.'

Entry 33 – 11:23pm

"We would never have recovered if you'd gone through with it. I'm not saying that to upset you. I'm not saying that to make you feel guilty. I'm saying it because I really think you need to hear it. I'm saying it because you need to understand how much you mean to us."

That's what Mrs Walters said to me earlier, when we talked, long after the kids had gone to bed. She made hot chocolate and we talked on the sofa in the front room. We cried together, and we talked. We talked a lot. We cried a lot too.

It's strange. All I seem to do at the moment is cry. I wonder if I'm broken.

Am I?

I wonder if she's ever cried with any of the kids in this way. I wonder if she waits until we've all gone to bed before she cries in the safety of her bedroom.

She held me, and she listened, in a way no adult has ever done before. I don't remember the last time Mum hugged me like that. I don't remember the last time anyone hugged me like that. Blaez has hugged me, and so has Lisa, and so have the kids, but they were comfort hugs. They were friendly hugs. They were hugs of support.

Mrs Walters' hug was a promise. Her hug was proof that she wanted me. Her hands had shaken while she held me close and whispered gentle things to me while I cried in her arms.

It wasn't embarrassing this time.

It was freeing.

I learned about passive suicide. I learned about suicide ideation. I learned about intrusive thoughts. I learned that what I was feeling was normal despite how terrifying my thoughts can sometimes be.

Things are making more and more sense to me now.

"Please promise me that, if you ever feel that urge again, that if you ever have those thoughts again, you'll come straight to me. It doesn't matter if it's in the middle of the night. It doesn't matter if I'm cooking dinner. It doesn't matter if I'm not in the house – call me. I will always answer."

I promised her I would.

I didn't sleep. How could I, after a talk like that? How could I sleep when everything was finally beginning to make sense?

She told me she loved me. She told me she was proud of me.

She hadn't told me she loved me before.

I think that's why I believed her in a heartbeat.

Chapter 48: Trust and Solace

Felan's phone pinged from inside his trouser pocket within seconds of him walking through the front door.

He shouted a quick hello and headed straight up to his room. Upon seeing the picture she'd sent him, his heart had burst with affection for his friend – his friend who had helped him from so far away.

The bramble bush had been cleared, and a headstone had been made. He considered hopping on a train to visit the grave, but he knew realistically it was a grave he would never have the courage to see again. The array of wildflowers strewn atop the grave (and the bluebell bulbs. Lots of bluebell bulbs that would flower next year, Blaez had said) joined the pieces of his broken heart together. Barely.

Blaez had remembered. Blaez always remembered.

He called her despite the tears rolling down his cheeks. He called her despite the little gasps he let out. She would understand. It wouldn't be the first time they had called each other in tears and tried to muddle through, and it definitely wouldn't be their last.

'Hi,' she said, when the call connected.

He let out a sob. 'Hi, Blaez.'

'Oh, it's okay, Felan,' she said softly. 'It's okay.'

'I don't think anyone ever bought her flowers before.'

'I'll be honest – Tristan paid for them. I just chose them.'

'I'll have to remember to thank him,' he said thickly. 'But you remembered that bluebells were her favourite. We only talked about it once, and you still remembered.'

'Of course. That's what family's for.'

Felan took his shoes off so he could lie down on his bed. He probably should have changed out of his work clothes before lying atop his covers, but who cared anymore? He was going to live a little for once. Screw what everyone else thought.

'Are you still with her?'

'Yes. She deserves to feel like she isn't alone. I meant what I said before – she will be remembered by me too.'

He remembered that day all too well. Oakley Church. Opening up to Blaez about his mum. Bruce. The Slum. Blaez lashing out – that had been a long time coming. The girl they saved from the drunkard. The Protrude. Running. So much running. The Warehouse. Nick. A lot could happen in the span of one day.

'I don't know what I'd do without you, Blaez,' Felan admitted.

'Probably something stupid.'

They chose to ignore the fact that Felan almost had.

He tapped repeatedly on his collarbone; that always did the trick when normal methods failed to calm him down. He had never been so in-tune with his body, and quite frankly, it was scary knowing himself so well. Before, he had only known what other people had told him. While he had believed it, there had always been a part of him, buried deep down, that had known it wasn't true.

He wasn't a mistake. He was important. It just took a long time to find that small part of himself. It took an even longer time to agree with it and to coax it out of the hole it had buried itself into.

'I heard about the brooch,' Blaez said suddenly, gently, an invitation to talk if Felan wanted to.

In all honesty, he had almost forgotten about it, too wrapped up in everything else that'd happened recently. Felan's gaze turned to the empty spot on his bedside table. 'I made Elliot cry,' he said with a heavy sigh. 'I can't believe I blew up at him like that. He didn't deserve it at all, and the look on his face... I never want to make someone that scared again.' Felan rested a hand on his stomach. 'I love these kids, Blaez. I really do.'

'From what I hear, they love you too.'

They fell into a comfortable silence, and it was at that moment he knew his friendship with Blaez would last forever. Sure, they might be a little trauma bonded, but the fact that they could sit on the phone in silence for long periods of time spoke volumes.

He loved spending time with her, even if they didn't speak. Just knowing she was *there* meant the world.

'I'll be seeing you really soon,' she said.

'Really?'

'Yeah. Really soon.'

'I can't wait.'

'Me neither.'

'I love you.'

'I love you too.'

The call ended. Felan turned to his notebook and he wrote about good feelings, but when it turned sad and melancholic, he switched to knitting. He was so close to finishing his latest project – a little brown bear for Blaez.

He knew she'd love it just as much as she loved him.

Chapter 49: Catharsis

Felan decided against going to the funeral in the end.

He didn't know Felicity well enough, even if he had been invited. No. There were other people who had known her for longer, people who deserved to be there.

Mrs Walters had given him some sound advice the night before: *'Listen to your body. Listen to yourself. If the thought of something makes you uncomfortable, then perhaps it's for the best that you don't do it. At least until you can figure out where the discomfort is coming from.'*

So, one week after the funeral, Felan visited Weisworth Community Church with a bunch of yellow roses in his hand.

It didn't take long to find Felicity's grave.

The flowers were all still in bloom, decorating the base of the large headstone, and Felan found a spot right in the middle to lay his own. Sitting on his knees, Felan placed the bunch of roses down. He traced the yellow petals with his fingertips and ran a finger down the green stems.

There were so many flowers.

This is what it means to be loved, he thought. *This is what it means to be known. This is what it means to be remembered.*

And yet his mother had been laid beneath an overgrown bramble bush without a single flower. Felan would never forgive himself for it. Even if he had been too young at the time to make the proper arrangements himself, he should have tried. He should have gone back to Guadalupe with Blaez and begged Tristan to fix it, yet without prompting her, and without asking her to, Blaez had sorted everything out for him.

This is what it means to be loved too. This is what it means to have people who care. This is what it means to be looked after.

But did he deserve it? Did he truly deserve Blaez's unwavering kindness and love after the way he'd treated her? She might have forgiven him, but Felan hadn't quite forgiven himself; he doubted he ever would.

The memory of his actions would always linger in the corner of his mind. He was by no means clean. He would never be clean. No amount of showering and scrubbing his body raw would ever cleanse him of his past.

Felan adjusted so he was sitting cross-legged beside Felicity's grave.

'I'm sorry I didn't show up last week. I wanted to, but it didn't feel right,' he said. 'I have your succulent living on my windowsill, and I have your favourite book on my bedside table.' Felan brushed his fingertips over the vast array of flowers. 'A lot of people loved you, and all of them miss you. Including me.' He sighed. 'I don't know if I have the right to say that to someone I barely knew, but it feels right. It feels right in here,' he said, pressing a hand to his chest. 'You changed me. I don't know how, or why, but you changed something within me.'

Every person that Felan had met had changed him in some way, and a large number of those people had changed him for the worse.

A scarily small number of those people had changed his life for the better.

First it had been Blaez and her steadfast loyalty to him, someone she had barely known, and in a matter of months she had given up all she knew to run away with him into unchartered territory with the help of Tristan and Mr Bailey. Then, it had been Mrs Walters and the kids, and Lisa and Hannah and Mark, and all of the kind people he had met during his time in Weisworth. Every smile and every friendly wave had changed something within him. They rewired him, they adjusted his default settings to something calmer, to something more alive.

For most of his life, Felan believed that there was something wrong with him. There must have been because why else would so many people bully him and degrade him? He accepted that behaviour towards himself because that's what he believed his existence was: a punching bag. Something to hit. Something to break. Something to bruise. Something to bleed dry.

Felan used to believe that good things only came to people who deserved them. It was a belief he'd followed long into his stay in Weisworth, and yet, did he deserve forgiveness for everything he'd done? Was he worthy of receiving it?

The earth didn't spin on the notion of forgiveness, or if people were deserving of something. It spun because of science, and to a degree, the enduring compassion of humanity.

And if he wanted forgiveness, then who was anybody to deny him that?

Here lies Felicity Barrow.
Beloved wife, mother, grandmother, auntie, sister and friend.

May you find peace at the hearth of indecision.
May your heart sing the truth your head refuses to hear.
May your wings guide you home.

Chapter 50: Evidence

Felan loved walking down by the river in the mornings. Or the afternoons. Or any time of day, really. It was nice to get out of the house and see the world whenever he wanted to.

Hundreds of daisies and buttercups flowered in the grassy fields that ran parallel with the river, down where the footpath took him, and where the sun beamed down upon the ground it looked like the field was aflame. Felan was so enraptured by the image that he took a photo with the intentions of sending it to Blaez later.

In his hand, Felan's phone rang. *Right on time*, he thought. He carried on walking down the footpath, following the river around the bend. Mrs Walters had told him that, if he followed it far enough, the river would go all the way to the sea.

Felan had never seen the sea before.

He answered his phone before it rung off. 'Hi,' he said.

'Felan!' Mr Bailey greeted. 'How are you?'

'Better. A lot better,' Felan admitted. It was strange how easy it was to talk to people now. 'How are you? How is everyone back in Guadalupe?'

'I'm well, Felan, as are the others. Blaez is missing you of course, but she's well. She's doing a lot better too.'

'I'm glad.' Felan spied a fallen tree up ahead and sat down on it. He was wrapped up in a hat and scarf, and his favourite purple jumper. For a sunny morning in June, it was bitterly cold. His knee bounced up and down in a poor effort to warm up.

'Are you free to have a chat?'

'I am,' Felan said quietly.

'Okay, so I know Tristan talked to you the other day about next steps about your mum's case. I want to give you a little more information, if that's okay?'

His knee stopped bouncing. 'It's more than okay.'

Something rustled down the line. 'Tristan managed to find footage of the accident, and of the car that did it, from a shop's security camera after going back through it. Luckily for us, the owner of the shop saved all of their recordings… however, it was blurry and pixelated, and they couldn't make out the licence plate. Only the make. A dark, blue Renault Clio. It's not all new information,' Mr Bailey admitted. 'The day it happened, Tristan had reported the colour of the car to us, to Harvey. He regrets not remembering more. He was too far away and the car was simply driving too fast.'

Felan shivered. 'It's still something, right?'

'It was a long time ago, Felan,' Mr Bailey said regretfully. 'But we'll do anything we can to get justice for you and your mum.'

'I know you will,' he said. 'I'm grateful. For everything you've done for me. I'm sorry I haven't expressed it sooner.'

'Don't be sorry – we get that the transition can be difficult. I'm glad you've found your way out.'

'Me too.'

Felan settled into the conversation more easily than he thought he would, and they talked about a lot of things. Mr Bailey asked about Felan's job, and the kids, and how he felt at the orphanage, and what he'd been doing to amuse himself. It was a rather pleasant conversation, one that he hadn't been expecting.

So, naturally, Felan had to ruin it. 'How are you getting on with stopping Nick?' he asked.

'There's a lot of planning that still needs to be done,' Mr Bailey eventually said. 'The thing is – you got out. They probably know that you and Blaez ratted out the whereabouts of the base. They've either doubled their defences, or they're planning on moving again. And we don't have an inside man now.'

Felan's heart sank. If Nick and the others moved on again, that would be it. Nick would get away with it. He'd get away with everything. Accalia and Edward wouldn't stand a chance.

They'd be trapped for the rest of their lives.

'But you're still watching them?'

'We've got people observing them around the clock.'

He focused on the red flowers at his feet whose name he had yet to learn. He clenched his jaw at the stark reminder of the girl he'd left behind. An adult. Barely. She was nineteen. She might even be twenty by now.

'I don't suppose you've seen a girl with red hair at all on those cameras? Or a young boy? He might be wearing an eyepatch of some kind.'

Mr Bailey sighed down the phone. 'It's best not to torture yourself like this, Felan.'

'Please.' He hadn't begged since he was in the throes of his nightmare. Not since Nick. The memory made his skin crawl. The residual anger built up inside of him like a volcano about to erupt.

'I've seen them both – it's rare that we see one without the other.'

The anger slowly dispersed, and relief filled him up instead. A few tears slipped out before he could rein them in.

'Okay,' he said. 'Okay. Thank you.'

'We're doing the best we can,' Mr Bailey said. 'The base is practically impenetrable, especially with the number of cameras set up – which isn't your fault at all,' he added hastily. 'But it's not impossible. We will catch them, Felan. We'll catch *him*.'

They said their goodbyes. Felan slipped his phone into his trouser pocket and released a shuddering breath. He did it a few more times to get the nervous jitters out from beneath his skin, his skin that itched with anxiety, and when he was sure he wasn't going to break down, Felan got to his feet and continued walking beside the river. He followed the twists and turns and the bends, and at one point he even crossed over an old, cobbled bridge.

A brilliant blue bird darted over the water top. Felan stopped in his tracks. It sat on a branch hanging over the water, and as if it had sensed him watching, it zoomed off seconds later, disappearing from view.

Felan watched it fly away in wonder.

Entry 34 – 2:38am

I can't believe it's taken me this long to piece together what really happened.

It's a stretch, but I think... I think it was you, Dad. I think this all happened because of you. I don't remember the make of your car, but it was blue, and you were drunk. You were quick to be rid of it, and you were also quick to blame me.

Maybe it wasn't you, and I'm reading too much into it. Maybe it had been another blue car with another drunk driver behind the wheel.

But you were drunk, and you were driving a blue car.

You turned up hours after Mum died, almost like you were hiding, almost like you were waiting until the coast was clear before you showed yourself.

Maybe it had been an accident. Maybe it was intentional. Maybe you were trying to get rid of us both. Maybe you were aiming for me, but Mum jumped in the way. Maybe you genuinely didn't realise anything had been amiss while you were driving. Maybe it wasn't you at all.

But you were drunk, and you were driving a blue car.

I debated calling back Mr Bailey; my heart is cold and so is the air. I've decided to keep my suspicions to myself.

The car is long gone, ten years long gone. Mum is dead and now so are you. Nothing good will come from this, other than a confirmation. If they're able to find the car, that is. It's been years.

And, strangely... I'd rather not know. Maybe sometime down the line, days or weeks or years from now, I'll tell Mr Bailey what I discovered, but for now I'm content with the information that the man who abused me is no longer here.

My dad is dead, and I am glad.

Chapter 51: Family of Choice

A few days later, Felan found himself back by the river accompanied by Jude and Josie, a rucksack slung over his shoulders with some essentials packed inside.

They crossed paths with a regular customer at the café, alongside her two golden retrievers. Both of the kids waited patiently by his side when Felan came to a stop. They were good kids, and he liked having them around – he felt braver knowing he wasn't on his own.

'You're not normally front of house, are you?' the customer asked. For the life of him, Felan didn't recall her name. Oh well. No one was perfect.

'No. I'm usually hiding out in the kitchen washing up,' he joked.

The lady let out a hearty laugh. 'There's nothing wrong with hiding from the general public. I must say, I was very impressed when I saw you on the till,' she continued. 'You acted like you knew exactly what you were doing.'

'I was terrified,' he admitted with a weak laugh. 'Sometimes I still am.'

Josie pressed against his side. Felan leaned into the touch, grateful for her company.

'It doesn't appear that way at all,' she said kindly. She offered the kids a warm smile. 'Now who are these lovely children?'

'My brother and sister,' he said. 'Jude and Josie.'

'Hi,' they said in unison.

'Ever so polite,' the lady said. She glanced down at her watch. 'I must get on – Ernie and Bertha have a nice, warm bath waiting for them.' The dogs at their feet whined. 'I'll see you around, Felan.'

He winced. He probably should have known her name. 'Yeah, see you around.'

He hurried the kids along the path without looking back.

'Who was that?' Josie asked.

'One of my customers,' Felan told her. 'She comes into the café.'

'Oh. Cool.'

'She knows your name,' Jude said.

'Yeah, she does.'

'Does it not weird you out?'

'It used to,' Felan said, dodging a muddy puddle. He grinned when Josie ran straight through it. 'Not so much anymore.' It meant that he existed outside of his room. It meant that people wanted to know him. 'It's nice to be known.'

Jude pulled a face. 'Does that mean that you weren't known before?'

'No, I *was* known. In fact, I was known really well… but not in the way I wanted to be known,' he said.

He'd decided weeks ago that he was going to protect the kids from his past for as long as possible. Realistically he knew that at some point he'd have to tell them the truth, especially after the fiasco that happened in the woods, but for now he was content to let them be in their blissful ignorance.

'You said you got into lots of fights – is that how you were known?' Jude asked. 'For fighting people?'

I wish, Felan thought darkly. He wondered how he could explain it without terrifying them. 'They knew me for other things,' he said carefully, trying not to give too much away.

Jude tugged on Felan's sleeve as they walked. Felan turned to look. 'We don't have to talk about it if you don't want to,' Jude said quietly.

'Thanks. I appreciate it,' Felan said. He reached out to ruffle the kid's hair. 'Maybe when you're older.'

Up ahead, Josie admired a rather fruitful blackberry bush. Jude ran after her. Felan walked on at a leisurely pace, and when he caught up to them, he took off his rucksack and took out the plastic tub he'd stashed inside earlier. 'Guys!' he shouted, raising the tub. The kids looked over. 'You fancy picking some? I thought we could make a crumble later with our bounty.'

He set the tub on the grassy floor, and between the three of them, it only took a few minutes to fill it. Felan sealed it up, slipped it into his rucksack and slung it back on. 'We'll just finish the loop around the river and then we'll head home.'

'Okay,' Jude said, popping a blackberry in his mouth.

Josie extracted herself from the brambles, and with Felan bringing up the rear, they continued on along the footpath, their fingers stained with blackberry juice.

He couldn't help but listen in to their conversation.

'Did you have any brothers or sisters before you came here?' Josie asked.

'No,' Jude said. 'It was just me and my mum. What about you?'

'Yeah! I had two older brothers. They were *way* older than me. Noah was the biggest – he was twenty I think, and Oliver. He was seventeen. They pulled my hair all the time. I kept telling them I didn't like it but they kept doing it anyway. I remember once they pulled out chunks and they left it all over the floor.'

'I won't pull your hair, Josie,' Jude promised.

'Thanks! And my dad used to smoke all the time in the house. I don't like the smell. It makes me feel sick.'

Felan pondered what he'd heard.

Josie's brothers had been old enough to know different. Her brothers had been old enough to look after Josie, had been old enough to protect her. Instead, they'd bullied her to the point where she had to be removed for her own safety.

He thought about stepping back a little because he didn't want to eavesdrop on such a private conversation, yet the kids knew he was there. He was sure they would tell him to go away if they wanted to talk privately.

'I didn't know any of that,' Jude said. 'Your brothers sound really mean.'

'They were. But they were my brothers,' she said sadly. 'Tell me about your mum, if you want.'

'She was mean, too,' Jude said. 'She shouted all the time. She said mean things. I wasn't allowed to talk much – she told me I had to be quiet.'

Rage filled Felan, hot and fast. He clenched his fists and breathed, trying to calm himself down before the kids noticed.

'I'm sorry she was mean to you,' Josie said. 'What about your dad? Was he nice?'

'I don't know,' Jude said. 'I never met him. I used to hope that he'd show up one day and take me away with him.'

Josie hummed. 'That sounds like a lovely dream.'

'Yeah.'

They turned around together. 'Felan?' Josie asked. 'Did you have any brothers or sisters?'

'No,' he answered truthfully. 'It was just me.'

The kids stopped to allow Felan time to catch up. They continued on together. 'What about your mum and dad?'

Felan tried to keep his face neutral. He'd known the question was coming. He'd known for weeks – of course the kids were going to get curious after a while.

'My mum died when I was seven,' Felan said, sadness clutching onto him with its jagged claws.

Josie's face fell. 'Oh.'

'She was lovely,' Felan said quickly. 'She was my best friend.'

But she left you. She left you alone with him.

She lied.

'And your dad?' Jude asked.

Felan fiddled with his sleeves and tugged them down further. He didn't know why – the kids had seen his arms in all their glory numerous times before. 'He wasn't a nice man,' he eventually said.

Jude clocked the movement with narrowed eyes. 'He gave you some of those scars, didn't he?'

'Yeah, he did,' Felan said. 'He was a very angry man, and to this day I don't know why.'

'Do you still love him?'

That was a good question. 'I don't know.'

'I still love my mum, even though she hurt me,' Jude said

matter-of-factly. 'She's my mum. You only get one.'

Felan stayed quiet.

'I miss my brothers,' Josie admitted. 'They could be mean, but there were days when they were nice to me. They played with me when Dad was away. Sometimes they looked after me.'

But sometimes wasn't always.

Sometimes wasn't good enough.

'It's okay to miss your families,' Felan said, managing to find his words again. 'You spent a lot of time with them before you came here.'

'Mrs Walters said that I can meet up with them when I'm older, if I want to,' Josie announced.

Felan raised his eyebrows. 'Really?'

'Yep. I'm going to think about it first though.'

'Good. That's good.' Felan glanced over to Jude. 'What about you, buddy? Are you going to try and see your mum at some point?'

'I don't know.' Jude seemed hesitant all of a sudden, and Felan understood completely. He didn't like talking much either. It was draining and it left him feeling vulnerable. 'Did you mean what you said to that lady?'

'What did I say?'

Jude blushed. 'Well, when she asked who we were, you said we were your brother and sister. Did you mean it, or were you just saying it?'

He felt like his heart might burst.

'I meant every word.'

***

'Does that make Blaez our big sister?' Josie asked on the way home, swinging hers and Felan's hands between them. Jude walked next to Felan, close enough that their arms bumped every few steps, but the kid didn't reach out.

Felan was happy to let Jude set his own boundaries.

'Yeah, if you want her to be,' Felan said.

'Do you think she'd want to be?'

Blaez had admitted to him on the phone the other night that she was missing the kids. Scrap that – *every* phone call she complained to him how much she missed them. She called them every week to speak to them, *'but it's not the same as seeing them in person. It's not the same as seeing them every day.'*

Felan felt the same way about a certain girl with a sarcastic temperament.

'I love them, Felan, and I'm scared they're forgetting me. What if they forget me?'

'Trust me when I say that they haven't forgotten about you. All they ever talk about is you,' he said, *feigning annoyance. 'You know, I'm getting kind of offended because they never seem to want to know about me anymore. It's always, Blaez this, and Blaez that.'*

'Oh, shut up,' she giggled.

Felan suddenly remembered that Josie was waiting for an answer. 'I think she'd be over the moon if you asked her,' he said, giving her hand a gentle squeeze.

'I'll do it when she comes back,' the girl decided. 'I've always wanted an older sister.' She squeezed Felan's hand in return. 'Out of all of my big brothers, you're my favourite.'

Felan wanted to wrap her up in bubble wrap, wanted to hold her close and never let the world hurt her again. The moment was ruined because, before Felan could come up with anything profound to respond with, Jude ran around Felan, tapped Josie on the hip, sprinted away and shouted, 'Tag, you're IT!'

Josie let go of Felan's hand and bolted after him. Felan watched on from behind, watched the kids chase each other and laugh. He was glad that they could still be kids. He was glad that they could still have fun, even after everything he'd learned today.

***

Dinner was ready when they got back home, so after a quick clean-up and a change of clothes, the three of them sat down at the table with everyone else to eat; dinner didn't take long to be demolished.

Once everyone had finished, Felan stood up and got to work on the blackberry crumble. Forty minutes later everyone tucked into it with a big scoop of vanilla ice cream each. Gemma had given herself purple lipstick and the other kids were practically licking their bowls clean.

It was a hit, if Felan didn't say so himself.

'I'll make more. I promise,' Felan said when the kids realised there wasn't any left for seconds. They made themselves scarce, leaving Felan and Mrs Walters to tidy up the kitchen. While they tidied, they talked about plans for future days out.

Felan welcomed those quiet moments the most, loved the easy interactions he could have with her.

Later, when he turned in for the night, he struggled to sleep.

What else was new?

He missed his mum. He found that her absence hit him quite strongly some nights, and other times it didn't affect him at all. He thought perhaps his chat with Jude and Josie earlier had been the main cause, but it wasn't their fault, of course.

He'd forgotten what her touch felt like and her face was beginning to lose focus in his memory; it was fading and blurring into a stranger and he had no way of fixing it. He had no photos of her to look at when he couldn't quite picture her loving smile. Even the echo of her laughter was distorted and crackly like a broken radio.

'I'm sorry,' he whispered into the darkness of his room. 'It's just so hard to remember. It's been so long.'

He tossed and turned for what seemed an age before he gave up. He turned on his desk lamp and wrote in his notebook until his hand ached and cramped, until he'd written out all of his thoughts. He leaned back in his chair and carried on knitting the little brown bear for Blaez.

There was nothing left but peace and calm and a thriving succulent in a terracotta pot on his windowsill.

Entry 35 – 5:19am

I used to wish you hadn't saved me.

I used to wish that you had let the car hit me. I thought things would've been better if I wasn't here anymore.

It's taken a while for me to realise that it isn't true.

Who was there for you, Mum? Did you have someone watching over you like you watched over me? I know what Dad did to me, and I hate myself for not knowing if he did it to you too.

Why did you save my life when there was no one there to save yours?

They're looking for the person who did it. Tristan found footage of that day from a shop's security camera. They're really trying ~~to help you...~~ to help me. ~~The thing is, I don't need their help. I know what happened. Or at least I think I do.~~

~~Mum, I think Dad...~~

They've given you a headstone too. I'm sorry I couldn't go and see it.

I took you for granted – but I was a kid. I didn't realise I was taking you for granted. That's what kids do. They have fun. They laugh. They play. They don't think for a second that their mum is going to die one day and never come back. Not once did that possibility ever occur to me. I didn't know. I didn't know what would happen.

Mrs Walters says I should stop waiting for an apology, but I feel cheated. She says that waiting for an apology gives power to the people who hurt me. I think she's right, don't you? But I can't help it. I deserve an apology for what I went through, and I'll never get one. Mrs Walters apologises on their behalf, and I appreciate the gesture, but she has nothing to apologise for. I want the city to apologise. I want Nick to apologise. I want Dad to apologise.

For a time, I wanted you to apologise too.

I wanted you to apologise for leaving me on my own, because if you had lived, none of this would have happened. You sacrificed yourself, and yet you forced a bigger sacrifice on me. You left, and no one saved me. No one came to help.

I was the one you left, and I guess at some point I was angry with you. I hated you too. I was upset and confused and hurting. But I realise now it wasn't you I was angry at. I was angry at the world, at the situation.

I was angry that you were gone.

I'm over that now.

I promise I'm not angry with you anymore.

There's another universe out there in which I had one more day with you, yet I'm glad we got to spend as much time together as we did in this one. I'm glad I can carry my memories of you to my grave, wherever and whenever that may be.

Also, I made a friend, Mum. For the first time. Ever.

Her name is Blaez... you would have *loved* her. I know you always wanted a daughter as well as a son. I really think Blaez could have been her. She visited your grave for me. She left bluebells there too. Of course, they're only bulbs at the moment but next year we're hopeful they'll flower. She remembered they were your favourite. Blaez remembers a lot of things. She remembers a lot of things that I'd rather forget.

I think that, after everything, you're proud of me... and maybe I'm proud of myself too.

I've made friends. I've gotten myself a job. I have hobbies. I'm *safe*. I am by no means clean, but I'm cleaner than I was before.

And I have a new family. Let me introduce you:

Gemma. She's four. She's adorable.

Elliot and Mary. They're eight-year-old twins. They're as thick as thieves, yet the complete polar opposite.

Jude. He's nine. He's a fighter. He's a real trooper. He's a mini-me.

Josie. She's also nine. She's probably one of the bravest kids I've ever met.

I know you're watching me. I know you've been watching me for a long time. I know you've probably been worried about me, and angry at me for what I've done, but you can rest easy now, Mum. I'm safe. I'm surrounded by good people.

You don't have to worry about me anymore.

I miss you, Mum. I really miss you.

I wish you were still here.

I'll be good from now on.

I won't take anything for granted ever again. I won't waste a moment, Mum. I promise. I won't waste any more moments.

I'll make you proud.

I love you, Mum.

I always will.

Chapter 52: Reunited

Weisworth train station had only one platform, and it was deemed 'the end of the line' since the trains couldn't go any further north.

Felan counted seven people on the platform waiting with luggage and a further four (excluding himself) who appeared to be waiting for friends and family – every single one of them had their faces buried in their phones. He didn't understand it – how could they go about their day completely unaware of the world around them?

Things were missed when people never looked up.

Despite the practically empty platform, Felan found himself looking over his shoulder. It was stupid, really. No one knew where he'd been moved to. He was safe in Weisworth. He had nothing to fear. Nothing, and no one, was waiting to pounce.

Well, the woman in the woods had been, and so had the man in the café, but they were outliers. Two people in one town wasn't bad.

The kids were in another art class in town for the morning – they were completely unaware that Blaez was coming home. Mrs Walters had dropped the kids off and then drove Felan to the train station under the guise of last-minute cover for the café. She was currently waiting for them in the car park. '*Take all the time you need,*' she had said.

Felan leant against an old post, his arms crossed, digging his fingers into his sides.

For a time, he feared that Blaez hated him, feared that she didn't need him anymore.

He wasn't afraid of that now.

He knew she still loved him, despite everything. It had taken a lot of convincing from Blaez's side for Felan to understand that, yet he had no idea what he was going to think, or say, or do, when the train arrived. He'd waited for her to come home for so long, to come home to him, and yet he didn't know what the plan was. He still hadn't decided what he was going to do about school; he took solace in the fact that Blaez hadn't decided either.

We can decide together, he thought. *Just like we always do.*

Even so, he was afraid. He was afraid of the dark thoughts in his head convincing him that doing something stupid would be a good idea. He was better now, but what if he got worse again? What if those intrusive thoughts and the ideations came back stronger?

Felan pulled his purple jumper tighter around himself. He wouldn't let it get worse. He refused to go down the same path for a second time. He refused to let his past govern his future.

He heard the train before he saw it, and when it rounded the corner a short while later he thought he might combust.

His sister was coming home. She was here.

Finally.

Through the sheer nerves he laughed to himself, remembering a conversation he'd had with Elliot and Mary a few weeks prior.

'Are you and Blaez together?'

'It's not like that between us.'

'But you want it to be?'

'What? No! She's my best friend – she's like a sister to me.'

'So you guys aren't going to get married?'

'She'll get married. And maybe, one day, I'll get married too. But Blaez and I... we're siblings. Like the two of you. There's nothing more to it.'

Yeah. That had been an interesting conversation. For some reason, they didn't understand that a girl and a boy could be friends without it being anything more. Gemma was too young to really understand, but all the kids had grown up with fairy tales, with princes and princesses who got married and lived happily ever after.

The world was slowly changing, but there was still a long way to go.

The train screeched to a stop. Moments later the doors opened and a handful of people spilled out. He pushed off the post and searched the small platform frantically for his friend, searching up and down.

There was no sign of her.

What if she had changed her mind and didn't come back? She hadn't called to let him know, but what if she didn't want to speak to him ever again? What the hell would he do then?

His vision blurred at the unbidden thought, and then he saw her, running, running to him, wearing the green, flowery trousers she'd told him about and a green headband in her hair to match.

She looked healthier than he'd ever seen her.

She dropped her bags and launched herself at him; he caught her and spun her around once. He held on tight, so tight he thought he might leave bruises. Blaez clung to him just as hard. He buried his face in her neck and breathed her in.

'Welcome home,' he said.

She began to shake in his arms, and he realised she was crying – he let his anxiety and relief out in sobs of his own.

At the back of his mind Felan was sure that people on the platform had the wrong idea, but he didn't care. They didn't know anything about his life, or about anything he'd gone through to get to where he was. They didn't know about his sleepless nights and his constant fear of never being good enough. They didn't see the flinches when someone moved too fast around him. They didn't see the scars that littered his arms. They didn't see his bitterness when he looked in the mirror after a particularly bad day.

They didn't know that, for a time, he wished he no longer existed.

'I'm so sorry,' he said. 'I'm so sorry for making your time there harder than it had to be.'

'No.' She pulled away. Tears streamed down her cheeks. Her eyeliner ran with them. 'Don't you dare apologise for that. The only thing that matters now is what we choose to be.'

She pulled him back in for another hug. Felan didn't want to let her go. He never wanted to let her go again. 'What do we do now?' she whispered.

Felan smiled into her shoulder. 'We go home.'

Entry 36 – 11:47pm

I'll say everything here because I don't know how to say it out loud.

I don't know if I'm going to let you read this, but anyway.

Here goes.

I've been so lost without you, to the point where I didn't realise how dependent I had been on you until you left. So I'm sorry about that. I'm sorry for leaning on you so much. You didn't need that. What you did need was my support. I'm ashamed to admit that I didn't give you what you needed, though I am grateful that Tristan and Mr Bailey did. I'm glad they were there for you when I wasn't, when I couldn't be. I'm glad you were able to talk to them about things you've never been able to talk about before.

Listen... I know there's more to the story that you haven't been able to bring yourself to say. I don't care that you haven't told me – I hope that one day you find the strength to be able to. I'll be here. I'll listen. I hope you know that.

And I know we've argued a lot over the last few months. I know the arguments were my fault. I'm sorry about that too. I'm sorry I got defensive and angry when you were pointing out the truth – I didn't want to admit it.

I have now.

I just want you to know that my anger is never aimed at you. I know I can be mean sometimes. I promise I'm trying to turn it around. Don't think for a second that I hate you. Quite the opposite, in fact.

My platonic soulmate, you know?

My best friend.

My other half.

My person.

The only person that truly understands what I'm going through because you were there at the worst time of my life. You've seen what I've seen... I only regret that you've seen more, that you spent more time there with *them*. I regret that you're hurting in ways I can't even begin to imagine. I regret that you got dragged into all of this in the first place.

But I don't regret meeting you. Meeting you has been the highlight of my life. You have brought me so much joy and love and comfort (more than I'll ever deserve), and I will spend the rest of my life learning how to repay you. I know you're going to tell me that I don't have to, but I want to. I want to make things right with you.

I've been alone for most of my life. I've been

alone with abusers and bullies and no one ever fought in my corner. I had no one by my side for the longest time.

Until I met you.

You didn't give up on me, even when I shouted at you, and even when I was downright awful to you. You gave me hope when I had nothing left; I know that you'll be by my side forever.

If it wasn't already obvious, just know that I'll be by your side forever too. Always. Even if I don't have the words to say, I will be there, no matter what.

I'm not going anywhere. I promised Gemma, I promised you, and I guess I promised myself too. I'm staying. I'm staying here for good. I don't want to start again. Not anymore. I don't want to disappear either.

The truth is – I was only hurting myself. By self-sabotaging and isolating myself, I caused irreparable damage. At least, I always believed it was irreparable. I know now that it isn't too late to turn things around. It isn't too late to make amends with the people I care about. It isn't too late to want to be alive.

It isn't too late to want to live.

I belong here, in Weisworth. With the kids, with Mrs Walters... and with you. It's freeing to finally get that off my chest because it feels like, ever since Mum died, I've been searching. I didn't even know what it was I was searching for.

I guess I just didn't want to admit that, all along, I had been looking for love, of any kind. The tinniest hint and I was on my knees. The simplest touch and I would short-circuit.

Hang on. Let me try that again.

I didn't love you because I was lonely. My love for you wasn't born from loneliness, or from fear. My love for you was born *from* you, because you were light, and I was stuck, steadfast, in the dark. I didn't see a way out until I met you. I didn't see a way out until I caught a glimpse of you that day in the clearing, already burning way *way* beyond my atmosphere, burning in and amongst the stars I used to watch every night as a kid, the same stars Mum used to tell me stories about, the same stars she told me to pray to if things ever went wrong… the very same stars I wished upon, begging for something good to finally happen to me.

And then you came along.

You were my very own wish upon a star.

You were proof that I was worthy of love, that I was worthy of compassion. You were proof that I deserved more. You were all the proof I ever needed, and all the proof I'll ever need.

You burned so bright, Blaez. You burned so bright that you made me want to step out of the darkness because I finally felt like I deserved to.

I started to love you because you made me feel like I could be seen.

Part of me never wanted to be seen again.

Part of me wanted to fade out of existence.

Part of me wanted everything to end.

And then you came along and changed my life forever. Because of you, I am forever changed, and I am eternally grateful that I get to spend the rest of my life loving you.

So, Blaez, if I ever let you read this... I'm glad it was you. I'm glad it was you who came up to me that day in the clearing. I'm glad you said hello.

I'm so, so glad it was you.

Author's Note

Around the world, over 700,000 people take their own life each year. That's one person every forty seconds.

One in five people have suicidal thoughts, many of which they never admit to. One in fourteen people self-harm. One in fifteen people attempt to take their own life, and 115 lives are lost every week to suicide. And this is just in the UK alone.

In the USA, more than 50,000 people died by suicide in 2023 – more than any year on record. Back in 2022, 13.2 million people thought about suicide, 3.8 million people made a plan for suicide, and 1.6 million people attempted to take their own life.

It's heartbreaking to hear that so many people around the world are in so much pain that they feel suicide is the only option left for them. Suicide is often associated with strong feelings of guilt – guilt which can stem from a dark past, a dark past such as involvement in dangerous gangs.

In the USA, gang membership is often associated with greater levels of depression, as well as a 67% increase in suicidal thoughts and a 104% increase in suicide attempts (especially in the aftermath).

It is reported that poor mental wellbeing can draw young people to gang life, however involvement in said gangs negatively impacts an already fragile identity and can ultimately worsen any, or all, existing mental health problems. On the surface, gangs offer support to isolated individuals who lack any form of relationships, providing a sense of belonging that these individuals are lacking.

If children are neglected, abused or exposed to trauma, the world can be a place of uncertainty and fear. Brain development will then focus on short-term survival, heightening stress responses and dulling emotions. Traumatised children can be overwhelmed when faced with stress (which can trigger the 'fight or flight' response) and have great difficulty expressing and controlling their emotions. It impedes their ability to communicate effectively which leads to further isolation of an already isolated individual.

In today's society, it is scarily easy to fall into the pit known as depression, so easy in fact you might not even realise you're in it, so easy that one in six adults in the UK are experiencing it right now. One in five children and young people aged eight to twenty-five had a probable mental disorder in 2023 (there are many more which weren't reported, many more which will *never* be reported).

Suicide ideation (also known as passive suicide) is an individual's desire to kill themselves without having a plan to act on said desire. They approach activities without concern for their safety, for example crossing a busy road without checking for oncoming traffic, and the notion is something that isn't talked about enough.

If not recognised, suicide ideation can lead to suicide. It's a stepping stone.

So please, check in with your friends. Ask after their wellbeing. Have a proper chat. It could very well save a life.

More people than you think are going through this every day – if this is you, you aren't alone.

And, if given the choice, be kind. You have no idea what someone could be going through.

Please be kind.

Helplines – UK

SUICIDE PREVENTION

CALM (Campaign Against Living Miserably): 0800 58 58 58; www.thecalmzone.net – a leading UK charity that stands against suicide because life is always worth living. Call 5pm to midnight 365 days a year, or speak via webchat.

Samaritans: 116 123, or text 'SHOUT' to 85258; www. samaritans.org – for anyone who's struggling to cope, who needs someone to listen without judgement or pressure. They provide solutions and ways to cope for anyone. Free helpline 24 hours a day, 7 days a week.

Support Line: 01708 765200; www.supportline.org.uk – they offer confidential emotional support to children, young adults and adults. They work with callers to develop healthy, positive coping strategies, an inner feeling of strength and increased self-esteem to encourage healing, recovery and moving forward with life. Free helpline on Tuesdays, Wednesdays and Thursdays from 6pm to 8pm.

SOS (Silence of Suicide): 0808 115 1505; www. sossilenceofsuicide.org – a registered mental wellbeing charity working to eradicate the shame, stigma and silence around mental health and suicide. Free helpline. Monday to Friday 8pm to midnight, Saturday to Sunday 4pm to midnight.

Papyrus UK – Prevention of Young Suicide: 0800 068 41 41, or text 07860 039967; www.papyrus-uk.org – a UK charity dedicated to the prevention of suicide and the promotion of positive mental health and emotional wellbeing in young people under 35. Free helpline, 24 hours a day, 7 days a week.

MENTAL HEALTH

Mind: 0300 123 3393; www.mind.org.uk – a UK charity dedicated to helping anyone who is struggling with their mental health. Answering calls between 9am and 6pm, Monday to Friday (except for bank holidays).

Young Minds: 0808 802 5544; www.youngminds.org.uk - the UK's leading charity fighting for children and young people's mental health.

SANE: 0300 304 7000; www.sane.org.uk – a UK mental health charity working to improve quality of life for people affected by mental illness. Answering calls between 4pm and 10pm, 365 days a year.

The Mix: 0808 808 4994; www.themix.org.uk – essential support for under 25s, from homelessness to break-ups.

SHOUT: Text SHOUT to 85258 – a free, confidential 24/7 text messaging service for anyone in the UK who needs help.

ABUSE

Childline: 0800 1111; www.childline.org.uk – free and confidential 24-hour helpline for children and young people.

NSPCC (National Society for the Prevention of Cruelty to Children): 0808 800 5000; www.nspcc.org.uk / help@nspcc.org.uk – free 24-hour helpline for children, or adults concerned about a child at risk.

HOMELESSNESS

Centrepoint (Ending Youth Homelessness): 0808 800 0661; www.centrepoint.org.uk – a charity providing accommodation and support to homeless people aged 16–25. Free helpline answering calls 9am to 5pm, Monday to Friday.

Runaway Helpline: 116 000; www.runawayhelpline.org.uk – for young people who feel like running away from home/who have run from home. Answering calls between 9am to 11pm every day.

MOVING BEYOND CRIME

Crime Stoppers: 0800 555 111; www.crimestoppers-uk.org – give crime information anonymously… for anyone.

Frank: 0300 1236600; www.talktofrank.com – honest information about drugs, for anyone.

Victim Support: 08 08 16 89 111; www.victimsupport.org.uk – free and confidential support to help you move beyond the impact of crime.

Word4Weapons: www.word4weapons.co.uk – a leading weapons surrender charity in the UK for the last 17 years, supplying knife bins to a number of police forces, community groups and faith organisations.

Gangsline: 01375 483 239 and 07753 351 256; www.gangsline.com – a non-profit organisation established in 2007 to provide help and support to young men and women involved in gang culture.

Helplines – USA

Victim Support Services: Call 425 252 6081; www. victimsupportservices.org – a non-profit agency providing peer support and advocacy for victims of crime

Childhelp National Child Abuse Hotline: Call or text 1800 422 4453; www.childhelphotline.org – the hotline is staffed 24 hours a day, 7 days a week, and offers crisis intervention, information and referrals to thousands of emergency, social service, and support resources for child abuse victims, parents, and concerned individuals.

Darkness to Light: Call 866 367 5444 or text 'LIGHT' to 741 741; www.d2l.org – a free helpline for children and adults needing local information or resources about sexual abuse.

National Parent Helpline: Call 1855 427 2736; www. nationalparenthelpline.org – available 10am–7pm Monday to Friday, this helpline offers emotional support and links to resources for parents and caregivers.

National Human Trafficking Hotline: Call 888 373 7888; www. humantraffickinghotline.org – available 24 hours a day, 7 days a week, this hotline offers support for victims of human trafficking and those reporting potential trafficking situations.

Child Find of America: Call 1 800 426 5678; www. childfindofamerica.org – a non-profit hotline for parents reporting lost or abducted children, including parental abductions.

National Centre for Missing and Exploited Children: Call 1 800 843 5678; www.missingkids.org – a non-profit corporation who help find missing children, reduce child sexual exploitation, and prevent child victimisation. NCMEC works with families, victims, private industry, law enforcement and the public to assist with preventing child abductions, recovering missing children, and providing services to deter and combat child sexual exploitation.

National Runaway Switchboard: Call 1 800 786 2929; www. youth.gov – assists youth who have run away or are considering running away and their families, linking youth and families across the country to shelters, counselling, medical assistance and other vital services. In addition, NRS works to prevent youth from running away.

PLEASE VISIT **CHILD WELFARE INFORMATION GATEWAY** FOR MORE INFORMATION (WWW.CHILDWELFARE.GOV)

Acknowledgements

I started writing *Convalescence* on a whim. I knew there was so much more of the story to tell. I also knew that I wasn't quite ready to say goodbye to Felan yet; I'd learned a lot from him and his story and I knew other people could learn a lot more too.

I couldn't stop thinking about the aftermath. I couldn't stop thinking about how Felan would integrate back into society, and how he would cope with accepting his past – how he would move forward, or not.

Thus *Convalescence* was born, and I am so proud of the story I have told.

Firstly, a huge thank you to my friends and family for your constant support. I'm always asked when the next book is coming out – here it is!

Secondly, a huge thank you to Dominic Wakeford for all of your help in making *Convalescence* what it is. You have been as fantastic as ever with your edits, always picking up on little things I often missed. I couldn't have done this without you. Thank you once again to Spiffing Publishing for a beautiful front cover and for your hard work and dedication in all areas to make this project work. *Convalescence* would still be an idea if it wasn't for all of your help.

Thirdly, thank you to everyone at Seagulls for your kindness and encouragement. Thank you to all at Washingpool for being as supportive and lovely as always.

And finally, thank you to all of my readers, old and new. Thank you for giving this book a chance, for giving this story a chance... for giving Felan and his story a chance.

Every child deserves to be fought for.

So, let's fight.

And please be kind.

About the Author

Convalescence is Maisie's second novel, which immediately follows on from the events of her first novel, *Opium*. She hopes her writing will inspire those who read it, and to make people think. She is an adventurer and a writer and is never short of ideas.

She is no stranger to a challenge, and is also no stranger to charity events. She walked the Jurassic Coast Challenge 2021 in support of the NSPCC and raised money for the amazing charity – the only charity fighting to end child abuse in the UK and Channel Islands.

She also took part in the Jurassic Coast Mighty Hike 2022 and Snowdon at Night 2024 to raise money for Macmillan Cancer Support. These adventures and long hikes always inspire story ideas and new characters. Training for the adventures helps even more so.

She lives in Dorset with her mum and their cat.

Follow Maisie on Instagram for writing snippets and updates:

@MKitton2206

Brief Explanations

Why *Convalescence*?

I chose *Convalescence* for its definition: time spent recuperating from an illness or medical treatment.

Following the title scheme, Felan is recovering from his time in Guadalupe. He is recuperating and healing from years of abuse in a quiet, reflective, safe place – a detox from a highly addictive drug.

A detox from *Opium*.

Why the use of different flowers?

I've always been fascinated by flowers and their meanings, so when I first started to work on *Opium*, and later on *Convalescence*, I wanted to include as many different kinds as was feasible. I used Felan as a way to channel my love for nature into my writing.

The poppy symbolises remembrance and conflict. Felan is remembering his past (the people he's lost and everything he's done) and he's conflicted. He's in inner turmoil with himself, a turmoil which lasts the entirety of the story.

The bluebells represent the presence of Felan's mother. They were her favourite flower and every time he sees them, he thinks of her. He feels it is the only way he can connect with her now and he cherishes those moments.

I included daisies because they're everywhere. Felan sees them in the fields by the river and then again in the back garden of the orphanage. They're representing the innocence of the children in the home, and furthermore the innocence of Felan. I also included them to show that simple beauty can grow easily in the most unexpected of places.

I included buttercups because they symbolise youth, purity and happiness. Felan sees them in the fields by the river too, and I used them to represent Felan and the kids: they're young, they're pure, and they're happy (despite what they've been through to get to where they are).

The cornflowers were included for my own personal love. As a kid, they were my favourite flower to grow and I'd always cut them and give them as a gift to my mum and my nan.

The yellow roses Felan leaves on Felicity's grave were used to reference their brief but impactful companionship on those Sunday mornings in the café.

I wrote in the sunflowers because they represent a long life and lasting happiness, as well as positivity. It was to hint towards a long and happy life for Felan now that he is safe from the constant danger and threats against his life in Guadalupe.

www.ingramcontent.com/pod-product-compliance
Lightning Source LLC
Chambersburg PA
CBHW030531190726
48283CB00006B/1856